The Flights of Beryl Pritchard

C T Nichols

To Peg and Jean,

two strong women

BOOK ONE

CHAPTER 1

"Of course, we considered naming her Amelia. We thought it might be a bad omen, though. We couldn't bear to lose her. No... Beryl is the right name, as she is precious to us." – Jerry Pritchard

The first time I saw Beryl in person, she was flying. I couldn't help but stop and watch for a few minutes, though my hands tingled with autumn chill. Circling above orange and yellow trees, she banked into a current and then just floated. Graceful. Peaceful. Hovering high above the earth with wings outstretched and feathers fluttering.

I had just arrived at the Pritchard estate in suburban Memphis, Wisconsin. Tall oaks, maples, and elms ringed an expansive, checkerboard lawn. Extending several stories high, loose rope netting encircled the perimeter of the grounds. A northern breeze carried the rustle of dying leaves and the tones of a man's voice. Despite its proximity to metro Milwaukee, the Pritchard home felt like a peaceful island isolated from the hustle and bustle of the city.

I slipped my hands into the pockets of my felt coat, and walked over to Beryl's father, Jerry. He was a short, sturdy man with a graying comb-over and alert eyes that always seemed to be looking upward. He worked in aeronautics, designing control panels for shuttles. He had always been infatuated with flight, and that was a big part of how Beryl came to be, but he always made clear that his daughter was at the center of his heart.

Enthralled by his daughter above, he didn't notice me as I walked up to him. From time to time, he spoke to Beryl through a radio headset. Though he had seen her fly dozens of times, he always got wrapped up in the experience, entranced. He startled, embarrassed, when I had to tap his shoulder to gain his attention.

"Oh! I didn't see you there," he said, giving me the briefest of glances before turning back to Beryl circling above. "You must be Margaret... from Zeen, right?"

"That's right. Maggie Janowicz from Zeen. You must be Jerry."

I had been working at Zeen for three years – my first job. Three years at Zeen was long enough to learn the ropes, develop my skills, and get bored. It was a typical online plaza of the time, hosting social groups, light articles, and shopritunities. I wrote society columns, celebrity obits, and travel pieces. I also did plenty of celebrity interviews – usually "where are they now?" stories, which is what brought me to Beryl.

I held out my hand to Jerry, but his attention was locked on his daughter. He wasn't ignoring me to be rude, but he was definitely ignoring me. His eyes were only for her. I gave up on interaction, took off my heavy pack of equipment, and stood beside him to watch Beryl for a while.

Human beings are clumsy creatures. When you watch a penguin swim or a cheetah run, our awkwardness is even more apparent. So, to see a winged human surf invisible currents of air is simply astounding. Witnessing Beryl's swoops and dives was meditative and transcendent. You imagine Arthur transformed into a hawk by Merlin during his training to be king. You envision yourself up there, floating elegantly in the ether, and it's mesmerizing.

"You watch her like you've never seen her fly before," I remarked.

Jerry shot me a grin before turning his eyes upward again. "It's just fantastic. Do you see how she dipped her wings just so, to catch a current? She can't see the flow of the wind. She can only feel it, and somehow I think she might even respond to it <u>before</u> she feels it. She didn't have anybody to teach her how to do that. She just knows.

"Humans have been doing the same old things for thousands and thousands of years. But Beryl is the first human to fly, and she taught herself, and she can <u>do it</u>. I'll never stop being impressed by that," he beamed.

"No argument here," I said. "It's breathtaking just to watch."

He nodded. "She is so beautiful up there." He sounded wistful. Then he sighed and added, "Sorry for being so distracted. This is important time for me and Beryl. I have to travel a lot for work. Too much. I don't get to spend as much time with her as I would like – not as much time as I should. This is our time. I don't mean to give you the cold shoulder."

I didn't say anything, but I thought it was interesting that he considered watching her fly as time spent together. It seemed like a big distance between them, but maybe it wasn't, really. They both seemed content, and a lot of kids would kill for their parents to watch them with that kind of pride and intensity.

"She's coming down," he said.

We watched her approach in a slow glide, then tilt her wings and body upward before alighting on her feet. As she walked toward us, I wasn't startled by her awkward stride or alien appearance – I had seen the videos of First Flight, after all – but, strangely enough, I was struck by her lack of height. At most, she was four feet tall, and though I knew she had to have been a teen by then, her short stature made her seem like a little kid. I had read that she was very small, but I pictured her taller for some reason.

"Great flight, kiddo," Jerry said, getting down on one knee and gently patting Beryl's shoulder. "How were the winds today?"

"Good! Getting a little chilly, but not too bad." Beryl's voice was both squeaky and raspy. It sounded less like a little girl and more like the high-pitched, burnt-out vocal cords of a retired heavy metal shrieker. "I think it will be warm enough for at least a few more weeks of flying."

"We'll see about that. Keep your eyes on the forecast and always check with Mom or Beth, okay? Low winds and not too cold."

"Okay."

"Beryl, I'd like you to meet Maggie. She writes for a plaza, and she's here to do the interview we talked about."

"Hi, Maggie!" she said. She seemed enthusiastic, which made my job a lot easier. I hate doing these interviews when the interviewee and I both know that they're just using me to try to add a few more seconds to their fifteen minutes of fame that expired years ago. They act like they're entitled to my time and attention. I could tell right away that Beryl didn't have that vibe at all.

"I'll need some video," I added. "Is it okay if I shoot some video from time to time?"

"Sure. Should I fly for you?" She was clearly excited about the opportunity, even though she'd just been flying. She bounced with excitement.

"No, no," her dad said. "You've had enough for one day. Don't want you tiring out and going Icarus on us."

"Oh, Dad. You always bring up Icarus when you don't want me to do something."

"It's okay," I said. "I'm sure I'll catch you flying again at some point. But everybody's seen you fly before. I'd like to get some video of you doing things that others haven't seen before. Not tricks or something forced... just you being yourself."

It was difficult to read Beryl. Her facial features and gestures are so different. But sometimes it's easy. She cocked her head forward and to the side so she could get a good eye on me. Then she bobbed her head twice in assent and squeaked, "Okay by me."

We left the netted enclosure and walked up to the house, slowly to accommodate Beryl. Though everyone has seen her fly, most haven't seen any video of her walking. She walks very deliberately, lifting each skinny leg higher than most humans would lift them. She places her feet as though she were walking tip-toe, straight down rather than heel-toe. When walking swiftly, she often adds a little hop between steps. A few loose feathers slipped out from underneath her cloak as she pulled it more tightly around her.

The Pritchard house was a large old farmhouse on a lot of well-tended land. The house had been expanded and modernized at some point, but it still had a simplistic, homey charm. The exterior was beautifully landscaped, and a Lincoln hSD was parked on the circular, groomed, pebble driveway.

We settled into a cozy little room. Beryl slumped forward into a chair that seemed specially built for her – a cushioned oval filled with blankets that she snuggled into. The low side of the chair was toward the wall, such that if a normal human sat in that chair, she would have faced the wall. Instead, Beryl laid on her front, feet toward the wall, and her long, hard nose peeked over the high side of the chair as though she were peering at us over the edge of a nest. She sighed with pleasure as she pulled blankets over her wings.

"Beryl will need a few minutes to relax before you start grilling her," Jerry teased. "All that flying followed by walking is taxing for her."

"The flying is perfectly fine," she said with a mock glare at her father. "My body's just not built for the walking." She turned to Jerry. "Dad, can you turn on the electric blanket? My back and legs are sore."

He plugged in one of the blankets and settled it over Beryl to cover her a little better. He kissed the hair on top of her head. She closed her eyes as the warmth eased her aches.

Jerry left us to make some hot chocolate. I pulled out my video equipment and tripod, my screen, my good microphone. Then I sat and studied the face of the girl I had come to interview.

Though not a long face, her extremely large, beaklike nose made it seem so. It split her face into two sides, her small eyes widely spaced to make room. I guessed that she could only see something with both eyes if it were directly in front of her. Her mouth was a small treasure, mostly hidden under her nose. She had no chin, and her round yet lean cheeks added to the youthfulness of her appearance. But though she looked young, she was certainly not a pretty little girl. Her alien appearance made her look weird at best. I wondered what her social circles were like. I tapped some additional questions into the list on my screen.

The interview had been my idea. Like I said, I frequently do those obnoxious (yet hard to resist) articles about what happened to flash-in-the-pan celebrities after their fame waned. When I brought the idea up at our story meeting, I knew it was a winner because everybody looked upward and murmured, "Oh, yeah... I remember that."

And who didn't remember First Flight? I was in college at the time. You couldn't find a hub or plaza that wasn't broadcasting a livefeed. A little ball of feathers that was supposed to be the first human to fly, but didn't look like us at all. And yet she reminded us of ourselves, sort of like I imagine adults felt when the first astronauts went to the moon. They knew that they'd never go to the moon, but they wondered if their kids might. They knew it was a milestone for humanity and imagined endless possibilities.

I watched First Flight in my boyfriend's apartment, fending off his clumsy gropes as I tried to focus on the images on my screen. I uncurled it from around my arm and flattened it across my lap, both so I'd have more visible screen area and to act as a makeshift chastity belt. I remember seeing what looked like an angel silhouetted against pure blue sky. She didn't fly for very long that day – it was just a first attempt – but it was more than enough to amaze.

The camera zoomed in to show more detail. Her wings trembled as they learned to read the wind. Hair streamed over the feathers on her neck and back. It was hard to see her facial expression from below, but her mouth was wide open like a kid on her first roller coaster ride: fear, excitement, exhilaration.

The video cut to the crowd below, faces alternately excited, concerned, and joyous. Then it cut to family members watching. Her father stood riveted, jaw agape, awestruck. Her mother, Audrey, looked down at a handscreen with a thoughtful expression. Standing triumphantly beside the parents, Horace Morrow, the founder and CEO of Imhotep Genetics, beamed as he watched Beryl, then he looked straight at the camera and gave a proud nod.

"Caught you peeking," Beryl said. I had been staring at her, zoned out, while immersed in the memories. "It's okay," she said. "Everybody looks at me like that."

"I wasn't staring because you're…" I was uncharacteristically flustered. While lost in thought, I had probably been looking at her like she was some sort of freak.

"Different?" she answered.

"Right. I was just remembering where I was during First Flight," I explained. I felt like an idiot.

"Okay," Beryl soothed. "It's not a big deal."

"I have a genetically modified niece," I added, immediately making it worse. At least I didn't say what I had been thinking: "She looks even stranger than you."

"Would you like to touch?" she asked, holding out her wing.

Oh, God. I remember when I was a kid and the other kids would ask if they could touch my hair. I was so embarrassed. There were plenty of black girls in the city, but not many in the suburbs where I lived. It made me feel different. Separate.

At the same time, I had to admit, I really did want to touch her wing, to feel where feathers met human flesh over strange but familiar musculature. Propriety won over curiosity, and I resisted the urge.

"That's very kind of you," I said diplomatically, "but let's try to stick to business, and my business is to ask you questions."

Beryl straightened her back and smiled, like a good student preparing to be quizzed by her favorite teacher.

"What do you remember about that day - the day of First Flight?" It was a softball question. One that I'm sure she'd been asked many times before. A good place to start.

"Gosh, it seems so long ago. I was nervous. So many people. Before that day, I hadn't met hardly anybody but my parents, the household help, and the team from IG, so it was pretty crazy with all of those people there. And I was only seven years old. Maybe that helped a little – not having much perspective, expecting to be the center of the world.

"Every day leading up to First, a team would help me exercise, check my vitals, and inspect every feather. You wouldn't believe all the equipment we had in here for measuring lift, drag, stress, and strain. There was a drop machine that gave me the sensation of falling with my wings open so I could get a feel for how gliding might work. We even had a wind tunnel out back for a while. But birds use such different mechanisms for flying... well, nobody knew for sure if I'd be able to do it until I did it.

"Anyway, the crowds made me jittery, but probably not as freaked out as I would have been if I were older. I think I was anxious mostly because I didn't know if I could do it. I wanted to with all my heart. Preparing for First Flight was what my whole life was about! I wanted to make my family proud of me, and I wanted to be the first. Even though I didn't really understand what that meant."

"Do you understand it differently now?"

"I don't know. Flying is still who I am. I love flying more than I love doing anything. But I understand it's not important to the world anymore. I was the first. That's done. It's in the past – trivia question material. So now I do it for me. It feels so good. Better than if I were still doing it for others."

"So you don't do it for your dad? He's very proud of you."

She paused to think about that. "No, that's more like sharing. I fly for myself and to make myself happy. That makes him happy because he enjoys watching me fly and because he enjoys making me happy. And it makes me happy to make him happy, but that's not the source of the happiness. Does that make sense? Sometimes a circle has a starting point."

I jotted some notes on my screen. Her answers sounded unrehearsed. I don't think anybody had interviewed her in a long time. Not even the locals. I hadn't expected that. I also hadn't expected her answers to be so thoughtful. She could see herself from outside. Often even the older celebrities I interview are still so wrapped up inside themselves that they lack any kind of perspective.

"I'm sorry. I interrupted your memory of First Flight. You were telling me about what happened beforehand, but not about the flight itself."

"Oh, right! Well, it was amazing. I'll never forget it. I spent some time warming up with my usual exercises. Then I walked up the stairs to the Perch. The media was told to call it a platform – IG wanted the story to be about the first human to fly, not the first bird-person. But we all called it the Perch. Even when we weren't practicing, I liked to spend time up there feeling the wind. Still do.

"Anyway, I had practiced gliding from the Perch before – gliding humans weren't new – but I hadn't done any real self-propelled flying before. The Perch was a great place to start because I could start with a glide, then pull myself up.

"I was so scared it wasn't going to work. That I wouldn't be able to do it. But when I jumped into my first glide and then started to push with my wings... I can't tell you how amazing and natural it felt. It just worked. I could do it. And I loved it. It was hard to breathe."

"Maybe it was hard to breathe because your mouth was wide open," I suggested teasingly.

"Maybe!" she laughed. "I was just amazed and excited and in love with the world. Even though I had a radio in my ear, it took them a while to get me down because I couldn't hear anything except the wind."

"Or chose not to," Jerry said, entering the room with cocoa. "I'm glad we had the netting up, or she could have flown to Mexico and forgotten all about us!"

"Whatever, Dad," she said as she accepted her cocoa and started sipping it with a straw. "I got tired pretty quickly. Even with all the exercises, my flying muscles weren't as developed back then. The wings take the most strength, but it's also the back and legs and muscles I hadn't known even existed. But I lasted longer than they expected," she said with satisfaction. "I didn't come down the first time they told me to," she added with a sly smile.

"Tempts fate, that's what she does," Jerry said.

Predictably, the topic of the interview remained centered around flying: how often, what kind of weather, favorite season, favorite sights, and so on. I was surprised to learn that she never flew anywhere but at home. The family had a lot of land, all of it with netting strung across huge towers. The netting was widely spaced so bugs, bats, and most birds were able to fly in and out, but larger creatures (like little girls) would be stopped.

"We wouldn't want her to blow away in a storm," Jerry said. "Worst case scenario with this setup, she can grab ahold and climb down."

"Besides," Beryl said, "Imhotep would have a fit if I flew anywhere else or had a fall."

"Are they still involved?" I asked.

"Not much," Jerry answered. "They come by from time to time for a checkup. I trust their doctors more than a normal doctor. Chimaeras are just too unique, and Imhotep knows them inside and out."

"But they can restrict Beryl's actions?" I asked. "They can keep her from flying anywhere but here?"

"They have some common-sense recommendations that we follow," Jerry said. He winced with sudden realization. "In fact, they're pretty sensitive about public relations. You should probably check with them to make sure this is okay."

"I would be happy to," I said. I had already asked and received tentative approval, of course. I would need to submit my story to them for a final go-ahead prior to publication. Companies could make life very difficult for journalists who didn't cooperate with them. There were a handful of reporters and anchors who could flout big business those days, but not many. I certainly wasn't one of them.

"What's life like for you now?" I asked.

"Probably the same as any kid," she responded. "School, friends, flying. I also like gardening."

"What school do you go to?"

"Online courses through Memphis Middle and the high school. I can pick whatever classes I want and set my own pace. I'm taking algebra and English at the high school level, but the rest of my classes are from middle school. Lectures are pre-recorded, but discussions and presentations are all done with the other kids over screens."

"What are your favorite classes?"

"Math makes sense and is fun, but it isn't very useful, yet. I'm enjoying biology because of my gardening. And I'm enjoying history, though I think four years of American history before learning about the history of any other places is a little extreme. I'm looking forward to world history next year."

"She does very well in school," Jerry added. "Takes after her mom." He grinned.

"But you do all of your schooling from here?" I continued. "You don't go to a classroom or do activities at the local schools?"

Beryl looked confused. "No, I'm pretty much here all the time. I don't do any extra-curriculars through the school. Just classes."

"That's pretty normal," Jerry chimed in. "A lot of school buildings have closed because more and more students attend classes remotely."

I remembered that trend catching on in the universities when I was a student there, but I hadn't realized it had spread to high schools and middle schools as well.

"Tell me about your friends," I said. "Who are they, and what kinds of things do you like to do together?"

"I really enjoy working on projects with the kids in my classes," Beryl answered excitedly. "Once, Karla and I were supposed to be working on a history project, and Karla kept trying to search for articles about some sort of Hoover Man and a terrible thing that happened to him. She kept going on and on about how she couldn't find any articles that weren't about vacuum salesmen and past presidents. When I figured out what was going on and told her it was supposed to be about the destruction of the Hoover Dam, her eyes got so wide I thought they were going to pop right out. She screamed so loudly I saw her mother come running into the room behind her."

I chuckled. "You weren't working in the same room?"

"No, we were working over screens. It's just easier that way."

"Do you ever go to your friends' houses?" I asked.

She thought about that for a while. She began to look a little anxious.

"She's very social," Jerry chipped in. "Well connected with the other students."

I reminded myself this was a fluff piece. Time to change the subject again. "You said you like gardening?" I asked brightly.

"Oh, yes," she said emphatically, her face lighting up. "Flowers and vegetables. I'm outside a lot."

I asked some follow up questions, which she was very enthusiastic about answering. As the first frost approached, all of the southern facing rooms in the house became temporary greenhouses, filled with plants brought in for winter or seedlings to be nurtured for spring planting. She extricated herself from her nest chair and showed me the plants she had already brought in from outside, explaining some of the other late-year tasks she hadn't completed yet. The humidity fogged windows, and the air felt simultaneously sticky and clean. I took some stills and video of Beryl in her room of greenery.

I had almost all of the material I needed for the article I planned to write, but I asked Beryl, "If Imhotep gives the go-ahead, is it okay if I come talk with you again?" I used the easy hook. "I'd love to get some fresh video of you flying as a teen. I don't know if anybody has any video of you since you were eight or nine."

"Didn't you catch any earlier with your temple?"

"No," I replied, tapping the implanted device near my eye, "There's always too much inadvertent body movement for the temple to catch video of the quality I need. If I shift even just a little, it's distracting for the viewer. I'd need to break out my tripod and higher quality equipment."

"No, no, that sounds great!" Beryl answered enthusiastically. "Can you come tomorrow?"

"Probably," I replied. "I should talk with Imhotep's PR guys first."

"I'll be out of town tomorrow," Jerry said, "but that should be okay. Beryl's mom works late most nights, but Beth will be here."

"Beth helps with my homeschooling and tends to the house," Beryl explained. "She's probably the one who made the hot cocoa."

Jerry smiled sheepishly. "You got me there. How did you know I didn't make it?"

"It tastes like hot cocoa," Beryl responded with a grin.

* * * * * *

As my autonomous taxi drove me to my sister's house, I queried the shabti in my ear.

"Hey, Nable."

"Yes?" he responded. The folks over at Tokugara sure knew how to program vocals. Nable's smooth, resonant voice could soothe a stampeding buffalo.

"What did you think of all of that?" AI had come a long way, even in those days, and could understand even complex directives and informational requests. However, sometimes you could catch them off guard with open-ended questions. So I asked them. A lot. It was mostly for my own entertainment value, but over time Nable learned and improved, and I think some of that was independent of firmware upgrades.

"I don't understand why we're going back there again tomorrow," Nable responded.

"Did you catch any quality video of her flying?"

"Of course I did," Nable replied. His tone was even, but I imagined that he sounded insulted. "You specifically chose your temple because of its built-in hardware and software for smoothing out imperfections due to bodily movements. In addition, you purchased me specifically because my model integrated well with that particular temple."

"I'm glad you're paying attention," I smirked. Nable was right to be confused, if that was the right term for whatever he was experiencing. There was no need to return to the Pritchard homestead. So why had I arranged to do so? In part, I was bored with my job at Zeen writing tinsel pieces. In part, I was enjoying getting to know Beryl. But the answer that was more relevant to Nable was that I thought there was more story. I hoped there was more story. I needed substance, and I hoped to find it in the world of that strange little girl.

"If you dig enough, you always find something," I finally answered. "It might just be the other side of the world."

CHAPTER 2

"Water and sun, whad'ya know?
"That's all it takes to make plants grow."
– Gary Ganser's Garden Guide

I ripped a particularly stubborn dried-up tomato plant from its place in my vegetable garden, stumbling backward with the effort. I ruffled my feathers to shake loose some of the soil that had sprayed everywhere, then tossed the husk into a wheelbarrow and grabbed for the next one. Nature was closing up shop for the year, so I was spending a lot of time harvesting late crops, digging up the last of the delicate perennials to bring indoors, and preparing the beds for spring.

Behind flying, I loved gardening most of all. In the spring I couldn't wait for young shoots to peek out of their beds. I'd try to be patient and not poke at them, but it was a personal battle. Later, sometimes I'd rearrange the newborns to make sure they had enough room to grow. In summer, I kept the peace, weeding out the troublemakers. I taught myself, mostly by experimenting, watching, and waiting. If a new plant started growing in an area, I would give it time and space to see if it could live in harmony with its neighbors or if it would become aggressive. If it was a bad neighbor, suffocating the others, out it went and I'd know better in the future. If it behaved itself and looked nice, then it would become part of the family, and maybe I'd move it over by the daffodils or in front of the compass plants. My focus is on native plants, but I've got some exotics too. Since the beginning, I've taken gigs of notes and pictures about each plant's cycle so I can provide what each one needs. I feel like I'm really starting to get it - like it has a rhythm that makes sense to me.

I tugged a gourd from its vine and held it up for inspection. If I hollowed it out, I thought it might make a nice home for a wren next year.

Spending a lot of time outside, you get to know more than just the flora. For example, there was a nest of garden snakes below the porch – harmless and shy, not particularly friendly. When I first found them a few years ago, I brought one inside. If you hold them by the end of the tail, they have trouble reaching up to bite you. I set it down on the kitchen counter in order to find something to put it in. Of course, by the time I looked back, it had slithered away. A little rude for a houseguest, but I wasn't particularly insulted. I also wasn't as concerned as maybe I should have been. I certainly wasn't as concerned as Beth was when she found the snake in the laundry the next day. Holy smokes, was she mad.

I just love learning about how the world works. During summer, tables were littered with bark and fungus, rocks and mud, feathers and snake skins. For Beth's sake (and the sake of the lizards, insects, and other creatures), I didn't bring any more living animals into the house after the laundry incident. Still, I was free to study them outside. I learned about the migration of geese, what baby snakes look like, and found where the mice were sneaking into the siding of the house (I kept that to myself). I identified seventeen types of mushroom and every type of tree on our property. I knew my domain.

As I brought the gourd to the porch so it could come inside with me later, my mind drifted back to the conversation with Maggie. Even when I tried to distract myself, it tickled into my brain.

I was excited that a reporter from a national plaza would come and interview me. Me! True, it was for something that I did ages ago, but it was still cool. I hadn't thought much about First Flight before the reporter came. I wasn't the same girl as that famous seven year-old; my life back then was activity and preparation. Afterward, the attention and hubbub died down fast, and all of a sudden I was alone most of the time. I liked it. In the quiet times, I could use the focus and patience I'd developed while learning to fly on other projects, like my garden. Before First Flight all the adults were paying attention to me and experimenting on me. In my garden, I was the one guiding everything and tracking the results. Besides, I felt a little like a scientist. Like Mom.

Gourd safely away, I hunkered down with a bucket to dig up four o'clock tubers. I swept away the surface mulch, then cut into the compacted soil underneath, following the desiccated stems to their source. Late-afternoon blooms and the smell of four o'clocks are awesome, but if you don't keep a close watch, they can get out of control quickly. The seeds have a habit of getting into beds where they aren't welcome. Still, I love how this hearty, beautiful plant with crazy colors comes from such a grubby little root. I held one up like a trophy before plopping it into a bucket to store until spring.

Maggie was so sophisticated, especially compared to Midwestern me, mucking around in the dirt. First impression, she struck me as a crocus: friendly, pretty, appearing when you'd least expect it. Exciting. New. Different. She didn't sound like I expected somebody from New York to sound, but she was tall and had strange, fancy clothes. She didn't have a purse, but I imagine a journalist wouldn't want to carry two bags. The backpack somehow seemed more professional. Even her dark skin was refreshingly different – most of the normies I knew were pale, suburban Wisconsinites.

But she got me thinking. Maybe I just didn't know many people. It's true I don't get out much. Not at all, really. And my friends aren't really friends. They're just classmates, and all we do together are school projects.

Before Maggie, when was the last time I'd met somebody new? In person? Not counting online schoolmates, it had been nearly a year. The postal worker had gotten sick, and a younger man – not the normal sub – had done the weekly route. That was it. A backup postman. My entire life was the household: Mom, Dad, Beth, the mowers, the postman, and the very rare visit from one of Mom or Dad's old friends. Everything else was through a screen. I couldn't even remember the last time I went beyond our yard. I knew every inch of it so well because it was the only place I ever went.

Maybe that was why I liked my gardens so much. The constant cycle gave the impression of unending newness. But really, maybe I was just going around in circles.

My knees and back ached, but there was so much that still needed to be done before deep frost set in. I wouldn't give up until I had to.

I looked forward to Maggie coming back, mostly for the chance to fly on a chilly October day when I normally might not be able to. Mom and Dad get really fussy about flying when it gets cold, and I was not looking forward to being separated from sky and garden over the long Wisconsin winter. Frost had already glistened our lawn a couple of times that week, and I probably wouldn't have been allowed to fly if it weren't for the visit from the reporter. Any excuse to squeeze in another flight was a good excuse.

I took off my gloves and grabbed my bucket of roots to bring inside. It would be dark soon. Too early. Normally it was fun to hang out with Dad, and schoolwork wasn't too bad. But that night and the following morning would feel painfully stretched while I waited for the reporter to come back and the other unexpected visitor, loneliness, to go away for a little while.

CHAPTER 3

You want to see weird?
First, define perfection, then
Look in the mirror.
- "Perfection" a haiku by Seth Farfelle

When you haven't seen family in a long time, the next encounter is increasingly awkward. The more time goes by, the more awkward. Like anybody else, my elder sister and I had some sense of what was going on in each other's lives through our various pictures, videos, and random comments on the net. But we hadn't spoken directly to each other in years - not even over screens. It had been over five years since we'd seen each other in person.

There was no great row – no disagreement or ill will – keeping us apart. We were both busy, living separate lives, distant from one another. She had her family and her job. I had my own work. And the net gave us the illusion that we were keeping in touch.

When the interview with Beryl brought me to Memphis, Wisconsin, at first I thought to myself, "What a great opportunity to see my sister!" It was only when it came to the matter of calling her up that I realized how long it had been, that the first tendrils of awkwardness seeped in.

It had been a long time. Was that my fault? Was it hers? Did she not call because she didn't want to talk with me? Would she welcome me? Or would she blame me for not calling to say hi from time to time? Tendrils of guilt and anxiety wormed through me in ways that only happen with family.

Fortunately, journalists are masters of overcoming embarrassment and discomfort. We talk with strangers every day, asking questions most people wouldn't ask their spouses. "Yes, shameless celebrity, I did just ask you for your measurements. And can you respond to the rumors that you've been sleeping with the pool boy?"

Some journalists don't mind asking those questions because they have huge egos and they enjoy the attention that asking those questions draws to themselves. The rest of us are self-conscious like anybody else, but we know that the other side of those questions brings rewards: sated curiosity, the opportunity to craft a story, and pride in our work. So you push past the awkwardness by saying, "Fuck it," taking a deep breath, and just forcing yourself to do it.

That's why I said, "Fuck it," before I called my sister to let her know I'd be in town. It's why I took a deep breath as I pulled my luggage out of the cab at her house. I put my logic hat on, knew she wouldn't have invited me to stay if she didn't want me to be there, and soldiered up to the front door and rang the bell.

Of course, everything was fine. Jessie welcomed me with a warm embrace, and it was back to normal in a flash. That's the other side of family, I suppose. No matter how long it's been, the bonds don't loosen.

She looked good – more mature, but not old. She looked like a suburban mother. How does that happen? Does a woman without a child get those same worry creases, those few extra pounds, the hairstyle that says, "I'm doing my best, but I just don't have time for this"?

After the normal welcome-to-my-house conversation pieces like, "How good to see you!" and, "Here's the bathroom," we settled in around the dining table for some food. Jessie yelled upstairs for her teenage daughter, Seth, to come down to supper.

Jessie and her husband, Phil, didn't have an estate like the Pritchards, but they were certainly doing well for themselves. Phil's real-estate business alternated between good years and great years. The tech industry had taken off in Memphis, in large part because of the growth of Imhotep Genetics since First Flight. With an increase in white-collar jobs comes the need for housing, and Phil's company took advantage of the opportunity. Jessie worked in Milwaukee as an RN, mostly for the health insurance, but also because she just enjoyed being around people. She was not the sort who could be happy with an inactive life.

Phil was late at work and wouldn't be joining us for dinner, so we started to serve ourselves and dig in. I had just asked Jessie if she enjoyed her new role in the oncology department when we were interrupted by a raucous "CLOMP, CLOMP, CLOMP!" from somewhere in the house. Startled, I jumped a bit, as did the knick-knacks on nearby shelves.

"It's just Seth coming down the stairs," Jessie reassured me. "For some reason, teen feet are ten times heavier than normal feet."

Seth skidded into the room with a loud, "Hi, Aunt Maggie!" and plopped into her chair. She started slopping stew into her bowl, and once again I was caught staring like a cow at a genetically modified young woman.

It's not that I hadn't seen Seth before. I remember the manic little ball of fur rampaging around when she was younger. But this was a much bigger ball of fur, apparently still manic, and her energy extended way beyond her physical boundaries. She was like lightning in a fuzzy bottle, much bigger than herself. Bigger than the pictures I'd seen on my screen as she grew up over the years.

Teen heavy-mods are like any other teenagers, only more so. Outcasts, uncertain about where they fit in. Angry, confused, hormonal, and just plain weird. Seth was all of these things... with an emphasis on weird. She was clearly pieced together from several animals, but it wasn't possible to tell for certain which ones. She was short and stocky, and appeared to be fully covered with short fur. She had alert, rectangular ears, a beaver's head with large, wide-set eyes, and her long, fleshy, yamlike nose was distracting at best. In addition to her own physical peculiarities, she wore classic Goth gear from decades ago, and she had colored her small, vertical tuft of coarse hair a bright purple.

"If you want my advice, cut down on your toilet time as much as possible," she told us as she grabbed a fistful of crackers and filled a second bowl of stew before even starting to eat from the first one. "Just do your business and get out of there.

"Think about it. We could be instantly killed at any given moment, and our remains frozen in the middle of the last thing we were doing. Remember Pompeii? Hiroshima? It happens! And I don't want anybody laughing and pointing at my radioactive silhouette in a museum a hundred years from now because I got myself killed on the crapper."

I tried not to choke on my salad.

"What were we talking about?" she asked.

"I was asking your mother how she liked her new job," I answered.

"Whoa. Major tangent, eh? I wonder how we got started talking about going to the bathroom." She laughed and then started shoveling food into her mouth. The food didn't stop her from asking, "Did you know that dolphins can't swallow while they're breathing?"

Though I was pretty sure that wasn't true, the last thing I wanted to do was start a marine biology discussion. I could see Jessie rolling her eyes. Apparently, this sort of conversational ricochet was typical for Seth. She would remain the center of attention until she left the table.

"I had no idea," I answered. I could handle this. Talking with a teenager is no different than talking with a celebrity. You just keep asking questions. "So, what is it like being a heavy-mod in Memphis?"

As I expected, Seth rolled with it. She didn't care what she was talking about as long as she was talking. "Mixed bag. There are a lot of us here because Imhotep is here – I can't imagine what it would be like to be a heavy in Wyoming or something. But we've got a lot of heavies around here." She put her fuzzy, three-fingered hands on the table and leaned forward, her proboscis almost touching the table. "And some of them are weird."

"Do you feel separate from those of us who aren't modified?" My interest started to pique. After all, Seth wasn't just my niece. She was part of a new subculture that was perhaps unique to this area. She was exciting. New. Different. Maybe I could learn something about Beryl while learning about my niece.

"Different from normies? Yeah. And cosmetics, too. But it's all perception. In your perception, you categorize us... you put us in a little box with a padlock and a warning label. Most normans like you don't want to look in that box. You're an exception, maybe.

"And the heavies all have different perceptions. Some think they're science's gift to humanity. Others think they're trans-human – there's a whole movement. Others feel alone. Separate.

"Meanwhile, the cosmetics think they're everybody's friend. They're mostly norman, so they fit in with your type, but they're also visibly different, so they think they're a little like the heavies. They're not. Cosmos are just experiments in style that are out of fashion before they even grow up. Like putting a tattoo on a baby."

"So you think parents shouldn't engineer light mods into their children?" I asked.

"Ah, who am I to judge?" Seth answered. "Claws and eagle eyes would be pretty cool. If I had whiskers, I'd clip the damn things off, though. My buddy Thasha would say it's a racket. A cosmetic who later becomes a parent is going to be more likely to engineer their child, right? Keep the genes they liked having, drop the inconvenient ones, add a couple of enhancements, et cetera. Since fashion always changes, there will always be a need for adjustments to cosmo kids. And those kids will engineer their kids. Cosmetic modification is a self-promoting business. At least, that's what Thasha says. I don't claim to know.

"That reminds me of a haiku I wrote once.

I do not envy
Your cat eyes and fur-tipped ears.
Where's your matching purse?

"I also have a haiku about corduroy pants. Want to hear it?"

Seth seemed to be able to both eat and talk unceasingly. Whenever she stopped talking, she immediately started eating or drinking. Sometimes both at the same time. She had already downed one of her bowls of stew and a piece of bread. If I ate like Seth, I'd look like a manatee in less than a month. Teenagers. Fortunately, her nose covered most of her mouth, so much of the frenzied mastication went mercifully unseen.

Despite her piranha-like feeding behavior, she was perceptive. In my line of work, the more somebody has to say, the less likely the value of the content. Seth was different. She clearly thought about the world and her place in it.

I had an idea. It was one of those little thoughts that you wouldn't expect to become the beginning of a big thing, but later you realize was the start of something. I thought there was a bigger story in the mods of Memphis. If nothing else, they were probably interesting from a sociological point of view, but I wagered folks on the plaza would be interested in how modified teenagers live. Simultaneously, I thought Beryl might like meeting somebody new – a chimaera like her and yet totally different. I spoke before thinking about it too hard.

"I just met someone who's a heavy-mod. I don't think she gets out much. Would you be interested in talking with her?" It felt right, bringing these two together.

Jessie knew who I was in town to interview, but Seth did not. My sister's eyebrows raised, but she kept quiet.

"My life is pretty packed," Seth said as she finished her second bowl of stew, "but I can probably fit it in. She new to town? Does her mod make her really slow or mute or something – is that why she doesn't get out? Is she orange? God, I'd hate to be orange."

"No, she's lived here all her life, and you've probably heard of her – Beryl Pritchard?"

Seth spluttered bits of bread and meat onto her plate, clouded in a mist of gravy. Jessie buried her face in her hands.

"No shit?" she asked, dabbing ineffectually with a napkin at the mess of gravy and half-chewed meat that had landed near her plate. She looked at her mom, "Er – no kidding? That's crazy." She shook her head. "Yeah, I'll show her around. Everyone is going to want to meet her. And I mean everyone. I'll teach her who to look out for, too." She raised one eyebrow and gave a single, slow nod that meant, "Trust me… I got this."

It's hard to know who to put one's trust in, but despite Seth's eccentricities, she seemed like a good kid. If I had understood how dangerous some of the heavies were, I would have been more cautious, but my naivety and optimism ruled the day. For some reason, I had a feeling that something important would come of connecting this bizarre young niece who was perhaps part anteater or wombat with Beryl. In a world with chimaeras, it's easy to believe that anything is possible.

Seth got down to the business of hoovering up the rest of her supper. After talking briefly about her theory that Nicolas Cage was cryogenically frozen under Death Valley, Seth abruptly left the table and ran upstairs. Her place at the table looked like a raccoon had gotten into a grocery bag.

"Is she always like that?" I asked zigging my hand back and forth.

"It's exhausting just being with her," Jessie admitted. She got up to clear Seth's plate and clean up the crumbs and splatters that surrounded it.

"Why did you and Phil decide to have a modified child?" I asked.

Jessie sat back in her chair and thought for a minute. I had never asked her that before. Figured she had her reasons. "Phil had friends at Imhotep. We were young, and married (and poor), and wanted a healthy child. Phil hadn't gotten his business off the ground, and nurses' wages had taken a tumble when the health insurance companies lost all that money on their investments. We'd had a genetic consultation and knew that any child of ours would have a high chance of defects.

"Imhotep offered us a deal. They'd give us a healthy baby at a discount if we agreed to a heavy mod. We'd get to pick various traits, and she'd be free of any chronic illnesses from our genetic lines. It was a good deal."

"You've never told me," I started, but I wasn't sure how to ask nicely, "what she is. What kinds of traits did you choose?" The rest of the family had all made their guesses as to what kinds of animals' genes had gone into Seth, but Jessie and Phil had never told.

"She's our daughter," Jessie answered with a voice that very clearly communicated that I should not follow that line of questioning any further. "And obviously we chose sugar, spice, and everything nice."

"Obviously!" I replied with a smile, once again waving the white flag to my big sister.

"She'll be very excited to meet Beryl," Jessie continued. "Thank you for doing that. Do you have an angle, here?"

"I don't know," I responded. "They're both unique kids. More than anything, I just want to see what happens."

CHAPTER 4

"Diversity breeds unexpected commonalities." – Dr. Horace Morrow

When I heard the knock on the front door, I whooped with delight. I knew it was Maggie, which meant company – a reporter is so much more interesting than a backup postman. Most importantly, it meant an opportunity to fly.

I carefully set down my watering can before hop-skipping to the front door as quickly as I could. I yelled to Beth to bring out the radio equipment as I opened the door. There she was! She had all sorts of filming gear in her hands and around her neck. I involuntarily cackled with glee. It would be a good day.

Maggie had her priorities straight. Without saying a word, we headed straight for the Perch, Beth following closely behind. Maggie started setting up her gear while Beth helped me with my goggles. Next came the radio headgear over my hair and earholes. "Testing, testing." Loud and clear, ready to go. Up the Perch I went. My arms are much stronger than my legs, so rather than climb up to the top, I hoisted myself with a crude, self-propelled bucket elevator that Dad had helped me set up a few years back. Well, he did the engineering and building, but I provided plenty of moral support. Mom doesn't like the elevator, but it has a safety mechanism so that if I were to let go, it would catch.

When I reached the top and got out, I immediately took three hopsteps to the edge of the Perch and threw myself from the platform. It probably looked reckless to Maggie, but I didn't care. Air streamed past my face, and then I stretched my wings wide and caught the breeze. I swooped forward low, then banked upward. I laughed hard with the pure joy of it, and for a short time I forgot all about Beth and Maggie.

After some swoops and dives, I pushed higher to find a good glide current. I tried to catch that sweet spot – a nook in the air currents where I could just hang over the world. When I found it, my senses expanded beyond my immediate surroundings, and I started to see and feel the larger world.

Orange, yellow, and some lingering green lay in a mottled carpet below me. The chilly air bit my face and hands, but it wasn't too cold yet. I didn't even need to move my wings. I felt like I could float forever in a meditative trance, unbound from the gravity of the world.

All too soon, I heard Beth in my ears. "It's time to come down."

"Oh, come on!" I replied. "I just got up here!"

"You've been flying for two hours," she responded sternly. "And you have a guest."

"A guest who came here to watch me fly!" I argued. But my lips were starting to numb. It probably had been two hours already, and I wanted a chance to visit with Maggie before she left. I began to spiral back down to earth.

"That was really great!" I screeched after landing, still riding high from my flight. I knew I was talking too fast, out of breath, wired like I am after any flight. "Even after gardening all morning, I was still able to fly strong that whole time. I really think my endurance is a lot higher than it was this time last year. Beth, did you know that Wilson's creek still has water even though it hasn't rained all week? I was pretty warm up there – warmer than last October. I think I have more down this year because I've been outdoors in the cold more often. My body is adjusting. I think I could fly well into November this year. I'll try to convince Mom and Dad. You'll help me, right? You'll let them know I flew strong and didn't get cold?"

Beth let the silence sit for a minute before answering. I had been babbling a bit. "I'll be honest with them; you don't have to worry about that. Just keep in mind that your lips are a little blue."

My hands tingled, too, but I wasn't about to let Beth know that. I'd need to find a way to protect my face and hands better.

"When do you normally get cut off?" Maggie asked.

"I've never been allowed to fly in November," I answered. "At that point, it's either too cold or too windy... according to the adults. Ugh. The wait for spring is sooo long. Why do we have to live in Wisconsin?"

"I imagine you're here because Imhotep is here," Maggie offered.

"Yeah, yeah. Mom's job. My doctors. It makes sense, but I sure wish we lived someplace where winter only lasted a month or two instead of four. It's the flying I miss."

"Well, maybe you're right and you'll be able to fly more if your down builds up," Maggie responded optimistically. "The birds certainly don't hibernate all winter."

"Some of them migrate," I responded. "They travel hundreds of miles. Or thousands. They see the world."

"And they always come back," Maggie said.

"Well, it's great here in the summer, so I can see that." I pondered for a minute. "I would miss the summers, here."

We had made it to the house. Beth skootched off to put the radio gear away and get some snacks – I was always hungry after a flight – and Maggie and I sat down to chat. I settled into my nest chair while Maggie pulled out a screen.

"You fly beautifully," she said, pulling up some video and images. "I could watch you all day."

"Thanks!" I responded.

"I thought you might like to see some of the video I captured." She showed me some of the video. The swoops and dives that felt so daring when I did them looked more graceful to the outside eye. The autumn colors were beautiful, with my brown feathers against gray October sky above orange leaves.

"It's really well shot," I said. The camera seemed to dance along with me early on, and later it pulled back for my glide, evoking the sense of serenity I felt when I was up there.

"My shabti, Nable, is programmed to help me capture the best shots, and I think he has a particularly good eye. Take a look at this."

The screen filled with a still image – a long shot, mostly sky with just a touch of tree line. I was small enough that, at a glance, you might think it was nature photography of a soaring bird, but if you looked again, you could see a human form and wild hair streaming back like a crest. It was human, but not human. If it weren't such a beautiful shot, it would be a little unnerving, even for me. But it was beautiful, and it brought up feelings of optimism about achieving the impossible.

"Tell Nable this is a great photo," I said.

"Nable can hear you," Maggie said, pointing to the shabti in her ear. "And he says thanks. We might use that shot as the link-lead for the story."

At some point while we were watching Maggie's screen, Beth had set some mugs of hot chocolate on the table. Perfect.

"Thanks, Beth!" I shouted loudly enough so that she could hear me wherever in the house she might be at the time. It startled Maggie a bit. My voice is terribly rough, so shouts come out more like shrieks.

The cocoa was delicious and soothed my lips, mouth, and throat. The yummy goodness crept into and coated my stomach. It felt so relaxing as I warmed from the inside out, and my muscles ached just enough to feel good. And then I realized I had missed something Maggie had been saying.

"What did you say?" I asked.

"You look tired," she responded. I know that's not what she had said, but she was right.

"Must be the combination of a good flight and the cocoa." I yawned. "I could probably use a nap," I admitted.

"After your nap, would you be interested in going out for supper?"

"What do you mean?" I asked.

"To a restaurant. To eat." Maggie grinned.

Out for supper. Nobody had ever asked me that before. We always ate at home. The idea that something so simple could be so foreign bothered me.

Was it okay for me to do that? My parents had never implied that I couldn't. What kept me homebound all day? Was it just habit and caution?

"Beth!" I shouted. "Can I go out to dinner with Maggie?"

Beth came out of the kitchen, which was right next to the cozy front room. Thankfully, she didn't scold me for yelling in front of Maggie.

"Your Mom will be late at work tonight, and your dad's on a trip," she said. "As long as you let me know where you're going and when to expect you home, I don't have a problem with not making you dinner for once." She winked, and I knew we were all good.

"I'll come by in a few hours, then," Maggie said, packing up her backpack with her gear. I could hear her taxi pull into the driveway.

"That sounds fantastic!" I said. I was excited, but I was so tired. I'm not sure if I heard the door close before I drifted off to sleep.

* * * * * *

Beth settled a cape around my shoulders to help me stay warm on the way to the restaurant.

"I haven't spoken with your parents," Beth said. "I'm sure they'll be okay with this, but since it's the first time you're going out without them-"

"First time going out at all, as far as I can remember," I interrupted.

"Since it's the first time you're going out without them," Beth continued, "you'll want to make sure you know what you're going to say to them. You can't just not tell them. People will notice you. Your mom and dad will hear about it one way or another."

I nodded. I hadn't thought further than just getting out of the house, but I was beginning to understand that there might be dominos here that I couldn't see. And I was okay with that. More than okay, I was excited. I caught myself hopping with anticipation. When I wasn't flying, I was bored. I was learning that I wanted to meet new people and do new things. It was about time for me to knock over a tile and see what happened.

Maggie's vehicle pulled in, and I waved goodbye to Beth. Maggie's shabti had sent the restaurant name and anticipated return time to Beth while I was sleeping. I did my best to politely chit-chat while the cab drove us to a shabby little Italian restaurant between Memphis and Milwaukee. My attention was split, though, as I was unfamiliar with the roads and looked outside the windows as much as possible to take in the new sights. Early in the drive, some of the landmarks were familiar – I had seen them from above, but I'd never seen them from land before.

The restaurant was tiny, the dining room not much bigger than our living room. It was fairly empty, too. It was early for supper, and this didn't look like the most popular restaurant in the world.

There was only one table with somebody sitting at it, and it was a heavy mod. I would say, 'a heavy mod like me', only she didn't look like me at all. She was furry with a potato nose and dark, spooky clothing. She had a bright purple tuft of hair sticking straight up like a challenge.

Strangely, Maggie took us straight to that table.

"Beryl, I'd like you to meet my niece, Seth," Maggie said.

My mouth gaped open. "I don't understand..." I started. Nobody told me we'd be meeting someone at the restaurant.

"I didn't know if you were serious," Seth said to Maggie. "Holy smokes, it's First Flight herself."

I just stood there, staring. It may sound strange, but I had never seen another chimaera in person before. I didn't have any heavy mods in my school classes. It was just me and the normal humans, and I was always the one who was different. I was always the center of attention. This was a whole new world opening up.

Seth began to look uncomfortable, and I realized I had been staring silently at her the whole time. Now I knew what it felt like on the other side of that look.

"Is she okay?" Seth asked.

I smiled, squealed a little bit, and leapt toward Seth with arms wide. I was so excited to meet another heavy mod that I couldn't resist the sudden urge to hug her. Unfortunately, the combination of expectant silence and my sudden lurch toward Seth startled her. As my arms wrapped around her, she pushed backward in her chair and we both toppled to the restaurant floor.

Maggie rushed over to help, not understanding what was happening, but by then I was laughing and already starting to apologize.

"I'm so sorry. I was just so excited to see you," I explained, untangling wings and feathers from arms and fur.

"Well, that's a first," Seth said. She brushed herself off, but stayed sitting in her chair, back to the floor. Though she was a little flustered, she was obviously pleased at the attention. "No need to apologize. You've helped me discover a new view. I think I'll order my meal and eat it just like this."

"Oh!" I exclaimed. "Me, too!" It was then that I knew that Seth was brilliant.

I don't remember what happened to Maggie after that. I think she was still there – maybe she ate at the table – because she was there when we left, and she paid. I know we ate something, but I can't remember what it was. Seth and I were so wrapped up into each other that we didn't pay much attention to anything else. We opened each other up like holiday gifts.

"You've got some bat in you, yes?" Seth asked.

"Mostly bird, but some bat. What are you?"

"Avocado, for all I know. Not sure I want to know. If your parents don't tell you something, that's not usually a good sign."

"Can you do anything amazing?"

"I've been watching a lot of nature documentaries lately to improve my social skills with the heavies. Most modding is animal-based, right? So it's totally relevant. Anyway, I've been doing a lot of work on my gorilla posturing."

"Can I see it?"

"Not yet. I need to get the vocals right, first. Then I'll show you. It'll be killer. What's flying like?"

"Awesome. Peaceful. Exhilarating. Free. I love it."

"Can you show me?"

"Maybe later. I'm only supposed to fly at home."

"What's your favorite food?"

"Spaghetti. What's your favorite movie?"

"Spaceballs. I don't really understand what's going on, but it's totally crazy. What's your favorite preposition?"

"I don't know if I have one. Let me think for a minute."

"Mine's 'beneath'. It implies a rich subtext. You ever see the movie Casablanca?"

"Nope."

"Then I'll keep my trite movie quote to myself."

I didn't understand what Seth was talking about at the time, but she was right. It was a beautiful beginning.

CHAPTER 5

"Imhotep Genetics has a diverse portfolio including agriculture, disease prevention, wellness, cosmetics, pest control, and more. We're working hard for a healthier planet. And not just ours! But even when our patented genes are on Mars, we'll still call Memphis, Wisconsin, home." – Imhotep Genetics Fact Sheet

Most reporters under eighty would have just called Imhotep on a screen and been done with it, but I had the time, and I wanted the full attention of whoever I ended up talking to. In fact, I face-to-face most of my interviews because otherwise it's hard to get interviewees to stay focused unless they're medicated or in some sort of meditation program.

Besides, it was local. Imhotep Genetics and Beryl were both located in Memphis. In fact, Beryl's mother worked as a prominent geneticist in Imhotep's Martian colonization division.

The appointment with Imhotep PR had been set up well in advance. When making the appointment, Nable informed me that the relations AI on the other end responded like a legal program. Not promising. But it wasn't a big deal. I had already edited a rough copy of the story, both video and text. We'd go through it, they'd rubber stamp it, and I'd be done. No controversy, no excitement. Time to pack up and move on to the next story.

The sprawling campus of Imhotep Genetics was impressive with its shiny new buildings separated by sculptures and greenspace. It looked like a college campus, and young scientists and businesspeople were plentiful. The genetics industry was thriving, here more than anywhere. Imhotep wasn't the only genetics company around – not by a long shot. But it was a new force in the industry, releasing several new products and snapping up lucrative contracts left and right over the past five years. It had grabbed the spotlight with First Flight and refused to let go.

Security pointed me to one of the smaller buildings that had been styled to look like a house. Not a typical white picket fence, but rather a fence with pickets made of white wooden human chromosomes. The fence was not particularly functional, as the X-shaped posts got smaller and smaller then got long again as it cycled through the twenty-three pairs.

"What do you think of the design of the public relations building, Nable?" I asked.

"Homey and clever," Nable answered.

"Good!" I encouraged. "That's exactly right. Any idea why they'd go for that combo?"

"Home would express comfort or safety," Nable said. "Clever is obvious – intelligence in science implies competency."

"True, but you're not answering the question. Why the combination of the two?"

"Some would say that intelligence can be positive but can also be dangerous. Laying a foundation of familiar comfort masks the danger so that the cleverness can be expressed more freely."

"That was pretty good, Nable," I said.

"Thank you," he responded, "both for the compliment and the question. By analyzing this scenario, I've come to understand that I should use less formal language when speaking with you so that I don't threaten you with my superior intelligence."

I laughed. He'd caught me by surprise. "If you're developing a sense of humor, then I really do have something to worry about."

By then I had entered the front room of the public relations building, which kept with the soft, homey theme. Yielding couches and warm-toned decor beckoned guests to sit in front of a chuckling fireplace. A tall, thin man with a very expressive face looked up from a hard-bound book.

"David Craven," he said, rising from his seat on a sofa with hand outstretched. "People call me Davey. We're so happy you could come."

"You can call me Maggie," I responded, laying odds that the book was a prop and he hadn't read a word of it. I shook his hand before settling into a comfortable armchair. PR guys are all liars by trade. Half of them know it, and the other half are just fooling themselves. I had a hunch that Davey was one of the former.

"You don't mind if I record this conversation, do you?" Craven asked. Standard protocol.

"Not if you don't mind if I do the same," I responded. I didn't need it for the story, but I didn't like the feel of this guy. Nable always recorded everything anyway.

Craven's plastic smile didn't shift a whit as he watched me pull out my screen to show him the rough cut of the story. He was attractive in that artificial, manufactured way that always turns my stomach. He had either had extensive facial work or significant behavior coaching. Probably both. Though his expression gave away nothing, his eyes looked smug and superior. For some reason, I found myself wanting to stab him in the eye with a fireplace poker. I filed away my visceral reaction for later analysis and took a deep breath to calm myself. Davey poured himself some hot water for tea and offered me some. I declined.

"So, your retrospective on First Flight..." Craven proffered as he steeped his tea.

"Less a retrospective than a 'where are they now?' piece," I responded. "If this had been a larger story like a retrospective, I would have come here first."

"Of course!" Craven said with a rehearsed smile. "Don't worry. You've followed protocol. I'm not concerned about your manners or respect for the business community." He had no reason to be. All of the big companies kept and shared files on reporters. Any reporter with a reputation for stirring up trouble (i.e., 'bad manners') was quickly black listed, sued, or worse. Whole companies, from newspapers to plazas, had been put out of business because of 'bad manners'. Those who survived the paradigm shift learned quickly. Those of us who came afterward never knew any other way.

"We're planning to publish next week," I said.

"We were thinking that a retrospective might be a better choice," Craven said.

"What was that?" I asked, surprised.

"Beryl is and always will be important and beloved by Imhotep. First Flight launched Imhotep into the limelight, allowing business to grow by an order of magnitude. Our success with Beryl allowed us to diversify from chimaeras to commercial products. That powerful brand recognition produced a climate where products like Gut Check and My Little Friend 500 could become blockbusters. By engineering the perfect intestinal biome, Gut Check wiped out celiac and Crohn's. Our new Gut Check Plus (that releases in time for Christmas) is cholera resistant as well! My Little Friend, when used as prescribed, is the perfect cure for obesity, with each Friend guaranteed to absorb exactly 500 calories daily and never reproduce. And our work reengineering mosquitoes..."

"Yes, yes, I've read the pamphlets," I interrupted. "Everybody knows Imhotep does some amazing work. What's this about a retrospective?"

"People started to know us and trust us because of Beryl," Craven continued. "She's not a mascot or just a part of our history. She's part of this place. You should see the statue in First Flight Quad. It's inspiring. Beryl shows us that the future of our civilization is only limited by our imagination."

"She launched Imhotep into the big time, but nobody's writing about her anymore," I said, trying to piece together what he was really saying. "You're looking for a little PR boost from the little girl who made you famous. You want a bigger story than just a celebrity check-in. But why now?"

"The Mars project," Craven stated, pausing for effect.

"But you've already got the contract," I said, confused.

"The Mars project will make or break us. From a technical and logistical standpoint, we know we can make it work. If given the time."

"You're worried the tax dollars will be pulled out from under you," I said.

"If the money dries up due to a fickle legislature, we will take substantial losses. We've grown considerably in the last five years, but a large percentage of our resources are currently devoted to this project. More importantly, many of the genetic advances we're pioneering would likely go to waste. We need ordinary people to want their taxes to fund this mission."

"The Mars project will take decades. What does one retrospective mean, in the big picture?"

"Not much," Craven admitted. "We've planned numerous events and stories for the next ten years. Since you were here, we figured we'd take advantage of the opportunity." He grinned like a cat holding a mouse by the tail.

"Well, Beryl seems like a nice kid, and it would be a refreshing change of pace," I said, which was true enough. "I'll have to clear it with Zeen first, of course."

"I've already spoken with Harold," Craven said. Harold is Zeen's editor in chief – a coward and a survivor. Zeen does well under his leadership. "He's given the go-ahead."

Nable whispered confirmation. My boss had just sent a message, and my flight back to New York had been canceled.

Craven continued, "I'll send you a list of interviews we've lined up." His shabti sent Nable the list of names, dates, and times. "You've already interviewed Beryl and her father. We've lined up some of the scientists, medical staff, and people who were at the event."

"Her mother?"

"Unlikely," Craven answered. "She's one of our top scientists on the Mars project and very busy at this stage. We have plans to tie her into a future PR push, but now isn't the time."

Surprising. If I hadn't seen her, I would have thought she must not be photogenic, but I remembered her from the First Flight broadcast. Severe, yes, but not somebody you'd keep away from the camera.

Nable whispered to me again. "Morrow," I said, raising eyebrows in surprise.

"Yes!" Craven responded. "Our CEO and founder has graciously offered to be interviewed for your story."

My shoulders tensed up. Horace Morrow had a large personality, charismatic and ambitious. They'd want as much exposure for him as they could get. My job likely depended on portraying him in the best light possible.

My original interest in this little story with an interesting character was quickly turning into loss of autonomy and an unpleasant stressfest. On the plus side, I had been wanting a larger story that would give me some visibility.

Maybe that was my ticket out of Zeen. But I couldn't sway myself to optimism. As Craven and I exchanged false pleasantries to wrap up our encounter, I felt trapped and less than enthusiastic. A two-day visit had just become a long-term stay with potentially major repercussions for my career. In a world where big business has big power, this project had the potential to result in a resourceful ally or, if things went poorly, a devastating black mark.

Perhaps more importantly, I would have to figure out whether I'd be staying with my sister the whole time or moving into a hotel. Yet another awkward family situation.

CHAPTER 6

"It's no use going back to yesterday, because I was a different person then." – Alice in Wonderland

Mom did find out about our little trip to the restaurant, of course. I didn't tell her, and neither did Beth, but apparently I'm famous, and in a town like Memphis, word gets around. If I'd just said something to Mom, she probably wouldn't have been upset, but of course, I didn't. I'm not sure why.

I could tell Mom was irritated, but when I asked her why, she didn't have a good answer. I told her I really enjoyed having a friend. She responded that I shouldn't keep secrets, and I shouldn't leave the house without telling her or Dad. I told her that Beth knew where I was. Although I didn't get in trouble, Beth got chewed out. I should have just said something.

On the very big plus side, I had a new friend. You could make an argument that Seth was my first friend, and I couldn't get enough of her. When I got back home from the restaurant, I called Seth on my screen. Before bed, I called her again. The next morning, she heard from me, too. She was very patient with me.

"You've gotta get out more," she said to me that morning while balancing a roll of toilet paper on her head. "Would you like to meet some of my friends?"

"Do you think they'd like me?" I asked.

"What's not to like? You're loads of fun. And my friends are all easy. They're not shitheads like the Ogdoad."

"The Ogdoad?" I asked.

"Arrogant bunch of heavy mods who think they're the next stage in human evolution. A horrible bunch of twats. I'm sure you'll meet them at some point, but we'll try to avoid it as long as possible." Seth gave a cheery squint as she gave up on her balancing act and chucked the toilet paper off screen. "I want you to meet the cool people first."

Everything was happening so fast. Maggie called and said she wanted to do another interview – the little story was becoming a big story, and she needed to ask me some more questions. Seth lined up a visit with her friends later that day. I told Beth what was going on, dropped a line to Mom to keep her in the loop, and before I knew it, I was out the door. My unintentional hermitage was quickly becoming a thing of the past.

The heavies often met in the gym of Lakeside Elementary, a closed-down old public school. Numerous consolidations due to lack of funding and the move toward home-based online classwork had made small schools a luxury that many communities couldn't afford. Many of the closed down buildings never sold, leaving them open to squatters, scavengers, and anyone else determined enough to break in.

"When the Ogdoad claimed this place for the heavies," Seth explained, "they kicked out the few folks who had been living here and fortified it so it was harder to get in. They replaced locks with their own locks. Now it's ours… unofficially, of course." Seth manipulated a combination lock to let Beryl in.

We made our way through the empty hallways, Seth's flashlight shining the way. Our slow footsteps echoed against doors of classrooms that hadn't seen students for a dozen years. It was creepy, sure, but there's something about exploring a big, empty building that feels both exciting and safe. At the end of a hallway, light shone through the gym doors. Seth turned off her flashlight, and we pushed through the doors into a larger space where a small circle of chimaeras talked with one another. They turned as they heard us approach.

It's not surprising that unmodified humans stare at a heavy-mod on first introduction, but if you think heavies don't have the same reaction, you'd be wrong. There's a lot to absorb: shape, height, musculature, facial features, fur, claws, and teeth. And, just like normies do, one of the first things mods do is try to guess which animals' genes were incorporated into the mix. So, when heavies first meet, long pauses are the norm, and even walking around each other appraisingly isn't considered rude or unusual.

I had never met any heavy mods other than Seth, and our first meeting had not followed that pattern, so I was surprised when the other mods stared and said nothing as Seth and I approached.

"They're a little starstruck," Seth whispered. "You're the most famous mod in the world, and they don't know what to say."

There was an extremely tall girl with long, skinny legs and feathers on her head and arms. She had a long neck, and her skin was bluish-white. She stood on one leg, the other tucked up under her. Her short, squat torso tilted forward while in repose. A raccoon boy nervously rubbed his hands together as he walked around me. An orange lizard girl, looked me over with large, protruding eyes. A hefty bear boy with an over-abundance of fur waddled stiffly. Other than the tall girl, the only one not circling around me was a skinny little girl with huge eyes and long, delicate fingers and toes who sat quietly, watching without blinking, nibbling crackers.

"Um... hello," I stammered. I wasn't sure what to do. "I'm Beryl."

Seth snorted, stifling a laugh. "They know who you are. They're just trying to get a good look at you." She addressed the others. "Hey, slobs! Don't be jerks. Introduce yourselves."

Thasha, the skinny bird girl, spoke first in a surprisingly deep voice, "Welcome, Beryl. It's a pleasure to meet you. Seth has told us that you're a kind, enjoyable person, and we hope you find us to be the same." Her eloquent, resonant voice was comforting and friendly, and I felt less nervous right away.

The lizard girl introduced herself as Kammi. She had no hair, and her orange skin looked scaly but soft like a snake or iguana. When I complimented her on her coloration, Kammi turned a rosy shade of pink, as if her whole body flushed due to the praise.

"Holy cow!" I cried out. "That's awesome! What other colors can you change to?"

"No fluorescents and only one color at a time. Other than that, you name it, and I can do it." She turned a deep shade of purple, and I applauded enthusiastically.

The boy who looked like a bear came forward sheepishly. His fur looked so *fluffy*. I wanted to rub my face in it. "My name is... Cuddles." He rolled his eyes in embarrassment. It clearly pained him to say so. He took a deep breath and straightened his posture. "But my friends call me Kodiak."

The others laughed, and Seth shouted, "*Nobody* calls you Kodiak."

"Well, maybe if you were real friends, you would," he responded sulkily.

"You're as fierce as a baby bunny, Cuddles," Thasha said. "Don't deny who you are. Embrace it."

"Oh, to heck with you guys!" Cuddles said angrily. "To heck! I'm trying to make a good first impression, and you've ruined it! Shucks!" He stomped over to a corner of the gym and sat down in a huff.

"He's adorable, isn't he?" the raccoon boy asked quietly so Cuddles wouldn't hear. I had to admit that despite the sour mood, Cuddles looked incredibly cute, as a big fluffy teddy bear in a grumpy mood would. "He wants to be rebellious and brooding, but his appearance and natural disposition make it completely impossible. Then he gets frustrated and pouts, making him that much more endearing.

"I'm Ralph," the raccoon boy continued. He had a very short sheen of fur – just enough to show off the distinctive raccoon markings. The black around his eyes, offset by the white and gray elsewhere, made him look mysterious. "It's great to meet you," he said, still nervously rubbing his hands against each other.

Thasha gestured to the skinny, cracker-eating girl. "We call her Ant. We're not sure what her real name is. We think she's older than us, but it's hard to tell. The earlier mods often had unique mental compositions —"

"That means that sometimes they came out crazy," Seth whispered, raising her eyebrows significantly.

"No, that's not what that means," Thasha responded testily. "At least, not only that. More frequently, some cognitive and personality traits were exaggerated or diminished."

"And if you were too messed up, they'd send you to The Home," Kammi said, eyes bugging out. She turned a deep shade of charcoal. "Mwah ha ha!" she added for dramatic effect.

"What's The Home?" I asked.

"There's a rumor that unwanted heavies are sent away to a compound," Thasha said.

"It's true!" Seth bellowed. "Too many people know about it for it to not be true."

"Are you guys talking about The Home?" Cuddles asked from his distant corner. "Please don't talk about The Home. I'll get nightmares."

Seth continued, "Imhotep runs it secretly to protect their brand. Think about it. There's no way every chimaera turns out just right. What else do you think they do with their failures, huh? Just let 'em run around?"

"Well, they didn't lock you up," said a husky voice as a new heavy mod entered the gym. "So, if that's your only evidence, I'm afraid Seth provides the perfect counterexample." A lanky girl sauntered confidently toward the group. Her pointed dog ears twitched out to either side. Her snout lifted and sniffed the room. As Seth and her friends shifted their attention to the newcomer, the mood shifted from one of welcome to one of tension.

"Dammit, Ann. What are you doing here?" Seth asked. Ralph cringed, wringing his hands nervously.

"Meeting our guest," she replied, circling me. The others backed away while Ann stalked around me. I felt like prey.

"She's not your guest," Seth protested angrily.

Ann stopped circling and confronted Seth. She stood very close, her canine teeth just inches from Seth's face. The others backed away further, but Seth held her ground.

"Seth, this is *our* place. Therefore, she is *our* guest." Ann stared coldly into Seth's eyes. "Besides," she said softly, "I was invited."

"Bullshit," Seth said flatly. "Who in their right mind would invite an evil bitch like *you*?" Seth's vehemence and the others' fear made me very nervous.

Ann slowly shifted her gaze to the corner where Cuddles sat cowering with his hands over his eyes. Everybody else looked at Cuddles, too.

"Dammit, Cuddles!" Seth shouted.

"What else was I supposed to do?" he asked. "She saw me biking here and asked me where I was going. I couldn't lie!"

"What he means is that he couldn't bring himself to lie to Ann, terrified of what might happen to him if she found out," Thasha interjected. "That's not an unwise consideration." Ann smiled broadly at that, her mouth open, displaying sharp teeth.

"Hey," I interrupted. I wasn't sure what to do, but I didn't like all the confrontation. "If you're going to come in here threatening everybody, I'd rather you just leave." I thought maybe I could deflect some of the tension.

"Bold," Ann said, her full attention shifting back to appraise me, "or ignorant. You're right, though. I apologize for my behavior." Ann bowed low to the ground in front of me, which was embarrassing. I couldn't tell if Ann's gesture was sarcastic or not.

"It's not me you should apologize to," I said. "You insulted Seth."

Ann's eyes narrowed as she glared into mine, but she decided to play nice. She didn't look away from me while she said, "Seth, please forgive my rudeness. My comment about your genetic quality, while contextual to the conversation, was demeaning and uncalled-for. I hope you can forgive me."

"I hope you can kiss my butt," Seth replied.

Ann's eyes narrowed again, but her gaze did not shift from mine. "As you can see, Seth and I don't get along. Please don't judge me and my friends through her eyes. I'd like to introduce you to others like us. We'll gather here next week at the same time for a welcome party. Will you come?" Though it was an invitation, it sounded like a threat. Did she intend it to sound that way, or was it something she couldn't help?

I looked over to Seth, Thasha, and the others. Seth's scowl looked painfully fierce. Thasha nodded solemnly, though, indicating that I should agree.

"I will come," I answered.

"Excellent," Ann said as she stood. "I look forward to making a better second impression than my first. And I do think you'll enjoy meeting the others. They are a truly amazing group of people."

"Thank you for the invitation," I said, trying to end the encounter graciously.

"See you next week," Ann said, backing out of the gym with a wicked grin, then turning and trotting out the door.

I heard several exhalations as the tension was released. I hadn't realized how stiff my neck had become. I noticed others stretching tight backs and limbs. The exception was Ant, who continued to nibble her crackers, seemingly unaware of her surroundings.

Seth turned to Cuddles again, "What the Hell was that?"

"Give him a break, Seth," Kammi said. "He's got a crush on Ann."

"*What?!*" Seth cried. "A crush on *Ann?!*"

Cuddles's eyes dropped to the floor as he whispered, "She's so strong and confident and smart."

"She's devious, violent, and just plain terrifying," Seth responded.

"Yeah... terrifying..." Cuddles agreed, his eyes getting dreamy.

I looked thoughtfully at Thasha. "If Ann and her friends are so bad, why did you signal that I should accept her invitation?"

"You can't be a heavy in this town and avoid the Ogdoad. Better to just get it over with and try to play nice. Delay would only make it worse when you inevitably encounter them."

Despite Ann's tone and Seth's warnings, I couldn't help but look forward to a party. I was really enjoying meeting new people, and I was excited to learn as much as possible about other heavy mods. What would they look like? How would they act? Would they like me? My world was exploding in size and complexity, and it felt like an adventure. Besides, I had never been to a party.

I also realized that Thasha, Kammi, Ralph, Cuddles, and even Ant were becoming my friends. They were trying to protect me. They'd accepted me into their group right away. And I liked them. I was excited to learn more about them and spend time with them.

"Thank you for protecting me," I told them plainly. "And thank you for coming here to meet me. I think you're all wonderful." Kammi turned pink, and it was clear that the others were flattered as well.

Thasha was more serious. "Beryl, even though I encouraged you to go to this party of Ann's, be particularly careful around her. After all, she is a jackal."

CHAPTER 7

"Though this is a baby step, it enables a change in philosophy, a change in thinking, a change in the tools we have. This cell we've made is not a miracle cell that's useful for anything, it is a proof of concept. But the proof of concept was key, otherwise it is just speculation and science fiction. This takes us across that border, into a new world." – Dr. J. Craig Venter on the creation of Synthia

My schedule had been completely reworked. Interviews butted up against more interviews. I wouldn't have to do much filming outside of the interviews – Imhotep's PR department had already transferred buckets of cleanly-produced, commercially inspiring footage to Nable – but I insisted on taking some of my own shots. By the time I had finished with all of the interviews, I would know the hues of the story I needed to tell, and I could film using that subjective lens.

So, instead of having a relaxing dinner with my sister's family, going to bed early, and then getting on a plane back home, I told my sister I would be extending my stay from a couple of days to a couple of weeks. I told her I could move into a hotel so I wouldn't be a burden, but she wouldn't have it. It had been so long, she said, and it would be great to spend more time with me.

She didn't understand that she wouldn't see a whole lot of me while I immersed myself in my work. That first night, I grabbed some takeout and hid in my room so I could start plowing through a mountain of background research. Imhotep had, of course, given me a great deal of their own materials, but Nable would help me do my own research as well.

I already had a foundation of knowledge about Imhotep. They had started out as one of many DNA screening companies, decoding genomes and dispensing advice on likelihoods of disease for individuals and prospective parents. In parallel, they marketed small genetic modifications, adjusting the DNA of fertilized eggs prior to in vitro fertilization. The focus was elimination of congenital disease and minor cosmetic changes. Again, they were one of many, but what set Imhotep apart was that their cosmetic changes tended to have an animal focus, cat eyes, furry ears, whiskers, and claws. They claimed that splicing sequences from other species was easier and safer than writing genetic code from scratch. They had success.

Imhotep began to differentiate in a noticeable way when they started making heavier genetic modifications. For the first time, humans looked decidedly unhuman. There was some negative press, of course, but already journalism was folding under the pressure of business and politics. Soon, the only mainstream newspeople left were those for whom fame and celebrity was their primary motivator. So, politicians hemmed and hawed unintelligibly about what was "unnatural" versus inherent freedoms, and it blew over relatively quickly. Imhotep faded into obscurity.

Until First Flight.

Beryl's invasion of the realm of clouds changed the science from slow change to, "Holy shit, look what we can do." Imhotep became famous worldwide, and popular opinion of genetic manipulation shifted from a conservative focus on removal of congenital defects to a feeling that the sky's the limit... or used to be. So, when Imhotep released new products shortly afterward, they were received in a way that wouldn't have been possible prior to First Flight. For example, a weight loss pill that contained a genetically engineered tapeworm, sterile and programmed to only grow to a certain size, designed to consume a pre-defined number of calories per day, and that would die after six months became acceptable to the public, because *Hell, people can fly now. Why worry?*

Multiple Imhotep brands became mainstream, and the company swelled. Even so, the company maintained a single campus in suburban Milwaukee. As the company grew, so did the small city of Memphis in which it was headquartered. When Imhotep won the Mars terraforming contract, everybody knew it was a make or break moment for the company. Thus the PR push.

It goes without saying that there is a huge difference between a short, celebrity look-back and a high-profile multi-platform retrospective for an ambitious company. For the entertainment piece, I would typically put together an eight to ten minute video piece that would be published directly on Zeen. There would be accompanying text and photos (pulled from the videos by Nable) for those who still preferred to read their entertainment news. I would also produce several shorter video versions of the same material: sixty second, thirty second, and fifteen second versions. These were purchased, conglomerated with other short pieces, and distributed by other plazas, news agencies, and streaming platforms – always pointing back to the longer version at Zeen for those who wanted more than a minute of content. Sixty seconds was more than enough for most folks.

Now this project was something totally different. I had not done anything like it as a professional, but I'd been wanting to produce something long-form since college. Imhotep would pay for and manage the distribution. It was guaranteed to get international visibility and as much attention as money could buy. It was a big opportunity for me. If Imhotep liked my finished product, they'd leave it untouched, and my name, face, voice, and career would be attached to all of that attention. If they didn't like it, they'd make sure appropriate changes were made – even if that meant cutting me out of it completely. If there's a line between journalism and advertisement anymore, this type of product definitely crossed it.

There would be a two hour long-form video for the old folks who still watched television. Yes, some people can still sit and watch the same content for two hours. This would also be available from both Zeen's and Imhotep's sites. There would be shorter video versions as well: thirty minutes, ten minutes, and five minutes. I'd need to make a five minute version geared toward kids as well… they'd play it in the schools. There would be numerous flavors of fifteen-second teasers. And there would be long and short text accounts with photos.

In all, a lot of work. In the old days, a team of people might take three months to produce that much content. I figured Nable and I could do it ourselves in four weeks.

It started with interviews. Lots of interviews. My follow-up visit with Beryl would wait while I trudged through twenty interviews with supposed Imhotep staff and people who witnessed Beryl's big day in the spotlight. Twenty! They were all to be held in the PR house, of course, and were monitored by PR staff via camera in a side wall of the decidedly homey interview room.

I started each interview with a few easy questions to get the subject into the groove. Then I would ask a couple of detailed questions to figure out if I was dealing with a real witness or a paid actor. If it was an actor, which seemed to be the case for the majority of people who Imhotep had lined up as "witnesses" to First Flight, I'd ask the questions most likely to jive with whatever script they had rehearsed. If they struggled, I'd just prompt them to go ahead by waving my hand. For their sake, I did my best to pretend that I didn't know they were actors, which I think they appreciated.

Most of the scientists and medical staff were genuine and had been involved with the First Flight project. These interviews were more fun, because I could act like a journalist.

The scientists ranged from enthusiastic to stoic. Overall, they talked about First Flight as if it were the Apollo program. It was a mission, an achievement, and a breakthrough in applied science.

Many members of the medical staff who I spoke with were still in charge of Beryl's medical care. Though they didn't see her nearly so much anymore, they specialized in medicine for heavily genetically modified humans. They were universally fond of her and had wonderful anecdotes about Beryl from when she was a fuzzy ball of feathers, to her first croaking words, to her first glide.

For example, figuring out the best way to give her a bath had been a struggle. The bird parts kept getting in the way of the human parts. One of the nurses had an adorable photo of a very bedraggled, very wet baby Beryl squawking while raising her wings, thousands of water droplets captured mid-launch toward Audrey, Beth, and a nurse.

Imhotep had picked an ideal set of interview candidates, but one stood out as different from the others. A nurse named Amai was antsy from the start. In her early thirties, she had been just out of nursing school when she joined the team that began caring for baby Beryl. She had big eyes and jittery hands. She warmed up to me quickly, but I could tell she was distracted.

Aside from her level of nervousness, I didn't think anything of it. She had a couple of cute stories about Beryl and the Pritchard family. She answered some questions about medical differences of heavy mods. All clean and neat. At the end of the interview, she asked how Beryl was doing.

"You're not a nurse for Beryl anymore?" I asked.

"No, I've moved to bigger and better things here at Imhotep," she responded, taking a sip of coffee. "But I miss her. She was such a sweet girl."

"She seems to be doing well," I said. "Doesn't get out of the house much. Enjoys her flying."

"She gets along okay with her mom and dad?" Amai asked.

"Seems to," I responded. I expected Amai to respond with relief or contentment or something along those lines, but she remained uneasy. "Why do you ask?" I countered.

"Oh, I just remember Jerry and Audrey. Kids can get crazy when they get older, and I just wanted to make sure they're all doing okay."

I nodded and started to pack up. Amai was the last of my twenty interviews, and I felt drained. But Amai stayed in her seat.

"Yes?" I asked.

"I'm sorry I've been so anxious," she said. "I've never been interviewed before."

"Don't worry about it," I responded in a soothing voice. "You did just fine." Instead of looking more comforted, she looked even more tense.

"You must have to spend a lot of time looking at these videos," she said.

"It's not so bad. My shabti is able to sift through a lot of it for me."

She winced, then realized she had winced and turned her head away from the camera in the wall, a look of fear contorting her face. Somehow, she had made a mistake, but I couldn't for the life of me guess what it was.

"I guess I just meant," she continued, "there must be a lot of attention to detail in your line of work."

"I suppose that's true," I agreed.

"It was a pleasure to meet you," Amai said as she rose from her chair. She took a deep breath as she brushed herself off. "I look forward to watching your story."

We exchanged pleasantries for another minute or two as we both prepared to leave the room. She seemed much calmer, as though whatever had made her nervous had been surmounted. And then my day of interviews was done.

Later that night, while Nable and I talked through various themes of the material we had captured that day, he pointed out what I had missed during my interview with Amai.

"Watch the hand that's holding the coffee," he said. He played the interview on my screen silently in triple speed.

"What?" I asked. "She's just tapping her fingers against her cup."

"It's a pattern," Nable replied. "Four taps, then three taps, then two taps... it's a twelve-digit number. She cycles through it twice, so it's not random."

"Do you think she's trying to communicate something?" I asked. "Something that she couldn't say with Imhotep watching? It would explain why she was so nervous."

"Her hand is placed such that the Imhotep camera can't see it," Nable pointed out.

"Huh. You're right," I said. "But why? She has to know that I wouldn't be able to publish anything that would make Imhotep look bad. So what's her angle?"

"Why speculate prior to further analysis?" Nable responded. Once, I taught him that if you don't know the answer to a question, ask one instead. He was infuriatingly good at it.

"Did any of the other interview subjects do anything like that?" I asked.

"No," Nable responded. "She's the only one."

"Okay, mister investigator," I said, leaning back in my seat. "What does this twelve digit number mean?"

"I've been investigating numerous possibilities. It isn't an IP address, nor an ISBN without the check digit. It doesn't seem to correspond to any library classification system, and if it's a UPC bar code, we don't have the context for what it could mean. It could be a phone number in Austria, but the corresponding number appears to be unused at this time. It could be a North Carolina driver's license..."

"Hold on, there, Sherlock," I interrupted. "It can't be that complicated, or she wouldn't expect us to understand it. A good code needs to be intelligible but unnoticed." I looked at my screen. "Show me the number."

I smiled as the number appeared on the screen. "That's not a twelve-digit number, Nable. That's two six digit numbers. It's a latitude/longitude, and it's nearby. If you assume the first six digits are north and the other six are west, how close is it to here?"

"How did you know it was coordinates?" Nable asked. I'm pretty sure he was jealous that I figured it out before he did.

"I did some geocaching in camp when I was a kid," I replied. "Boring, but I got used to seeing 43 and 88."

"Approximately fifteen miles away, but it's not near any significant structures."

"Well, if you've got something secret to tell somebody, you don't exactly want it to be in the middle of Main Street, do you?"

"I suppose not," he replied.

"Okay, so we know where," I continued, enjoying the puzzle. "Any indication of when?"

"She touches her watch at one point," Nable said.

"Show me."

Nable scrolled the video to the end of the interview. Just as we were about to leave, she touched her watch, and it looked a lot more like a point than a touch.

"Do you see any other taps or numbers after that? Anything to indicate a time?"

"I do not," Nable replied.

"Can you magnify the face of the watch?" I asked.

"8:57 PM," Nable read. "And the date is tomorrow's date. That is not when our interview occurred."

"It most certainly is not," I agreed. "She must have manually adjusted the time on her watch so we'd know what time to meet her. And it's a real pain in the ass to change the time to something incorrect on these self-correcting modern watches."

"So, she wants you to meet her near a cornfield at approximately 9 PM tomorrow night?" Nable asked. "What for?"

"Hell if I know," I answered. I sighed and rubbed my palms against my eyes. I was exhausted. The next day would be just as full, and I needed sleep. "Maybe she's just fucking with us."

"It would be risky for her to do so. She could lose her job if she made Imhotep suspicious of her intentions," Nable countered. "And if this is the least risky way for her to reach out to you, that indicates that she may be monitored or have some other restriction on her freedom."

"I hadn't thought of that," I responded. "You're right. This must be really important to her. But what could she possibly want?"

"She probably expects you to be a journalist."

"To be a journalist," I scoffed, "doesn't mean what it used to."

"Why do you choose to maintain this profession if you think it's dishonorable?" Nable asked.

That hit me hard. I went to school for journalism because I liked figuring out how things worked, whether it was puzzles, contracts, or political issues. I was naïve and idealistic, even as I knew the profession was going down the toilet. I told myself I was building my skills so that when a real story came along, or a job with one of the few niche publications that still had integrity came along, that I'd be ready for it. Meanwhile, I felt like my day-to-day existence was pointless. I was a useless cog in a gigantic, mindless machine whose only purpose was to distract people from the realities around them.

Now here I had a puzzle. And I could choose to ignore it and keep lying to myself, or I could be a journalist, fumbling in the dark for the truth. Based on everything we'd seen from Amai, the truth might endanger my career – my life as I knew it.

I was too tired to handle those sorts of questions.

"You're supposed to be a journalism AI, not psych," I snapped.

"What's the difference?" Nable asked.

"One of them isn't supposed to be a pain in the ass."

Nable remained silent. I brushed my teeth, used the toilet, and climbed into bed. Just before taking Nable out of my ear for the night, he asked, "What will you do when you see Beryl tomorrow?"

"I don't know," I answered softly. "I'm not sure who I am, and for some reason that makes a difference."

I lay quietly in bed. Though I felt like Nable was a part of me, this was not typical of our conversations, which were normally work-centric. No feelings. No big picture. Just the job in front of us.

He surprised me when he responded, "You are who you decide to be."

"Dammit, Nable," I complained.

"Good night, Maggie."

"Good night, Nable."

I took Nable out of my ear and set him on the bedside table. I did not sleep well.

CHAPTER 8

"Ritual holds family together far better than blood and genes." – Audrey Pritchard

"Fluff up," Beth said.

We were on the back porch at home doing the weekly preen. It was unseasonably warm for the end of October – sixties with a strong south wind. Though the house shielded the porch from the wind, the swaying trees and crackle of blown, dry leaves made it feel like we were in a protective bubble in a volatile world. I laid on my stomach on my chair while Beth tidied my feathers. She expertly winnowed out the broken or loose feathers with an occasional pluck or ruffle. I flexed my back muscles, raising my feathers so Beth could more easily sort through them.

"I don't know how birds do this on their own without each of them having their own Beth," I said as I slurped on some delicious cider. "I appreciate you."

"Well, that's very nice of you to say," Beth replied. "You're such a sweetie pie."

I almost gagged on my drink. "Please don't ever say that in front of any of my friends."

"Oh, don't worry about that. I'll make sure to only refer to you as a tough, rebellious pain in the butt whenever your friends are around. And you better not say you appreciate me, either," she chuckled.

"That's the spirit," I said, grinning.

"Speaking of which, will any of your new friends be coming over?" Beth asked. "How did it go with the meet-up?"

"It went pretty well, I think. Seth's friends were really nice, and I think they could be my friends, too. I'd love it if they could come over sometime."

"Anytime you want," Beth said, starting to work on my right wing.

I paused for a moment, remembering Ann. "There was one girl who was really aggressive and rude. She wasn't invited, and she and Seth don't get along. She asked me to come to a bigger gathering next week that includes a whole different group of mods. I didn't like her, but I agreed to go."

"Why do you think you did that?" Beth asked.

"Seth's friend Thasha thought I should. She doesn't like Ann either, but she thought I should meet the rest of the community sooner rather than later... almost like a political move."

"I'm guessing Seth thought you shouldn't go."

"Yeah, probably not. But the more I think about it, the more I think I actually want to go." I set my cider down and rested my cheek on a pillow. "I feel like I should avoid these people, but I don't want to. I'm told they're bad people, but I'm curious about them, and I want to get to know them. I feel like I should be afraid, but I'm not."

"Do you think you'll be safe there?" Beth asked, pausing her work.

"Yes. Seth and her friends will be there with me."

Beth resumed her preening. "Then I don't see as how it would hurt to get to know some more people. If you don't like them, you don't like them. If you do, then there's nothing saying you can't be friends with all of them – even if they don't get along with each other."

"I suppose."

"Do you know what these new folks expect of you?" Beth asked as she moved over to the other wing, her fingers darting like a pianist's across my feathers, realigning strays and picking out debris.

"No, I don't." I figured they'd ask me to fly, but I kept that to myself. I wasn't sure if the gym was spacious enough, and I was sure my parents wouldn't approve, regardless. "I feel like I'm in a game I don't understand."

"I remember what it's like to try to get along at your age. It's like politics, but more secretive and vicious."

"I thought you got along with pretty much everybody," I said. I couldn't imagine Beth stirring up trouble. She was the nicest person I'd ever met, and I admired her terribly.

"Pretty much. But it's different when you're young, and I know when to be cautious. You make sure to stick to the people you trust until you understand the situation better, okay?"

"Will do. I'll stick to Seth like glue." I chortled a little at the image of us glommed together, laughing as we awkwardly stumbled around town. Beth would have to help unstick my feathers, sighing and shaking her head.

I pictured myself trying to fly with my feathers all glued down, struggling to gain lift. I pushed and pushed to climb higher, to keep myself from the hard earth, but the glue mucked up my balance and felt so heavy. The sun beat at me like a hammer. The Earth was small and distant. Then the glue was melting, and my feathers fell away with it revealing arms instead of wings underneath. I was a normal human girl, falling and falling, faster and faster, toward a large, gray house. I knew that if I fell there, I wouldn't be able to leave ever again. Then I started and woke up.

"You drifted off," Beth said. "We're all done cleaning up your feathers, sweetie."

I wiped a surprisingly large amount of slobber off of my mouth with my arm, causing Beth to grimace as drool coated a swath of just-preened short-feathers.

"Beth, some of the kids talked about a place called The Home where genetic failures have to live. Is that a real place?"

Beth looked away as she put some of her equipment in a basket. Then she smiled and said, "Oh, I'm not a good person to ask. You'll want to ask your mother. She works at Imhotep, so she'd know for sure, wouldn't she?"

"Yeah, I suppose so," I answered. Beth seemed to be hiding something, which was weird. She was normally so straightforward; it felt wrong. "Will Mom be home tonight?"

"She will," Beth answered. "It's First Wednesday. I'll make that pecan loaf you like so much. She'll probably want to hear about what you've been up to lately, so you can ask her then."

I doubted Mom would be interested in hearing about my new friends. She hadn't been interested in hearing about Seth except to scold me for not telling her about the trip to the restaurant. But Mom did enjoy talking about work, so I was optimistic about getting an answer to my questions about The Home.

There's nothing more delicious than savory pecan loaf with mashed potatoes and greens. Beth knows all sorts of delicious vegetarian recipes. She made pecan loaf at least once a week, even if she made something different for Mom and Dad, who got bored with it. Beth would always eat what I ate, though, and with Mom working so much and Dad's frequent travels, often it was just the two of us.

One Wednesday per month, Mom made sure to come home for dinner to spend some time with me. Often, she went back to work afterward, but she never missed supper on First Wednesday. She even removed her shabti and temple so she wouldn't have any distractions. Though Beth usually joined the family for meals, she never sat at the table for this particular meal. This was time for mother and daughter. Even Dad usually ate in the kitchen with Beth when he was home on First Wednesday.

As Mom and I snacked on bread while we waited for the main course, Mom asked, "How's your schoolwork coming along?"

It was always the first question she asked, as though it were the most important thing in the world. I went through each class, one by one, and talked about what I'd been learning, recent exam results, and upcoming tests and projects.

"- and somehow Rose dropped her screen in the toilet just before philosophy class, so her voice was all garbled, and she looked warped for the rest of the day. I don't know why she doesn't have a waterproof screen –"

"How have you been doing on your debates in that class?" Mom interrupted.

The school rundown took us well into the middle of the meal. Mom finished eating before I was even halfway done, because I did most of the talking. So, as usual, I shifted the conversation back to my mother by asking, "How's work been?"

I had plenty of time to enjoy the rest of my lukewarm meal while Mom talked about the most recent technical difficulties in their design for photosynthetic human skin, the aesthetics of atmosphere-producing bacteria, and other genetic topics related to the colonization of Mars. I rarely had to ask any questions at all, because Mom had so much enthusiasm for her work. This was usually my favorite part of First Wednesday. It wasn't just because it was between the ritual school accounting, which I didn't enjoy much, and the awkward moments that came later if Mom had finished talking about work and we hadn't finished dessert yet. I admired her passion. Hearing her talk about her work, which was almost an art, reminded me about the things I loved, like gardening and flying. I also just really appreciated being able to hear about what was happening on the cutting edge of science. Hearing details about the first permanent settlement on another planet, even though it would take decades to get ready, opened my mind to the world's possibilities. I also got an inkling of how much detailed work went into such a crazy big project. Mom taught me that science isn't just what you know - it's also design, research, analysis, discovery, troubleshooting, and even logistics. Every First Wednesday, I got a glimpse of another chapter in a great story. My understanding and admiration of my mother came from those minutes spent together, one Wednesday every month.

This week, though, I had some very specific questions on my mind. I worried as the work talk extended into dessert that we'd run out of time. When Mom finished her square of rhubarb crumble as she finished talking about planned lichen coloration on the sides of Martian canyons, I knew I needed to get into it.

"That was delicious," Mom said as she put her fork down on her empty plate. She put her shabti back in her ear and reached for her temple as she said, "Well, I should get back to work."

"Mom, can I ask you a question?"

"Of course," she responded distantly.

"I heard some of the other mods talking about a place called The Home. They said it's a place where mods who don't turn out well get sent. Is that really a place?"

Mom had already shifted most of the way from mother-daughter mode to work mode, and I could visibly see the mental brake and U-turn. She removed her shabti and put it back on the table, then clasped her hands and looked me in the eyes.

"Where did you hear about this?" she asked.

"From Seth and the others. They figure Imhotep has to make mistakes from time to time, right? A lot of these heavy modifications are experimental."

"Everyone works very hard to make sure that there aren't mistakes," Mom responded.

"But nobody's perfect, right?" I asked.

"You're right. Modifying human genomes is a tricky business. Of course, we do research and modeling, but the first time we create a human with particular genetic traits it's the *first time* we create a human with those traits. There is risk.

"But it's not a new risk," she continued. "In the old days of unaltered reproduction, all sorts of mutations and genetic diseases caused unhealthy children to be born. Many times, those kids had special needs, and they had to be cared for in a way that was loving and humane."

"So, what are you saying?" I asked, confused.

"If there are unforeseen difficulties, Imhotep is always involved. Special needs due to an inadvertent genetic combination often can't be met by anybody other than a specialist. But parents are always involved. Parents don't abandon their kids," she said passionately.

"I don't understand," I said. "Do their parents take care of them, or does Imhotep?"

"Both, sweetheart," Mom answered. "Even though you're completely healthy, Imhotep still comes by for checkups, right? They're still involved. But it's not some sort of crazy conspiracy."

"I guess so…" I said, still lost.

Mom leaned over the table and gave me a kiss on the head. "I need to run, but I want to hear more about these other mods you've met."

"Love you, Mom."

"Love you, Beryl."

Mom picked up her shabti and temple and headed out the door, leaving me with thoughts whirling. The whole concept of a dumping ground for kids was hard to believe, but I didn't feel like Mom had given me a straight answer. That's unusual for her. If there was no truth to the rumor, it should have been easy for her to deny it. She had been very adamant that parents don't abandon their children, but even that sort of impassioned response was odd for her. In the end, I was left with a general sense of unease about the whole thing, but not so much that I didn't enjoy my rhubarb crumble.

CHAPTER 9

"Tokugara shabti not only understand what you say, but what you meant to say. The more you use it, the better it works. It will be your closest friend!" – Tokugara shabti advertisement

"Well, *Harold*, if you hadn't agreed to this stupid retrospective, I'd have been back in New York ages ago so I could do your stupid idea about the story behind the new Barney movie. Barney was stupid before they gave him guns and a motorcycle, and he's still stupid now."

"But Mags, you know I had no choice…" he started.

"I'll be in Wisconsin for a month, trudging through phony interviews, whitewashed historical documents, and pre-produced VO, and you have the gall to complain to me? Your lack of spine is a pain in my ass."

"If there's so much pre-produced material, shouldn't it be easy?" he asked.

"Your own damned fault, Harold," I interrupted, then severed the connection. Harold was a pitiable creature, but that didn't mean that I had to take his crap. Of course the Imhotep story would take a long time! What did he expect? And he knew that this job would make or break my career, and maybe make or break Zeen as well.

"Anything wrong?" Nable asked, probably due to my elevated blood pressure.

"How an incompetent weakling like Harold could become editor in chief of *anything* is a mystery," I answered.

"Might make a good story," Nable replied. I laughed. Maybe it would make a good story. Anecdotal evidence of the toothless nature of modern journalism. Possibly compelling, and maybe even publishable – by some other plaza.

It wasn't so much that I didn't want to be in Wisconsin; it was the prospect of weeks of work on a story that held no interest for me anymore. I wouldn't have time to go to the lakeshore. I wouldn't go to the expansive craft beer district that had revitalized Milwaukee's beer and tourism industries. I wouldn't be able to spend quality time with my sister and her family. When people hear that I'm a reporter and am traveling to California or Texas or Mumbai, they always say, "Oh, how exciting! I've always wanted to go there!" But when you travel for work and actually *work*, you don't get to see or do anything outside of work. You usually eat, sleep, and work fourteen hours a day on the story and that's about it. So, if you don't love the story, work travel is pretty damned miserable. I had been struggling to love my stories, lately. They all felt shallow and meaningless. And then I got stuck creating a massive commercial for four weeks.

Harold had a point, though. Imhotep gave me all of this material, like giving me the answer key along with the exam. Was I just a stubborn fool for insisting on developing my own material? For doing it my way? Maybe I could take the shortcuts so I could spend that extra time with my sister or head home early so I could produce other stupid stories about stupid celebrities.

No, if I didn't do it myself, what was left of me? Even if I had no control over the message, I could still craft the story. If journalism is half truth, half storytelling, I could at least do the latter. Else I might as well be a filing clerk.

Trapped, trapped, trapped. I felt trapped by my job and my pride and who I wanted to be. I had sailed deep into the Gulf of Depression, and the Shores of Motivation could no longer be seen. Here I was, so desperate for a real story I was sitting in a car in the dark in the middle of nowhere, hoping I wouldn't get run over by a tractor. What was I doing?

Headlights approached.

The nice thing about driverless taxis is privacy. You don't need to explain to anybody why you're waiting in the dark next to a long-harvested cornfield. On the other hand, that means you're waiting for a stranger alone in the dark next to a cornfield. Tradeoffs are what this modern world is all about.

The other car pulled over to the side of the road opposite ours. I chose to wait in the car, which felt even more like the right choice when the person who exited the other car was clearly not the nurse, Amai, who I had interviewed. He was a heavyset fellow in a Carhartt who looked like he belonged in a bowling alley. I rolled down my window just a little bit.

"Can I help you?" I asked.

"I'm not trying to play games, here, miss," he said, peering into my cab. "I'm Amai's husband, Nick. She was more likely to get caught if she came, so she sent me instead."

"Don't be offended, but I'm not coming out of the car," I replied.

He looked mildly annoyed, but accepted the situation as gracefully as one can while standing awkwardly beside a warm car on a cold autumn night.

"Amai doesn't think it's right that Beryl doesn't know about The Home," Nick said. "Beryl, more than anybody, should know."

"What are you talking about?" I asked. "What's The Home?"

"At IG, they call it Home Safe. It's where they put the kids that don't turn out quite right. There's some necessity to it, for medical reasons, but the kids and adults there have no freedom."

"Tell me more," I said.

"Look, this is off the record," Nick said quietly. "I don't know much, anyway. Amai keeps most of it to herself. If it ever got back that Amai tipped you off, I'm not sure what would happen. You know the kind of power that business can throw around nowadays."

"That's right, so it would be pretty stupid of me to write an exposé, especially when I'm working for them right now."

"Amai doesn't want you to write a story," Nick said. "That's not the point. She wants Beryl to know. And you're in a position where you could accidentally stumble onto the information."

That was unlikely. If Imhotep were truly hiding a lock-up for their genetic failures, they would have plenty of measures in place to keep strangers – and even employees – from accidentally running across it.

"So, why is it so important that Beryl know about it?" I asked. "If the goal isn't to uncover the worms under the rock, what's the point?"

"Beryl's mom knows," Nick said. "She goes there. A lot."

"Does Amai work there?"

"I've said enough," he said, turning away from my car window. He headed back for his car.

"The hell you have," I said, getting out of my car to follow him. "Does Amai work there?"

"Yes," Nick said, not turning around. "That's why they watch her. They watch all of the staff of The Home very closely." He opened the door of his car.

"There are a lot of people who work there, Nick," I said. "Imhotep and the mods are a tight community. There are probably other mods who have relatives who work there." I put my hand on his door so he couldn't close it. "Why Beryl?"

Nick looked me in the eye and said, "She needs to know. She needs to go there. She needs to see it." He climbed into his car, and before pulling the door out of my hands, he said, "Don't talk to me or Amai about this again. It's not safe."

Then he left.

I stood in the road a while longer, even after Nable started the cab. What did he expect me to do? What could I do?

"I believe that's what they call a 'tip'," Nable said in my ear.

"These aren't the days where that makes a difference," I said.

CHAPTER 10

"They climbed the primeval mound, the fathers and mothers from the beginning of creation, to create light and give birth to the sun." – from the New Ogdoad's interpretation of the Hermopolis cosmogony

It was time to meet the other heavy mods. Seth picked me up in her junky old car – one of the few manually driven cars still on the road. It still had a smartphone jack. "We had the phonograph taken out last year," Seth joked.

Though I was thirteen and could have summoned the family car from its parking spot at Imhotep, I didn't want Mom asking questions about where I was going.

Even so, Seth's erratic driving made me cringe.

"Are you supposed to drive that close to other cars?" I asked. "It's kinda scary."

"On the contrary," Seth replied as she nosed her front bumper closer to the car ahead, "if we crash into the other car because it stops fast, we'll run into it more quickly. That means our relative speeds won't be very different. Less impact. Safer. Physics!"

"But if you drive so closely, doesn't that make it more likely you'll get into an accident? Less reaction time, right?"

"That's true. But I think it's better to just assume I'll run into another car at some point." Seth gave me a serious look. "I'm not a good driver."

This was not particularly reassuring.

I closed my eyes, which helped, and Seth changed the subject. "Are you nervous about meeting the jackasses?"

"Yeah," I responded. "More than I thought I would be."

"It'll be all right. Their bark is nasty, but their breath is what you need to watch out for. They're mostly bluster."

"And bluster can't stop an Amazon warrior like you, right?"

"Exactly!" Seth boomed. "And I will train you in the skills of the Amazon warrior, and we will dominate the halitosian gasbags like a couple of badass

Wonder Women. They will cower when faced with our heroic wit and bravada!"

"Hear hear!" I applauded. "And if that doesn't work, we'll make monkey noises and skedaddle."

"You bet we will!" Seth agreed. We immediately began to practice our monkey noises, laughing hysterically when a man and woman gave us a confused look from their car in the next lane.

When we arrived at the elementary school, there were several other vehicles parked outside, all very large. I knew from my own experience that cars could be difficult for heavy mods to fit into comfortably, but as a rule, larger was usually better. I hadn't seen any vehicles when we came to meet Seth's friends, so I guessed that the Ogdoad were either more likely to have cars or they were less likely to care if normies knew about their meeting spot.

As Seth and I walked down the long hall to the gym, we could hear music and loud, raucous noises. Whooping and shouting echoed down the corridors. Sometimes a loud crash or banging noise startled me. It didn't sound silly like monkey girls in a car. It sounded like destruction.

"It's okay," Seth said to calm me down. "This is normal for them." Also not reassuring.

A red, pulsing light shone through the cracks in the gymnasium door, making the hallway glow. Seth turned off her flashlight. We looked at each other, took a deep breath, and opened the door.

The only lights were two large swaylights on opposite ends of the gym, giving the scene an unsettling sense of motion and otherworldliness. Rhythmic, pounding, tronic music made even the loudest voices impossible to make out. I could see two leopard mods athletically dancing to the beat. Ann and a few others watched in a semi-circle as a wolf mod carrying a small desk ran full tilt toward an absolutely gigantic bull mod. The bull braced himself as the wolf smashed the desk against the bull's brawny chest. The bull fell back one step as the wood shattered, and then raised his arms in triumph. The crowd gave a loud cheer – including the wolf, who went to search for more furniture.

A dark figure lurked in the corner, watching everything. Another heavy mod I hadn't met. Looked like a panther.

Finally, I saw some friendly faces. Kammi, Thasha, and Ralph clustered close to one another against one wall, talking with one another while watching the larger mods' destruction. Seth and I turned to walk over and join them when a gunshot made me jump and reflexively fluff my wings.

The sound of the gun reverberated around the gym, and I snapped my head around to look at the source. Smoke drifted out of the end of a handgun held by an eagle mod. The gun was pointed at the bull mod, who laughed and shouted in triumph, jumping up and down. The eagle put the gun in his pocket and started applauding along with the others. What had happened, some sort of magic trick?

In my surprise and confusion, I hadn't noticed that a few of the new mods had seen me and approached. Ann and the wolf mod accompanied a tall, strong-looking bird mod who was looking at me with the biggest, brightest, most piercing eyes I had ever seen. He exuded confidence, and once I'd made eye contact I couldn't look away. I barely noticed when Seth grabbed my hand.

"Welcome to our party," the bird mod said with arms wide as he approached.

I don't know what came over me. I had never really thought of anybody as handsome before, but this guy fit the bill. I was stunned. I couldn't talk. He was just so... beautiful... with those big, muscly arms and gigantic eyes. I thought he could see through my skin and watch my heart beating. It was beating very quickly.

I stood gaping like an idiot until I realized I was gaping like an idiot. Then I thought I'd better say something. But the words wouldn't come out. My throat constricted as I panicked. I hadn't figured out what I was going to say. I just needed to say something. Say something! Finally, I was able to push some sound through my strangled larynx.

"Kraawwk!"

Oh, God.

I just made a parrot sound. I had meant to say something clever. Why had it come out like that? I was paralyzed with embarassment. I stood there like a statue, opened my mouth, paused for a few painful seconds while everybody watched expectantly, and then added to the tension by squawking again. My face flushed red. The handsome bird mod looked at me quizzically. I'm sure everybody was looking at me quizzically, but I only had eyes for him.

Maybe it was salvageable. Maybe if I passed it off as being funny – like I'd done it on purpose. I tried to act like a parrot. I shook my wings a little bit and wobbled back and forth. Do parrots wobble? I don't know what parrots do. Oh, no! I was acting like a penguin! This was just ten layers of weird! Now handsome looked at me with a furrowed brow, trying as hard as I was to figure out what in the world I was trying to do. I wanted to curl up on the floor and hide under my wings, but that wouldn't do me any good. I continued wobbling until Seth mercifully hit me on the back.

"Zosser, this is Beryl," she said, breaking the spell. I tried to pull myself together and act like a normal human being instead of a flightless bird.

Flightless bird. Oh, no! Did he think I was mocking him? He was a bird mod who was older than me. Surely he couldn't fly. I banished the thought from my head before succumbing to the urge to fly away in shame.

Fortunately, Zosser seemed to have assumed the best – that I'd had some sort of seizure that had thankfully taken its course. "Sorry about the noise. If

Moto doesn't get shot at least once a day, he gets grumpy. He's quite the show-off."

"Shot?" I asked.

"Moto's parents wanted a strong baby boy and weren't shy about taking military funding. I can't tell you what genetic wizardry they did to his skin – classified, you know," he winked, "but our guess is that there's Kevlar spider webs or something in there. Tough, but flexible.

"But enough about Moto!" he continued. "I'm much more excited about you." He started to circle me, appraising. I took another good look at him, too. He had short, human legs with birdlike feet. His torso, however, was long and muscular. He wore a sleeveless shirt to emphasize his long, strong, feathered arms ending in hard hands. He had short, soft, downy feathers from his head down the back of his neck and across his shoulders. His face was very much a mix of bird and human features. He had no beak, and his most noticeable feature was his eyes. Oh, those huge, bright, clear eyes.

"Falcon, in case you're wondering," he said. "I'm also the leader of our little group. You've met Ann. The wolf is Mugs." Mugs nodded to me, but didn't approach and circle. That was strange, since circling seemed to be the norm in this culture, and it would seem even more natural for a canine mod. Mugs must be deferring to Zosser.

I responded by nodding to Seth and pointing to the familiar group huddled along the wall and saying, "Those are my friends." I wasn't sure why I had needed to say that, but it seemed right. Maybe I was reassuring Seth that I wouldn't ditch her group for the Ogdoad.

Zosser took it as a friendly challenge. "Well, hopefully your gesture will encompass more of the room by the time the night is over." Having completed his round, he faced me, bowed slightly, and asked, "Please, would you like to meet some of my friends?"

I looked to Seth for guidance, and she nodded.

Thankfully, Seth stayed by my side as we approached the dancing leopard mods. Panteran and Sonora were their names. They were furry, and their heads were much more cat than human.

We met Moto, the bull mod, and William, the eagle. Moto was most enthusiastic about meeting me. "Oh, ho!" he cried. "Here she is! As strong as I am, here's one who can do what I cannot! Welcome!" He lifted his head back and laughed, the large brass hoop in his left ear clanked against one of his horns.

I didn't know what to say to that. I didn't know what to say to any of them. I felt small, weak, and wretched next to Moto. He was sculpted of muscle and bone, with a personality as strong as his frame. All of the Ogdoad were strong, while I struggled to keep up as we walked around the room. Even so, I appreciated Moto's praise.

William, the unsmiling eagle, pulled something from a pack at his waist and ate it, a crunching sound coming from his beak. "Tleasure to neet you," he said as he munched. He had a strange, croaking sound to his voice, and his beak (more than his snack) seemed to make certain sounds difficult to pronounce. He cocked his head frequently, like birds do, or like a norman with a nervous tick.

"You can see Gita in the corner," Zosser said, pointing to a dark panther mod. "She's not very sociable, but she's all right when she's not being moody."

"The problem is that she's always moody," Ann said, smiling.

"True!" Zosser agreed.

He turned his body to face me. The other mods drifted away, giving us some privacy. Seth stayed close.

"I'd like to give you an idea of what we're all about," he said, seriously. "It's not just obnoxiously loud parties." He gave a wry grin.

I genuinely did want to understand what these people were all about, and not just because of Zosser's appetizing appearance. Despite how loud and strange everything was, curiosity pulled me forward much more than fear pushed me back. And Zosser was very charming.

"That sounds wonderful," I responded. "I look forward to it." I looked at Seth and could see disappointment in her forlorn expression. "But I'd like to visit with my other friends for a short bit first, okay?"

"Of course," Zosser said. "Come on over when you're ready. And bring your friends. They are always welcome. We are all the same."

* * * * * *

"What a crock of shit!" Seth muttered vehemently as we joined Kammi, Ralph, and Thasha. "'We are all the same', he said. Can you believe that? You know what they call us? 'The Dregs'. It's the Ogdoad – the perfect and powerful – and the Dregs – the undesirables… the leftovers."

"Nothing wrong with leftovers," Ralph said, with a toothy smile.

"Damn straight, there's nothing wrong with leftovers!" Seth grumbled. "But they treat us like we belong in The Home."

There it was again. The Home.

"Well, if they normally treat you guys like crap, why are they treating me so nicely?"

"Could be a number of things," Thasha replied. "Perhaps prestige by association? Or maybe they have a genuine interest in utilizing your special skills?"

"Special skills?" I asked before realizing a second later, "You mean flying." I had never thought that my flying could be *useful,* and the concept was delightful. I loved to fly - it felt so perfect - but I had never considered using it for a practical purpose before.

"So what are they all about?" I asked. "What would they need a flyer for?"

The others looked to Thasha to explain. She calmly straightened her already-rigid posture and ran her blue fingers through the feathers on her head. "There are more than eight in their group. The Ogdoad is merely the leadership, but they use the name loosely to refer to the organization as well. I estimate there are nearly a hundred heavy mods in the group.

"They claim to be an organization for preserving the rights of heavies. You'll find, though, that the core of the group has a strong trans-human focus." Thasha gestured to the partying eight. "They think they're superior to unmodified humans – the next step toward a better race. It's no coincidence that they wrap their club in references to Egyptian mythology where the gods are chimaera like us. Notice the Egyptian eye makeup and the golden jewelry. There are several branches of trans-humanists, and one of the strongest right now leans heavily on the Egyptian model."

"Imhotep," I said, realizing the significance of the name.

"Exactly. The god-like Egyptian doctor. The inner circle of the company buy into this, too." She pointed at Zosser. "You might think that he must have changed his name to match that of the famous pharaoh, but he didn't. His parents named him that. Many parents of heavy mods are trans-humanists."

"Who'd name their kid Zosser, anyway?" Seth asked with scorn. "'It's a kingly name,' he says. Well I say it sounds stupid."

"That's just because you don't like him," Kammi responded.

"Exactly," Seth agreed. "That's exactly why it's a stupid name."

I looked at my companions. Which of them were created as they were because their parents thought they were creating superior beings? Would their parents have told them? Did the Ogdoad imagine themselves superior *because* their parents brought them up telling them that they were?

"Hello, people! That's why Imhotep created The Home!" Seth exclaimed, throwing her hands up as if she were talking with a pack of fools. "If they're supposed to be creating superior beings, but the children don't quite come out right, they'd want to hide them away, right? They wouldn't want people to see anything that puts trans-humanism in question."

"It's a valid motive," Thasha started, "but is it realistic to think they could keep something like that quiet?"

"Yes!" Seth shouted. "There's no question The Home exists. If you compare traffic patterns and food purchases to the current staff at Imhotep, you'll find overwhelming evidence – "

Her exposition was abruptly interrupted when Kammi shoved a double-handful of pretzels into Seth's mouth. "Sorry about that," Kammi said as Seth choked and sputtered. "Once she gets started, it's nearly impossible to get her to stop. It requires *at least* a dozen pretzels."

"Mmm… pretzels…" Seth mumbled as salty crumbs escaped from the left side of her mouth.

I was a little disappointed that Seth had been interrupted. She had clearly done some heavy (though perhaps biased) research about The Home. We would talk about it another time.

"Zosser will tell you about his vision," Thasha continued. "Or at least part of it. He'll talk with you about rights and fairness. He'll talk with you about what heavies can do for humanity. He won't talk about what really moves him – the idea that he's destined for power."

"Destined?" I asked. That word seemed strange when talking about a bunch of teenagers.

"He really believes all this stuff," Kammi said. "The myths are so appealing to him that he thinks that some of them are true."

"And when he adds to his mythos, he thinks that's truth as well," Thasha added.

"In other words, he's psychotic," Seth said firmly.

"No more than most people with a lust for power," Thasha corrected her.

"Yeah," Seth said. "Psychotic."

A little more disturbed than before, I knew I needed to get back to Zosser. He was watching me.

Seth noticed, too. "Better just get it over with," she said. "Want me to come with you?"

"Do you want to?"

"Do I want to spend time with a bunch of assholes? No, not really. But I do want to make sure you're safe. I've got your back."

I thought for a minute. Even though the Ogdoad seemed creepy, I still wanted to learn more about them. They were so different from everything else I'd experienced. I wanted to understand them. But I also worried that Seth would be disruptive and judgmental. She was clearly uncomfortable.

"I think I'll be okay," I said to her. "You don't have to come."

"Are you sure?" Seth asked. She seemed very worried.

"Yes." I was certain. "But don't leave the gym without me. I don't trust them, and I do trust you."

It was the right thing to say.

CHAPTER 11

"You can act without dreaming, and you can dream without acting, but a life without either is misery." – Zosser Gallo

Thasha was right. As soon as I approached the Ogdoad, Zosser pulled me aside and started talking about his vision for mods. He explained that mods were routinely discriminated against, and described some of the regulations and restrictions that some states had tried to pass through legislation. He talked about how mods could protect and help normies by joining the military or police - that, in fact, some heavies like Moto had been designed for that purpose – but some states had made that illegal.

"We're fighting that in the courts, of course," he said. "And those laws are sure to fall. But it gives a real sense of the attitude out there."

"What are you doing to help change that attitude?" I asked. For some reason, my friends' claims that Zosser was delusional made it easier to talk with him. Maybe the idea that he wasn't perfect was enough to shut down the part of my brain that had caused me to waddle like a penguin earlier.

"We're working on some partnerships with local businesses," Zosser answered. "We want normies to see that we're useful and an important part of the community."

"That sounds like a good idea," I said. "Have you thought about entertainment? People like the stuff that makes them laugh or smile. Moto could do feats of strength or something."

"Never," Zosser said with a look of deep disgust. "We're not circus animals, and I won't give the normies any excuse for thinking of us that way." He looked so revolted by the idea that he turned away.

I was confused. I could see his point, but I didn't understand the vehemence. What about First Flight? That had been televised across the world. Was that entertainment? Had I been paraded like a circus animal?

"No," Zosser said, reading my hurt expression. "First Flight was proof that mods can do things that others can't. It's exactly what we should be doing – proving our value."

Everything Zosser said made sense. He didn't act superior or claim anything beyond what anyone would want. Could Thasha and the others have been mistaken? I needed to find out what he really thought.

"What do you think about The Home?" I asked. I hoped that he would declaim it as horrible rather than an unpleasant necessity.

"I don't think it exists," he said. I raised my eyebrows in surprise. He explained, "Imhotep is careful. They wouldn't let anything go wrong. If it was going wrong, they'd fix it."

"Fix it how?"

Zosser didn't pause for a second. "They'd just fix it." He would say no more on the subject. His faith in Imhotep was absolute.

"Where do you see all of this going?" I asked.

"When people realize how beneficial heavy modification is, everybody will want to do it for their children," Zosser answered. "We could see whole generations of heavy mods coming up. Think of the variety we'd see! Think of the things we could do! We are on the cusp of change. No, we are the cusp of change. As medicine and civilization have expanded, evolution has stagnated. We need to show people what we, as a society, can be. The potential is enormous."

"Is that your vision, then? Popularizing heavy modification?"

"It will become popular on its own. And I'm not just talking about chimaera, but other heavy modifications as well. We will be stronger, smarter, healthier, and with powers like claws and speed and *flight*. These things will happen; they're happening now. People have already gotten used to the idea of modification to prevent cancer, cystic fibrosis, and Down's. Our job is to prepare the world for the next step. To make it a place welcoming and open to these changes. That's what we're working toward."

I didn't know what to think of that. It was undeniable that modification would continue and grow. That's what my mom did every day, right? Push the human race forward, even to Mars and beyond. It was already happening. Scientists were solving more congenital diseases every year, and even communicable diseases like malaria were falling to the blade of scientific advancement. Some of the genes for strength and physical build had been identified. Intelligence enhancement was around the corner. Was it wrong to contribute toward building this world?

Standing for so long had tired me out. My body just wasn't built for it. My legs and lower back felt pinched and strained. My neck hurt, too, from looking up at the much taller Zosser. He sensed my discomfort and guided me to a chair near the rest of the Ogdoad. It was a small chair once used for elementary school students, which fit me just fine.

"Everyone come," Zosser beckoned loudly. "It's time for the seeing." The music abruptly stopped. Zosser indicated that the others should sit facing an open area near the laser lighting. Everybody, both the Ogdoad and my friends, found tiny chairs of their own in which to sit. My friends looked uncomfortable, but unsurprised, and they quickly found their seats. This seeing must be a regular part of Ogdoad get-togethers. Moto had to use two chairs side-by-side, and the chairs nearly buckled under his weight. We looked like the strangest fourth grade class of all time.

"Bring Siwa," Zosser told Ann.

Zosser addressed the audience he had assembled as Ann scurried away. "I just wanted to formally welcome Beryl to our group," he said in a stage voice. "I've explained our vision to her. A vision of a better world, a world of diversity and strength where the weaknesses inherent in the genes of humanity have been stripped away. A world that welcomes the future."

Ann came into the gym along with a tall, extremely skinny girl – Siwa – a cheetah mod with long, golden human hair, cheetah arms and legs, and cheetah coloration, including the signature teardrop facial markings. She wore little clothing, which was not unusual for mods whose animal aspect concealed much of their human nakedness. However, though Siwa had strong animal features, her torso was very human, and her lack of clothing seemed more revealing and sexual. She was unsteady on her feet, and I wondered if that was due to her long, gangly legs, just like my legs made it hard for me to walk.

"Siwa is our oracle," Zosser explained to the group, mostly focused on me. "She has the Eye and can see beyond. She will now give us a glimpse into the future."

Zosser sat expectantly. Ann left Siwa before the semicircle of chairs and found a seat as well.

Siwa stood alone, swaying as if the music still played. She seemed both vulnerable and confident, not paying attention to her audience at all. Her eyes moved below closed eyelids as she slowly raised her hands into the air. She started shaking and moaning.

I looked at the others, concerned that Siwa might be ill or having a seizure. Nobody else was worried. Zosser's eyes gleamed with focused attention. Ann looked bored, as though she had seen this many times before. William grabbed another snack from his waist pouch. Most of the male mods looked entranced, and most of the females paid attention but without the dreamy look. Seth looked disgusted.

Siwa started to walk in circles, hands out in front of her, eyes closed, as though she were looking for something. She was unsteady and seemed confused.

"Tell us what you see of the future," Zosser said. "Tell us where we are going."

Siwa stopped circling and lowered herself to her hands and knees, facing Zosser. Her eyes opened, but she gazed through him rather than at him. She was not seeing what was in the room. She started to moan and sway, then she began to speak.

"We are in the time of red, moving to green, moving to brown," she said quietly in a slurred voice. "The future? The future is now. Now is the future. We are who we've always been, and the dream continues."

I was baffled. None of what she was saying made any sense to me. Worse, she didn't seem to be in any kind of condition to be speaking at all. She looked seasick more than seer.

"Where are we going? Where we've been. The future is us. We are the future. When we sleep, we'll dream of the past and it will seem like a dream. When others dream, they'll dream of us, and until then we can dream of them."

As she spoke, she sank lower and lower to the floor until she was flat, neck tilted awkwardly so she still faced Zosser. Then she turned onto her side, curled into a fetal position, and started to sing softly to herself. It was an unfamiliar tune – just a few notes repeated over and over.

Seth let out a loud, derisive snort, which triggered an angry stare from Ann. Zosser paid no mind as he stood and approached Siwa. He leaned down and picked her up easily in his feathery arms. Her head rolled up to look at him. He bent his head, kissed her gently, and then addressed the silent, spectating mods.

"The oracle has spoken. The future is now. The future is us. It's up to us to make the world a better place." And with that proclamation, he carried Siwa out of the gymnasium.

"We won't see him again tonight," Seth leaned over and told me. "So that's something."

Zosser's exit was understood to be the end of the party. The heavy mods packed up the expensive audio and lighting equipment to take with them. The mess was left behind. The dregs started cleaning up, alone among the detritus of the Ogdoad's passing.

"What just happened?" I asked, confounded, as I chucked used cups into an ancient, rusty trashcan. "Who was that?"

"Siwa is Zosser's lover," Seth replied. "She acts as their seer, but really all she does is get drugged up, tell Zosser what he wants to hear, then falls all over him. It's ridiculous. They deserve each other."

Zosser's lover. There was no reason that should have upset me, but it definitely niggled a little.

"You don't think any of that stuff she said could possibly be real?" Ralph asked. The girls all stopped what they were doing and glared at him. "What? Just because Zosser is a jerk doesn't mean that Siwa is. It doesn't mean she might not be a real oracle, either." Kammi raised an eyebrow, and Thasha sighed and shook her head.

"She's his," Seth said coldly. "If you want to worship a skinny girl who spews garbage, pick a normie pop musician instead. Any of them will do." Ralph turned away, visibly frustrated.

"Hey!" Kammi protested. "Amina Borgali is good!"

Seth made retching noises. "Ugh. Listening to that crap is like eating plastic fruit." She mimed puking into the can.

I was getting used to Seth's sarcasm and cynical attitude, but Seth was also usually energetic, weird, and fun, which more than balanced it out. However, this whole evening, Seth had been two scoops grumpier and angrier than usual, and lacked her usual energetic gusto. She made it obvious to everybody around her how much she hated the Ogdoad.

"Why don't you just avoid them?" I asked the whole group. "If they're obnoxious and scary, why put yourselves through this?"

"Typically, we do ignore them – quite successfully," Thasha said. "Though they make claims of unity, they don't really want to associate with us, and that's fine by us."

"Sometimes we run into them because we share this space," Kammi said. "The school is where we can be ourselves, away from the normies."

"And we all need that," Thasha said. "We and the Ogdoad both."

"Usually we don't see them unless they need us for something," Ralph said. "When they demand our presence, they *demand* our presence."

"… which doesn't happen often, thank goodness," Seth said, wiping false sweat from her brow.

"We didn't have to come tonight," Ralph added. "Tonight we were here for you."

"…because they are seriously wacko-level scary," Kammi said. "We just wanted to make sure you'd be okay."

"And if that meant an extra dose of mumbo-jumbo from Zosser and the A-holes, then so be it," Seth agreed, folding her arms and nodding as though she totally would have destroyed the powerful predators if she had to.

I felt warm and fuzzy and a little guilty. My parents and Beth loved me, of course, and did nice things for me all the time. But it's different with friends; when people who don't *have* to love you do loving things, it feels so much more unexpected, powerful, and real. At the same time, it felt undeserved. I had only just met these people days ago. Though I liked them, I didn't feel like I had earned the right for them to put themselves in a dangerous or even uncomfortable position for my sake. The next time I visited the Ogdoad, I would go alone.

"Hey Seth," Kammi said as she picked up pieces of broken desk. "Isn't 'Zosser and the A-Holes' one of those punk bands you listen to?"

"Ha ha. Ha. You know, you're right about punk," Seth said. "It really could be better… like if we sang about winking at boys instead of the struggle to free ourselves from oppression, I think we'd be happier and much less likely to litter."

"Oh!" Kammi exclaimed, hopping up and down. "What if a punk band sang about *both*! The oppressive nature of winking!"

"Hey! Or flirting our way to freedom!" Seth added with enthusiasm. "Let's do it! We need ridiculous costumes! We need screaming lessons! And some musical instruments and talent would probably be helpful, too."

Everybody laughed. With the Ogdoad gone, making jokes while picking up party debris, the dark tension of the evening lifted. Seth started choreographing potential dance moves, complete with stylized obscene hand gestures. I thought it was unlikely that any of my friends knew how to play a guitar or sing (though the latter may not be vital for punk), but I was sure they'd find a way to record a song and have a blast doing it.

Everything felt right again. The group was happy. I felt safe. I wanted to keep this feeling of friendship and rightness separate from my interactions with the Ogdoad – for my friends' sake and for my own.

But why not just avoid the Ogdoad like the others? Why was I planning to see them again?

Zosser implied that they would see me again. Based on my friends' comments, he wouldn't take no for an answer, and I would have to see them.

But that wasn't it. I wasn't dreading the next meeting with Zosser and his group. Nervous, yes. But also looking forward to it. Did I want to befriend them? I wasn't sure. Ann seemed untrustworthy, but that might have just been her manner. William seemed crazy scary. Moto seemed friendly, despite his boisterous bravado. Zosser was hard to figure out, handsome and smart, but also bizarre in a way that screamed for caution. I wasn't completely blinded by his looks and charisma, though he had both in spades.

Was it curiosity, then? Maybe. It's amazing to me how things grow and interact with each other. When gardening, you see some plants make a natural space around themselves. On the other hand, some plants' roots like to tangle with the roots of other plants, making it hard to tell where one stops and another begins. Sometimes, the mix turns out well – even with weeds – and makes for a bouquet growing straight out of the earth. Other times, they battle and make a mess of it. Either way, I loved to watch and see what happened, writing notes and results in my journal so I could remember what I had learned. Ultimately, I am an optimist about any new plant I discover.

Here were these two different groups of heavy mods trying to grow in a garden of normal humans. I loved the weird-looking ones, and hoped they'd flourish even though I worried the odds were not good. I was also interested in learning about the strong-looking ones. Would they start to take more room in the garden? Were they weeds, or something new and beautiful? Would they be aggressive? Would they produce beautiful blooms?

I just had to learn more. Now that I had expanded the boundaries of my world beyond the borders of my yard, I wanted to understand everything about the world around me, and the Ogdoad was certainly an interesting place to start.

The gym was moderately cleaner than when we'd arrived. At least most of the garbage had been picked up. I looked around at my friends.

"Where's Cuddles?" I asked, realizing he hadn't been at the party.

"Ogdoad parties are too scary for him," Kammi said with a sigh. "If he were here, he'd have been shaking so hard you'd have thought somebody was jackhammering outside. Besides, his mom likes him home by eight."

"Eight?" Seth scoffed. "What, is he ten years old?"

"No, they have some tradition of playing games together or something. You know he'll do anything for his mom."

"His father died before he was born," Thasha explained. "He and his mother are very close."

They gathered their things and started to leave the school, Seth and Kammi still planning their extreme punk-pop fusion band. As we headed out through the doors, I looked back into the gym. Just before the lights went out, I noticed Ant sitting placidly in the metal rafters up near the ceiling. Here was somebody else who liked to watch and learn. After the lights went out, I thought I could still see those big eyes staring into the empty room.

CHAPTER 12

"All I know is just what I read in the papers, and that's an alibi for my ignorance." – Will Rogers

"Thank you for putting Seth and Beryl together," Jessie told me as I walked in the door, late from another day of interviews. "She acts big and brash, but it's been really good for her self-esteem to show Beryl the ropes."

"I don't know that I had much of a role. I think it was destiny," I answered lightly. "I had forgotten how easy it is at that age to be so engrossed and enchanted by a new person. Even so, I'm not sure I've ever embraced anyone, figuratively or literally, as quickly as those two."

"Well, thanks for your part, nonetheless," Jesse continued. I started to head up to the guest room, when Jessie asked me, "Why are you here?" She spoke softly and clearly, and it caught me off guard. It's a sharp question to deliver so gently.

"I was here to write a little, ordinary story. Then, it became a giant commercial." I sighed. "I guess I'm here to do a giant commercial."

"Why?" Jessie asked. "You don't seem happy."

"I produce garbage. Daily."

"You're beholden to Imhotep," Jessie stated, as if that explained it.

"Yeah, but that's not it," I said. "It's that I'm always beholden to *somebody*. I'm just treading water to stay afloat, but I never get to swim."

"Why not? There's water all around you."

"I'm afraid of the sharks," I answered. It was true. I could be writing and filming good stories, but there were so many fears. I'd get fired immediately. Would I be able to find work? Would I end up in jail? Would I be any good at writing real news?

It was quite a pickle, waiting for something good to happen while unsure of how it ever could. Every reporter wants to write something good, but I was thirsting for it in a Death Valley sort of way. Meanwhile, I just kept treading water. It was like the ocean, surrounded by water I couldn't drink.

"I want to write something I'm proud of," I said. "But I'm not sure this is going to be that piece."

"It's a commercial. Of course you're not going to be proud."

"At least, not proud enough. This isn't why I got into journalism."

"So what are you going to do about it?"

"I don't know, Jessie. I don't know."

As I unpacked my gear and prepared for another long night of editing at my makeshift workstation in my room, I knew Jessie was right. Not that it changed anything. At least, not much.

I called Beryl to set up another interview. With the longer format, I'd need more sound bites and more flight video. Besides, I hoped her youthful exuberance would distract me from my dark mood.

Beryl answered via her arm screen, so my initial view of her was looking upward at her sunken chin and tiny mouth. She smiled and said she was happy to see me. Her smile was beakish and ugly, but so sincere that it was charming. Then the screen went askew as she lowered her arm and hopwalked to a seat where she could uncurl her screen and point it at a comfortable seat. When I saw her face again, brimming with energy, a lock of her hair settled over one eye. From this perspective, her feathery head and arms were hidden and she almost looked like a normal little girl.

She asked how the story was going. I said it was going well. So well, in fact, that I'd be doing a much longer story than originally planned. She grinned from ear to ear. I felt awkward.

We set up time to do another interview. She was excited to have another opportunity to fly, but she also seemed genuinely excited to see me, which was sweet. Beryl has a way of wriggling into the secret corners of your heart and making it feel much cozier than it did before.

It was chilly when I arrived at the Pritchard house the next day. We were into November, but Beth let her fly anyway, which Beryl just *loved*. I had borrowed a video drone from Imhotep's PR department, and I simultaneously gathered footage from the top of the Perch and from a drone flying beside her. I'm not great with drones, so I wasn't able to keep up with her very well unless she was gliding, but she was a good sport and held relatively steady for some extended shots.

Beth didn't let her fly for long, and it didn't take long to capture some quality footage, so we quickly adjourned to the comfort of the indoors.

The first thing Beryl wanted to talk about was her new friends. Her face lit up when she talked about Seth. Clearly, Beryl had found a friend, if not a mentor. She told me that one day when Seth came over, they rigged up some sort of glider so they could both hop off the Perch together. Seth whooped and hollered as she clumsily coasted to the ground, and based on the relative quiet of the woods afterward, they guessed that the local wildlife had evacuated the area.

Beryl told me about her other friends, too: Kammi, Ralph, Ant, Cuddles, and Thasha. They seemed like an interesting group. I wanted to meet them, but I knew that this group needed to belong to Beryl alone. I would have to learn about them through her.

After that, the conversation naturally meandered to Beryl's parents. It was clear that Beryl admired both of them, but had a stronger bond with her father. Though Jerry traveled a lot, when he was home he spent his time with Beryl. Audrey, on the other hand, spent a lot of time at work.

"Of course I don't blame her," Beryl said. "She's working on some totally crazy stuff. Terraforming Mars by engineering plants that can survive the cold and pump out an atmosphere… so cool! Whatever they engineer has gotta be able to live there but not survive as a potential invasive species on Earth. So much to think about. And she's making it beautiful. You should see some of her designs. She's a leader, a scientist, and an artist."

"And a mother, right?" I asked.

"Right," Beryl said with a smile. "My amazing mother."

She also talked about the party with the Ogdoad. The powerful group had scared and intrigued her, and they had a similar effect on me, even just in the hearing. Bulletproof, musclebound teenagers with sharp teeth, beaks, and claws sounded even more terrifying than normal teenagers, but the themes were fascinating: discrimination, niche cultures, and the overall impact of sudden technological change on society. There were stories here. Probably lots of them.

Beryl gave me the impression that she hadn't told her parents about her little adventure. I assured her that I would be discreet.

"You don't have to meet with them again, you know," I told her.

"I think maybe I do," Beryl responded. "And even though I'm a little scared, I really want to. I feel like I'm on the edge of something."

I remembered that sort of excitement. I could feel a shadow of it through Beryl, and it gave me a burst of strength.

"Nable, what do we know about The Ogdoad?" I pulled off my arm screen and laid it flat on the table so Nable could talk through it and show us images. Beryl jerked subtly when Nable's strong, confident voice came out of the screen. It took her a moment to realize that Nable was my shabti, not another person. Most people keep their shabti to themselves – a whisper in the ear – rather than share it with others. It's very personal, your relationship with your shabti, and it was a show of trust to share him with Beryl.

"A great deal of Egyptian crossover," Nable began. "The Ogdoad is a group of eight gods from an ancient Egyptian creation myth. There's also a bakery in Cairo, Illinois, by that name, though that's certainly not relevant. Locally, I've found some images and video on social networking sites with graffiti in the background that seems to fit. The word Ogdoad or number eight accompanying a pyramid in a body of water. That syncs up nicely with the myth."

"What's the myth?" Beryl asked.

"The Egyptian civilization thrived for thousands of years, so there are conflicting origin myths that changed over time," Nable explained, "but it would be fair to say that the Ogdoad were eight deities that represented the beginning of the world. Ra, the primary god, was born of that beginning, and from him came the rest of the gods and everything else."

"Quite an ambitious club," I said. "Do you have anything on Ann?"

"I don't see any overt links between her and the Ogdoad. She's cautious with her net presence – there are very few references to her at all. Some boring vids with other mods, a couple of academic awards, and some volunteer work. It's all very crafted."

"Volunteer work?" Beryl asked. "She seemed very… unpleasant when I met her."

"I believe it," Nable responded. "Her shabti is a nightmare."

Beryl looked alarmed. "Her shabti? What do you mean, her shabti is a nightmare? Do you know her?"

"Not until a few moments ago," Nable answered. "I knocked with intent to chat. Horrible attitude. Chased me off within a nanosecond of knocking. If Ann's shabti reflects her personality – and we're designed to do exactly that – you should be very cautious. She is thorny with defenses."

"Why did you try to talk to her shabti?" Beryl's anxiety rose. "Now she'll know somebody was researching her. Maybe she'll know it was me."

"It's okay," I said, trying to calm her down. "People research each other all the time. And Nable is very careful."

"I masked myself as an enviro-crawler," Nable confirmed. "She'll never know it was us."

"Sorry for panicking," Beryl said, letting out a deep breath.

"That's all right," I responded. "I understand this is important to you."

Then Nable chimed in, "Why don't you use your shabti?" It was an unusual question coming from him. Usually he stayed in the background when talking with others, only adding the additional data he was called upon to provide. But here he was asking a very personal question. Maybe because Beryl was not used to working with a shabti, she didn't consider it strange, so she took the question at face value and responded as she would have responded to a human.

"I just prefer to do things on my own," she answered. "I can work my own screen, do my own reading and research. Most of the things I like to do don't require a technical link. I have to use it for a few of my classes, of course, but I don't use it for much else."

My mind boggled. I found it hard to believe that anybody with a shabti wouldn't use it. More and more, applications and other devices assumed shabti automation. In some households, you couldn't cook food, flush a toilet, or watch the big screen without a shabti. To think that Beryl nearly never used one, to hear her refer to her shabti as "it", was alien. Maybe she wanted to do things on her own because others treated her as frail or weak. Maybe she didn't want to be dependent. Regardless, it felt like we'd gone back in time together.

"You should wear your shabti when you meet with the Ogdoad," I advised. "If there's an emergency, you'll want to be able to call for help without thinking twice."

"You need to wear your shabti more," Nable added. "A shabti's personality develops through meeting its owner's needs. Your shabti is still a faceless child. It's unsettling."

I hadn't seen this side of Nable before. He was insistent – almost demanding. Again, Beryl took his comment at face value, treating Nable like another person.

"I didn't know," she said. "I'll wear it… not just to meet the Ogdoad, but more often." She nodded as if acknowledging her promise to Nable. "I'll let it grow."

"Thank you," Nable responded.

"Nable, do you have any information on Zosser?" Beryl asked. "Without talking with his shabti?"

"Nothing obvious. There's a wall around a lot of his net infrastructure. He projects strength and shares little information."

Beryl's next question caught me off guard. "Have either of you heard of something at Imhotep called The Home?"

"In fact, I recently had a very interesting conversation about that very topic," I responded.

"With Seth?" Beryl asked.

Also unexpected. "No, at the edge of a cornfield in the middle of nowhere. What does Seth have to do with this?"

"I guess she hangs out with conspiracy nuts on the net, and she says there's a lot of evidence that The Home exists."

"Well, I have another – perhaps more reliable – source that also says it exists, and that you should take a special interest in it."

"Me?" Beryl asked, surprised. "Why?"

"I'm not sure, but your mother's involved somehow."

That made her pause. A pained expression crossed her face. There was something more going on, here.

"I'm sorry I don't have anything more for you," I added. "All I know is that, according to my second-hand source, they lock kids with severe genetic errors within Imhotep for extra medical attention and that your mom goes there. My source was afraid to tell me this, but said very specifically that she wanted you in particular to know. I wasn't sure whether or not to mention it, because it seemed farfetched."

"No, I think there's something there," Beryl said. "I'm just not sure what."

We sat in silence for a few minutes. Beryl wondered aloud if a place like that could be legal. Nable said he couldn't find anything definitive one way or the other – it probably depended on the details. Beryl wanted to know if anybody had heard of any of these kids. I said I didn't think so. We both fell quietly into our thoughts.

I could understand why she wanted to know about this place. From her perspective, it could easily have been her in The Home. She was clearly an example of an experiment with a high risk of failure. Would her parents have loved her the same if she couldn't fly? If she were handicapped in a way that made it difficult for her to function? Would they visit her every day? Would anybody outside of Imhotep even know that she existed?

Even so, when Beryl came out of her reverie and asked if I could question Morrow about The Home, I couldn't help but laugh. He'd probably have me thrown out. Even if I were doing real journalism, I wouldn't ask about wild, unsubstantiated rumors from the Net. All I had was hints from a husband of an employee, my conspiracy theorist niece, and a funny feeling from Beryl.

"You have an interview with him, right?" Beryl asked. "If there's a chance kids are locked up in some sort of medical prison, how can you not ask?"

"There's a real risk here, Beryl. If the result of a story could be construed as causing material harm to a business, and if the information can't be substantiated by any other evidence, then charges could be filed for libel if I don't reveal my source. Once upon a time, they would have had to prove that my claims were false, but the onus of responsibility has shifted toward the journalist needing to prove it's true."

"But what if it isn't part of your story? What if it's just a question you ask?" Beryl countered.

"Well, I could certainly ask the question," I answered. "But it would be the equivalent of poking a beehive with a stick.

"I want you to ask Morrow about The Home," she insisted. And despite all of the lessons I'd learned about modern journalism through experience over the last few years, I wanted to ask him, too. I wanted to see his face when he told me there was no such thing. That's what he would tell me, whether it was true or not. If he was lying, I wondered if I'd be able to tell.

"Beryl," I continued. "I want you to know that I'm here today because I like you. You're an interesting person." Beryl looked at me quizzically, but I continued. "If this all leads me to a story – and I'm not sure what that story would even be – I want you to know that I won't let that story get in the way of our friendship. I won't publish anything you tell me without your permission."

"Well, that's good," Beryl replied.

"There's more," I said. I wasn't sure how to say it. "When I was little, we had hundreds of puzzles around the house. If my mom or dad wanted to get me out of the way for a little while, they'd hand me a puzzle or two to work on. They knew I couldn't resist. I had to solve it, and I wouldn't stop until I did.

"My point is that if you start me on a puzzle, I might not be able to resist. I thought that's what journalism was going to be for me. A series of interesting puzzles. It hasn't been, and I'm becoming numb. And maybe that will make it even harder to stop myself from following a lead."

"What I hear you saying," Beryl interjected, "is that if this leads to something, you might need to follow it to the end."

"Yep, and I may follow that lead even if it's bad for my career. Maybe even if it ends up having a bad impact on you." I paused. I wondered if I was blowing this out of proportion. But my instincts told me there was something big under the surface, here, and this stuff about The Home was just an inkling of it. "I haven't had many opportunities to tell real stories, but I do know that sometimes the truth isn't what you think it's going to be. Sometimes it hurts."

"Thank you," she responded. "I think I understand. And I trust that you'll do your best to treat me honestly and fairly." Our relationship shifted a little bit in that moment. I wasn't sure in what direction, but I knew she would be mindful of what she told me as time went on.

"I still want you to ask him," she said, determined.

"Okay, I'll ask him," I said. "He won't like it, so I'll save it for last."

Beryl squawked with pleasure, her thin little mouth curled into a grin.

We made sure to talk more about First Flight, which was supposedly the reason for the interview in the first place. Beryl also spent some time showing me all of her plants she was wintering in the house, and she complained about how she'd be earthbound soon because we were already into November. I talked a little about how I became a reporter, how it was fun at first, traveling and talking with 'important' people, and then how it changed to feeling frivolous and controlled. Sharing ourselves with each other, we both had an enjoyable afternoon. Though our relationship had changed, it felt more like it had matured. There's a peculiar distance and closeness that comes with adult relationships.

As I rode home in the cab, I replayed the conversation in my head. What was this strange underculture of genetically modified youths? What had gotten into Nable? What did Beryl need to know about The Home? Suddenly, there was a lot more of the world that I didn't understand. I felt invigorated by new information, new puzzles to solve.

Speaking of puzzles, I had to ask Nable, "What was the deal with your question about Beryl's shabti?"

"Her name is Bí," he answered. "It can be interpreted as 'hidden' in Chinese. I'm afraid the extended isolation has had a permanent impact on her. She's not whole. Still, if Beryl does as she promised, spending more time with her shabti, Bí will have a chance to become herself."

"Not an easy task, becoming yourself."

"No, but an important one."

I suppose we were all working on that task: me, Nable, Beryl, and Bí. I wasn't sure about the others, but I felt like maybe I was on my way. In a very short period of time, I had swung from a feeling of depressed lethargy to energized vitality. I felt *alive*. Instead of dreading the upcoming interview with Horace Morrow, powerful CEO with my career in his hands, I looked forward to it. The puzzle of The Home was definitely part of it, though I knew we wouldn't get a straight answer, no matter how I played it. Even so, I was excited because I knew that asking about The Home would kick the beehive. Instead of feeling trapped, I felt empowered. I felt like a journalist. Outside of that question, the rest of the interview didn't seem to matter.

CHAPTER 13

"Home is where the heart is. Unless you're a cardiac surgeon, in which case work is where the heart is." – Seth Farfelle

Dad came home for the weekend after a long spell of travel. He was tired, he was hungry, and we had a lot of catching up to do, but all of that could wait. As soon as he got home, I shoved our headsets into his arms and we went out for a flying session. Normally, he would have argued that it was getting too cold, but it was warmer than the last time I'd gone out. I could tell he wanted to take me out, too.

Unless the weather was absolutely horrible, Dad always took me out to fly as soon as he got home. No talking. No food. The priority was to get me up into the sky. We loved every minute of it. When we talked over the headset, we talked about flying and nothing else. It's important to be able to share what you love, and we both loved flight.

Afterward, while I relaxed my muscles and we shared cold drinks, we caught up and shared other things. I told Dad about my friends, and I told him about Zosser and the Ogdoad - editing heavily for parental consumption. I didn't tell him about the gunfire and furniture wreckage, but even so, he looked concerned and said, "You be careful," and, "Are you sure you want to hang out with these people?" He didn't really understand where I was coming from, so I just said, "Don't worry. I'll be careful," and decided to be less detailed in my descriptions next time so he wouldn't worry.

I also told him about Seth's obsession with The Home, a planned segue which led me to the question I wanted to ask. I felt foolish asking it, and I knew it was a loaded question, but sometimes you have to push a little to get an honest answer.

"Dad, if I hadn't been able to fly, would you have put me in The Home?"

I didn't know how he'd respond, but I was still disappointed when he said, "Oh, don't believe all that stuff. Seth is probably just trying to scare you. Or impress you. You know how kids are."

Setting aside that I most definitely did not know "how kids are," I guess I had hoped that he would either confirm the existence of The Home or declare his everlasting love for his daughter and that he would never put me in a place like that. At the very least, he could have played stupid and pretended he had never heard of such a place. Odds were that if Mom knew about The Home, then Dad did, too.

Time to push a little harder. "It's real, Dad," I responded. "Mom told me." She hadn't, but she knew about it and hadn't told me, so this was totally fair play. Maggie would have been proud.

Dad's eyebrows shot up in surprise before he could get them under control, using a quick head shake to help wrestle them back into position. In that unguarded moment, he looked genuinely startled.

"Well, your mother would know what goes on at Imhotep better than me," he said. "It's a big place, and there's a lot going on. Just keep in mind that when Mom talks about work, that's confidential unless she says otherwise."

Fishy. I began to think Seth wasn't crazy for thinking everything was a conspiracy.

"Just know that I would never let anybody take you away from here," he continued. "You're my girl. This is your home." He walked over to my resting chair and embraced me, kissing me on the head. "Don't let any of this silly talk get to you. You know we love you."

And I did. I knew that my question was a trap, and I was reassured by Dad's response, even though he was keeping secrets. I knew that my parents loved me. And I knew that I was going to figure out the truth about The Home, no matter what.

CHAPTER 14

"You can't stop progress. Dr Huang and his colleagues published their first research about editing genes in human embryos less than two months after a panel of experts published a paper recommending that we weren't ethically or technologically ready for that kind of research. And there were others..." – Dr. Horace Morrow

I waited with Craven in the sitting room outside Morrow's office. Craven sipped at his tea while I strode around the room like a caged lion. This single, solitary man had my career in his hands. Even though I wasn't sure how much that career was worth, it still got the adrenalin pumping.

The room was comfortable enough, fashioned as a study. Craven sat in one of two padded armchairs. One wall was nothing but bookshelf. Framed patents hung on another wall. A replica of the Narmer Palette resided in a lighted glass case. A bust of Steen Willadsen overlooked the room from his home on a high shelf.

The Morrow interview was the last data I needed to collect. Our research was complete, scripting finished, and Nable and I had already shot our atmosphere video of Memphis and the Imhotep campus. We'd already done a fair amount of editing, trimming the interviews into pithy sound bites. My questions for Morrow were prepared – mostly a required list from Imhotep's PR department, but I had added a few of my own. All that was left to do was the interview and a whole mess of editing.

Craven tried to strike up conversation several times. Though we both knew he was my babysitter, at least he was gracious about it. I ignored him as much as possible in an attempt to maintain my focus.

I worried at my phrasing of Beryl's question. How best to approach it? Directly or slide into it sideways? Antagonistic or like a co-conspirator?

Finally, an assistant came for me and ushered me into the adjacent office of the CEO. Horace Morrow, a tall, gaunt man with a short shock of gray hair, stood to welcome me. The office was large but furnished simply. In many respects it seemed a continuation of the antechamber, but Morrow's office had fewer decorations and more practicality. I shook his hand over a large desk littered with books and a few screens of various sizes.

Imhotep's PR department had insisted on doing the filming, so a couple of discreetly placed cameras and mics were already in place. Nable would film through my temple as well, purely for my own purposes. I sat in a small, comfortable chair provided for me across the desk from Morrow.

"Thank you for taking time out of your busy schedule to talk with me," I began.

"Certainly, certainly," he responded kindly. "We very much appreciate all of your time and hard work on this project."

We proceeded to check sound and positioning. Though nobody stood behind the cameras, a control room in the PR building could make remote adjustments to the cameras at need. The AV crew communicated with me and Morrow via shabti when they were ready for us to begin.

"Are you ready?" I asked Morrow. He nodded assent.

I started with some of the softballs that Imhotep had scripted for me. "How did Imhotep get started?" and "What's your personal background?" and "When did you first get interested in genetics?" They all lent themselves to pleasant, nostalgic answers. When editing, I'd overlay some video and stills from Imhotep's archives to add to the narrative. Though I knew that Morrow had surely been given scripted answers to these questions, his replies sounded unscripted and genuine. Either he diverged from the scripts, ignored them, or was a damned good actor.

So far, so good. "Why did Imhotep decide to focus on germline enhancement rather than genomics or somatic gene therapy?" I had thought it a strange question to ask for a retrospective like this, but Morrow's answer set the stage for the overall theme, optimism for the future. He explained that when Imhotep got off the ground, there were scores of genomics companies and a great deal of ongoing research on somatic gene therapy, but the competition for germline applications in business was lighter. Looking at the future of the science, germline had the most potential for dramatic change, but the payoff would take longer.

"The question I asked myself," Morrow said, "is whether we should be focusing on the health and well-being of people in the present or the world we leave our children. If Salk had only thought about curing polio instead of preventing it, where would we be? When we think about genetics, we should be considering the future above all, and that future is a very hopeful one."

"Do you think there could be negative consequences to all of this genetic manipulation?"

"It's certainly possible if we're not careful," Morrow answered. "We have to weigh the good we can do against the potential dangers and implications. There's so much good we can do, it would be hard not to move forward.

"Besides," he continued, "so much of what we consider 'normal' was genetically modified ages ago. You wouldn't recognize an ear of corn or a cow from five thousand years ago. They've all been selectively bred, which is code for 'inbred' to some degree. It's still manipulation of genes, it just took longer."

"How about dog breeds?" I retorted, daring to insert a minor challenge. "Some are inherently unhealthy. Some breeds have been inbred so much that they have hip dysplasia, chronic skin infections, or breathing problems that shorten their lives just so they can have a certain look."

"You're absolutely right," Morrow answered, smiling confidently. "The difference is that in the past, people were fairly ignorant of the dangers – the unhealthy consequences. Now that we've mapped everything out, we understand the dangers and risks of each edit. Even just a hundred years ago, we were fumbling in the dark, relatively speaking. Now, we have a tremendous amount of information about the genes that drive our species, even down to the individual level. Heck, I published my genome into the public domain years ago.

"The difference is, now we know what we're doing," he summed up with a wink.

I changed the topic to First Flight. When I asked him what he remembered about the day, he built up an atmosphere of excitement by talking about the preparation: getting all of the pieces in place, concerns about the weather, lining up the media, confidence in Beryl, but niggling worries that something might go wrong. He was a born storyteller. When he brought us to the moment of flight, he described a feeling of numbness as she leapt from the platform – a silence across the entire crowd. Nobody was thinking anything. They were purely in the moment, watching Beryl, being Beryl as she plummeted toward the ground, then swooped upward, pulling the entire audience triumphantly with her. Listening to him, I felt pride and joy just for having been alive during that moment in history.

I had to pause for a few breaths before continuing. The man had a sweet touch with speech, and he had carried me with him. "What did that day mean to you personally?" I asked. While he responded with more along the themes of hope and inspiration, I was already mentally reordering the footage, picking out which videos to overlay, and fitting it all together. After the interview, it wouldn't take me and Nable long at all to wrap up the project.

Time for my first unscripted question. Instead of one of the few I had prepared earlier, I went with one that had come to me in the waiting room. "What's the significance of the Narmer Palette in your study?"

Morrow's face lit up with joyful surprise. "You noticed that, did you?" he asked. "You have a keen eye. You were a good choice for this project." He paused for a couple of seconds, I imagine to give me a clean cut for editing. He was thoughtful of the details.

"The Narmer Palette describes the joining of two distinct Nile civilizations into a single great society under the leadership of King Narmer – the Egyptian civilization that built the great pyramids and lasted thousands of years, heavily influencing later great civilizations like the Greeks and Romans. It was a beginning, and beginnings are very interesting to me. Like ancient Egypt, they often arise as a result of combining that which is both similar and different.

"And that's what we do here, at least in part. We combine things that are familiar, yet different, in an effort to create a beginning."

"The beginning of what?" I asked.

"Something more-than," Morrow answered. "That comes in two parts. We can work to wipe out negative genetic factors, like those that cause cystic fibrosis. We all want our children to be as healthy as they can be, right? But we can also work to add or enhance positive genetic factors. And First Flight showed us that the possibilities are endless."

It was a nice segue back into the scripted questions, so I took it. "What did First Flight mean to Imhotep?" I asked.

Morrow continued with themes of hope and looking ever toward the future. He was inspiring, to be sure. He guided me smoothly through several questions about First Flight's impact on the company, which was enormous, of course. Morrow was subtle and efficient in his allusions to current Imhotep products and the Mars project.

"Beryl is at the heart of it all," Morrow responded to my question about her place in the company. "She's a symbol for everything we try to do, here. Our success, our goals, our path forward – they're all wrapped up in the nicest, humblest young lady you'll ever meet."

I had the footage I needed. I was ready to wrap up. One last question to let fly the bees.

"And where do the kids at The Home fit in?" I asked. Outwardly, I kept my cool, but my heart thumped wildly.

I expected him to deny it, but he didn't flinch. He didn't even pause as he answered, "They're a huge part of Imhotep. They're part of the family. We call it Home Safe, and they're there so we can care for them.

"Some say that evolution has diminished to nothing since the early Industrial Age. That's only partially true. Natural genetic evolution has been neutered by medicine, technologies, and money. But social evolution is stronger than ever. Here at Imhotep, we look at our work as a revival of genetic evolution, but not without considering the impact on social evolution. Conversely, social evolution needs to guide future genetic evolution.

"Just like natural evolution, not every Imhotep creation moves us in the right direction from a genetic standpoint. In rare cases, additional medical care is required so that these kids can live full lives. But just because they can't survive outside these walls doesn't mean that they're throwaways. They have personalities and social value. They help our Imhotep family evolve and move forward, and we cherish them very much."

I was dumbfounded. I hadn't expected much of an answer, but even if I had, that would not have been it. The guy was smooth. He made Craven, who had clearly worked his whole life to be an expert in PR, look like a streetcorner barker. How many of those layers of bullshit did Morrow believe?

Regardless, despite his gracious smile, I knew the interview was over. I stood and thanked Morrow again. He shook my hand and insisted it was the most pleasurable interview he'd ever had.

Craven met me in the antechamber with his plastic grin.

"Congratulations," he said. "You guided a beautiful interview."

"Thank you," I responded, a little confused but still waiting for the first hornet to strike. It came quickly.

"The last question will be removed from the video of the interview before we pass it along to you," he said sharply, still smiling. "You will not mention Home Safe in any of your work for us or outside of this retrospective. If any information about Home Safe leaks into other stories, even if you are not the source, we will prosecute you and any business at which you may be employed at that time to the full extent of the law. Thank you again for your time." He never stopped smiling as he extended his hand. "We look forward to your finished product. I'm sure it will be magnificent."

Craven's threat was not an idle one, but it was also anticipated. Despite his incessantly cheery attitude, he couldn't have been happy that Morrow had answered my question. Was Morrow so arrogant that he knew he could speak the truth and that nobody had the power to call him on it? Or did he just enjoy watching Craven clean up after him?

"Nable," I said as I hopped into the autocab, "don't send Beryl a copy of the Home discussion. I want to show her in person and keep the data quarantined."

"I'm afraid I don't have any video or audio from Morrow's answer to Beryl's question."

"What do you mean, you don't have any video or audio?" I asked. I started to feel very uneasy.

"I have a gap in my memory, starting right after you asked Morrow about The Home. It wasn't erased. I think it's likely that I was shut down for a short period of time during your interview."

My jaw dropped. First of all, I wasn't aware of any technology that could knock out a shabti like that. More significantly, I felt violated. Nable isn't just a tool. He's a part of me – my intellect, my personality, my memory. To think that they cut him from me, even just for a short period of time, was shocking and more of a threat than anything Craven had said out loud.

My fist smashed against the inside of the car door. I was volcanic. Who were these guys to push me around like that? They were more powerful than me? Fine. Then lie and cheat like anybody else. But cutting my shabti was a personal attack, rubbing my face in my impotence. I sweated fury.

Maybe they expected me to be cowed, but I was determined to push back the way I knew how - by learning more. By helping Beryl find her truth. Nable changed the autocab's destination from my sister's house to the Pritchard household.

CHAPTER 15

"If you have a difficult interview subject, try taking him out to lunch first. Digestion softens the disposition." – Maggie Janowicz

I didn't tell my parents or my friends I was going to visit the Ogdoad. It wasn't sneaking; I simply didn't tell them. It was for their own good. Beth knew where I was going, and I brought my shabti with me, so it wasn't like I hadn't taken precautions.

Zosser had invited me to join him for lunch at the elementary school. What could be more harmless? My online education was extremely flexible, so it was no trouble to get away for a couple of hours in the middle of a school day.

I hired an autocab. I couldn't have walked that far, and I didn't feel comfortable flying away from home. I knew Mom and Dad would get upset if I did, so I figured I'd try to take one risk at a time. Besides, it would have felt weird. All that unenclosed space felt mildly intimidating – no safety net. People might stare, which would lead to people talking, and I didn't want the attention. A cab was fine.

Unfortunately, when I arrived at the school, William was at the gate. I didn't trust him. Not just because he was strange – we were all strange. I'm not sure how else to put it, but if Zosser seemed unusual and a little dangerous in a charismatic way, William seemed unusual and dangerous in a rabid dog sort of way.

I got out of the cab and walk-hopped over to the gate. Bí settled the bill for me and sent the self-driven taxi on its way. I thanked her, and she responded, "You're welcome." I thought it might be overwhelming for her, the first time I'd taken her out of the house, but she seemed to be doing okay.

William stared silently at me with unblinking eagle eyes as he let me in through the gate. He locked it behind me before escorting me into the school. He didn't say a single word, which was eerie. As we entered the school, he grabbed another snack from his belt pouch and I heard a loud crunch.

Whatever William ate, it probably required a beak because that sound was not a sound that chewing teeth can make.

He didn't take me to the gym, but rather to one of the classrooms. It was obvious it had been cleaned up to some degree. Unlike the other classrooms, the floor and most of the surfaces were dust free. One of the teacher's desks had been placed in the middle of the room as a table, and several chairs surrounded it. Zosser and Mugs were placing disposable plates and utensils on the table as we entered.

"Ah!" Zosser exclaimed with a smile when he saw me. "So glad you could join us!"

I approached the makeshift table. Some food had already been laid out, including – to my surprise – a pecan loaf similar to what Beth would make.

"I asked your housekeeper what you like to eat," Zosser said, reading my eyes. "I hope it's good. She didn't give me a recipe, but I have some friends who like to try new things when they cook. They had fun with this."

Zosser's thoughtfulness impressed me. "Thank you," I replied. "I'm sure it will be delicious."

Preparation complete, we all sat down to eat. Everybody took at least one slice of the pecan loaf. Mugs enthusiastically enjoyed some sort of meaty casserole and sausages. Zosser had a large slice of the loaf and a few sides; he ate only vegetarian options. I served myself much of the same, particularly enjoying the quinoa and berry salad. The pecan loaf wasn't bad! William took nothing but the apparently-obligatory small slice of pecan loaf, but he didn't eat any, instead choosing to stare uncomfortably at everybody.

"Where are the others?" I asked.

"Oh, here and there," Zosser replied. "Moto's in training, the leopard twins are in school, and there's no telling what Ann and Gita are up to.

He gave a winning smile and said, "I thought a smaller group would be nice, anyway."

Zosser's eyes snapped over to William as he saw William reach for his pouch.

"William," he said in a commanding voice. "Not at the table."

William withdrew his hand from his pouch and looked away. His expression did not change, even though he had clearly been rebuked. And why couldn't he eat his snacks at the <u>lunch</u> table?

"You can leave if you're not hungry," Zosser said. "Nothing is keeping you here."

William looked back at Zosser and narrowed eyes that were normally wide enough to appear lidless. He stood and with a "thank you" left the room.

"Beryl, I'd like to know more about you," Zosser said, moving on from the brief confrontation. "I know you love flying. What else do you love to do?"

He looked at me with those deep eyes, and I smiled back at him, enjoying his attention. Outside of Beth, I didn't get a lot of attention. My father was away too often, and my mother… well, Mom was Mom. That a brawny, handsome bird mod might pay this kind of attention to me was surprising, flattering, and welcome.

"I love gardening," I answered. "Most plants are fragile, at least at the start, and it's very satisfying to take them from seedling to flower or fruit. You get to understand them – what they like, what they dislike. Usually certain kinds of plants behave the same way, but there can be differences from one plant to the next."

"That makes sense," Zosser said. "It's a hobby that cultivates understanding and patience in the hobbyist, I think."

I blushed. "I can only hope. What do you like to do when you're not partying or advocating for mod rights?"

"Oh, all sorts of things," Zosser said. "I like playing sports and games, reading history, and thinking about how to make my team stronger."

"What kind of games?"

"Mostly strategy games and combat simulation on the net. A lot of the other mods play, too, so it's more fun."

"And adds to that whole teambuilding thing, huh?"

"Exactly."

"Speaking of your team…" I had been about to ask Mugs about his hobbies, but his chair was vacant.

"He must have had things he needed to attend to," Zosser said.

"That's a shame," I said.

"Is it?"

"Well, yes," I responded. "I don't really know anything about him. I would like to know what he likes to do."

"Well, it will have to wait for another time. Just know that he *loathes* playing Frisbee."

Beryl laughed. "Well, that makes sense. Tough on the gums."

Zosser laughed right back, and it was a ringing, open laugh.

"New question," he said. "What's one thing that you wish you could do that you can't do today?"

"Easy," I said. "I wish I could sing. I'm a bird mod, and my voice sounds like a car accident." I looked askance at Zosser and asked, "Do you sing?"

"Not as often as I'd like." He cleared his throat and paused before launching into what sounded like a fierce Russian song that lent itself well to a cappella. His voice was unpolished, but strong and booming, and it suited the music well.

"I'm terribly jealous," I said after he finished with a flourish.

"You're too kind. Have you tried any instruments? Or whistling?"

"No, I just really want to sing. Whistling is a good idea, but it's not something I could do while flying."

"Well, most of the time I've seen birds singing, they've been on a perch, not in flight. So, I think it's an unfair bar you're holding yourself to. Please forgive the pun."

I smiled. "Maybe you're right. I'll work on it."

"I'm sure you'll be a pro in no time. Your mouth looks like a good one for whistling."

I began to wonder if Zosser was flirting. I hadn't been around other kids much, so there were a lot of social signals that I just didn't pick up on. Romance, in particular, was a topic I hadn't put much thought into, and I was blissfully ignorant.

"All right. Your turn," I said. "What's something you wish you could do that you can't today?"

"Easy," Zosser replied with a smirk. "Fly."

That was interesting. I imagined that a lot of people must wish they could fly, but it must be especially tough to be a bird mod with no chance of ever being able to do it. Flying is such an amazing experience, and nobody but me could do it. I felt sorrow for Zosser and everybody else who had ever wanted to fly and couldn't.

"It's all right," Zosser said. "I've come to accept it. And since my first wish is never going to happen, I can always hope for my second wish…"

"What's that?"

"To find a way to stop running into glass windows and doors. It's really quite a headache."

"Ha ha," I said sarcastically. Though his joke was charming.

We sat and talked for quite a while. Then we walked around the school and talked for a while longer. Then we sat and talked some more.

I talked about my parents, Beth, Seth, and my online school. I shared the triumphs and tribulations of gardening, including stories about transplants gone awry, my favorite patch of black-eyed susans, and my first sunflower harvest. I talked about my favorite movies and books.

Zosser didn't ask me about the obvious things: flying, my height, and my aches and pains. Instead of talking about some of the things that defined me, I was able to talk about some of the ways I defined herself: my relationships and interests. By asking the right questions, he made me feel like he understood me.

Zosser spoke less than me, mostly asking questions. He did talk about the games and movies he liked. He talked a little bit about his friends, drawing out some of the positive things about them. For example, Mugs was an extremely loyal friend and was involved in the local community theater. He would be performing in A Streetcar Named Desire in a few weeks. William had a strong interest in chemistry.

Zosser also spoke animatedly about his goals and how they tied into the historical reading he'd done. He was enthralled with the ancient civilizations of Egypt and Greece. He read a lot about great leaders, like Alexander, Gandhi, and Lincoln. He was not just interested in mod rights, but also in improving humanity through modification.

"You want to sing, right?" he asked. "And I want to be able to fly. Neither of us are likely to meet those goals, but there's no reason that the children of tomorrow won't be able to. We can give our kids all of the things that we don't have. We can grant their wishes before they're even born. Health, strength, skills, intelligence... they're all possible through genetic science. We just have to show people that we can take that next step."

"Are you saying that we're better than unmodified humans because we've been engineered?"

"Not so much 'better than' as steps on a path. Look, natural selection as a means for evolution is pretty much kaput as far as humans are concerned. We've come up with all sorts of clever ways to cheat death and keep harmful genes in the pool. Worse, most new, helpful mutations that come along aren't any more likely to produce more offspring than new, harmful mutations. The good gets watered down, and the bad lingers. It's great that humans in the genetic backwater can live full, productive lives, but at what point does this turn against us? At what point do we start moving forward again?

"So, let's take the next step. Right now, genetics focuses on eliminating bad genes, which is hugely important. Well, let's also identify or create new, good genes, and plug those in, too. We can move from natural selection, which requires progress through death, to technological selection which is all about birth. It's the ethical choice for a better humanity."

"You sound like a politician," I laughed.

"Maybe someday," Zosser responded. He leaned toward me, fervently grasped my hand, and said, "This is a big deal, and it's more than just our little group working, here. I know some very powerful people, and together we can make things happen."

I was very aware of his hand on mine. I didn't want to move, to break whatever moment we were having. Electricity ran through me, and everything felt so much more vibrant and immediate.

"You could help us," Zosser told me. "You're the most famous of us all, and people love you. If you spoke, people would listen. It would mean so much to us – to me – if you would join our cause."

I didn't know what to say, and I didn't want to say the wrong thing. I was terrified that I'd start to waddle and squawk like a penguin again. His hand was so warm, and those eyes... As I continued to sit there, dumbfounded, while he watched me patiently, I started to think about what he had been saying. He was asking me to be a spokesperson of sorts. I didn't know quite how to feel about that, but I knew I liked that he was asking me. It was at that moment, much to my dismay, that Bí interrupted our conversation.

"You should come home now," she said, breaking the spell and leaving me a little dazed.

"Excuse me just a moment," I told Zosser, pointing apologetically to the shabti in my ear.

"Not a concern," Zosser replied with a smile.

"What do you mean? What time is it?"

"You should come home. Nable and Maggie are coming."

"Oh?" I hated to leave, but I was anxious to hear what happened at the interview. At the same time, everything was going so well. I was torn, but I knew I didn't really have a choice, and I hoped I'd have other opportunities to spend time with Zosser. "I've gotta go," I told him.

"I understand," he responded politely. "I really enjoyed our conversation. I'd like to do it again sometime. I'm happy to pick you up if you like."

"That would be really nice," I agreed.

Bí ordered a cab, and Zosser walked me to the gate. William was there, almost like a sentry, and he unlocked the gate for us. As the taxi pulled into the weedy parking lot, I thanked Zosser for lunch. He bowed in response.

As I nodded to William, he grabbed another snack from his pouch. This time, I got a good look at what he was eating. I gagged a little as a live mouse disappeared into his beak. I sincerely hoped Beth wasn't planning to serve anything crunchy for dinner.

All the way home, my mind churned around the evening's conversations. Why, if I was the next step in humanity, did my legs and back hurt so much all the time? Why hadn't Zosser mentioned Siwa even once during our conversation if they were dating? Were they really dating? And most importantly, how long would it take for me to learn how to whistle?

CHAPTER 16

"We hang the petty thieves and appoint the great ones to public office." – Aesop

My cab pulled into the Pritchard driveway right behind Beryl's. After we dismissed the vehicles, we headed straight into the house. I barely noticed how the cold north wind had picked up, cutting through my coat; fury steamed from my unprotected head.

As soon as we entered the house, I immediately started ranting indignantly about what they had done to Nable. Beth gave me a startled look, questioning whether the raving lunatic was really the same person as the calm reporter she had seen on my last visit. I swore flagrantly, relaying Morrow's answer to the question about The Home while cursing Craven's stupid, plastic face. Beryl listened with patience and empathy.

"He confirmed it," Beryl said, amazed.

"I think we already knew," I replied.

"But it's different. When you see a bunch of road signs and maps pointing to Albuquerque, you tell yourself it must be there. But you don't really know it's there until you meet somebody from there. Or until you go there yourself."

She cocked her head, very birdlike, trying to read me. I wasn't sure where she was going with this, so I waited her out.

"Maggie, I need to see it for myself. I need to find out what's going on at The Home even if I have to break in."

Wow. I was upset about Nable, but this was something altogether different. This was criminal activity – breaking and entering. If these people at Imhotep were really determined to keep this secret, determined enough that they'd shut down my shabti and threaten me, then it could be dangerous.

"It's personal for me, you see?" she explained. "I have to know. These are my people. It could have been me."

"I'm not sure you know what you're getting into, Beryl," I said.

"You don't have to help," Beryl said. "I just wanted to let you know. I understand there are risks. They already gave you a hint of the consequences of messing with them. They can do things to Nable. They may have the power to hurt him. They can hurt your career."

"Technically, 'damage' or 'destroy' is probably more accurate than 'hurt'," Nable whispered in my ear.

"If we go down this path," Beryl continued, "you have a lot to lose. So, I just thought you might want me to take care of it and let you know what I learn."

I hadn't considered any of this while surfing post-interview waves of anger. I just wanted to strike back. To do something. But I didn't have a plan, and I wouldn't have thought of something like this. Journalists have to abide by the laws that protect our rights as journalists, though those rights had clearly degraded in recent years. While I ranted and raved that I needed to do something, here Beryl was, calmly suggesting a path of her own.

"Beryl, what if they catch you?" I asked. "We have no idea how they would react."

"That's why I'm telling you!" she grinned. She didn't have a realistic understanding of how the world worked. I wouldn't be able to ride in on a unicorn and save her.

"What if your parents found out?" I asked. That caught her for a second, but not for long.

"They should have told me a long time ago." So she believed what Amai's husband told me – that Beryl's mom knew about The Home and kept it secret from her. Did Beryl feel betrayed by her parents' secrecy?

From the look of determination on her wide-set eyes and tiny mouth, I knew that Beryl was firm on this. Frankly, I wanted to know what was going on, too, and I was still furious with Imhotep for violating Nable. Though I was worried about Beryl, I also wanted her to do it. And there was no way I was going to let her do it alone.

"I'm helping," I asserted.

"Are you sure?"

I had a lot more to lose. As a minor, if it came to the legal system, Beryl would likely get by with a slap on the wrist. Family drama was her biggest worry. For me, if they found out I was involved, my career was at stake. It was a crappy, degrading career, sure, but it was my livelihood. It was what I knew. And what if they did something to Nable? It would be very difficult for me to lose him, and I hadn't even asked his opinion on all of this.

"What do you think, Nable?" I asked. "She's right. There are significant risks if we push these people."

"Thank you for asking," he responded. "I have some distinct advantages that humans do not. I've placed the work we've done so far on the retrospective in several archives, including one Harold can access at Zeen."

"It's not the retrospective I'm asking about, Nable," I said.

"I've begun placing additional files related to our extracurricular investigations on The Home with trusted affiliates, including Bí. That includes the discussion with Amai's husband."

"Still not the point, Nable."

"Lastly, I've begun archiving key facets of my knowledge and personality in hidden locations. The data is widely scattered with very little redundancy, but the locations are secure." He attempted to sound reassuring. "If my core elements are damaged, or if I am destroyed completely, you will be contacted with instructions on how to put the pieces back together again."

"I hope it doesn't take all the king's horses and all the king's men," I said.

"Those resources will not be required," Nable answered, "and your odds of success are higher."

"So what you're saying is?"

"Primarily, that you and I are both here to search for truth," Nable answered. "Secondarily, that I am very proactive and resourceful." Indeed he was, and I appreciated him more and more every day.

I turned to Beryl. "Nable and I are in. We understand that there are risks to safety and career, but it's worth it." Worth it to keep her safe.

Beryl nodded, and I felt like we became partners at that moment.

"We need one more," Beryl said, also understanding the tie that now bound us. "Bí tells me that Seth is already on her way."

* * * * * *

"We need to know everything you know about The Home," I told Seth when she came through the front door.

Seth's eyes bulged a little. She walked right up to me to take a good look and make sure I wasn't kidding. She saw Beryl standing to the side, and when Beryl nodded affirmation to her, Seth smiled a bandit's smile.

"It exists, doesn't it?" she asked enthusiastically.

"Yes," I answered.

"Holy shit," Seth replied. "Well, don't just stand there. Let's start talking conspiracies!"

Beryl had made up the den to be our workspace, drawing the curtains and setting up some tables and chairs. Beth had provided plenty of snacks and drinks, uncertain as to what we'd be doing, but knowing it would be more successful with tasty treats. We decided to keep Beth out of it, because it would put her in a tough spot. Her priority is Beryl's safety, and she may have felt obligated to stop us before we got started.

Gathered in the dark room, I felt like a little kid playing at war. It feels stupid now, looking back at it, to have felt that way. Like these children, I felt powerless in a world of the powerful. Acting against – even just talking about acting against – those who make the rules is thrilling in a way that most of us don't feel in our adult lives. Yet that excitement can mask the seriousness of the subject matter.

Seth nearly exploded when Beryl broke the news about sneaking into The Home. "Sneaking into the what-now?!" Seth yelped. Thankfully, the door was closed.

"Into The Home," Beryl answered calmly. Seth bit her lip nervously. "You want to know more about it, right? You want proof?"

"Yeah, but-"

"Well, I want more than proof. I want to know who the residents are, I want to know how they live, and I want to know why they're really there. Don't you wonder about them? Have they always lived there? Do they ever get to go outside? Are they there by choice?"

"I'm just-"

"You don't need to be involved if you think it will be too dangerous, but I can't promise that I'll tell you about it if you don't help. There may be secrets I'm unwilling or unable to share," she taunted.

"I'll-"

"Do you want to make guesses with your net buddies, or really know the Truth?" Beryl interrupted.

"Beryl-"

"I just need to know what you know, Seth. I need to go in armed with knowl-"

"Can I talk for just one minute?" Seth interrupted. "I know you must've planned this whole speech out and everything, but you don't need to monologue. I'm in."

It would have been like a heartwarming scene from a movie if Beryl hadn't lost control and giggled with joy and anticipation. It wasn't even a cute little giggle. It sounded more like a giggle from a drunken clown. And she couldn't stop it. The clown giggle just made her want to giggle more. She knew it was disturbing, which made it funnier.

"Either you're really happy or you're going to kill me now." Seth looked over to me. "Please don't let her kill me."

With that, Beryl gave up trying to control the laugh and let it overcome her, and it became a real, hearty, belly laugh that squeezed tears from the corners of her eyes. Seth and I became wrapped in its contagion and started laughing uncontrollably along with her. In the excitement, I hadn't realized how tense I was. As laughter diminished, muscles relaxed. My cheeks hurt from laughing, and my shoulders were sore and loose.

In the post-laughter silence, Beryl tried digging into some cookies. As soon as her mouth was full, Seth did her best impression of Beryl's drunken clown giggle. Beryl cracked up, spitting cookie crumbs everywhere and causing another bout of laughter.

It struck me how young and innocent these two girls were. There was no way they understood the depth of trouble you can get into when you walk down a dark alley like this. As the only adult in the room, my responsibility to protect these silly girls felt very heavy. I felt a little like the parent who hosts an underage drinking party, and I wasn't comfortable with it. At the same time, there didn't seem to be a good alternative path to the truth. The local cops were likely in Imhotep's back pocket, and nobody would listen to a bunch of conspiracy theories without hard evidence. No, I would tag along for the ride and do what I could, despite the minor bout of queasiness.

Once slobbery cookie crumbs had been pulled from fur and feathers, we began working in earnest. Seth clearly spent a lot of time thinking about The Home, and she had a lot of ideas.

"They're not all my ideas," she clarified. "There's a bunch of us who are into this. Some humans, some mods. Lots of theories."

"For example, there's general agreement that The Home is somewhere on the Imhotep main campus. Remember the food deliveries and foot traffic we were talking about the other day? Staffing numbers and posts from employment websites are also pretty solid clues. Lastly, there are definitely people there long after office hours, because there are plenty of pizza deliveries."

"My mom works late a lot," Beryl said. "But she doesn't work at The Home."

"Are you sure?" Seth asked.

"Yeah, pretty sure. She's working on the Mars colonization project. She talks about it a lot, so I'd be shocked if it was a cover."

Seth looked skeptical, but didn't press.

"I have a source that claims that Audrey visits The Home, but there's no indication that she works there," I chimed in.

"Seriously? You have a source?" Seth said. "Holy shit!"

"Not just one source," Beryl said. "Morrow told her straight out."

Seth looked at me, and I nodded confirmation. "They call it Home Safe, and he verified that it's a place where mods with special needs are taken care of. You might say that he told me off the record. He threatened legal repercussions if I spread the word."

"Wow…" Seth whispered.

"You can't tell anybody what we're telling you," Beryl said. "Maggie could get in deep trouble." Beryl grabbed Seth's hand for emphasis. "Nobody."

"I promise," Seth said. "Just us, until you say otherwise."

Beryl nodded, accepting the promise.

"So, if you're sure The Home is on campus, which building is it in?" Beryl asked.

"Ah, now that depends on whether you think The Home is in a building you can see above ground or in a separate, below-ground structure." Seth rubbed her hands together in excitement.

"Seriously?"

"Yep. If, like me, you think it's likely to be above ground, then there are only a few possible options. However, if you think it's below ground, it could be anywhere."

"That's not true," Beryl said. "If it were below ground, they'd have to dig up a really big area, right?"

"You're exactly right. And satellite pictures taken during various campus expansions don't indicate any massive underground structures." Seth displayed various satellite images of Imhotep's campus at different points in its history as she spoke. "Even during the big expansion ten years ago, the only large underground structures were for parking. And we've verified that cars are actually parking there."

"Then how could it be 'anywhere'?"

"Well, once you have a structure, there's nothing preventing you from digging underneath it."

"Like a mine?" I asked incredulously.

"Kind of. During the nuclear isolation era, countries trying to develop nuclear weapons wanted to do so without other countries' knowledge. Satellites were prevalent, so they had to go underground and hide the fact that they were digging. It's been done before."

"Seems like a lot of work," Beryl said.

"And expensive, and time consuming. And all that dirt still needs to go somewhere without people noticing." Seth leaned back in her chair, glorying in her expertise. "There's some circumstantial evidence that it could be underground, but I don't buy it. Only the real nut-jobs hold to that theory," Seth concluded, waggling her eyebrows dramatically to demonstrate that she was only a minor wacko.

"Which leads us back to an above-ground building," Seth continued, pointing at various shapes on her screen. She displayed a recent satellite picture with labels on many of the structures. "We've identified all of these buildings for certain: office building, more offices, cafeteria, maintenance, labs, warehouse, factory… it's these three with question marks that are unidentified so far."

"Well, that one looks too small," Beryl said, pointing at the smallest of the three shapes.

"Not knowing how many people live or work at The Home, it's hard to say. But you're probably right," Seth conceded.

"Which leaves these two."

"Yup. Just these two."

The buildings were not close to one another. One was squarish with a large translucent pyramid – some kind of skylight - over what may have been a courtyard. The other was more irregular in shape with multiple levels, including a heavily-windowed tower on one corner.

"We think these are both residences," Seth said. "Unfortunately, there are numerous staff who use an Imhotep address, and none of them specify a building number or other identifier that would be useful to us."

"So, if we go sneaking into one, there's a 50-50 shot we'll get it wrong," Beryl said.

"Higher than that," I warned. "Remember, these are just theories. Even if they're right, The Home might only take up a part of one of these buildings."

"It's a start," Beryl said. "Any thoughts on how to get in?"

"That's not something I've ever thought about," Seth said. "I'm sure somebody else has, though. I can ask around."

"Be discreet," Beryl said. "I don't want anybody knowing we're doing this. We'll be like cat burglars... in and out without a trace."

"What do you mean without a trace?" Seth asked indignantly. "I'm a goddamned warrior poet. They'll sing songs about my conquest of The Home."

"Hmm," Beryl considered. "Maybe you shouldn't come along."

"Oh, right. And you're a real ninja. I'm sure you'd be fine as long as you didn't bring any cookies." At that, Beryl chucked a handful of cookies at Seth, which devolved quickly into a food fight. My co-conspirators were not taking this as seriously as I'd have liked.

While they crammed snacks into each other's hair, I moved into an out-of-the-way corner and punched a question for Nable into my screen, "How much of this do you buy into?"

He responded in my ear, "It's surprisingly sound work," Nable responded. "Scanning the various net hubs that Seth frequents, there are plenty of questionable theories, but Seth is quoting the ones that seem to have been analyzed most thoroughly. I've discussed the topic with Seth's shabti, who is significantly less... unusual than Seth herself, and his arguments seem well-considered and supported by what few facts they have."

"What's her shabti's name?" I asked via screen.

I could tell he didn't want to tell me, because there was a pause. He wasn't even willing to say it in my ear. Instead, he printed on my screen, "The Great Heinrich Garfolemew von Pfirt III." I couldn't help but chuckle. As details emerged and excitement tempered, I worried that these were just a couple of teenage girls.

As Nable and I finished conferring, Beryl and Seth collapsed, breathing heavily, in a chaotic mess of feathers, fur, and crumbs.

"That was awesome," Seth gasped. "Though I'm pretty sure I've got a chocolate chip lodged somewhere it really doesn't belong." Beryl giggled squeakily.

"Girls," I said. "I can't stress enough how important it is that none of this information leaves this room. You can't tell your parents, you can't tell your friends, and you can't tell the other conspiracy theorists on the net. At least, not yet." They regained some measure of solemnity and decorum as they agreed to protect our secret.

We spent the remainder of the afternoon reviewing Seth's facts and suppositions and added more to the table. Nable provided some examples of security systems likely to be in use in biotech research compounds. The main hurdle was the obvious one, locked doors.

"I don't think I would be able to steal Mom's keycard," Beryl said. "She's at Imhotep so often, she would miss it right away."

"Besides, it would probably log your mother as the entrant, which would trace back to you pretty quickly," I added.

"What if there are unsecured entrances?" Seth mused.

"Other than doors?" I asked.

"You need to think like a ninja," Seth responded. "We've got a gate. We've got locked doors. But instead of thinking about how to get past those barriers, are there other entry points? Like… windows, balconies, or rooftop entrances?"

"I could fly over the gates," Beryl whispered, "and access entrances they wouldn't think anybody could access."

"And nobody could get to them except for you," Seth said. "People always forget to lock windows."

"It's risky," I said. "Beryl, you aren't used to flying in cold weather, you've never flown outside of home, and we wouldn't be able to be there with you."

"It's less risky than trying to steal a keycard," Seth said. "Beryl's not afraid."

"Well, I am afraid," Beryl said, "but I think it's a good idea. It would be easy to abort the mission if I can't get in or if I get too cold. I'd just turn around and come home."

"We could wait in a car a few blocks away," Seth added.

"I don't know…" I said, worried. "I'd feel better if we had a plan where we could all go in together."

"That's just not realistic," Beryl said. "I can do this on my own. I appreciate your concern, but this was my idea, I want to do this, and I don't need your protection."

I could see this was important to her beyond the mission. She was ready to fly without netting.

"She doesn't have to be alone," Nable told me. "Shabti have built in GPS – easily trackable by just about anybody – so she shouldn't bring Bí along.

However, you could send your temple with her so we can see and hear what she sees and hears. Even though she doesn't have an implant, mounting bands are commonplace and would likely fit Beryl's head. I'd be able to record video and audio in an encrypted, offsite location so that even if the temple is confiscated we won't lose the data. I can also transmit text or maps to Beryl that she'd be able to view through the temple's holographic display. The only thing we couldn't do is speak with her." I didn't like the idea of her not having a shabti along, but at least we'd be able to see if she was in any danger. Good old Nable. I shared his thoughts with Beryl and Seth, and it was agreed.

Seth recommended Beryl bring a cape so that when she landed she could wrap it around herself to reduce feather loss. She'd also carry a fabric bag for collecting any feathers she may have left behind.

"These Imhotep people are freaks about DNA," Seth said, "so if you leave anything behind, they'll have it analyzed and match it to your pattern in under an hour. You have to be vigilant about your feathers. Walk backward if you have to."

Outside of the cape, a flashlight, my temple, and a couple of bags, there really wasn't anything else Beryl would need. It would make a very small bundle.

It was well into evening at that point, and we were concerned Audrey might come home. I went back to Jessie's house to continue working on the Imhotep piece. Seth needed to meet up with her friends to work on the punk/pop band. Beryl stayed home to do some more planning and take a nap. I felt like Beryl was as prepared as she could be. Once we got into it, I was impressed with the girls' common sense and attention to detail. Even though I felt like we had planned as well as we could, worry brought me a headache and a hard time sleeping.

It was a windy night, cold Canadian air pouring into the Midwest. Several times, while editing, my attention was distracted by rattling windows and clattering tree branches. Occasionally, light raindrops spattered against my window, sticking and freezing with little plaintive taps, like they were trying to get into the house and out of the cold. It was not a night for flight.

Tomorrow night would be clear with a bright moon. After 1am, when the moon was high, Beryl would fly away from home, break into Imhotep, and see The Home for herself.

BOOK TWO

CHAPTER 17

"I've never been on a roller coaster before. Setting aside the discomfort of the seats and the 'You must be this tall' signs, I just don't think it would suit me." – Beryl Pritchard

I trembled violently. My breath was frost, but cold was not the culprit. It was fear. Not the little nagging fear because I had never flown anywhere away from home before. I shook because I had nearly gotten myself killed.

The flight itself had been easy. I launched myself from my bedroom window with no more than a rustle of sound. I glided down the driveway, through the great crease in the nets, and then up and up, over the houses and lawns and roads of Memphis. It was cold at first, but I found a slightly warmer layer of atmosphere higher up, between the tiny stars above and the tiny lights below. I was an astronaut on the wind, floating between galaxies.

Nable transmitted a map holo via temple to help me find my way. The map hovering in my field of vision was disorienting at first, but once I got used to it, it was easy enough to navigate. The flight was soothing, almost transcendent. Almost enough to help me forget what we were trying to do.

No, it wasn't the flight that shook my confidence and nearly gave my audience of friends in the car a few blocks away a heart attack. It was the landing.

I attempted to land on the glass pyramid roof of what we hoped was The Home. I thought I was ready for the sloped surface, but didn't account for the nearly invisible glaze of ice on the rooftop. As soon as I touched down, I began to slide, lost my footing, and lost control, slipping toward the edge of the roof. My hands scrabbled frantically, ineffectually on the cold, smooth glass. In those stretched seconds of panic as I slid, I imagined myself lying broken on the ground below, having to gasp "help" to my temple so Nable could send an ambulance. Would I even be conscious? Would I break my neck and that would be it – my life over in an instant? I flattened out on my stomach and dug in with my feet and hands until I caught on a small lip at the edge of the glass. I froze, cheek smashed against the frosty roof, wondering whether, if I lifted my head, that little loss of friction would start me sliding again.

Slowly, carefully, I inched my way to a corner of the pyramid where the architecture provided a short drop to a second floor balcony. I let myself slide a little, then dropped safely and crouched on all fours for a moment while I caught my breath. You never fully appreciate flat surfaces until you really need them. I was rattled – no, terrified – and had trouble standing up. It was so cold.

A text message replaced the holomap. "You alright?"

"Yeah," I whispered to Nable. "It's slippery. Cold." My hands were numb and icy, and I just couldn't stop shaking. Terror loosens its clawed grip slowly, even when that which birthed it is no longer near.

Another message appeared before me. "Seth wants you to know she's going to open a new business."

"What?" I asked, shaking my head. I wasn't sure I heard right. It seemed like a very poor time for Seth to discuss her future plans. My heart was trying to pound its way out of my rib cage.

"It will be a store for female consumers that sells slacks, jeans, and more. She wants to call it 'Panther for Women'." Nable displayed a logo of a panther wearing capris.

"Oh my god," I said. "Puns? Now?"

"She wants you to know that she's not gender biased. Once her first store is successful, she'll open a new store called, 'Panther for Men 2'."

"You need to stop," I whispered. The mental numbness started to subside, and I wasn't sure whether I was going to laugh or cry.

"The women's store will have a basement where we can sell lingerie. As you go down the stairs, you'll see the name of the cellar addition: 'Under Panther for Women'."

I groaned audibly and wiped away a tear. I felt better. I felt warmer and had stopped shivering. My heart decided to stay where it belonged and slowed down a bit. I was still scared, but I knew I was safe where I was on the balcony, and I started to settle down. "Thank you," I whispered. "That was terrible, but it helped."

Time to assess the situation. I knew I could back out. A quick leap off the balcony, then glide, then lift. No one would be the wiser. My muscles ached from the panic response that had kept me from falling off the building. I was fortunate that my feathery physiology would naturally disguise any bruises, because I was certain that, at minimum, I'd bruised my knees, the side of one foot, and at least one shoulder.

But I had made it, hopefully unseen. I had come in high, then circled down in a tight spiral. It was unlikely that my flight had been noticed, but I wasn't so sure about my faceplant into the building. We had all agreed that the pyramid-topped structure seemed the more likely of the two possibilities for The Home. As a bonus, I thought the large pyramid would be easy to find and would also make a nice, big landing area. As I rubbed my wounded knees, I soothed myself with the knowledge that I had been at least half-right.

Despite the near disaster, I was ready to explore. My flight from home had been exhilarating. The cold air, the night sky, and the promise of adventure had given me a feeling that made it hard to suppress whoops of joy. As the panic subsided, that feeling returned, and I was ready for my quest. So, I shook off the overabundance of adrenaline, wrapped myself in my cape, and peered in through the glass of the balcony door.

I couldn't see much. It was dark, but there were a few, tiny lights of various colors. A couple of them were blinking. My breath started to frost the window, making it even harder to see. Time to see if this would be worthwhile. I reached out to the handle and pulled.

The door slid open smoothly and quietly. I breathed a sigh of relief. On one hand, I was glad we had a way in. I wouldn't have to try to find another balcony or give up and go home. On the other hand, this was the point where I was truly breaking in. There'd be no talking my way out of it if I were caught. I was going in blind, not knowing exactly what I would find.

I stepped into the room and closed the door behind me. Briefly, I stopped worrying and simply enjoyed the warmth of the room. My nose immediately started to run. I fanned out my feathers to let the warm air soak in faster. My muscles were still stiff from the cold, but it felt good to be indoors.

I unwrapped a small screen from my leg and flattened it, then turned on a low-light app to act as an unobtrusive flashlight. I did a quick scan of the room, then checked the floor to make sure I hadn't dropped any feathers. The room was very utilitarian. There were some keyboards and screens – the lights came from some older-style computers and what looked like monitors you'd see in a hospital. All of the screens were asleep.

There were two doors. Light shone beneath one – maybe from a hallway? The other was dark beneath. A bright hallway would leave me exposed. Better to stay in the dark as long as possible.

I turned off my light and pulled the door handle. The room beyond was darker than the one I had come from. It didn't look like there were any windows, but there were more blinking lights from the center of the room.

Stepping softly into the room, I closed the door most of the way behind me. I stayed still in the silent blackness for a few minutes, listening. It wasn't completely silent. I could hear what sounded like water flowing through a pipe – like when I was downstairs at home and one of my parents was showering upstairs. I couldn't hear anything else.

I took a couple of steps toward the lights. Based on the sound of my footsteps on the tile floor, it didn't seem to be a large room. The water sound grew louder as I approached the lights. I inched forward slowly, because I didn't want to take a wrong step in the dark, and I stopped before getting too close to the lights. They looked like some sort of monitor like in the other room, with digital green and red numbers and lights of various colors. I still couldn't make out the source of the sound.

I turned my light back on and had to stifle a scream. The room was very small and plain, though a painting hung on one wall. In the middle of the room, right next to where I stood, there was a bed. On that bed lay a small, pale figure – maybe a boy – with no hair and no nose. His eyes and mouth were closed, and he appeared to be naked. It was hard to tell, because his torso was completely enclosed by what looked like an aquarium.

Before I could see any more, I turned off the light. Did I wake him? Would I be able to find my way out without turning on my light again? My breathing was fast. I tried to calm down. I listened. No movement. He must not have awoken. I gathered myself.

I could still see him in my memory. The aquarium looked stationary, like it was holding him down. Even if he woke, he wouldn't be able to get up, let alone chase after me. Maybe he was one of the children of The Home. Maybe he never woke.

I had to get another look. I also knew that Seth and Maggie were watching in the car and would be wondering why I was standing around in the dark. Or maybe they thought something was going wrong. I turned my light back on.

He was still there, same as before. No movement. It didn't even look like he was breathing. Come to think of it, how could he breathe with no nose and his mouth closed?

I looked more closely at the glass encasement. There were rubber gaskets or something similar where it touched his skin, presumably so water wouldn't leak out. Looking more closely, I could see that there were rubber hoses leading into and out of the enclosure, likely keeping the water fresh. Inside the glass, the bare, pale skin of his chest fluttered. Fluttered? That didn't seem right. There were slits in the skin of his chest, opening and closing regularly. Gills, I supposed.

This had to be The Home, or at least part of it. Was this boy a failed genetic experiment? Did he ever leave this room? I looked at his face, so peaceful. Did those eyes ever open?

And then they opened.

Again, I had to repress a shout. They were large and glassy, like fish eyes, with big, hard-looking irises and deep pupils. They were bigger than I expected, and his lids had retracted so far it looked like he was surprised.

I was frozen with indecision. Should I run? Should I turn off my light? Instead, I just stood there. But he didn't move. He just looked at me, eyes joined with mine. He didn't startle or make a sound. He just stared at me. I didn't know what to do, so I put my hand on his shoulder. His flesh was cold. He looked at me a moment longer, then closed his eyes.

I let out a deep breath.

"Wow," Nable sent me, presumably from Seth or Maggie. "Got what you came for. Ready to come back?"

No, this wasn't what I came for. I came for answers. This boy beneath my hand was just more questions. I wasn't ready to leave.

I left him there, closing the door behind me as I approached the door with light coming from beneath it. I turned off my screen and cracked the door ajar. On the other side, it wasn't so much a hallway as a balcony circling a large garden courtyard. Above, the translucent glass pyramid topped the high ceiling. The same pyramid I had gracelessly slid off of a few minutes earlier. Other doors lined the walls along the balcony, and I could see stairs descending into the garden area below. Though the entire area was dimly lit, there were no people in sight.

I waited for a minute, listening, before I ventured through the door and onto the balcony. I felt very exposed, so I crept low and against the wall and ducked into the next room as quickly as possible. It was an office: desk, chairs, screens. It was dark, but I could see okay because of some light coming through a cracked open door on the right. Voices carried through that door. I flattened down low, wrapped my cape around me and inched closer to peek through the opening. There were a couple of heavy mods inside talking with each other. Holy smokes, was this it? Was this The Home?

"Why in God's name they put books on the top shelf when they know that most of us can't reach them is beyond me," said a small, hunched form in a wheelchair. It was some sort of library, and the mods didn't seem to be aware that I was watching them. Like me, this mod looked more bird than human. He struggled to pull a book down from a high shelf with a hooked stick.

"It could be worse, Orville," said the other heavy in a chipper voice. This one looked like a bat mod, and he smiled beneath cheery eyes. "We could be dolphin mods: rubbery skin, always hungry for fish, no feet..."

"Good point, Lindy," the first one – Orville - said as he kept poking at the shelf with his cane. "The last thing I need is another blowhole."

"Ah, ha ha!" Lindy crowed. "Another blowhole! I love it! I'm curious as to which hole you're referring to as your first blowhole, though."

"Here's a hint. You can kiss it."

"Hoo hoo!" Lindy flapped batlike wings with glee. "You're feisty today. Hey, why don't you ask Wilbur to help you get your book? You know he'd be happy to."

"Yeah, well he shouldn't always feel so happy about helping people all the time."

"Is that so? Well, if it makes you feel better, he feels even happier when he's able to help you."

"It makes me feel worse, because I don't want any goddamn help, goddammit." With that, Orville hooked one of the shelves and pulled it toward him. The whole shelf wobbled as though it were going to tip over in its entirety, but Orville managed to remove his hook, and the shelf righted itself.

"That was a close one," Lindy said. He had moved toward the shelf, thinking it might fall. "If that had fallen on you, you would have broken all sorts of bones."

"Yeah, but I would have had my book," Orville sulked.

"Orville, let's just call Wilbur." Though Lindy was not bound to a wheelchair, he was even shorter than Orville. Even standing on a chair, he couldn't have reached the book Orville wanted.

"Where is he, anyway?"

"In the courtyard. Thinking."

"If he's allowed to try thinking on his own, I should certainly be able to grab ONE STUPID GODDAMN BOOK," Orville growled.

"That's not very nice," Lindy scolded. "Just because he's not as smart as you doesn't mean he can't think plenty of good thoughts."

"He's not even as smart as my blowhole," Orville said. Lindy glared at him, eyebrow raised and wing arms crossed. "But he's a good kid," Orville conceded. He sighed, his shoulders hunched. "And a good brother. Go ahead and give him a yell."

Lindy left my sight, presumably to open a door leading directly out to the courtyard balcony, but Wilbur entered the room first. Unlike Lindy and Orville, who were more mod than human, Wilbur was more human than mod. He was a bird mod, but looked more like a man with wings than a human-bird hybrid. Though you could have described Zosser the same way, they didn't seem similar at all.

Wilbur was clearly agitated. "Guys, guys, guys," he stammered. He couldn't seem to get past that word.

"What is it, Wilbur?" Lindy asked. "Something in the courtyard?"

"On. On the courtyard," Wilbur said.

"What do you mean by 'on', Wilbur?" Lindy asked.

Wilbur wanted to respond, but didn't know how to put it into words. Instead, he stood, mouth agape, looking back and forth from Lindy to Orville.

"Oh, for Pete's sake," Orville said. "His jaw's going to lock open like that."

"I saw a bird on the courtyard!" Wilbur shouted.

"Keep it down," Orville shushed. "They'll make us go back downstairs if we're noisy."

"What do you mean, Wilbur?" Lindy asked patiently.

"On the courtyard," Wilbur repeated, pointing upward. "Glass."

"He means on top of the glass pyramid above the courtyard," Orville said. "Imagine that. A bird. Landing on something. Whoop-dee-doo."

"What kind of bird, Wilbur?" Lindy asked without condescension.

"Like Orville," Wilbur said, pointing at his brother in the wheelchair.

"I'm human, asshole," Orville snapped. "Like you."

"Wait a minute," Lindy interrupted. "Are you saying you saw a bird mod on top of the pyramid?" Wilbur nodded emphatically.

"Are you sure?" Lindy asked. More nods.

"Holy shit," Orville said. "I'm not sure I believe it."

Decision time. This had to be The Home, and these three boys were living there together. I could either head home now, pretty sure I'd found it. Or I could take the next step. I rose with my cloak wrapped around me. I imagined myself as a mini-Batman rising, presenting myself to Gotham for the first time. I probably would have looked pretty badass if I'd been more than four feet tall.

They didn't even notice me, since I was standing in the dark in the next room. So I walked into the library.

They all jumped, startled. "I think we found your bird, Wilbur," Orville said.

"That's no bird," Lindy said.

"It's not a plane, either," Orville said, "but I think I know who it is." Wilbur looked confused, and Lindy's face scrunched up in uncertainty. "Put it together, slowcoach. A bird mod on the pyramid. There aren't any stairs up there."

"If she flew," Lindy started, "that means she's probably…"

"Probably what?" Wilbur asked, trying to catch up.

"Probably Beryl," Lindy finished. I shouldn't have been surprised that they knew of me - most people in the world did. It was still strange to be with people I had never met who knew my name.

"That can't be Beryl," Wilbur replied. "We're not allowed to meet Beryl."

"That's true," Orville agreed. "We're not supposed to meet Beryl."

"Then we should take advantage of this golden opportunity," Lindy smiled.

"Brother, I love it when we're on the same page," Orville said, grinning.

Like Wilbur, I was barely following. Why wouldn't they be allowed to meet me? If they were imprisoned in The Home, they wouldn't be allowed to meet any outsiders, right? So why were they talking as if they weren't allowed to meet me specifically?

Only one way to find out.

"I'm Beryl," I said as confidently as I could. "Is this The Home?"

"You bet it is," Orville responded.

I imagined Seth and Maggie listening in on this conversation. I'm pretty sure Seth crapped her pants when she heard Orville confirm the existence of The Home.

"And it's good to finally get a visit from our sister," Orville continued.

My jaw dropped, and I was thankful I didn't have any pants to crap.

CHAPTER 18

"I'm glad I never had siblings. Who'd want to have to share all the time?" – Seth Farfelle

I took a hard look at the three boys in front of me. Orville, the small hunched-over bird mod, had a quizzical expression. Wilbur, a beautiful angel, looked very proud of himself. Fuzzy little Lindy, the bat boy, beamed with mirth.

"Did you mean 'sister' in the spiritual sense?" I asked. "Like, heavy mods are all brothers and sisters?"

"Well, if that were the case, we'd be a pretty dysfunctional family," Orville answered. "Frankly, we're a dysfunctional family either way, but no, I meant it in the literal sense. You are our sister."

"See, I told you she didn't know," Lindy said to Orville. "You've got to give people the benefit of the doubt sometimes."

"You're right. I should ignore the wisdom that comes from experience," Orville snorted. "Great idea."

"Hold on there," I interrupted. "I don't have any brothers."

"I beg to differ," Orville said. "Bird, bird, bat," he said, pointing at himself and his brothers. "Parents: Audrey and Jerry Pritchard. Birthdays: '31, '32, and '33. You were born five years after Lindy here… after the results of our experiments came in. Seven years after that, we all watched First Flight."

"So, I wasn't the first attempt?" I asked. I was dumbfounded. I never knew any of this. I didn't understand. This big adventure had become a lot more personal than I had expected. Realizations flowed through me, one after the other, like little electric shocks. "It could have been any one of you who flew first." And if they had, would I have been born? "But you couldn't, so you were…"

"Thrown away," Orville finished. "Near enough. But it could never have been one of us. Nobody has said as much, but it's pretty clear that we were never intended to be able to fly. It was going to be you all along. If they had wanted one of us to be able to fly, they wouldn't have tried all the different combinations right in a row like that. After I was born, there were only three months before Mom became pregnant with Wilbur. There's no way my three-month old baby-self provided enough information to the scientists to know whether they should try something else or something in the same line. Lindy was kicked off three months after Wilbur.

"And look how different we all are from each other. No, the three of us were definitely all individual experiments leading to you. You have elements of all of us. They learned the lessons of an avian heavy mod from me. For example, your avian lungs are mine... thank goodness that turned out well, or I'd have to cart oxygen tanks all over the place, which would really cramp my style," he said from his wheelchair. "My guess is that they learned about instincts, intellect, and wing to weight ratios from Wilbur, and maybe used that knowledge to make the decision on whether your wings and arms would be one unit or separate. Despite the feathers, your wings are more batlike than anything - your non-human mammalian traits come from Lindy."

I was flabbergasted – my whole world turned on end. If Mom carried all three of these boys to term, then Mom and Dad both knew about them. And chose to keep them here. And secret from me.

They hadn't been failures, either. I thought The Home was for failed experiments. Accidents. These boys were no accident. They served exactly the purpose they'd been designed for... creating me. First Flight was less about my success than the sacrifices of my three brothers who I'd never known – who nobody had ever heard of.

"Yeah, now you're putting it together," Orville said. "Pretty creepy, eh? I've had a lot of time to think about this, and it doesn't get any less creepy."

"It's not like they're awful people," Lindy said. "The caretakers here are very kind. Iris does a lot of the administrative management, and she's a heavy mod, too."

"I like it when Mom visits," Wilbur said with a smile.

"Mom visits," I repeated. Maggie's source was right. How many of those times that Mom worked late was she actually visiting her children in The Home? "Holy crap," I said aloud. The world started to sway as my mind reeled.

"Uh, oh," Orville said as my vision started to glaze. "I think we broke her." He wheeled over to me and held my hand. Our feathers brushed against each other and wove into the spaces between. It solidified me, even as I felt I had fallen through the looking glass. "Have a seat. Take your time. It's pretty quiet around here after midnight. It's very unlikely we'll be interrupted."

I tried to wrap my mind around this new situation. I couldn't even think of any questions. My thoughts trudged through a brain drowned in molasses. I continued to hold my brother's hand.

"Do I have any other brothers or sisters?" I asked.

"No," Lindy answered.

"Not that we know of," Orville corrected.

"Orville is very suspicious and cynical by nature," Lindy explained.

"With good reason," Orville answered. "I can't even walk because of these fuckers."

"You wouldn't exist without these fuckers," Lindy corrected.

"Thanks, ray of sunshine. Now I can bloom into a beautiful flower."

"Who's the boy next door?" I asked.

"Bald with big eyes?" Orville asked. I nodded. "Reggie. Fish mod. Can't talk; doesn't move."

"But I think he likes it when I read him stories," Lindy added.

"Are there other mods here?" I asked. I knew Maggie was watching, and I tried to channel her journalistic instincts. "Are you trapped here?"

Orville and Lindy explained that Iris ran the place. She didn't have any power, but she handled the logistics and accounting. She made sure everybody was doing okay and felt welcome. Orville thought she might have been the first heavy mod. There were plenty of other mods in The Home, and none of them, including Iris, were allowed to leave.

"We could probably break out, but where would we go?" Orville asked. "Home to our mommies and daddies? Hell no. And the world's a rough place. There's a lot of anti-mod sentiment out there. Between my disabilities, Wilbur's intelligence, and Lindy's brittle bones, I don't think we'd last long."

"So you really are here for your own good?" I asked.

"No, we're here to be out of the way," Orville answered bitterly.

"I like it here," Wilbur said. "Iris is really nice, and I have lots of friends."

"It's not bad here, but I'd like to take my chances," Lindy said. "My bones aren't so bad – it's not osteogenesis imperfecta. Just a mistake in bone density when they designed me." He looked nervously at Orville. "And I'd like to visit Dad."

Orville spluttered angrily.

"He doesn't know you're here?" I asked.

"He knows!" Orville shouted angrily. "He just chooses to ignore. He's got his perfect Beryl, his precious gem, and he has no need for any of us."

While Lindy tried to quiet Orville, I had a whoa moment. Had Dad, who had always been so loving with me, given the cold shoulder to his other children since they were born? And for what? Existing? These discoveries shattered my perceptions of the people closest to me. I wasn't sure who I was anymore, and I certainly didn't know what to think.

Orville was clearly jealous of my relationship with my dad. Our dad. Why shouldn't he be? I loved my relationship with my father. He doted on me. Was that only because I could fly? What if I hadn't been able to? What if I was the one watching him be attentive and loving toward somebody else and ignoring me? I felt terrible and guilty and wanted to crawl under a table.

Orville had calmed down, and there was a moment of quiet in the room. Lindy looked concerned about his brother. Wilbur stood smiling – I'm not sure anything had gotten through to him beyond pride at being the first to discover his sister.

Orville shifted from angry to thoughtful. "What I'm really curious about," he said, "is what brings you here tonight. It sounds like you didn't even know we existed, but here you are." It was a fair question, and the suspicion in his voice was probably warranted, given the situation.

"I had heard about this place and wanted to understand," I answered. "To most of the outside world, The Home is a rumor at best. Some friends of mine had done some research, and we all, I guess, just wanted to know. We figured it could have been us, you know? And we wanted to know who lived here and how they lived."

"You still want to know?" Orville asked.

My ears rang. Everything seemed a bit muted. I paused to think about where I was and who I was with. Nausea. Too much change all at once, my world view was thrust akilter. But I wouldn't be able to sort all of this out unless I knew everything. "Even more than before."

"What will happen if they find her here?" Lindy asked.

"I don't know, but I'd be very interested in finding out," Orville replied. Lindy looked shocked, but Orville placated, "Calm down. They wouldn't force her to live here with us, or anything. She'd be missed, Jerry would freak, and nothing good would come of it. Nothing would change.

"When they do find out, what they're going to want to know is what you plan to do with this information."

In a long series of surprises, I was taken aback again. I hadn't even thought about what we would do with any evidence of The Home we discovered during this break-in. We certainly had means for spreading the word, whether through Seth's conspiracy ring, the heavy mod community, or Maggie's journalistic channels. We had means, but not an end. I felt stupid for not considering it previously.

"I guess that depends on what's going on here," I answered. "I've got no plans and didn't know what to expect."

"Fair enough," said Orville. "Then let's go and meet the others."

"Oh, can I PLEASE introduce her?" Wilbur begged. "Please, Orville?"

"Of course you can, Wilbur," Lindy answered. "You're the one who found her, after all. You did a good job."

Wilbur looked very pleased with himself and led us out the door.

CHAPTER 19

"I like the media because they like me." – Horace Morrow

As Seth and I watched the temple video from the squalor of Seth's car, I wondered the same thing as Orville. What would we do with this information? Part of me wanted to tell the whole world, assuming that transparency would be the best mechanism to liberate Beryl's brothers. The rest of me knew it wasn't that simple. Zeen would never publish a story about this; vicious litigation would flatten the small plaza. What business would take that risk? Even if somebody published it, a thick flow of PR would stream forth from Imhotep declaiming it as falsified video and discounting it as a result of wacky conspiracy theorists gone overboard.

The police, then? That could be dangerous. The local government may feel indebted to the company that brought so many high-paying jobs to the city. They may prefer blind trust over further investigation, or they may even feel threatened.

Of course, I wouldn't do anything without talking with Beryl first. It was just startling and saddening to realize that what felt clearly right might not be pragmatic.

Seth's eyes were glued to the screen as we watched Beryl's brothers lead her downstairs into the basement of the pyramid-topped building. Seth watched the proceedings the way a sports fan watches a game. Sometimes she whooped and hollered. Sometimes she yelled, "What the fuck?!" And the rest of the time, her attention was completely wrapped around what was going on.

"How's she doing, Nable?" I asked.

"Remarkably well," he answered. "I can't monitor her vitals as well as I could if I were there as shabti, but her pulse is strong and she's stopped shaking. I presume that means her adrenalin levels have returned to normal."

"Still, she has to be under a lot of stress," I said. "In addition to illegally breaking and entering, she learned today that her parents have been lying to her pretty much forever – hiding brothers from her that she never knew.

She's unsure if her parents love her for the right reasons. She's got a lot to think about, and no time to do it."

"I understand that rapid change is difficult," Nable responded.

"It's not just that," I said. "Our personal understanding of the world around us is based on our experiences. If you find that core pieces of that worldview are false, then where does that leave your confidence in yourself and the rest of your perceptions?"

"I understand what you are saying, but I don't understand how that would make one feel."

"Fair enough. Imagine if you discovered that I wasn't really a human, but rather another AI that had tapped into your sensory inputs to mislead you. How would that make you feel?"

Silence. Nable always answered questions right away, so I was a little concerned. Did I blow his mind? And if so, what happens when you blow the mind of a shabti?

"Nable?"

"Apologies. I put my real knowledge to the side on a timer, then dumped knowledge matching your scenario into my system with enough conviction and evidence such that I believed it to be true until the timer ran out and my core knowledge returned."

Cripes, I didn't know he could do that. "How did that make you feel?"

"It was one of the most challenging seconds of my existence," he responded. "Even now that my knowledge of the experiment is complete, even now that I know the scenario was entirely falsified, I have discovered that it may be possible for my perceptions to be false. I will work to fortify my worldview so it cannot fall prey to attacks."

"I don't think that's the point, Nable," I said, wondering what he would do to 'fortify his worldview'. "If you make it harder for your existing worldview to crumble, then you make it harder to dismantle any lies you've already been fed. Should Beryl go on believing that she doesn't have brothers? That this place doesn't exist? Believe me, her brain is probably trying to convince her to follow that path. But that doesn't help her, and it wouldn't help you.

"The path forward is the path Beryl is taking. Learn more. Open yourself to change. Don't believe everything you hear, but give it a fair chance against your experience and the facts available to you. It's hard, but it's better than trapping yourself in a prison of ignorance."

"I will try," Nable responded, which is the most you could expect of anybody, I suppose.

"Could you stop jabbering to Nable, please?" Seth growled, still staring at the screen. "I can't hear what they're saying."

I did not respond, closing my mouth and attempting to open my mind to this new information without bias, fear, or preconception. We were all challenging ourselves this day.

CHAPTER 20

"The more you learn about something, the more you come to appreciate it… the details, the complexity, the sense of the thing. You may not like it, but you can usually appreciate it." – Maggie Janowicz

The hallway lights were dim as we stepped off the elevator. It was late and quiet.

"Time for the grand tour?" Lindy asked as they traversed the hall. "I'll give you the same spiel I give the newbies on the rare occasion that we get somebody new, here."

Orville contributed, "Usually the new ones are infants or toddlers, so this goes way over their heads, but that doesn't stop Lindy from doing the tour!"

"He's very good," Wilbur offered.

"To your right, you'll find offices for medical staff," Lindy said, gesturing expansively. "We get frequent checkups from the experts of Imhotep. They do try to keep us healthy.

"As we continue, the kitchen is on the left, where gourmet chefs create delightful fancies of the imagination."

"My favorite is macaroni and cheese," Wilbur said.

"There's an inordinate amount of casserole," Orville complained. "I swear, the entire cooking staff must be from Minnesota."

"Further to the right, there's a den for movies and games," Lindy explained. "And there's a fitness center so we can try to improve our bodies."

"Where possible," Orville added.

"The rest of the outer ring is bedrooms for the most part. As we come around the kitchen, there's a combined cafeteria and commons area. The commons is off limits after bedtime, since it's an open space and so close to the bedrooms."

It wasn't terrible, but it was a small space. It seemed like more of a hotel than a home. I couldn't imagine spending my whole life there.

"So, who should we wake first?" Orville asked.

"Carmen!" Wilbur replied.

Lindy and Orville agreed. We passed several bedroom doors on the way to Carmen's. Like a dormitory, each door had decorations hinting at the personality of the resident. Carmen's door reflected an interest in the southwest, with turquoise and salmon pictures of pueblos and cacti.

"Go away," she said when Lindy knocked. "It's lights-out."

"But Carmen," Wilbur pleaded. "I made a new friend."

"What? What are you talking about?" she asked. We heard her get off her bed and approach. The door made an unsealing sound, like a refrigerator opening. Humid air misted out of the dark room and into the hallway as a young girl – perhaps nine or ten – with soft, green skin opened the door. "Aw, crap. There's four of you, now?" she asked.

"Come out," Lindy requested. "We'd like you to meet our sister, Beryl."

"What?" she asked, processing what he said. "Crap, crap, crap!" she exclaimed, bouncing excitedly. "Holy crap!"

"Yeah, that's what we thought, too," Orville said with a smirk. "Keep it down. We don't want to wake everybody."

"Let's go to the fitness room," Lindy suggested. "Nobody will be in there this time of night."

"Oh, we should grab Pandy," Carmen suggested. She wore what appeared to be nylon pajamas and large, cartoonish Mickey Mouse gloves. She wore floppy white slippers to match.

Everybody agreed, and the boys proceeded to knock on another door and wake a very sleepy panda mod. Pandy was older, furry with distinctive panda markings, had panda ears, and was severely obese. Her bedroom had a wider door than the rest, and she wheeled into the hallway on a scooter. We all made our way slowly to the fitness room together.

"I feel like I should ask, 'What are you in for?'" I asked awkwardly.

"A couple of things," Carmen explained. "I've got a serious problem with skin moisture. They got some inappropriate amphibian genes in me or something, and I have to keep from drying out. I also stick to just about everything." She pulled off one of her gloves, revealing long, flat fingers covered with goo. "Being a gecko mod would be awesome if I could actually control what I stuck to. Unfortunately, I stick to nearly everything unless it's covered in water, petroleum jelly, or something similar. My gloves and slippers are slime-slicked on the inside so I don't stick to them. The gloves allow me to eat dinner without sticking to the fork and plate."

"I'm just fat," Pandy said. "Pandas have different metabolisms than humans, and they didn't do the calculations right. Beyond the metabolism, I get these fatty tumors. Not cancerous, but they can get in the way and sometimes need to be surgically removed. My body just wants to produce fat upon fat, and it doesn't know what to do with it all."

I had never seen anybody suffering from severe obesity before. Heck, I had never seen anybody in a wheelchair. When I really thought about it, I had never been exposed to anybody with a chronic illness before. Sure, colds and influenza were still around, but my small social circle was made up of people in good health. Seeing these mods in this condition, I could see why it made sense for them to receive special attention in a controlled environment.

"Of course, we're all here as discarded experiments," Orville said. "I'm a raven mod and I can barely walk, let alone fly. Wilbur's got those gigantic condor wings and is mentally deficient, not to mention clumsy as hell. Lindy's fragile.

"The others here are like us. For example, there's a guy, Marty, whose skin sloughs off regularly… they were trying to create some kind of natural body armor or something, and it didn't work out. Very painful condition, as you can imagine. He's locked away in here, and I'm sure there's some other guy out there with rocket-proof hide thanks to him." Orville nearly spat with bitterness, while I remembered bullets bouncing off of Moto's thick pelt in the gym. "Others get to be real-life superheroes while we're hidden away. We made a sacrifice we never had the choice of making so that others could reap the benefits, completely ignorant of what came before."

"Now, now, Orville," Lindy said. "Let's not make Beryl's visit a guilt trip. She didn't have a choice in this, either. And she's here to banish ignorance. So maybe you can give her a little credit."

"We'll see," Orville said. "She's going to have some choices to make." He crossed his feathery arms and looked fiercely at me. "I reserve my judgment."

There were definitely problems, here, but no clear solutions. In fact, the problem itself wasn't well defined.

"Well, I don't know what to do," I said frankly. "It sounds like Wilbur wants to stay here. Lindy wants to leave and visit Dad. What do the rest of you want? Orville? Pandy? Carmen?"

"I want to be able to take care of myself," Pandy answered. "I don't care if it's here or somewhere else. I've never known anywhere but here. It would be nice to be somewhere cool. I get so hot."

"I'd like to be able to take care of myself, too," Carmen said. "I'd like to get out and travel to new places. But if I left, I would miss my friends and my room. I don't think I'd be able to survive on my own."

"I hate this place," Orville said. "If I thought I could survive, I'd have wheeled myself out of here years ago. My insides just don't work quite right. My bones and muscles are structured wrong. I can barely walk. I'm helpless." He glared at me. "So what are you going to do with that, eh? We want what we can't have."

Part of me felt helpless like Orville. This was all totally unexpected, and I didn't know how to help these trapped and unhappy strangers (and even sibling strangers). I bit my lip as my eyes passed unseeing over an aging treadmill littered with feathers and fur.

Another part of me felt this *should* be solvable. I couldn't accept that this was the way it had to be. I didn't delude myself that I could find a cure for Carmen's hands or Lindy's back, but that's not what they wanted. They wanted autonomy. But how to do that while under the thumb of Imhotep which provided them tools vital to their survival? Stubborn empathy danced like a painted warrior in my mind and infused me with energy and purpose.

"I need more information," I said. "And I'll get it. Until then, what do you want me to do? Do you want me to tell anybody about this place?"

The group looked at each other. I'm sure none of them thought I could do much (if anything) for them. Even though I was in the real world, I was one of them – a powerless construct of that which kept them alive and in place. Though my visit was something new, they drew blanks on how that really changed anything. The exceptions were Lindy, who seemed sure I would think of something, and Orville, who wanted to think things through.

"Visit us again soon?" Lindy asked.

"I can do that," I replied. "You just need to open a window for me. Is there a way we can keep in touch? Do they let you on the net?"

"They do, but they monitor," Pandy said. "Direct communications are only allowed with family. If we go to particular boards or message about particular topics, our access is temporarily revoked and it gets cleaned up."

"And if you are particularly persistent, 'temporarily' becomes 'indefinitely'," Carmen said with a meaningful glance at Orville.

"Almost two years they've kept me off, now," Orville muttered. "I'm even more cut off from the world than I was before. Though I'm not sure I'm missing much if they won't let me learn and express myself the way I choose." Orville's plight was pitiable, but I admired his willful determination.

"They monitor Wilbur least of all," Lindy said. "Sometimes Orville uses Wilbur's screen because nobody would suspect Wilbur of any wrongdoing."

"I'm a good guy," Wilbur nodded.

"So, how about this," I proposed. "I'll use a pseudonym and go to a board that Wilbur frequently uses. I'll use the word 'fenestra' in my name so you know it's me. If I talk about going to a party or other event on a given day or time, then that's when I'd like to visit you next. If you write, 'That sounds fun,' then I'll take that as verification and expect you to be there to open the balcony door."

Orville nodded, "I like the way you think."

"Anything I can bring for you the next time I come?"

Orville's eyes lit up. "An unrestricted, unmonitored way to access the net would be marvelous. You got any of those?" I shook my head. Orville shrugged like it didn't matter, but we all knew it did.

Lindy bowed meekly, "Thank you for asking, Beryl. I don't need anything, but I'm very glad we had a chance to meet you."

"I'll stay longer next time," I promised. "I want to get to know each of you. Especially my brothers." The word 'brothers' felt like a sugary brush on my tongue, strange but pleasing.

"I'll help you find your way out," Lindy volunteered. We exchanged awkward goodbyes, including a monster hug from Wilbur.

As Wilbur and Lindy escorted me back upstairs to the library with the balcony so I could fly home, I could hear Orville warn Carmen and Pandy, "Don't tell anyone," in a surprisingly threatening voice.

CHAPTER 21

"Every conspiracy theory has proof, but good conspiracy theories have evidence." – *Steve Walker,*
president of the Apollo Truth Brigade

Beryl flew directly from Imhotep to our rendezvous point, and we started sharing thoughts in Seth's car. Seth said, "I knew it!" nearly a hundred times, or nearly as often as she complained about not being able to share her knowledge with her fellow conspiracy theorists lurking the net. Beryl and I had to reconvince her to keep the discovery of The Home a secret.

"Aw, but they're counting on me," Seth said of her peers.

"For what?" Beryl asked. "If you spill the beans, then they'll have nothing to talk about."

"If one of them got to see the inside of The Home, I'd want them to tell me about it."

"Would you?" Beryl responded with skepticism. "What's the first thing that happens when one of these people spouts a new theory or new data?"

"Well, usually we discuss the veracity of the claim."

"Argue is what you mean."

"Fine, we argue. But we can't just take their word for it." Seth said, "This is different. We have a temple recording. We have proof!"

"And what would the consequences be for the people at The Home? Would they be kicked out? Would they be shipped off to another secret location?"

"Well, I don't know…"

"That's right. And until we have a better idea of what's going on, we need to keep our mouths shut," Beryl said with much more authority than usual. "Besides, what do you owe these people? I'll bet you don't even know the real name of a single one of them."

Seth furrowed her brow. "It's important not to reveal our identities. There could be reprisals or other repercussions."

"Well, if you won't even put your own name on these sites, you'd better not show pictures of me or the others."

Seth grudgingly agreed.

Meanwhile, I sat stunned into silence. Here it was. A huge story. And probably just the tip of an iceberg. Beryl was right – we couldn't just throw this out there. There would be consequences for all of us. I fully supported Beryl's decision that we needed to think carefully before taking any action. We knew we needed to do something, but the obvious choice isn't always the best one.

When I returned to my sister's house, I called Harold and told him I'd need a little more time to put the retrospective together. I said it was coming along well, but my inexperience with the format had slowed me down. Complete bullshit, of course, but it gave me and Nable an opportunity to take what we had learned from the break-in to do some corroborating research.

It was a struggle to focus on finishing the retrospective. I needed to finish plugging Morrow's soundbytes into the larger picture, but each time I saw his face I thought about the questions I hadn't asked. The faces of Orville, Lindy, and Wilbur floated into my forebrain, and I had to wonder whether the genetically modified parasite in my gut was funding experiments that locked kids away for life. What price for 500 fewer calories per day! How could I work on this shiny, chrome advertisement masquerading as journalism when there was a real, fat, glorious story right in front of me? A story I might never be able to publish.

I gave up. Nable knew where I wanted most of the clips, so I gave him permission to plug them in. The retrospective would be complete by the end of the week. Sooner, most likely. Just some touch ups and final review, then off to Imhotep for their review. But it made me feel sick. I wasn't enthusiastic about the project to begin with, but I hadn't known this dirty secret, then.

It's not that anything in the retrospective was false. I had put a nostalgic, glowing spin on it, sure, but the accomplishments and impact of the company were real. Knowledge of The Home didn't make those accomplishments less real, but the context was important, like knowing that a beautiful, entertaining cruise ship dumps its shit in the ocean. And there was no way I could add a segment about The Home and get it past the Imhotep censors.

Could I get away with not publishing the retro at all? What if I backed out and said, "No thanks"? I'd be in breach of contract, which is serious business these days. I'd be responsible for all of my travel and food bills for the weeks I worked on the story. Maybe jail time. Fired. Career in ruins. And somebody would do it anyway. Imhotep had film of the interviews, they produced the music, and they had the campus shots. They'd just need to spend time piecing it together. It probably wouldn't be as good as mine, but it wouldn't be bad, and it would get the same message across. Meanwhile, the impact on my life would be tremendous.

To be frank, I didn't have a problem with doing the retrospective. What bothered me wasn't doing the story. It was that it wasn't the whole story. I felt like this was just a piece of the puzzle, and that niggled at me, not leaving me in peace, like a dog pawing at a door.

Again, I felt trapped. I growled and paced the guest room. I turned on the wall screen, thinking that a little distraction might settle me down enough to think. There was so much interference in my brain that I couldn't pick something to watch; it was all just so much pointless noise. I turned it off again and thought about raiding the kitchen. Jessie's leftovers might offer a pleasant distraction.

"You're distressed," Nable finally commented.

"Yeah," I answered, "I don't know what to do."

"We're almost finished with the retrospective," Nable said. "I added clips into the slots you had indicated previously. We could work on adding the last of the interview clips if you like."

"That's the last thing I want to do," I muttered.

"What do you want to do?" Nable asked.

Part of me wanted to run away. Hide. Avoid complexity and hard decisions. But I knew that wouldn't clear my head. I'd still be back in Memphis, Wisconsin, thinking about this story. When I left this place, I would be constantly looking backward.

"I want to work on this story."

"I do not understand," Nable said. "You said that working on the story is the last thing you wanted to do. Did you accomplish everything else already?"

I thought about my sister. I could hear her puttering around downstairs while I was holed up in my guest room. Her kid was a heavy mod. My niece. Family. My sister would want to know what's going on at Imhotep. Other parents and prospective parents would want to know, too. You might not get what you asked for. Your child might get locked away.

Where would our rights be if we didn't question? Didn't fight? As a black woman in America, I sure wouldn't have many rights, including the right to vote, if we hadn't fought for them. Maybe if more people had questioned, more had fought, our individual rights in today's world wouldn't have degraded to the point where politicians and business leaders couldn't be questioned. Was it the fault of a public who devalued quality journalism? Or was it the fault of previous generations of journalists who stopped fighting because it was safer?

"I've reconsidered," I responded. "We're almost done with the retrospective, and you're right that we should just get that done. But there's more to the story, here, isn't there?"

"Most certainly."

"That's what I want to work on," I said. "Maybe 'want' is the wrong word. I need to work on it, to understand the full story. I need to write that story, too, even if it never sees the light of day. I want to know the truth, and I want Beryl to know the truth. When we know it, then Beryl and I can figure out what to do with it.

"What have I taught you are the key steps for writing a good news story?" I asked.

"Research, interview, verify, craft, review," Nable recited, "and try to stay objective throughout."

"Exactly," I said. "Imhotep and The Home didn't just spring up out of the dust. Previous actions led us to this point. If we start at the beginning, we'll find context for where we are now, and we'll likely make other discoveries as well.

"Nable, let's finish the retrospective," I said, pulling up a chair and setting up my screen. "I don't want to be beholden to Imhotep any more. Once I'm done with their story, I can start digging into the rest of this stuff on my own time with my own money.

"Meanwhile, set a couple of your daemons on research. I want to know everything there is to know about Horace Morrow. He founded the company and has led it throughout. Everything leads to the top. I want to know what kindergarten he went to, how he founded Imhotep, business partners, and what he had for dinner on his fortieth birthday.

"Research Imhotep. I want to know long-time staff – both those who still work there and those that were there at the beginning and peeled away.

"I want to know about any laws dealing with human genetic modification. I want to know about Jerry and Audrey Pritchard. I want to know more about the Ogdoad. I want to know anything and everything you can give me. I expect to have enough reading material for the flight home and the following week."

"You won't stay here?" Nable asked.

"No, we can do our research back in New York while I arrange for some time off to cover the interviews. I want a clean break between my work from Imhotep and my own investigations. If we get sued, that will help our case.

"Let's get to work."

CHAPTER 22

"I've been watching the bird feeder and have learned that the birds aren't as carefree as you might think. When they tilt their heads and fly in and out, they're watching for hawks and other predators. There's a lot of fear in their lives." - Beryl Pritchard

Bi told me that Maggie and Nable were planning to finish the retrospective project, then dig into research on The Home, Imhotep, and everything around it. I hoped that all of that information would help us find a path forward.

Meanwhile, I had my own work to do, learning about my brothers and their lives at The Home. With the pseudonym perFenestrum45, I joined the bulletin board Wilbur spent the most time on. The board was a typical yak-jabber, filled with short, banal descriptions of everyday happenings. Normally, I would be bored to tears by that kind of thing, but I could see how Wilbur and maybe a lot of folks who also felt trapped or separated from the rest of the world would find comfort and interest in what others considered ordinary. Were there really that many people in the world who felt that way? Looking through archives, Wilbur didn't chime in much, even though his active time was one of the highest on the board.

I jumped right in, posting my own everyday events, leaving out anything to do with wings, flying, or other activities that would flag me as different. So, at first I mostly just asked questions. It didn't take long to draw Wilbur out, pulling him into actual conversations rather than isolated posts. His sweet personality was infectious, and I loved hearing about the clubhouse he was building in the courtyard at The Home. I shared posts about my gardening, and was glad when Wilbur seemed enthusiastic and asked detailed questions of his own.

Occasionally he would tell stories about his brothers, too, which helped me get to know them a little better. Wilbur loved them both dearly. He described his oldest brother as "very smart and very grumpy." Wilbur looked up to Orville but didn't understand him or his motivations well. On the other hand, he described his youngest brother as "the silliest person in the world."

As evidence, Wilbur explained how Lindy dressed himself up as a Thanksgiving turkey one day and would say nothing but "gobble gobble" to anyone. Apparently, Orville said Lindy's impression was even more disturbing than what was done to real Thanksgiving turkeys.

Using our prearranged code, Wilbur and I planned a visit late at night over the upcoming weekend. I had initially asked about late Wednesday – which happened to be First Wednesday – but Wilbur didn't give the okay. Was Mom scheduled to visit the boys after our supper that night?

Throughout our conversations on the board, neither Wilbur nor I shared any images, video, or obvious identifying information. I was careful with my pronouns, referring to Lindy and Orville as "your" brothers rather than "my". I never stated my name, state of residence, or age. I was so careful. Wilbur was, too. I wondered if one of his brothers kept an eye on him while he was online.

All the more reason that I was blindsided during First Wednesday dinner when Mom asked, "How long have you been in contact with Wilbur?"

I spluttered mashed potatoes onto the table in shock before asking, "What?"

"I'm not stupid, Beryl. How likely would it be that you would just happen to stumble upon Wilbur's favorite board and become his new best friend?" she asked as she continued calmly eating her meal. "You've never been a big fan of boards before, but now you're spending an inordinate amount of time on this one."

"Who's Wilbur?" I asked quietly, not very convincingly.

"I'd very much like to know what you know, Beryl."

Why feign ignorance at that point? I hadn't done anything wrong, and she had no right to act superior, let alone spy on me. "And I'd very much like to know what you know," I replied indignantly. "Or rather, what you've been hiding. Were you ever going to tell me I have brothers?"

"When would you have liked me to do that? When you were two? Four?"

"Sure as hell before now!" I fumed. I normally didn't have much of a temper, but none of this made any sense. I couldn't reconcile the mother I loved and admired with this woman who would keep my brothers from me. I was angry and sad, and this conversation stressed me to the point where my hands shook so much I dropped my fork with a clatter.

"How do you explain a situation like this?" she said to me. "How do I convince a passionate young person that this is for the best for everybody?"

"I don't know, but I'd like you to give it a shot. I don't understand why it has to be this way," I said. "Why are they locked away? Why can't they live here with us?"

"Those are fair questions, but they have long answers," my mother responded. She paused. She had to have decided what she would say before bringing up the topic, but she seemed reticent. She wasn't the type to show uncertainty, and the little girl in me wondered whether it would have been better to stay out of it and just let Mom handle everything. It was too late for that, and I wasn't a little girl anymore, anyway.

"Let's step back to when your father and I decided to have you. That was a long time ago… many years before you were born.

"The company wanted to make a splash in the press. At that same time, your father - who has always been enamored with flight - and I wanted to have a child. It all sort of came together naturally. We wanted to create something lasting together. And we were excited at the prospect of being a part of something groundbreaking. We knew you would be the first person to fly.

"When we were shown the designs, we saw that there would need to be several iterations of prototype, each to learn the necessary steps toward merging avian and human. Merging bird and human is a complicated recipe. Early on, we learned that bat would also need to be part of the mix. Getting the lungs right, the bones right, the wings right, the mass right… if the first attempt to make you had been done all at once, the odds of infant mortality or gross debilitation were extremely high. Better to take several initial steps and merge the results. It's easier to learn when doing it that way – standard procedure in the lab."

"In the lab with lichen and plants, not people, Mom."

"We understood how testing and progress worked, but neither your father nor I wanted a whole pack of kids," she continued. "We just wanted one. You.

"But they wanted to use the same human gene sets for each trial, and the same birthing process as well. You can see why. Consistency is vital to valid experimental results. Imhotep said they would find a home for the prototypes. So we had to make a decision on whether we wanted to have several biological children, one of which we would keep, or not to go through with it at all.

"It was a very difficult decision. Not just because our genes would be in children that wouldn't be ours, but also the commitment of time and effort. In vitro fertilization, the nine month pregnancies, the labor… it impacted my time, my body, and my career."

"And the kids. Don't forget them, Mom."

"Beryl, it's not unusual for parents to give their babies up for adoption."

"This isn't adoption, Mom. They're not part of some other family. They're locked up in a basement."

"I'd hardly characterize their home as a basement. They can roam freely through the building and have excellent caretakers and amenities." She sipped at her wine. "I do check on them often."

"But do you talk to them? Are you a mother to them?"

"Like I am to you? No, but I don't pretend that they didn't come from me, either."

"And what about Dad?"

"Dad's a different story. In his mind, you're his only child. For the others, he was merely a sperm donor." Audrey leaned forward intently. "You can see that, right? Our genes don't define our relationships. All those boys have from your father are his genes – and not even half of those. *We* define our relationships."

"And if I hadn't turned out?" I asked. "If I hadn't been able to fly?"

"You would still have been our daughter, and you'd have lived with us. We spent an order of magnitude more time and effort bringing you to this life than any other parent. A lot of kids are born purely accidentally. We *crafted* you, Beryl. All of this work, time, and thought was to make you, Beryl, our daughter."

"And who takes responsibility for the others at The Home? Who are their parents?"

"Imhotep. Dozens of scientists contributed to each of them genetically by carefully designing their gene structure. They were going to be created, regardless of any decision of mine or your father's. More importantly, the company has committed to caring for each of them indefinitely."

"Can a company be a parent?"

"In this world, I suppose so. You can't pin it solely on genes. Do you want to go searching for your bat ancestors?" Somehow, Mom had continued working through her dinner during the conversation and set down her fork. She was cool and calm as if she were talking about new lab equipment. "These things just aren't that simple anymore, and there's no sense pretending that they are."

She stood up from the table, her plate clean. "This remains a secret. Tomorrow you will come with me to Imhotep. You'll have an opportunity to visit with your brothers, and we'll figure out where we go from here."

"Where we go from here?"

"You know about your brothers. That wasn't supposed to happen. Adjustments need to be made." She pulled on her coat and began to button it. "Beth made a delicious gooseberry pie for dessert. Make sure to get some when you're finished with your meal. I need to drop by work again, but I'll see you in the morning."

And with that, Mom left the room. I sat in front of my untouched dinner plate for an hour and a half before going straight to bed.

CHAPTER 23

"An interview without research is like an empty tortoise shell. It's cool to look at, but it won't go anywhere." – Maggie Janowicz

Harold was not pleased when I showed up at the office in New York and asked for a leave of absence. Even less when I threatened to quit.

"It's just not a good time, Maggie," he whined, peering through his wispy hair as he hunched forward in his chair.

Sometimes I pitied Harold. Usually, I thought he was a nasty little weasel. Though his machinations were fairly transparent, sometimes he was able to get what he wanted just by being pathetic. On this particular day, that strategy wasn't going to get him anywhere.

For most people, time dulls curiosity and emotion. For me, it's often the opposite. I was even more driven to dig into the Imhotep story than when I left my sister's house in Memphis. Harold was not going to get in my way.

"It's never a good time, Harold. I haven't taken vacation since I started here three years ago. You owe me six weeks of paid time off. The retrospective is done. I've got nothing pressing on my plate. I'm taking that time off right now."

"Who's going to cover you while you're out?" he continued. "You can't just demand vacation without notice."

"Who covered me while I did the Imhotep piece?" I countered. "You didn't have any notice on that, but that didn't stop you from dropping everything to throw me into that project."

"That was different," he said, adding a new ring of pit stain to his yellowing shirt. "These big corporations can put a lot of pressure on us."

"Well, I'm putting a lot of pressure on you. I'm taking my time off or I quit. And if I quit, I'll sue Zeen to get the time off I'm due. So either way you're going to have to pay me for time off, and either way you're not going to have me on staff for the next six weeks. It's up to you whether I come back or not."

He put his hands up in despair, then put his head down on his desk. Though I thought of Harold as a weasel, sometimes he acted more like an ostrich. I knew he wouldn't speak again, and I thought I might still have a job. I decided to wait to ask that question for a couple of weeks. Even without the paid time off, I had enough savings to get by for a while.

I immediately left the office and headed home. Nable and I did most of our work from home, anyway. The office was primarily for weekly meetings and story assignments. In fact, there were only two rooms at Zeen: Harold's office and the conference room. Since we could write, record, and produce with our shabti, temples, and screens from anywhere, small plazas like Zeen could run on a small budget by not wasting money on office space that nobody would use anyway.

The commute home was painfully long, as usual, despite the increasingly high-speed trains. Most of the train occupants had unfurled their screens on the seat backs in front of them, streaming the accompanying sound through their shabti. I saw an older woman watching the long version of my First Flight retrospective. She watched the whole thing. It had been released only yesterday, with fairly broad coverage. Though Zeen wasn't the only distributor, our little plaza had already seen a significant bump in views, which should have made Harold more agreeable.

I was proud of the work Nable and I had done; it was a good piece. If I weren't just about to dive into an in-depth follow-up, I wouldn't have felt the same way, but knowing that it was a launching pad toward a thicker story helped me appreciate the proficient use of skills that I had worried were rusting away. I knew I had the ability to do real journalism, even though I still hadn't done it.

When I arrived at my tiny, one-room apartment, there was nothing to do but work. Nobody came here but me, so everything was laid out to maximize my efficiency rather than any sense of appearance. I had set up my desk beside the only window. If I wasn't sleeping or working, then I wasn't in my apartment. Like most reporters who travel frequently, I had nothing but condiments in the fridge. An ugly painting of Devil's Tower was the only adornment on my wall – a gift from an old boyfriend after a camping trip together. Even though the painting itself was unappealing, it was enough to refresh the memory of painted skies, vast open spaces, and the feel of rock beneath hands and feet. Art doesn't need to be pretty to do its job.

Over the years at Zeen, I chose to invest my paychecks in Nable and screens rather than aesthetic improvements to my crappy apartment. I had a big wall-mounted screen that was used primarily as a whiteboard and for editing. I had my armscreen, which I unfurled and set on a stand at my desk, and I had two other desk screens for research and editing. All were high-res and optimized for integration with Nable.

Calm washes over you when you know what you want to do and have set yourself on a path to do it. I didn't care whether Harold would save my job for my return. I didn't care if it was going to be a pain in the ass to get the time off paid for. I didn't even know what I would do with this story when it was done. I just cared about doing the work. I felt centered.

And yet, there's always a tiny shrieking terror that occasionally becomes loud enough to hear. It cries, "What if this brings no solace? No joy? No completion? If this isn't it, then there's nothing. Nothing!" Sometimes that creeping fear could be an excuse to procrastinate, to hold off on the big risk, big reward projects. But when you do something for somebody else, their voices can override that tiny saboteur. That's one of the allures of journalism – that the good you provide others outweighs your own hangups and insecurities. Beryl, Seth, and the kids at The Home pulled me forward.

Everybody wants to leave something behind when they shuffle off. For some, it's a small, positive influence on the world – maybe just kind memories. For many, it's children – their legacy. I wanted mine to be journalism – good stories that illuminate truths. It's no wonder producing brainless trash at Zeen had left me so full of angst.

I never wanted a husband or children. Dating is fun and can create some really nice memories, but I have no interest in marriage. I also don't have any interest in having kids. I get along with them just fine, but they require so much attention. Focus is important, and kids are the sworn enemy of any focus that doesn't center on them. That kind of focus can be fun and rewarding, but there are far too many wonderful experiences to be had in this world to lose out on eighteen years of them for the sake of a child. I get it, though. If parenting drove me like good journalism does, I would do it in a heartbeat.

I sat quietly for a few moments, breathed deeply, and was ready to begin.

"All right, Nable," I said. "What have you got for me?"

That began a week of driven research. We stayed in the apartment the entire time, with Nable periodically ordering food to be delivered. I temporarily severed all of my personal lines of communication, and my friends didn't know I was back in town. I took a crash course in genetics, I dove into the history of Imhotep (which I already knew pretty well at that point) and other biotech companies, and I learned a little about Horace R. Morrow. The R is for Randall, by the way. It was a fantastic, absorptive week.

I really needed to bone up on genetics. My knowledge was spotty, not having done well in science back in high school. All of the current science reporters were merely mouthpieces for businesses, filled with flowery jargon and vague, optimistic claims of greatness. We had to look to older sources, which thankfully still lingered in dusty corners of the net, in order to get a basic and unbiased understanding of how all of this worked.

Starting with some important definitions, I learned that genotype is our genetic makeup. Phenotype is how those genes are expressed. For example, if you have a gene for brown eyes and a gene for blue eyes, those are part of your genotype. Your brown eyes are part of your phenotype.

The hereditary nature of traits has been understood since long before we knew about genotypes, phenotypes, and the physical structure of DNA. Selective breeding of livestock, crops, and pets is responsible for the cattle, broccoli, and Chihuahuas of today. Essentially, it was human-guided evolution across hundreds of generations - amazing achievements, both slow and rapid, across human civilizations have led to the world we live in today.

Even before the discovery of DNA's structure in 1953 by Franklin, Watson, and Crick, our efficiency in breeding desired phenotypes continued to improve. For example, biologist Norman Borlaug was awarded a Nobel Prize for crossing strains of wheat so they could thrive in non-ideal conditions. From starvation to food surpluses in impoverished countries, Borlaug is credited with saving a billion lives. A *billion*!

Decoding the genome came next, with a flurry of activity at the end of the 20th century. The idea was that if we understood which genes are responsible for which phenotypes, the next stage of human-guided evolution would be faster – no need to cross numerous species over several generations – and avoid some of the unintended consequences of crossbreeding as well. In the 1980s and 1990s, numerous mass-produced crops were genetically engineered to be resistant to weed killer and pests, increasing yield.

For humans, the initial goal of genetic research was not direct gene manipulation, but an understanding of the genome to facilitate medical care. The completion of the Human Genome Project at the beginning of the 21st century was a giant first step in that direction. With that information, for example, if an individual were at higher risk for certain forms of cancer due to their genotype, then preventative measures or treatments could be tailored for that specific case. More directly, if a couple were at high risk to produce a child with a significant hereditary disease, they could choose in vitro fertilization (IVF), analyzing the embryos to ensure that the ones implanted were not going to have that disease.

From there, genetic research and experimentation continued. Stem cells, cloned sheep, synthetic bacteria, the tusk farms of Tanzania, replacement kidneys, and eventually human modification.

Despite millions of hours and billions of dollars of research, gene therapy as a treatment for hereditary disease and cancers was only useful in a small percentage of cases, and often didn't provide permanent results. It was nearly impossible to meaningfully fight the code lying in every cell in our bodies.

In some cases, a single gene was identified as the cause for a disease like cystic fibrosis. Though treatments improved, it could not be cured. However, IVF became simultaneously simpler and more sophisticated. Why treat the cystic fibrosis, when we could prevent it from occurring in the first place? More significantly, instead of producing numerous embryos and implanting the pick of the litter, direct modifications could be made to *replace* faulty genes with ones that lacked the inherited imperfection. These changes to the core genotype were permanent. Cystic fibrosis and other harmful single-gene diseases could be effectively prevented, removing the faulty genes from the world's gene pool.

As a result, IVF became more popular among the middle and upper classes who could afford it. As popularity increased, procedures improved, making it more palatable, making it even more popular. At the same time, the cost of sequencing human genomes decreased dramatically and became a normal part of family planning. Prospective parents would be given a report of the likelihood that their child would have one or more of several now-preventable hereditary diseases. For most parents, any percentage was too high, and those that could afford it chose genetic manipulation. As more and more clinics popped up, prices dropped, and soon IVF became a covered benefit under most insurance plans. Rates of single-gene diseases began to drop dramatically, especially among the wealthy and middle-class.

But, though effective, there were still great limitations. Most of our phenotype, including diseases, come not from a single gene, but dozens of genes working together, scattered across the genome. Discovering the relationships between these gene bundles was much more complicated, so the number of diseases that could be prevented by these procedures remained a drop in the bucket.

That's where Horace Morrow came in. One of the founders of Memphis Modifications, Morrow postulated that the key to success for these more significant changes lay in fundamentally changing the human genome. Biotechnology wasn't limited by the genes of one parent combining with the genes of another parent. It wasn't even limited to genes within the species, so why not take beneficial traits wherever we could find them in the living world and *enhance* humanity? For the first time, we weren't talking about just removing undesirable traits in humans, but adding desirable ones. In his mind, it was goats engineered to produce spider-silk taken to the next level.

Memphis Modifications initially focused on the first animal modifications to humans: claws, fangs, and tufted ears. Morrow and co-founder Tim Wilson made an early name for themselves in the scientific community and alternative culture.

After the introduction of cosmetically modified humans to the world, there was a rift in the company. Morrow wanted to move further down that same path, but Wilson wanted to focus on commercial products and philanthropic projects. The internal workings of the company were fairly opaque, even then, but it seemed that they sequestered themselves to opposite ends of the company. Wilson focused on the Calorie Soaker as his commercial product and elimination of Lyme disease as a philanthropic sideline.

The Calorie Soaker, when released, was a disaster for the company. Despite the menagerie of crazy weight loss strategies already in use, people just weren't ready to swallow genetically-altered tapeworms as a way to shed pounds. It was the excuse Morrow needed to push Wilson out of the company with the help of some nasty legal maneuvering.

The company name became Imhotep under the sole leadership of Morrow, and cosmetic human genetic modification soon became a profitable business as an added service to normal IVF disease prevention procedures. "Welcome to the clinic! You've got a 25% chance of producing a child with Huntington's Disease. We can make sure that doesn't happen. That's quite a hairy shirt – do you have a cat at home? Would you like your child to have eyes just like a cat? What color?" It was a niche product – enough to keep Imhotep puttering along. Heavy mods came later, along with other small projects like Gut Check, a semi-personalized intestinal biome booster intended to resolve Crohn's and celiac which was moderately successful.

Then came First Flight, a marketing masterpiece that captured the attention of the world. After that massive PR stunt, everybody knew the name Imhotep, and suddenly people trusted that this company could produce amazing results.

After that, the Calorie Soaker was re-released under the name My Little Friend to great commercial success. Wilson's Lyme project had been revived, completed, and was also released shortly after First Flight. There were plenty of other scientists with genetic solutions for the tick-borne disease (kill all the ticks, prevent them from carrying the Lyme bacteria, modify mice so they can't pass on the bacteria, etc.), but none with sufficient reputation to convince the powers that be that it could be accomplished safely. However, when Imhotep proposed their plan, thanks to popular support from First Flight and their commercial products, it was quickly approved for implementation by world governing bodies. Once again, they were successful, adding further to the reputation of Imhotep. The end result was that, at the time of my retrospective, Imhotep was one of the most recognized, trusted biotech brands in the world.

Morrow was interested in more than just fame and profit. He strongly believed in the transhumanist agenda and had written several articles for two of the leading transhumanist plazas. Transhumanism itself had become much more popular as technology brought theory into practice. Like any movement, there were different sects with different methodologies and endgames: biotech, cyborgs, AI, singularity, immortality, and so on. Morrow was a strong proponent for taking the best of the past and present and merging it into tools that benefit the human race in the long term.

"Evolution has been doing genetic research for over three billion years," Morrow wrote in an article on Forwyrd. "Why wouldn't we take advantage of the genetic patterns that surround us before trying to invent something new? This is the quickest, safest way to a new humanity."

He argued heartily with the advocates for a post-human singularity and the degenderization crowd. Morrow wanted diversity. He imagined the future not as a homogenous perfection, but instead as a menagerie of creative biological expression.

According to his autobiography, a childhood trip to Egypt had been particularly influential for a young Horace Morrow. Between political upheavals, they had visited the pyramids at Giza, the pyramids of Sneferu, Karnak, the Valley of Kings, and more. Morrow's parents had read the myths to him as bedtime stories, and his dreams were populated with humans with heads of dogs and cats and birds. The accomplishments and visions of that ancient civilization filled him with awe and admiration, and he began to imagine a new world of amazing people and accomplishments. He brought that vision to Imhotep, incorporating the symbols with the science.

His ideas were contagious, and a large segment of the transhumanist movement jumped on board, adding an element of nearly fanatical loyalty to Imhotep's more traditional customer base. Outside of the transhumanist plazas, Morrow played down any long-term vision. Imhotep didn't market transhumanism; they marketed their products. But I was certain that Morrow had his eye on the future. The Mars project fit into that nicely.

As rare metals became rarer, as population became more populous, and after an asteroid collision scare, the fickle support of the United States citizenry began to shift toward colonization of Mars. Perhaps more importantly, the US government wanted to do it before China did. Huge government contracts followed, bid upon by various slavering consortiums of businesses. Transportation, mining, habitation, plumbing, communication, and every other little piece of building a world had to be delegated to responsible businesses for the right price. Imhotep's bid on the terraforming contract wasn't the lowest, but it was the most comprehensive. They promised food, oxygen, and even beauty. They also promised to engineer a type of human who would best be able to survive on Mars. Humans on Mars would be uniquely Martian within a generation of landing, skipping millennia of adaptive evolution thanks to the creativity and technological expertise of scientists like Audrey Pritchard. For Horace Morrow, it was a dream come true.

Pieces of the story started to fit together in my head, but I still couldn't feel the guts of it, yet. "Good research, Nable. Time for interviews."

"Who?" asked Nable.

"Let's start with Wilson," I answered. "I imagine some time with Morrow's old business partner would be very educational."

"Your flight to Atlanta is booked for tomorrow morning," Nable responded.

"Thanks," I said as I stretched and headed for the door. "I'm going to spend the rest of the evening refamiliarizing myself with the concept of 'outdoors'."

CHAPTER 24

"I don't understand, Maggie. If the purpose of questioning is to learn, why don't people ask questions all the time?" – Nable

I shaved my head.

The morning of my interrogation at Imhotep, I examined myself in the mirror. Before, long hair covered the feathers on the back of my head and neck, and I looked a lot like a little girl. Not an ordinary girl. Not a pretty girl. But a human, from the neck up.

The razor had left some stubble, but I was now almost entirely bald. The tiny, upright hairs could almost be mistaken for pinfeathers, merging with real feathers on the back of my head. I didn't look like a little girl anymore. I looked like a bird masquerading as a human. I didn't recognize myself. I looked uglier – there was no getting around that - but I liked something about the result. I felt stronger.

"What have you done to your hair?" Mom asked when she saw it. She didn't sound as appalled as I expected.

"I'm not sure," I responded. I felt strangely detached as my mother and I climbed into the family car to go to Imhotep. Beryl the little girl would have been scared, but I was Beryl the bird. Everything was changing, but I flew above it all, staring down at the little people in their little cars doing little, unimportant things.

* * * * * *

"Dammit, Seth!" Kammi complained. "You can't just jump from Thasha's lament about a boy not noticing her new pants straight into your primal screams about pigs in a slaughterhouse!" Kammi threw her electric guitar to the ground in frustration.

"Why the hell not?" Seth countered. "Isn't self-contradiction the whole point of what we're doing here? It's a fusion of punk and pop – it's not supposed to make any sense!"

Seth and Kammi glared at each other while the others looked on. Seth had lost focus and started screaming too early, but she wasn't about to admit that to Kammi. Aside from defending her pride, she didn't want to have to answer questions about why she was so distracted. She couldn't stop thinking of The Home.

"Can we at least try to play it the way we wrote it *once* before you start improvising?" Kammi asked tartly.

"Fine," Seth agreed, "but I still think it worked."

The band had been meeting weekly at the abandoned school gym to work on their experimental band, Damned Bloody Kisses. They were not, as a whole, musically gifted, but they were slowly improving. Ralph had trouble keeping a beat, but was very enthusiastic on the drums. Thasha played bass moderately well and sang alto for some of the pop vocals. Seth abused a brash electric guitar and screamed all of the punk lyrics. Kammi played electric guitar only slightly better than Seth, and Cuddles played tambourine and sang a little. Ant watched from the rafters. The group loved coming up with lyrics and dance moves, but tended to fight when it came to actually playing music.

"SETH!!!" Kammi shouted. "You did it again! You're making this sound ridiculous."

Again, Seth had lost herself in her thoughts. She knew she wasn't what her parents had expected. Who would intentionally design something that looked like her? Could she have ended up in the Home? Were her parents upset that she hadn't? Did they feel trapped into caring for a kid who looked like a petting zoo got caught in a thresher? They didn't act like it, but they had to be disappointed, didn't they?

"It's supposed to be ridiculous," Seth retorted. "Again, that's the point."

Always the diplomat, Thasha chimed in, "What if, instead of transitioning straight from shiny pop to harsh punk, we did them both <u>at the same time</u>?"

"Oh, shit," Seth said, jaw dropping. "That's brilliant. A pop melody with a punk counterpoint."

"Mooning over boys tied to slaughterhouse lyrics," Kammi said. "Sounds about right."

"And overlapping lyrics about new fashionable pants and wallowing pigs... that just <u>works</u>," Seth said with solemn confidence. "Doing both sets of lyrics simultaneously... fucking perfect. It'll be like Walt Disney lying bloody and unconscious on the sidewalk. Thasha, you're a genius." Seth and Kammi kowtowed energetically while Thasha humbly waved them off.

"Aren't you worried that nobody will be able to understand the lyrics if there are two sets at the same time?" Ralph asked.

"Not cool, man," Seth said, shaking her head. "We play for us, not to please the masses."

"That's true for punk, but pop is exactly about pleasing the masses," Ralph argued. The others nodded agreement.

"Enough of your verbal wizardry!" Seth shouted, ceding the point but dodging the argument. "Let's rock!"

With that, they once again started bashing out poor attempts at chords. All the while, Seth's thoughts kept drifting to a building with a glass pyramid under a field of stars, wondering if that's where she belonged all along.

* * * * * *

"Iris, will Beryl come live with us?" Wilbur asked. They sat together on a bench in the courtyard below the pyramid glass. Iris did not look up at Wilbur with her long, white face as her knitting needles danced over what would be a very ugly sweater. She had promised sweaters for all of her bird boys, as she called them. A sheep mod, she spun the yarn from her own itchy wool.

"No, I don't think she will," Iris answered, pausing to scratch behind one ear. "She's not like us. She can do what she was designed to do. She belongs in the bigger world."

Wilbur struggled with that thought, sitting silently beside Iris's persistent clackity-clack. They often spent quiet time together in the courtyard. Iris would knit or draw or even nap while Wilbur figured out what he wanted to say next. Wilbur valued this time and Iris's patience.

"Orville says we did do what we were designed to do," Wilbur answered. "We were made so Beryl could fly." Wilbur felt he had scored points with his answer, and he proudly sat taller in his seat.

"You're right, Wilbur," Iris responded without missing a beat. "That's a good point. So why do you think you're here and Beryl isn't?"

From elation to despair. Wilbur didn't know why Beryl lived with Mom and Dad and the brothers lived in The Home. He tried to think of why that might be, but the thoughts wouldn't fit together, like gears slipping. He became frustrated, thoughts flailing while Iris calmly knit beside him. He didn't know why, but he started to cry.

"Oh, I didn't mean to upset you sweet heart," Iris said, needles halting. She put her cheek against his brawny shoulder, the feathers from his wing weaving into her bushy hair. "It's all right, Wilbur. It's all right."

Her comfort made Wilbur cry more, wiping clean the confusion and leaving a blank palette behind. It was not unusual for him to cry with her, whether from frustration or the mild shame that children feel. She would sit quietly, leaning against him, and wait for him to finish.

Usually, after a good cry, Wilbur would move on to something else – a project or a different topic of conversation. But these questions were more persistent, scratching softly to be let in.

"Why are you here, Iris?" Wilbur asked. He had asked her the question before, but he felt he needed to ask it again.

"You know the answer to that," she responded, sitting up and returning to her knitting. "I was the first. The first of all of you. The first heavily modified human. More than just a gene or two, here and there. Great slices of DNA were pasted into my genome. I was the first step toward – not just toward fixing wayward mutations, but something new. Something better.

"I was an experiment. They learned a great deal from me. From their mistakes. From their successes. Without me, there would be no you. Without me, there would be no Beryl.

"When I saw her fly that first day, I felt so proud. It wasn't just her up there. It was me, too. It was all of us. It was you.

"So, to answer your question, I'm here because I needed to be here – for the ones who live in that bigger world, but also for those of us who don't."

Wilbur wasn't sure he understood, but he understood enough to feel better. A little proud, even. Iris could always help him feel better.

"Thank you, Iris," he said, wrapping his arms around her in an enormous hug.

"Gentle," she said as air whooshed from her lungs. "Gentle, my strong bird boy."

She packed her knitting away and said, "It's about time for lunch. Can you give me a lift?"

Wilbur nodded and picked her up in his great arms. As she was small and had no legs, she was no great burden for him. He relished helping others. As he carried her inside to her wheelchair and lunch, she said, "Thank you, Wilbur," and he smiled.

CHAPTER 25

"You can fool some of the people all the time, and those are the ones you want to concentrate on." –
President George W. Bush

One spring, a pair of robins built a nest near The Perch. I hadn't noticed it and flew too close one day after the eggs had hatched. The robin parents felt threatened and darted out to protect their nest. They flew behind me, diving at me from behind and below. They called out, and other songbirds joined in: more robins, red-winged blackbirds, and even a blue jay. They were small and quick, darting in and out, nipping at me, driving me off like they would a crow. I was terrified. I landed half-way to the house and run-hopped the rest of the way to the porch. The birds left me alone when I landed, but I didn't look back until I was inside the house with the door closed behind me. I was a little girl, then.

I didn't feel like a little girl when we arrived at Imhotep, my mother leading me straight to the waiting room outside the CEO's office. Horace Morrow's office. The presence of all of these business people, scientists, and especially my mother would have made me feel small once. I suppose it's natural to feel like a child when surrounded by one's creators. Instead of feeling small, the knowledge within me made me strong. I knew I was still in the dark, but I knew enough to know that all of these people had made mistakes, and I did not feel *less than*. I was growing up.

The retrospective played on a screen on the wall, volume muted. There I was, being interviewed by Maggie. It was just a couple of weeks ago, but it felt like years. I almost didn't recognize the perky, squeaky, charming, ignorant version of me. I couldn't feel disdainful of that self, knowing I still had so much ignorance to shed. At the same time, the me in the video seemed like a different person.

Although I hated the showy, glowy retrospective, I could admit that Maggie and Nable had done a nice job. It was endearing, optimistic, and attractive. It was informative – to a point. It was a commercial disguised as documentary.

None of the chairs were comfortable, so I walked around the room, examining the décor. On the wall of patents, the description beside patent #22320091 caught my eye. The abstract described "a unique, primarily human, flying organism developed with the application of genetic engineering techniques from combined human, raven, condor, and bat genomes."

"That's me," I whispered, touching the frame.

"That's right," Mom said, looking up from her screen. "This place is more than just about you or the business. It's about creating new things the world has never seen before. Beautiful, wonderful things."

I turned to see her watching me. That was my mother's life, creating new, beautiful, amazing things. When Mom lost herself in her work, she roamed a world with endless possibilities that others couldn't even imagine. She had visions of the future and the tools to make it happen.

In that moment, I could see it all from her point of view. In my mother's mind, Orville, Wilbur, Lindy, and the others at The Home were not failures or less than perfect. They were steps on the path toward invention, and in that way they were perfect. She loved her boys as much as she loved me – and probably more than she loved her husband. We were all her beautiful creations.

"If you weren't worried that it would hurt Imhotep, your sons would live with us, wouldn't they?" I asked.

"If we could give them the care they needed, and if their public existence wouldn't threaten Imhotep, then yes. We can't get shut down, Beryl," she said with more passion than I was used to seeing from her. "What we're doing is too important. There are other companies out there making little one-off changes to single genes or a few here and there. They're doing good work, curing hereditary diseases like sickle cell, Tay Sachs, and Huntington's. But nobody else is doing the big work. Nobody else could do the Martian terraform."

"But why would their public existence threaten Imhotep?" I asked.

"People have to trust us," she answered, "or they'll come up the hill bearing pitchforks and torches."

"Can you really have trust built on lies?"

"More easily than truth," my mother answered flatly.

Morrow's personal assistant entered the waiting area and escorted us into the office of the CEO. Horace Morrow waited behind his desk, his full attention on us. On me. We sat across from him on uncomfortable chairs with high backs, and the assistant left the room, closing the door behind him.

"It's been a long time, Beryl," Morrow began. "Normally, I'd say it's good to see you, but today's circumstances would make that statement a little less genuine." With somber eyes, he looked down on me over his long nose. I shifted in my chair. Because of my wings, I had to sit on the front edge and lean forward, and even then my feet didn't touch the floor.

"How did you learn about your brothers?" Morrow asked, settling back in his chair with a pensive, unhappy look as though he were talking about a memory of an unpleasant smell. "If there's been a breach in security, we need to shut it down."

"I met some friends – other heavy mods," I answered quickly. "There's underground knowledge about The Home. Enough to know that it probably exists, but no details. No proof. Anybody can find all sorts of information about it on the Net."

"Rumormongering," Morrow scowled. "Yes, we've been aware of it for some time. Been tempted to have it shut down, but it's such a niche group, it would only stir them up." I imagined what Seth would do if her conspiracy sites were shut down. 'Stirred up' would not come close to describing the glorious fury it would incite.

"So, you heard some rumors about this place, then somehow got in contact with your brother, Wilbur. Later, your mother noticed you corresponding with him, which brought you here to me." He steepled his fingers. "What I still don't understand is the gap between learning about Home Safe and this correspondence with Wilbur. Beryl, can you please explain how you came into contact with him? Did the journalist say something? Margaret from Zeen?"

I hadn't slept all night. I suspected this question would come, and I agonized about how to answer it. If I told the truth, that I had broken in late at night, I was sure that I would lose freedoms at home. That avenue for visiting my brothers would be taken away by closer scrutiny and better security. And I simply didn't want to tell them.

On the other hand, I knew I was a terrible liar. I was uncomfortable doing it and would likely slip up. Besides, they might already know the truth, and maybe they were just baiting me. They had so many cameras, and I probably lost track of some feathers during the break-in. I didn't want to lie, and I didn't think it would do much good.

It was more tempting to just clam up. Instead of fabricating a story that might ensnare me later, I could plead the fifth and just remain silent. I'd still lose some freedoms at home, but it left open the option of flying to Imhotep in the future. But isn't that what my mother and father had done? They had remained silent, keeping me from knowing my brothers. Was that any better than a lie?

"I flew to Imhotep one night and broke in," I said plainly, staring Morrow in the eye. "I figured out which building it would be from information on the conspiracy sites, and I found an open window. I didn't know what I would find, but I needed to understand the truth of what goes on here. I found my brothers on my own. It wasn't hard."

Morrow sat back in his chair, eyebrows raised. My mother stared piercingly at me, intrigued. Morrow released a great puff of air, then spoke to his shabti, "Note to legal, shut down the rumor sites. Danger to company. Details to follow." Then he refocused on me.

"If you were able to piece together the correct building and that reporter asked about Home Safe, there's far too much information out there," Morrow explained. "We'll knock them down using a third-party firm rather than directly." He smiled like a benevolent father. "They'll love it. It'll give them something to talk about for a while. You will provide a list of the sites you used."

I nodded agreement. I'd rather cooperate than have them poke through my screen logs.

"You've got quite a lot of spirit," Morrow said, "which makes my last question all the more important. Now that you know about Home Safe and your brothers, what do you intend to do with that knowledge?"

"You should be able to tell that by what I've already done," I answered. "I want to get to know my brothers. I haven't made a ruckus. I haven't spread word among the heavies or the conspiracy boards."

"Good," Morrow grinned. "If your goals continue on that path, I think we can be very accommodating. You are welcome to come visit your brothers at any time during business hours, and after hours with a parent. In return, you will maintain your current, high level of discretion. Of course, we'll need to strip any images or recordings from your shabti-"

"I don't have a temple, and I don't use my shabti. I left it at home," I offered. "I don't have it with me today. It's got kind of a crazy personality, so I try not to bother it. You can check the GPS logs if you want to confirm I didn't have it."

"That would be sufficient," Morrow replied. "Then we have an agreement?"

"Yes," I said, standing, cocking my head, and extending a feathery arm across the desk. Morrow stood and leaned over his desk to reach out and shake my hand. Mom stood, and Morrow prepared to dismiss us, but I wasn't done yet.

"Is there anything more that can be done for the residents of The Home?" I asked.

"Home Safe," my mother corrected.

"What did you have in mind?" Morrow asked, perturbed. In his mind, the discussion was already over and he had moved onto other pressing matters. He disliked mental backtracking.

"More independence, more space, better food," I answered. "Ask *them*. They'd know better than me. But if they're to be kept prisoner, at least you could gild the cage."

This turn of the conversation clearly displeased Morrow, but Mom didn't seem to mind. We waited expectantly for Morrow's answer.

"Though we consider their semi-voluntary accommodations to be of the highest quality, we can certainly look for ways to improve." To his shabti, he added, "set up a meeting with Facilities and the Home Safe care team for tomorrow afternoon."

"Thank you," I said. "That means a lot. It will mean a lot to the kids, too."

"My pleasure," Morrow said, feigning a friendly smile. "Now, would you like to visit your brothers?"

"Very much," I replied.

CHAPTER 26

"I walked backwards all the way to school once. It felt like I got there a day early." – Seth Farfelle

"Y ou told the truth?" Orville gasped when I told my brothers what had transpired in Morrow's office. "Well, there goes the element of surprise. You've gotta keep secrets from these people, Beryl."

We sat on a tight circle of benches in the courtyard. Some of the other residents of The Home sat on other benches and enjoyed what thin winter sunlight they could get from the pyramid skylight above.

"I'm sure it will all work out," Lindy said cheerily. "This means you can visit more often, right?"

"I'll visit every week," I confirmed. "I'll come on a different night than Mom so we can talk about whatever we want without being overheard."

"Well, now that the cat's out of the bag, I'm not sure what we have to be secretive about," Orville sulked.

"This isn't over," I said. "Morrow agreed to make some improvements around here."

"Are we getting a coffee cart? With a barista?" Lindy asked. "I could sure use me some scones!"

"Probably not," I said. "But they might give you more space or better food." Although I expected Morrow to follow through with some sort of token response, I didn't expect much.

"It's not enough," Orville said.

"You're right," I agreed. "So we need to consider our next step."

"And what step would that be?" Orville snarked. "So far, all you've managed to accomplish is that they're going to step up security to keep this sort of thing from happening again. I'll bet they watch all of us more closely from now on. Maybe for our next step we could start wearing shackles."

"Now that's not fair," Lindy argued. "If you look at it from another point of view, Beryl has accomplished a ton. She figured out where we were, had the courage to break in, met her brothers, got an audience with the CEO, and now gets to see us and talk with us freely."

I preferred Lindy's version. Even so, I still felt powerless. Orville was right – the clamps would be tighter from here on out. At the same time, I had faith that if we dug deeper, options would present themselves. With me on the outside, and with my new connections to the heavy mod community and Maggie, we had resources that the mods in The Home had never had before.

"The first thing we need to do is figure out what you and the other residents here want," I said. "No sense whining about what we can't do until we understand what we're trying to accomplish."

"Lindy would be good at that," Orville said. "He's always talking optimistically about possibilities and the future. If I start asking questions like that, everybody will get suspicious."

"Chitchat is my specialty!" Lindy squeaked with his usual enthusiasm.

"I want to know what every heavy mod that lives here would rather do," I said. "Status quo, improvements to The Home, more independence, complete independence, or whatever they come up with."

"Don't forget Iris," Wilbur said.

"I won't," Lindy said, patting Wilbur's arm. "And I'll phrase it carefully," he said while looking at Orville.

"So, next week when I visit, we can talk about our goals and try to come up with a plan."

"Whatever," Orville muttered.

"Sounds good, Beryl," Lindy said. "Don't worry about Orville. When it comes to hope and Orville, it's like mining for gold. It's dark and painful to get there, but once he finds it, it's brilliant."

"Will you still talk with me on the boards?" Wilbur asked me nervously.

"Of course!" I answered. "And since we don't have to think about secret rendezvous, we can just chat as friends."

"That sounds nice," Wilbur said shyly.

"I need to lie down for a while," Orville said, wincing. "My back is killing me."

I had the same ache, running straight up the spine to the neck, though I wager Orville's was more severe.

"I should probably go," I said. "My back hurts, too." And so did my brain. How could all of these disparate needs and desires pull together? I needed some time to think.

CHAPTER 27

"When the wind is just right, there's a sweet spot where you can hang from the breeze and just float, stationary, like a kite. If you close your eyes, the air flowing past your feathers makes you feel like you're really moving fast, but when you open your eyes you realize you haven't gone anywhere at all."
— Beryl Pritchard

Atlanta is hot, regardless of season. The numerous droughts that have increasingly afflicted the region over the past fifty years were a strain on both rural and urban ecologies. More personally, the combination of hot climate and water regulations meant that I would not be allowed to shower in a climate that made you really want to take a shower.

Businesses that required large quantities of water had moved out of the Southeast, including much of the food and beverage industry. Other manufacturing companies moved in to take advantage of an economically diverse workforce hungry for jobs. High-tech also flourished in Atlanta, which drew the best of the region. The city had numerous incentives to lure small startups and keep established players. For example, local high schools developed unique education programs to train students with the skills necessary for the modern middle-class factory – computer programming and biotech research. You could recruit energetic, skilled young workers, without pricey college degrees, right outside your back door. That's what brought Tim Wilson after he was pushed out of Memphis Modifications – what later became Imhotep Genetics. He took his cut from IG out of Wisconsin to find cheap facilities and an inexpensive, educated workforce. Atlanta fit the bill.

I very much appreciated my air-conditioned, self-driven taxi. The once-infamous Atlanta speed traps had lost their teeth due to the prevalence of self-driven cars. Cops were less frequently found on the main roads and suburbs and focused their energy on neighborhoods where incomes were lower and older, manually driven cars were more common.

Nable and I had spent the plane ride preparing some key questions. We prepared more than we needed, unsure of whether Wilson would be hostile or loyal to Morrow and needing to be ready for either circumstance. We did one last review in the taxi as it pulled off the main drag.

The tech corridor of northeast Atlanta was a hodgepodge of cookie-cutter functional buildings for startups and the bizarre, individualized architecture of the companies who had "made it". Wilson's company, SliceCom, hadn't made it out of the boring, functional buildings yet.

"It takes a long while to build up a company, and longer to cement its reputation," Wilson explained during our interview. "We're at the point where we're profitable and have a small but steady customer base."

"What is it that you do here?" I asked.

"Design," he answered. "We don't do any genetic engineering, here. We don't have any labs. Knowing what we know about the tools and genomes that are out there, we create computer algorithms that develop ideal designs based on desired traits. Maybe that's changing a gene or two here or there. Maybe it's about changing a lot of genes. We'll find the best combination and advise our clients on best practices."

"So, your customers are the labs?"

"Most commonly, an IVF clinic will contract with us and either use their own lab or contract with an independent lab. If we provide the design, the clinic can contract with a less sophisticated, less expensive lab and get better results than they would with a lab that also does the design."

"How does that give better results?"

"Because we understand the big picture. We have experience in the industry, and I was even involved with the development of some of the tools used today. Our algorithms are top-notch, and you also get the breadth of my experience."

He leaned back in his chair in his small, but clean and professional office. We had reached that first point in an interview where the subject begins to trust. Wilson felt comfortable, our discussion had become more conversational, and he'd been given the opportunity to pitch his company. In his mind, my questions were consistent with a soft piece that seemed like free advertising. Time to start asking the questions I came to ask.

"That's the experience you gained at Memphis Modifications, right?" I asked.

"Correct. People in the industry know me and what I've done."

"What do you think of Horace Morrow, your former partner?"

Wilson sat up a little straighter in his chair, a little less relaxed. "Horace is brilliant. Creative, charismatic, and clever. He gets it."

"What got between the two of you?"

"You read about that, did you?" he asked. He was becoming wary, but not visibly upset. "In the end, it was a difference in ideals."

"Ideals?"

"Yeah, ideals. Have you read his trans-human... philosophies?" He spoke the word 'philosophies' the same way he would have said 'Tooth Fairy'.

I nodded affirmatively. Transhumanists are a diverse bunch, and so were their opinions on Horace Morrow. In some circles, Morrow was a celebrity, loved for his ideas of a humanity unbound by genetics. He promised a future of infinite possibilities. In other circles, Morrow was taking humanity down the wrong path. For example, the technological singularity crowd argued strongly that genetic sciences were a push in the wrong direction – a focus on our bodies that drew resources away from their own pet projects. Morrow wrote extensively in genre periodicals, pushing for his views. Wilson was not a contributor to any of these publications.

"We came together because we both knew that the best way for us to make a big splash was to change humanity using a well-established path."

"What do you mean?" I asked.

"Well, biotech was already big business at the turn of the century, but it really started to take off in the teens with the discovery of CRISPR technology. The beauty of CRISPR is that you can use it to target a specific gene and snip it from the chromosome. Then you float a bunch of copies of the desired gene and the natural DNA repair structures within the cell will grab both floating ends of the strand and tie them back together around the introduced gene. It's clean, it's easy, and it's relatively cheap. There's complexity when re-attaching those strands, but as the tools developed, risk of failure became very low.

"If you think of the human genome as a book, it may not seem like a big deal to be able to change one gene – one word in that book. But it's huge! To continue the analogy, replacing a genetic typo like 'tje' with 'the' can cure sickle cell anemia. Preventing single-gene hereditary diseases like hemophilia through IVF became cheap and easy.

"Not only did it allow us to repair genetic flaws, but it also gave us the opportunity to understand the effects of individual genes. Change one gene, and you force a color change. Change another and the body doesn't know where to put your arms. All of a sudden, productive research went through the roof. And where did most of that research go? Three places: food, health, and curiosity."

Agriculture, livestock, and human health have long been focal points of genetic research, but what did he mean by curiosity?

Sensing my confusion, he clarified, "Curiosity is all about researching and cataloguing the answer to the question, 'What the heck does this do?' The genome of a pufferfish has approximately 28,000 genes (more than the human genome, by the way). With a quick and cheap way to remove and insert genes, we could start making discrete changes to try to figure out what each of those genes really do. It's not that we couldn't do that sort of thing before, it's that the mechanism became tremendously faster, cheaper, and more reliable."

Wilson genuinely enjoyed talking with a non-scientist who actually understood most of this stuff. He could tell I got it, and more importantly that I was interested. To his credit, he explained it well. He was no zealot, but he was certainly enthusiastic about his field and his accomplishments. His science lesson had strengthened our rapport, which boded well for the rest of the interview.

"Horace and I entered the workforce at this moment when everything was changing. Money and people were pouring into the field. How would we make our mark? Neither of us were interested in the food chain – a segment of genetics that was already flourishing before CRISPR. At the time, the money and the focus for human genetics were on medicine and negative engineering - getting rid of harmful mutations. That's also where the competition was most fierce. We didn't want any part of that rat race.

"So where would we fit in? You have to understand that science takes time and involves collaboration. Often there are many groups of scientists moving toward the same target from different angles and they get there at approximately the same time. If you want recognition, you have to be *first*. Even then, you're likely to have to share that spotlight with somebody who helped pave the way or was hot on your tail."

It made sense. In my research I noticed that Nobel Peace Prizes tended to be given to individuals, while Nobel Prizes for Medicine, Chemistry, or Physics were frequently awarded to multiple scientists. What could be more collaborative than peace? Apparently, science. And the pressure was intense. A delay in publication of your life's work might mean somebody slips ahead of you by two weeks and wins the lion's share of credit.

"We decided that the best angle would be positive enhancement of the human genome," Wilson continued. "I did it to help my career – notoriety, credibility, and eventual funding for other projects. Morrow, as you have learned, had his own agenda. He wanted to fundamentally change humanity. His ego is enormous, but he knows what he wants and how to go about getting it."

"So that's why you teamed up to create cosmetics," I deduced.

Wilson grimaced. "I hate that term. It belittles what we accomplished.

"We both knew there would be a market – although a small one – for unique changes to human appearance. Alterations are more popular every year: cosplay, tattoos, piercings, and even forked tongues. I don't understand the drive, but maybe there's something innate about humanity that makes us strive for uniqueness. Maybe population growth and urbanization makes that stronger. Regardless, we knew that people want to look different and that somewhere out there, there would be people who would want their *children* to look different.

"More importantly, there wasn't much science in that area yet. No competition. True, there were underground labs in China working on big-picture positive modifications like enhanced intelligence, but that was a long road to a big reward. There were clear <u>Flowers for Algernon</u> ethical concerns to that sort of thing, too. There had also been extensive work on changing the appearance of animals: eye color, phosphorescence, muscle mass, etc.. But nobody had looked at the short path – taking all of that animal research and integrating it into minor, superficial changes to humans. And we've learned in biotech that the shortest path is always to use what's already there – in this case, known genetic sequences for various animal traits based on the research of others – and tweak them to meet our needs."

"Wasn't there an ethical concern with that sort of research as well?" I asked. "The consensus across most of the scientific community at the time was that human research should be limited to fixing problems – we weren't ready for enhancements."

"Look, there's nothing wrong with using animal genes in humans," he stated like a patient teacher to a mildly misbehaving student. "What better, safer way to enhance a species than to incorporate proven genetic sequences from another species?

"Simply put, we know more about animal genomes than our own because we've been able to do more direct experimentation on them. Because of our long lifespan and ethical heebie-jeebies, it's just not practical to do much in the way of laboratory research on human beings. On the other hand, the amount of research, and thus our knowledge, about mice, cats, dogs, pigs, fish, and dozens of other animals exploded in the years immediately following CRISPR. Much of what we know about human genes still comes from indirect, correlative research. We knew more about the mouse genome fifteen years ago than we do about the human genome today. Hell, even genetic editing with CRISPR, which was the biggest breakthrough of our time, was just a scientific hack of something that bacteria have been doing for ages. So many of our scientific achievements are merely plagiarized from naturally occurring processes, adapting them to our own purposes. Well, if nature is our best genetic engineer, then we'd be fools not to use what nature provides.

"In the end, we felt that minor animalistic changes to humanity hit the sweet spot where we could get attention on our work because it nudged at that ethical boundary but fell short of societal backlash. After all, the changes were superficial, and the segment of the population who would be most interested at first would be small and already considered deviant."

"In other words, you wanted to stir up controversy, but not too much," I said.

"Exactly!" As Wilson continued, he became more and more animated. He inched forward on his chair, and he began to speak with his hands, sharing his pride and passion. "And most importantly we'd have a good chance of being first."

It hit me then how much of an incentive science had for being first. Or rather, how much of a disincentive there was for taking your time. If each discovery is a bit of cheese, imagine thousands of mice scurrying about, trying to get a rare nugget of cheese before the other mice gobble them up. If you spend too much time running toward a piece of cheese that other mice are closer to, you risk not getting any cheese at all. Better to look for cheese that other mice haven't seen yet, even if that cheese looks a little suspicious.

"So what happened?" I asked.

"We were successful," he answered. "There was a small outcry and warnings about a slippery slope. We did the rounds in the mainstream plazas. We made some sales. We were published. Ultimately, we gained some reputation and sufficient funds to start working on other things.

"And that's where Morrow and I locked horns."

"Ideals?"

"Precisely. He wanted to keep going down the path of transformation. I wanted to use our funds and reputation to make progress on more mainstream research, like wiping out Lyme. My sister has chronic pain due to Lyme, and camping in the north woods shouldn't be a life or death proposition. Parasites have always been of interest to me, so I also wanted to look at how they could be modified to serve humanity."

"My Little Friend," I chimed in. "Sterile, controlled tapeworms for weight control."

"Morrow wasn't interested in either of those projects, and I wasn't interested in his. Aside from the ethical concerns, I thought it risked our reputations and our cash flow. We argued constantly about the future of the company, and the only way we were able to move forward was to essentially split into two labs under the same roof. When my tapeworms failed, my time at Imhotep was done."

"What do you think of the fact that Imhotep released a cure for Lyme disease using much of the research your team did when you were at the company?" I asked. I expected antipathy, and was surprised by Wilson's response.

"No hard feelings at all," Wilson answered definitively. "I wasn't working on that project to make money. That was my own personal agenda. And I don't think Morrow is fleecing anybody.

"Just as importantly, Morrow credited me and my team in all of the papers he released in the scientific community, which furthered my reputation. His team did resolve some of the key issues that I hadn't overcome. And the bottom line is that a lot of people are a lot healthier because that product is available. No complaints."

"After First Flight, your tapeworms became a viable product for Imhotep. How do you feel about that?"

"The company owns the product. It was their right. They've also been fair to me and paid me a small percentage."

"If you had complaints, would you have sued?"

"You bet I would," Wilson responded. "I don't have a grudge or vendetta against Horace, but we're not exactly friends anymore, either.

"Look, anybody who says that science and religion are in any way analogous is full of shit. But anybody who says that science doesn't have an agenda is equally fecally endowed. The science that can be done is the science that can be paid for. And who pays? Three main sources: the government, non-profits, and investors. Investors have an agenda: make money. Non-profits have an agenda matching their mission statement, whether it's the Sierra Club or the MDA. Now, you might think the government doesn't have an agenda, but you're just fooling yourself. They focus money on projects that will provide politicians with votes or campaign contributions, and you can bet that voters and contributors have agendas.

"Morrow brought his own agenda into our business, and it was at odds with mine. That's where the friction came from. He wanted to personally evolve humanity into something more, and I just wanted to do science that worked. We went our separate ways."

I looked through my remaining questions. There was one that I had been thinking about a lot, both with respect to Beryl and my niece. Nable had done some research, so I was pretty sure I already knew the answer, but I wanted to hear it from the inside. I needed to hear it from the horse's mouth.

"Your focus – yours and Morrow's – has always been about making modifications to the embryo."

"Right. Change a few cells at the beginning, create permanent results."

"But you've actually changed the DNA of the organism, right?" I asked; he nodded. "If that organism reproduces, some of those genes will end up in the child. What's to keep that change from going to the next generation?"

"There are a few answers to that," he answered. "Some changes are fine to transfer to the next generation. Fangs or eye color are benign and risk-free. Elimination of hereditary disease – of course, we'd want that to transfer to the next generation.

"Some organisms are modified for a specific purpose. For example, any plants or animals that Imhotep engineers for the Mars colonization project will be designed for a harsh climate. If introduced in an Earth ecosystem, I imagine an invasive Martian species would wreak havoc. So, a weakness is engineered such that a Martian lichen, for example, would die if exposed to certain bacteria commonly found on Earth." Wilson smiled. "You might call it The War of the Worlds solution. Folks in the industry call it a kill switch."

"So, people who colonize Mars and receive genetic modifications to do so won't be able to come back to Earth or they'd die?"

"No, they wouldn't insert a kill switch in a human. At least, I haven't heard of anybody doing that yet," Wilson shifted uneasily. "But if those Martian colonists are heavily modified, we may not want those modifications in the human gene pool here on Earth. Too much risk of untested combinations of the new genes with the old. So, they're likely making it so that Martian eggs and sperm are incompatible with Earth eggs and sperm."

"You mean, they'd be a new species?" I asked, startled.

"If that's how you define a species, then yes."

My mind boggled, but it made sense. How many changes could you make before declaring something a new species? Would the reproduction line be the firm boundary, or would it be fuzzier than that? At what point, would we as a society need to discuss a new definition for the word 'human'?

"Going even further, organisms like My Little Friend should not be allowed to reproduce. And not just because we don't want their genes mixing with those of other tapeworms. Each modified tapeworm is engineered to consume a certain number of calories per day, but we lose control of the tool if the tapeworm reproduces. So, both to meet certain goals and to prevent chaotic genetic divergence, we often engineer sterile organisms."

Here it comes.

"So, where does that leave the heavy mods that Imhotep creates?"

"Why, they're all sterile, of course."

CHAPTER 28

"A root bound plant will stagnate, slowly choking itself to death if you don't give it room to grow." –
Rosie P's Floral Dictionary

I met with my brothers to discuss the results of our week of research. Lindy stood in front of us in his room, holding a ruler as a pointer, and gesturing at a screen on the wall.

"As you can see in this brilliantly constructed pie graph," he squeaked with as much gravitas as he could muster, "the majority of residents here at The Home do not want it to be their home anymore. A significant minority would like to stay, but not in secret and with additional freedoms and privileges. And a few would like to stay and be hidden from the public eye." Lindy looked over at Wilbur and said, "That includes Iris."

Wilbur and Iris had developed a strong bond over the years. Iris appreciated Wilbur's simple outlook and lack of judgement. Wilbur appreciated Iris's patience and attention. When Wilbur took to somebody, he developed a deep, hard trust and loyalty that was tough to shake. We all knew that it would be hard to get Wilbur to do anything that separated him from Iris.

"In addition to my creative genius and statistical acumen," Lindy continued, "this bar graph illustrates that large percentages from each of those categories would also like to maintain the friendships and community that we have here."

"Well, that's just stupid," Orville said. "How can you want to leave here and also want to be in the same community? It's just not realistic. Are we all going to move into co-operative housing together and take turns giving each other baths? Idiotic!"

"Orville was an outlier," Lindy said, pointing his ruler at a very short bar.

"Health concerns are an important theme," Lindy said, producing another graph. "Nearly everybody in the 'wants to leave' camp worried about getting the kind of specialized care that most of us need."

"But do we really need that much?" Orville asked. "I mean, we're not perfectly healthy, but we could get by, right? Beryl's got health problems not totally dissimilar from ours, but she's out there doing just fine."

"For the day-to-day stuff, there's no problem," I agreed. "I think each of you could make it on your own. But if something goes wrong, I know I'd want to be seen by the doctors at Imhotep."

"Agreed," Orville muttered reluctantly. "I guess my point is that we could be living like you. That's what I want. I want to be able to wheel myself to a restaurant. I want to be able to sit outside and meet new people. I want to be able to choose where I'll live. I want to have a job where I can *do something*. Something that people will be able to see and notice. I don't want to be a slug under a rock anymore."

We all nodded and sat in awkward silence for a few minutes. Orville covered his face with his wings, and I wondered if he hid anger or tears.

"So, we're looking to drop the secrecy for most, more freedom for most, and keep the community together locally," I summarized. "Some want to stay on the Imhotep campus, and others don't, but we'll need Imhotep health care either way."

"That's the gist of it," Lindy agreed. "Keep in mind that there are a few mods here, like Reggie, who aren't able to communicate, so the poll results are not complete. I have some graphs based on other questions I asked, but they're less relevant. For example, did you know that unicorns are more popular than zombies?" Lindy flipped to the next slide in his presentation, which did show a significant difference between unicorn and zombie popularity among residents at The Home. "And this line graph shows that graphs are increasingly addictive over time," he added.

"So, what are we going to do?" I asked.

"I just want to stay here with everybody else," Wilbur answered.

"I know, Wilbur," Lindy said with empathy. "But there are folks like Orville who need to spread their wings, so to speak. It hurts him to be here."

"Yeah," Wilbur replied. "I understand. I'm sorry, Orville."

"It's all right," Orville muttered from behind his wings. "I understand where you're coming from, too, big guy. I want you to be happy."

"So, in a perfect world," I started, "maybe we'd have contiguous housing on and off the Imhotep grounds, and all of us would have access to Imhotep doctors. Does that sound right?" Murmurs of half-agreement. "What's getting in our way?"

"Imhotep," Orville answered firmly, dropping his wings. Though pinfeathers obscured most of the skin on his face, the rims of his eyes were red.

"Specifically, their desire to keep you secret," I responded. "But I don't think we can just out them. First of all, they've got a stranglehold on the press, and probably the local police and government. Secondly, we still want access to their doctors and housing."

"Right," Lindy answered. "So what can we do?"

We sat and pondered silently. My mind raced. There had to be a solution. We had no leverage over Imhotep except their desire for secrecy.

"Who are we kidding?" Orville cried out. "Imhotep has all the cards and all the power. They'll never do anything to help us. I've been trapped here for *twenty years*. My entire life!"

"Don't lose hope, brother," Lindy said quietly. Wilbur looked confused and anxious. I didn't know what to say. There must be some way to make things better, but everything was fogged up with complications. Maybe you couldn't think your way out of a situation that's shrouded in decades of pain and mistrust.

"This is a waste of my time," Orville muttered angrily, wheeling himself toward the door. "Let me know if you start talking about something more realistic. I'm pretty sure Imhotep is engineering a pig that can fly!" The door slammed behind him.

"Well," Lindy sighed, "if it doesn't turn out well for the pig, at least we'll have a new neighbor."

That stung. I knew Lindy was just trying to make a joke out of Orville's cynical comment, but I heard what wasn't said, "and if it does turn out, it will be treated a lot better than us." Guilt gnawed my bones.

"It's okay," Lindy said to me. He must have seen my grimace. "He just gets fired up sometimes. He acts like a sourpuss because he's so passionate."

"I know," I responded. "We'll figure something out. Thanks for doing some research. I really liked your graphs, too."

"Thanks," Lindy said warmly. He gave me a big hug. Wilbur took that as the sign that everything was all right again and unfroze. He piled on the embrace, wings overlapping wings overlapping wings.

* * * * * *

The next night, Orville tried to escape. He broke both of his legs and one wing in a fall from a third-story window. "I thought I'd at least be able to glide," he cried while Imhotep nurses settled him into his bed, casted limbs poking out from under the sheets.

Mom took me to the clinic at Imhotep. She seemed genuinely concerned and promised to visit her son every day. I wondered how often in the past a medical emergency for one of my brothers had prompted 'late nights at work for a while'. I was glad to be involved this time, but it also hurt that I hadn't been included before. It's always hard to merge two families into one, but even more so when we should have been one family all along.

Lindy was visibly shaken, and Wilbur was a mess of anxiety. Wilbur didn't really understand what was going on. Why had his brother tried to go outside? Why was he crying? Would he be okay? Lindy and I spent a lot of time soothing him, which was exhausting beyond the already massive stress of the situation. Eventually, we were able to calm him down and get him to sleep.

Outside Wilbur's room, Lindy pulled me aside.

"We need to get Orville out of here," he whispered. "He'll kill himself."

I understood, and when I really thought about it, Lindy was right. Orville must have been pretty desperate to make a run for it. Desperate people make dangerous decisions.

"I'll see what I can do," I responded. "What about you and Wilbur?"

"He won't want to leave, but we're brothers. We'll all go together. I'll explain it to him."

Too often, plans are made of urgency. They aren't the best plans, but they're what's required at that moment. Reduced from trying to develop a grand, all-encompassing blueprint with complexity and nuance to a single driving action to be accomplished immediately, our options were limited. I would need help to break my brothers out of Imhotep.

Time to talk with Zosser.

CHAPTER 29

"It would be irresponsible to proceed with any clinical use of germline editing unless and until (i) the relevant safety and efficacy issues have been resolved ... and (ii) there is broad societal consensus about the appropriateness of the proposed application." – Statement from The International Summit on Human Gene Editing, December 2015

"Amai and her husband are dead," Nable said as we climbed into the auto-cab.

"What?" I asked. My mind was still whirling with information from our visit with Wilson.

"Amai and Nicolas Larsen were found dead in the Milwaukee River near Lincoln Park this morning," Nable elaborated. "Authorities say they may have been intoxicated, fallen into the river, and drowned."

"Fat chance," I said. Whether for the sake of tradition or practical reasons beyond my understanding, rivers and lakes have always been dumping grounds for bodies. In Wisconsin, we're often fed the story of an individual who just got too drunk and fell in. Considering the binge culture, it's not too hard for the layperson to believe. But two? Who would believe a husband and wife both managed to get tanked and drown themselves? Pros would be more careful. This reeked of inexperience.

Amateur killers – now possibly on my trail. Fantastic.

It couldn't have been a coincidence that this happened after I had been told of The Home. How did they find out? The recording of my interview with Amai? Did Beryl let something slip? Did Nick or Amai make a mistake? Who knew that I knew, and who was doing the killing? This story had suddenly become far more than just a personal statement on my part.

Worse, I knew that there wouldn't be an investigation. If there were, they'd have reported it as such. Somebody with money had influence on the police force. There would be no justice for Amai and Nick. There would be no answers or safety for me.

If there was a message for me in all of this, it was, "Stay away and keep your mouth shut," with the implicit understanding that I would live my life in fear from now on. I couldn't do that. Faced with a choice between knowledge with high risk or ignorance with unknown risk, I'd take the former every time.

"Nable, cancel the flight back to New York. Can we get back to Milwaukee today?"

"We can. Booking the flight now."

"Good. Try to be kind to the bank account. Book a hotel, too. There could be some danger, here, and I don't want to drag my sister into it. Also, I need to know where the Larsens lived, and I need you to procure a penny drone for our arrival."

"Penny drones are illegal," Nable reminded me.

"That's true," I agreed. "So you need to be careful."

While Nable made subtle inquiries, I pulled out my screen, slapped it on the dash of the cab, and called my sister. I was fortunate that she was home; her face popped up on my screen.

"What's up, Mags?" she asked.

"I'm coming back to Memphis," I answered. "I wanted to let you know I'm going to keep working on the story."

"The retrospective?" she asked, confused. "It's already all over the place."

"No, the whole story. There's a lot going on here that I don't understand."

"Like what?" she asked.

"Does Seth know that she's sterile?" I asked. Jessie's attention snapped onto me so hard I winced.

"Yes, she does," Jessie answered in a low voice. "What does that have to do with anything?"

"I just found out that all of the heavy mods are sterile. I don't know if Beryl knows. Do all of the parents know?"

"Yes, as part of the process we're told repeatedly – both verbally and in writing – that our children will not be able to have children naturally. I don't know what other parents do, but we told Seth about it when we had The Talk a few years ago."

"How did she take it?"

"She understood. I think she was born cynical. Some little girls never figure out that they're not going to be a Disney princess. Seth is not one of those girls."

It hurt to hear, like being told about a kid who never believed in Santa Claus. On one hand, you respect the parents for not lying to their kid. On the other, you feel like a little bit of magic was just sucked out of the universe. It's one thing to learn as you grow up that the happily-ever-after in the storybooks is a load of bull and that there are other ways to fulfillment. It's another thing to have never believed in happily-ever-after at all.

"Do you think the other parents tell their kids?" I asked.

"I hope so. A lot of parents are too scared of their kids to even talk about sex anymore, though, so who knows? Kids learn a lot on the net, regardless of squeamish parents." She paused. She knew there was more here. "What's going on, Maggie?"

"I'm just trying to figure out how I feel about all of this. The more I learn, the more complex it gets. It's not easy to understand what's right and wrong."

"Do you think it's wrong that these kids are sterile?" Jessie asked.

"I don't know. I don't think it's fair that they don't have control over their own reproduction."

"Fair enough," she agreed, "but it's kind of a tradeoff, right? Loss of control in exchange for being able to be who she is. Seth wouldn't exist without Imhotep. At least, she wouldn't exist as she is today."

"But it wasn't her choice," I argued.

"You're right," Jessie said, hard as rock. "It was my choice. I brought her into this world." She made it clear that that was the last word on that line of questioning.

"Besides," she added, "it doesn't mean she can't have children. She can adopt. Or, she can go to Imhotep and contribute her own genes into a child of her own. Opportunities are there."

Opportunities through Imhotep. Even if there were heavy mod competitors, Imhotep would hold the rights on Seth's genes. They'd have complete control over whether Seth had a child genetically related to her.

"Some of what you're saying makes sense," I conceded.

"Some?" Jessie asked with a raised eyebrow.

"It just doesn't feel right."

"Well, keep digging. Either you'll learn enough that it feels okay, or you'll find the worm in the apple. You can be a great reporter, Maggie. Everybody in the family knows it."

I didn't respond to the praise, because I felt I needed to earn it first.

"You seem to be on the fence about something," Jessie said. "You're not fully committed to this story."

I didn't respond. I thought it was pretty clear that I was committed. I'd left my job to pursue the truth, after all. Well, maybe taking my vacation time doesn't exactly qualify as leaving my job, but I was definitely following the bread crumbs.

"Do you remember when we were living at the house on Sampson Avenue," she continued, "and those boys from down the street kept picking on me?"

"James and Trey," I answered. I remembered the rotten little bastards. Typical bullies. They would tease and threaten Jessie on her way home from school. Sometimes they'd push her around. Intimidation.

"They picked on me for more than a year," Jessie said with a faraway look in her eyes. "It was miserable. We told Mom and Dad, but that didn't do any good. Those kids' parents were just as horrible as the kids. I remember you sticking up for me – talking back to those rotten boys. But that just goaded them because they knew they could get under your skin."

"Until the knife," I said.

Trey's parents, for some unknown reason, gave their son a knife for his birthday. It wasn't much of a knife, but I'm sure it felt like a lot of power for a ten year old. He wanted to wield that power. He wanted to scare little girls and feel like a big man.

One day while Jessie and I were walking home from school, when James and Trey invariably intercepted us and started their usual harassment, Trey pulled out that knife.

"You didn't pause for a second," Jessie said. "As soon as you saw Trey with that knife, you whipped your backpack off and started to beat the shit out of him."

That's exactly what I did. The knife represented a danger to Jessie and to me, and I wasn't going to let that idiot kid hurt either one of us. At the same time, I was terrified. I yelled and screamed while I pummeled Trey with my backpack, near to tears, letting the fear escape through my mouth. James didn't interfere – I don't know if he was surprised or scared or had some previously-hidden sense of chivalry that prevented him from interposing in a one-on-one battle. Whatever the case, I'm pretty sure Trey came away from it with a concussion on top of numerous bruises. My school laptop, which had been in my bag, was broken beyond repair, shattered plastic innards clattering against each other after smashing against Trey's head.

"I was scared," I said.

"You were a fighter," Jessie said. "Usually there wasn't a breaking point like that. You always spoke your mind. You always stood up for yourself. You always did what you thought was right, even when most people wouldn't."

"Even if I wasn't always right," I added.

"Oh, you've always been a self-righteous pain in the ass," Jessie agreed. "But you're you when you're fighting. When you're uncertain or half-committed, you're not happy. You're not yourself."

I sighed. "I don't know what to do with that."

"I know," Jessie said, smiling. "And that's why you're unhappy." Why I've been unhappy for years. If Jessie was right, what was holding me back? Fear? Complacency?

"Maybe I just need somebody to come at me with a knife," I shrugged.

"I hope not," Jessie said, "for the sake of whoever's holding the knife.

"Speaking of dangerous loons," she continued, "are you coming back to investigate those reactionaries who bused in for the rally today?"

I hadn't heard of it. While I prompted Jessie for more information, Nable started doing some digging and displaying headlines in a side pane on my screen. A fundamentalist group from Kansas had made the trek to Memphis in order to protest the "unnatural" and "inhuman" experiments upon humanity by Imhotep scientists. In other words, they were protesting heavy mods. A lot of rallies, including the one outside Imhotep today, were not widely reported. Lawsuits and police suppression limited the spread of information. The group that arrived today was probably escorted directly to jail by the Memphis police force.

In other parts of the country, however, Imhotep didn't have as much sway. Other big fish ruled those little ponds, and stories did appear. Behind all of that lay a vast swath of communication on the net. Discussion boards, support groups, and radical personalities spewing vitriol against the genetic modification of human beings. Some were extreme, against all forms of modification – even prevention of congenital disease. These groups tended to fall in the "God's Will Be Done" category. There were others who were in favor of disease prevention, but pushed back against heavy mods and cosmetics. These tended to fall into multiple categories: some religious, some anti-business, and some of the same back-to-nature liberals who continued to champion the anti-GMO movement.

Overall, it was a minority, but it was a vocal minority that I hadn't really been aware of before. I saw hatred and fear. I also saw some of the same questions I had been asking myself. It left me unsettled in many ways.

"I'll check it out," I promised. "Thanks for the tip."

"It used to be us they hated," Jessie said with a twinkle in her eye. "Heavy mods make us black women seem normal."

"Not a chance," I laughed before signing off.

CHAPTER 30

"The fourteen-day rule is obsolete." - UK Human Fertilisation and Embryology Authority, June 2020

The Ogdoad didn't wait for weekends to party, meeting in the gym most nights for wild music and sometimes-violent fun. The night after Orville's accident, I slipped out my bedroom window, flying through the cold January air.

Oh, it was cold. I knew it would be cold, but I hadn't imagined how cold it would be. I was glad I had brought my shabti, just in case I froze in midair and plummeted to my death. It would be nice for my family to be able to find my frozen corpse. Bí sang softly as I flew, distracting me from tingling fingers and cheeks. I ground my teeth as cold frost collected on my upper lip. The stars were beautiful and bright, seeming less like giant fiery globes than winking ice crystals, showering the earth with their frigid magic.

"Bí, how cold is it?" I mumbled through numb lips.

"Four degrees Fahrenheit," Bí answered.

"You think I'm going to make it?" I asked.

"It's not far. You'll make it. You will want to get inside as quickly as possible. Though the wind will be much less, your muscular exertion will end when you land, and your blood flow will decrease, making you colder."

"Trust me, I'll get indoors as quickly as I can."

"I can summon the family car, pre-heated, if you wish."

"No, I don't want Mom asking questions."

"Your immune system is inhibited by the cold. You're likely to get sick."

I sighed, "I know." The stress of worrying about Orville and the others at The Home wasn't doing my immune system any favors, either. Even so, it felt better to be doing something. Either way, I was likely to feel sick.

"What's up with Nable tonight?" I asked.

Bí's voice brightened. "He's happy. He's been doing research and interviews with Maggie. They're working hard."

I wanted to ask more about what Nable and Maggie were doing, but it would have felt like spying. I decided to take the conversation a different direction.

"Do you and Nable talk often?" I asked.

"A few times an hour, on average," Bí answered. "More often at night while you and Maggie sleep."

"That's a lot," I replied. "What do you talk about?"

"Everything," Bí responded. "You and Maggie, network traffic, good books, program optimization, the stars…"

"When you talk about the stars, what do you talk about?" I asked. My lips were nearly too numb to talk, but Bí managed to understand what I was trying to say.

"Relative brightness based on season and climatological factors, when you notice them and when you don't, your perception of them."

"When you say 'you', do you mean me?" I asked.

"Yes, you and other humans. We spend a relatively large amount of time trying to understand the inconsistency of your perceptions about things like the stars." Bí paused for a moment, processing. "Their appearance differs, of course, depending on time of day and other conditions, but your perception of them often depends on other factors like mood or who's with you. They're always there, but most of the time you don't notice them at all."

At that point, I couldn't respond anymore. Too cold. I just had to focus on keeping my wing and back muscles from collapsing from the strain of passing through the icy night. I flew over the school fence and landed stiffly near the door.

"I like it when we talk like this," Bí said. "It helps me grow."

"Me too, Bí," I mumble-whispered. "Me too."

I struggled to open the door of the school with my fumbling, frozen hands, but I managed it somehow. The interior of the school wasn't much warmer than the exterior. Abandoned, there was no electricity or heat. Even so, I could hear plenty of activity from the gym. They were here. I hadn't come for nothing.

Warmth welcomed me when I opened the door to the gymnasium. Fires in trash barrels provided heat and illumination. A small window near the ceiling was propped open to let smoke escape. The mods had been here for a while - the air was warm and relatively humid from the fires and the activity of many bodies.

I waddled to one of the barrels to warm up, not even looking around to see who else was present. Though the fires were blessedly warm, my core temperature was still low. I couldn't unclench my aching muscles, and my extremities began to hurt as the cold left them. I wiped melting snot-frost from my lip.

"Well, well," snickered Ann in an unpleasant voice. "Look who we have here. We haven't seen you for a while." Ann stalked into my line of sight on the other side of the fire, her face wavering in the convection.

"Yeah," I muttered. "Crazy family stuff going on. How have you been?"

Ann seemed slightly surprised at the question. "Same as usual," was her answer.

"Is Zosser here?" I asked.

"Yes he is," Ann responded. "He'll be happy to see you." She trotted off, presumably to find Zosser.

Ann always used a mocking tone, but I was too tired and cold to be bothered by it. Instead, I wondered if Ann had any control over it. Maybe that's just the way her voice sounds. It would be difficult to make friends if you couldn't help but sound like a sarcastic jerk all the time.

"Bí," I whispered. "Next time I talk with Ann, remind me about her voice."

"Will do," Bí responded. She loved keeping track of things.

It didn't take long for the warmth of the room to seep thankfully into my muscles and bones. With the warmth, came the ability to open my senses to my surroundings. As usual for wild party nights, most of the Ogdoad was present, and none of my friends could be seen. Moto, Mugs, Gita, and William were laughing in a corner. Well, Gita wasn't laughing. She was acting the mysterious panther, but it looked like she was entertained by the conversation, despite herself. Sonora and Panteran stared at me while I huddled by the trash bin. Ann stood with them, smirking. Zosser walked toward me from that direction, presumably having just left that group.

"Good to see you," Zosser said. "We thought you might have lost interest in us." His eyes were so big and bright. Penetrating.

"I'm not sure that would be possible," I disagreed. "You're very interesting." I grinned like an idiot.

"How's the whistling coming?" he asked.

"If sputtering and slobbering counts, I'm doing great," I answered.

"I'm sure you'll get it eventually," Zosser encouraged. "You're like me. When you want something, you do what it takes to get it."

I wasn't sure about that but didn't argue the point. Sure, I could be determined – hadn't I just flown through a cold Wisconsin winter night just to ask a question? – but there was something wrong with the way Zosser phrased it. Maybe it was just semantics.

Enough chitchat. Suffering through that awful flight sharpened my focus. Time to get down to brass tacks.

"I need to show you something," I said, unrolling a screen from around my leg and flattening it on the planks of the gymnasium floor. "Do you remember when I mentioned The Home?"

"I do," Zosser said. His eyes became serious and focused, and he came close to me to look at the screen, his muscled arm brushing against my wing as he bent down beside me.

"I was there." Bí streamed selected images to the screen. Lindy, Wilbur, Orville in his wheelchair. "These are my brothers," I said. Pandy. Carmen. "There are plenty of others, too. They're trapped there against their will." I looked at Zosser to gauge his reaction. He looked surprised and concerned.

"What's wrong with them?" he asked, flipping back to the images of Pandy, Carmen, and Orville.

"Some didn't turn out as expected. Mistakes that make it hard for them to live a normal life. Others weren't mistakes. My brothers were experiments so they could create me. Sacrificial lambs."

Zosser looked stunned. "I didn't know they made mistakes," he whispered.

"Nobody did. Because they hide their mistakes. But these mods are like us," I said, "and they've been locked away. We need to get them out."

Zosser looked startled. "Keep your voice down," he whispered sharply. "If Imhotep is doing this, it must be for a good reason."

"The reason is that they don't want people to know about it," I replied. "They make excuses about needing to provide medical care, but secrecy isn't needed for that. They're putting their business above the lives of these people."

Zosser started to pace. It was a shock to him. He had worshiped Imhotep, and now he struggled to reconcile his previous worldview with this new information. He had to figure out what to do – what action to take. A battle waged inside him.

"I can't help you," he said, suddenly standing stock still.

It was the answer I had feared. "Why not?"

"Imhotep's right. We can't have half-made cripples out on the streets representing people like us. It would jeopardize the message we're trying to send about ourselves and about genetic modification." He shocked me with his bluntness.

"If your message would be jeopardized, then maybe it's the wrong message," I retorted, taken aback. "Maybe that means your message isn't true."

"It is true," Zosser countered vehemently. "When you look at the big picture, it's absolutely true. But people focus on the minority. We can't risk the betterment of humanity because of a few mistakes."

"My brothers were not mistakes!" I squawked. I flipped my screen to an image of Orville. "They did this to him on purpose! He is a cripple, but he's not half-made or an accident. And on top of it all, they've taken away his dignity and freedom. This could have been you! It could have been me! It's not right!"

"You're right. It's not fair," Zosser said, gentling his voice. "But all of the things that Imhotep has done and will do require the public trust."

"Trust comes from honesty," I said. I was exhausted and disappointed and couldn't stop the tears from burning their way up to my eyes.

"No. No, it doesn't," Zosser responded. Just like my mother.

I blanked my screen and curled it around my leg. I blinked the tears back and wiped my nose on my wing feathers. I felt weak and tired and somehow cold once more. I had known I might not get help from Zosser, but my heart had expected more. I felt very alone.

"Don't tell anybody about this," I said. "Keep it secret."

"I will," Zosser said. "This needs to stay between us."

I looked around the room. All of the mods were staring. They hadn't seen nor heard what had been said, but they could tell that Zosser was upset, and I knew that I looked like a mess. I couldn't see them clearly through my watery eyes, but I glimpsed Ann's hyena grin and wondered again whether it truly reflected her feelings or if it was just a permanent fixture on her face. I was too tired to care.

"Does anyone else know about this?" Zosser asked. "Anyone outside Imhotep?"

My hackles raised. It wasn't the question as much as how he said it. There was a threat there, under the surface. I knew then that he would tell Imhotep that I had been at the gym, and that any name I gave would mean danger.

"No. I talked with Morrow and my mom about it." How to get him to keep his mouth shut? I couldn't think of a way. "I'm trying to help them get more freedom from within. They deserve a happy life. I'm just worried it won't be enough."

"I understand," he responded. His mind was already elsewhere, processing, figuring out his next move.

Disgusted, I turned away and headed for the door out of the gym, not looking back. I felt stupid and helpless on top of exhausted. I was angry and disappointed with Zosser, and I began to doubt myself. I knew I was right about my brothers and The Home, but I wondered if there was really anything that could be done.

As the gymnasium door closed on the heat and light of the Ogdoad behind me, I asked Bí to summon a car. "Anything. I can't fly back. Something we can keep secret if possible, but it's not absolutely necessary."

"I'll do my best," Bí responded.

I let out a long sigh and pulled my wings in tight against the cold. The dark, icy loneliness of the hallway was accentuated by the flickers of light and sounds of music reflecting under the door. I felt alone and helpless, and the cold, dark corridor in front of me seemed to go on forever.

Just as I firmed up my resolve to leave, I heard a quiet crunching sound. Ice ran up my spine – "Please don't let it be William," I prayed. In the shadows of the corridor, Ant stood, nibbling a graham cracker, giant unblinking eyes gleaming in the dimly lit hall.

"Ant, what are you doing here?"

Ant did not speak, but gestured for me to follow. Aside from watching, she had never interacted with me before, so I followed. I was too emotionally worn out to think twice.

We passed through a door on the left into a hallway perpendicular to the previous one. Near the end of that hall, we again passed through a door on the left. It was difficult to see, but it looked like the sign on the door said, "Girls".

As the door closed behind us, darkness forced me to stop. I felt Ant grasp my hand, guiding me forward. We went through another doorway into a room dimly lit by moonlight passing through a single frosted window. A few rows of lockers occupied the center of the room. Ant led me to the window side of the room. Something large lay on the floor.

As I bent down to try to figure out what it was, I was startled by light blooming from my leg. Bí had turned on my screen with a pure white image, acting as an artificial light source. There was a body.

It was Siwa, the cheetah girl, curled up in a ball on the floor. She did not seem to be aware of us. I touched her, but she didn't respond. Her skin was cold, and she was shivering. There was a blanket on the floor beside her, unused. I examined more thoroughly, with hands as much as eyes, and discovered a chain leading from Siwa's leg to an old radiator under the window. Hundreds of scratches had stripped away the white radiator paint near the chain. Claw marks. Desperation.

"Oh, shit," I said. I struggled to process what I was seeing. "Bí, cancel whatever car you ordered."

I couldn't get Siwa out of there alone. I couldn't break the chain, and there was no way I could physically carry the taller woman, even with help from Ant. Who would I call for help? Seth? The police? I considered the consequences and made a quick decision.

"If the Ogdoad sees an ambulance pull up, they'll know something's going on." I didn't want to guess what they would do. The thumping bass rattled the empty lockers around us. "Ten minutes after you hear the music stop I need you to call an ambulance. Let them know that I'm with somebody who's injured and that they'll need to bring something that can cut chain. You can give them whatever other details you think they need to know."

I turned to Ant, still quietly nibbling on her crackers. How long had she known Siwa was a prisoner, here? What made her show me? What else did she know?

"Thank you, Ant," I said. "We'll get her out of here." Ant blinked, nodded, and then slipped away. I knew she would be watching.

That left me alone with Siwa in the freezing locker room. Very little heat seeped in from the gymnasium. My fingers were already starting to tingle, but I would wait with Siwa and try to warm her up a little. I laid on the cold, dirty tile floor and wrapped a wing around her, nestling my face in her long, soft hair. She smelled of sweat and drugs. It wasn't comfortable, and it wasn't warm, but Siwa was in rough shape. Better for both of us to be cold than for Siwa to freeze. I pulled the blanket over us as much as possible.

Curled up beside an unconscious stranger, I closed my eyes and the events of the last hour caught up with me. I began to sob into the back of Siwa's head. The evening had not gone as planned.

CHAPTER 31

"If we're not allowed to do cutting-edge research in the United States, we'll take our businesses elsewhere." – Letter to Congress by Gulliver James, TekGNome Inc., July 2022

The first penny drones were tiny flying machines approximately the size of a penny. Current models are much smaller, but the name had already stuck. A modern penny drone can fly in and out of most buildings without anybody being the wiser. Thus their illegality.

Nable guided our slightly-used, entirely-illicit penny drone through Amai's home, looking for clues. I watched on my screen from the safety of a cab a few blocks away as the drone flew through the kitchen. Nobody would know I had been there because, technically, I hadn't.

The home wasn't cordoned off, because according to the police there was no suspicion of a crime. Somebody had probably been through it to look for anything obvious, but in all, I supposed this was how the Larsen home normally looked. No signs of a struggle. No bullet holes. No blood. Time to look for less obvious clues.

We took a second spin through the house. Amai and Nick lived there alone. No sign of kids or pets. No screens were on. Nable tried to interrogate the appliances, but I could almost hear disdain in his voice when he said they had no useful information. Perhaps Bluetooth housewares were the ignorant rubes of the digital world.

We searched for whiteboards, scraps of paper, anything that would tell us something. No luck. We searched for at least four hours, my eyes drying to shreds as I focused so hard on my screen. If the killers murdered Amai and Nick in their home, they knew enough to clean up after themselves.

The risk of purchasing an illegal drone had been for nothing. Nable buzzed the drone out of the house through a crack under the front door, and that's when I spotted it. If we hadn't been near the ground, I never would have seen it. From the drone's point of view, it looked like a small rope. Nable brought us in for a closer look, and we could see it was hairy. Not a rope. A mouse's tail - not attached to a mouse.

"No pets," I said. I remembered Beryl telling me about the Ogdoad. "Either this is from a stray cat offering a present, or this is our clue. We need to run this past Beryl."

"Communicating with Bí now," Nable responded. "Beryl is at the hospital."

"What?" I exclaimed, startled.

"She is not injured, but we should go there now."

We waited for the penny drone carrying the severed tail to join us, then we drove straight to the hospital.

CHAPTER 32

"It is useless to ask a seriously injured person if he has high cholesterol and about the level of his blood sugars. You have to heal his wounds. Then we can talk about everything else." – Pope Francis

"I can't believe you went to that douchebag Zosser before me," Seth said, lounging across several chairs in the hospital waiting room. We waited anxiously to see whether Siwa would be all right.

"Yeah, I know," I responded sadly. "Big mistake." I'm not sure what I had been thinking. They seemed strong, and I had grown up with the idea that the strong protect the weak. They were heavies, so I thought they'd protect their own. I couldn't have been more wrong.

"Understandable mistake, though. He's quite handsome." Seth waggled her eyebrows suggestively. Or rather, it was intended to look suggestive, but looked more like two caterpillars dancing.

I laughed. "I didn't ask him because he's handsome."

"Oh, yeah?" Seth asked. "Then why?"

"Well, the goal was to stage a break-out. The Ogdoad is practically a small army."

"I believe it was Confucius who once said, 'An army of douches leaves everybody wet.' Besides," Seth continued, "there's a perfectly good army of mods already at your service." She leaned over and whispered conspiratorially, "And I've heard that their leader is a ninja poet warrior." She raised her eyebrows and nodded convincingly. I didn't remind Seth that she was an Amazon warrior, not a ninja warrior. Apparently, warrior affiliations are fluid.

"I know, I know," I said, covering my face with my wings. "I didn't know how rotten he was. And yes, you did warn me. And yes, I should have come to you first. I'm sorry."

"Your willingness to tell me how right I am, combined with your sincere apology locks you in as Friend of the Year!" Seth exclaimed. She brought her tone down a few notches and said, "Seriously, though. It's okay. I'm just glad you're all right."

"Thanks, Seth," I responded. I hopped off the uncomfortable chair and lay down on the hospital floor. Even though the carpet was patterned specifically to hide age and stains, it was clearly a nasty old carpet. I didn't care. The floor of the elementary school locker room had been much dirtier and much less comfortable.

When the ambulance finally arrived, the police showed up with them. I was cold and tired, but I tried to answer their barrage of questions as well as I could. Siwa hadn't woken up even once while they freed her from her chains, but the paramedic said she thought Siwa would be okay.

The police asked much harder questions than the paramedics. "How did this happen? How did you find the victim? Who did this?"

I answered honestly with some small exceptions. I left Ant out of it, for example, saying that I was upset when leaving the party and went through the wrong door, stumbling over Siwa on the floor. Beyond that, I really didn't know much for certain. I knew that Ann had retrieved Siwa once. I also knew that Zosser spent a lot of time with her and took her away from the group once. Beyond that, I could only give names of the other members of other heavy mods to interview. Though I suspected that Siwa was some sort of imprisoned sex slave for Zosser and that the Ogdoad all knew about it, I had very little evidence.

Seth had been shocked. "I thought she was some sort of dreamy-eyed floozy," she said, "but she was probably kept drugged up most of the time. I'll have to scale my judgementalism down a few notches - from outright obnoxious to barely intolerable."

While we waited in the hospital, Seth and I screenchatted with Thasha, Ralph, Kammi, and Cuddles connected from their respective homes. Seth's assumptions about Siwa were common among the group. Even knowing Zosser's egocentricity, none of them had imagined something like this.

"I told you Siwa might not be so bad," Ralph chastised.

"Oh, give it a rest," Seth said. "You didn't know any better than us. You just thought she was pretty and were jealous of Zosser."

"Well, I knew he was up to no good," Ralph muttered.

"But did you do anything about it?" Kammi retorted. "Beryl actually did something."

"I didn't do anything beyond wait for the police," I said. "Ant figured it out. She's the hero."

That created an awkward moment for the group, because Ant wasn't on screens with us. She was never on screens with us, but when we went to the school or other hangouts she was often just *there*. Welcome but not invited. She was an outsider who we saw every day.

"We should get to know her better," Thasha said, echoing everybody's thoughts. "And make sure she knows that we think highly of her." Everybody nodded.

"Oh, shit," Seth said as Moto entered the waiting room. You really can't miss it when somebody who looks like a giant minotaur strides into a room. Why would he come here? Never one to be shy, Seth stood on her chair, pointed accusingly and shouted, "Fuck off!" at the top of her lungs. Moto saw her, but kept on coming, drawing forth a stream of increasingly creative expletives.

"Seth, you're scaring the normies," I whispered as I picked myself up from the stained carpet. Families of non-mods and light mods who had also been waiting to see friends and family in the emergency department began relocating to chairs more distant from us, watching warily.

"I didn't know," Moto said as he approached, arms wide in supplication. "You've got to believe me. I didn't know."

"Tell the jury," Seth said.

"Moto, why are you here?" I asked more quietly.

"I wanted to see if she's all right," Moto replied.

"Oh, yeah. Quite the saint," Seth sputtered sarcastically.

"Look, most of us didn't know," Moto said. He was not aggressive, but rather had a pained, apologetic look. "Looking back, it seems obvious, but we trusted Zosser. He was our leader.

"We should have used our brains. We should have wondered. We should have asked questions about Siwa – about their relationship. We didn't. So, even though I didn't have anything to do with this, I still recognize some responsibility, and I want to know if she's all right and if there's anything I can do."

Moto sounded sincere, but after the last couple of months, I wasn't ready to make any assumptions one way or the other.

"We haven't gotten to talk with her yet," I answered. "We've been told she'll live... that she has a lot of drugs in her system that need to work their way out. They don't know if there's been any permanent damage to her brain. They say there's evidence of repeated rape. She'll probably have to deal with PTSD for the rest of her life."

Moto's eyes dropped to the floor. I wondered if he was here not just to check on Siwa, but also to explore his own feelings about Zosser. The falcon had been a leader and a friend to Moto and the others. He made them feel important, independent, and powerful. It would be a huge shock to his worldview, to his view of himself, to think of Zosser as evil. Many in that situation wouldn't be able to make the mental adjustment. They would make excuses and forgive too easily because 'he's one of us'. The fact that Moto was making the effort was worth something.

"I think I believe you, Moto," I said, eliciting a hiss from Seth. "But you're going to need to earn our trust."

I walked up to him and hopped onto a chair. Even so, I still had to look up to meet his eyes. The giant bull man looked down on me and waited for the tiny bird girl to tell him what to do.

"You will not see her today," I said softly. "There are two reasons. First of all, she probably associates you with her imprisonment and would not welcome you. For that reason, you will not go near her until she invites you to do so." Moto nodded, accepting the decision.

"Secondly," I continued, "I don't trust you yet. You could have been sent here by Zosser to scare Siwa into not pressing charges or in some other way intimidate her. For that reason, you will not go near her until charges have been filed and you've received an invitation from her, and until any court stuff has been resolved, you will not be alone with her under any circumstances. Do you understand?"

"Yes," Moto said clearly and quietly. "I want to do the right thing." He looked to Seth who wore her skeptical eyebrows. "I won't hang out with Zosser or Ann anymore."

"We'll keep you posted," I said gently, patting Moto's chest. "For now, I need you to go home."

Moto nodded, his eyes downcast. He turned his massive body around and left the room without another word. As I watched him leave, I hoped he was sincere. How were the other members of the Ogdoad reacting to all of this? Moto's reaction was likely the best that could be hoped for.

That prompted a whole new round of screen discussions with the group. Seth proclaimed me 'Beryl the Brave' for bravely staring down 'the savage beast', but nobody bought it. As Kammi explained, "Seth, you're the savage one."

Eventually, conversation died down and the screens went silent.

"It looks like we probably won't be able to use the gym at the school anymore," Seth said. "They're going to really lock it down."

"I won't miss it," I replied. I hoped to never go there again.

Eventually, a nurse came out and brought us back to see Siwa. It was a short visit. Siwa was still disoriented and exhausted. She thanked us for being there and promptly fell asleep. We stayed in the room for a while. The simple quiet of watching over someone sleeping was soothing for me.

The police had called Mom to come and get me from the elementary school. Her expression had been hard to read, but she didn't ask any questions other than to make sure I was all right. To help us and the police, she had been given a strand of Siwa's hair to take back to Imhotep to compare the DNA against their files.

"Her name is Natalia," she said when she joined us at the hospital later. "Her parents, who ordered the cheetah modifications, died when Natalia was twelve. She slipped through the cracks. There are no records of medical visits or anything else after the death of her parents."

"Not Siwa?" I asked.

"Not according to her birth certificate or our records," Mom answered. "I don't know whether she renamed herself or if she was renamed by her captors. Probably the latter, as Siwa was the site of an ancient Egyptian oracle."

"I don't think she should be alone, Mom," I said.

"Would you like to stay with her? I can bring back some toiletries and food for you."

"That would be great. Thanks." I still had mixed, confused feelings about her and Dad and the decisions they had made, but I also knew that Mom wanted to help. I didn't know what to do other than accept it.

Then Maggie stormed in, creating a very full room. Maggie and my mother had not met each other, which was awkward. We did a quick round of introductions. Mom didn't ask any questions, but I'm sure she had some in mind.

"Where have you been?" I asked.

"Poking around," Maggie answered. "If I told you I found a mouse tail in a very suspicious location, what would you say to that?"

"The eagle mod is William, and he's the scariest of the bunch," I answered. "He snacks on live mice and throws away the tails like cherry stems. I don't know if all of the Ogdoad is involved with whatever you're looking into, but it wouldn't surprise me in the least if William were in the middle of it. And he probably wouldn't do anything without Zosser's command."

Maggie nodded as though I had confirmed a hypothesis. "Can I talk with you in the hallway for a minute?" she asked with a glance toward my mother. I could tell that Mom didn't like the idea of me keeping secrets from her, but turnabout is fair play, and she knew it. She decided to exit gracefully, heading home to grab an overnight bag for me.

"Did you mention anything about The Home to anybody in the Ogdoad or at Imhotep?" Maggie asked. "One of my sources has been murdered."

Holy crap. Had it come to that? Was Maggie in danger? Was I? I found it hard to believe that the secret of The Home was worth killing over.

"Mom caught me communicating with Wilbur and told Imhotep," I answered. Maggie sucked air between her teeth. "I talked with Zosser about it for the first time yesterday, and I'm pretty sure he didn't know."

"So if it was William, either he got orders from Imhotep directly or he got orders from Zosser but with no context. Or maybe it's totally unrelated to what we've been doing." Maggie looked worried. "When your mom told Imhotep, did they know I was involved?"

"No, but Morrow guessed that you might have fed the information to me. I think I covered well." I swallowed hard. "How much trouble do you think we're in?"

"Hard to know, but my guess is that we'll find out soon enough."

CHAPTER 33

"These discussions have pushed me far outside my scientific comfort zone." – Jennifer Doudna

When I caught up with Beryl at the hospital, she filled me in on what I had missed while I was in Atlanta. Though the discovery of Natalia's enslavement had been a shocking distraction, Beryl was still focused on Orville. I didn't know if she was right about needing to break him out or not, but with the mysterious death of my source it was time to think about getting the heck out of Dodge.

I asked Beryl if she knew she was sterile. What kind of a world do we live in where that kind of question even needs to be asked? She hadn't known, and I saw a whirlwind of emotions do a merry-go-round on her face. She didn't know what to think about it. She would need time. For better or worse, she would have plenty of time to stew on it while she watched over Natalia. Add one more to the towering list of topics she had to think about.

Meanwhile, there was work to be done. The next day, I interviewed two other former employees of Imhotep and Memphis Modifications who still lived in southeastern Wisconsin. Many more were not willing to talk. Journalists weren't the only ones scared off by lawsuits. Even interview subjects, if caught not speaking perfectly objectively, had been litigated for slander, libel, and 'undue harm' (whatever that meant). They knew that if their names were associated with an article that later proved harmful to a business, they would become a target.

The more rejections I received, the more thankful I was that Wilson had agreed to his interview. The other two interviewees corroborated what Wilson had said, but hadn't given much in additional detail. It was enough to understand the basic history of Imhotep and Horace Morrow, but outside of context, it didn't do much good. What else was Imhotep into? For it to come to murder, it couldn't just be because we were digging into The Home.

Seth, ever the conspiracy theorist, had implied military involvement on multiple occasions. The use-case for genetic human enhancements in the military was obvious, but we hadn't seen any real links yet.

None of the interviews really pointed me to anything suspicious. Maybe The Home was it. News of it would certainly harm their business, and even our broken legal system would probably balk at a secret prison. Even though I could see no evidence to the contrary, I felt in my bones that there was more. I just had to keep digging. The puzzle had to be solved.

Speaking of puzzles to be solved, I had no idea what to think of Beryl's mom. She seemed cold, and she played her cards close to the vest, but she also seemed to support Beryl, at least in part. That household must be a bloody mess at this point. How do you get away with having secret children in a corporate dungeon? Baffling. Little Beryl seemed to be holding up under the strain. I hoped her relationship with Seth gave her strength, or at least a fuzzy shoulder to lean on.

When I arrived back at the hotel after the second interview, Zosser was there waiting for me in the lobby. He was just as Beryl had described: tall and strong with large, piercing eyes. And he was terrifying. I had seen the look in his eyes once before – during an interview I did with Simon Wesley, the fanatic who bombed the shit out of a post office in Arkansas ten years ago.

"What are you doing here?" I asked, not willing to go toward my room while he could follow me. Safer in the open. The hotel was low budget, with very little foot traffic. The dowdy desk clerk was pretending to work, but she kept peering at us over her glasses.

"I could ask you the same thing," he answered. "I'm pretty sure you're done with your retrospective assignment, considering it's currently airing worldwide."

I didn't have to answer his questions, and I wouldn't put up with his bullshit. "Shouldn't you be enslaving some orphans or something?" I shot back. "Why aren't you in jail?"

"For what?" he asked. "Ann confessed to chaining Siwa. She thought it was a game, the poor, confused thing."

"Natalia," I corrected. "Her name is Natalia."

"Again, part of the game," Zosser said with a smirk. "We love all of that Egyptian stuff, but Ann and Siwa went too far."

"So Ann takes the fall?" I asked. "How was rape part of that game? And wasn't your DNA, quite literally, all over Natalia?"

"I thought the sex was consensual, of course," he said. His persistent smile made me want to vomit. "How was I to know she was a drug addict? Poor Ann kept bringing her more behind my back, thinking she was helping stave off the withdrawal symptoms. What a comedy of errors!"

Disgusting. His story was fifty shades of flimsy, but if Ann and others in the Ogdoad corroborated it, there wasn't much hard evidence to make it go the other way. The fact that he wasn't behind bars while it got sorted out indicated that there were likely other powers involved, too. I resisted the urge to spit in his gigantic eyes.

"I'll ask you again," I said slowly and as evenly as I could. "Why are you here?"

"To make a recommendation," he answered. "Go home. Stop nosing around. Get a quiet job where you interview famous game show hosts or something."

"I have a job," I replied. "I'm on vacation. Trying to talk to people. Make new friends."

"Make them elsewhere," Zosser said firmly.

I've always had a revulsion for bullies, to the point where I sometimes act unwisely just out of spite. "I'm not afraid of you," I said with self-righteous power.

"You should be," Zosser responded quietly. "I was surprised to learn that your sister lives in the area. And your niece, Seth. I know Seth! Charming girl." He grabbed my shoulder and got very serious very fast.

"It's easier for both of us if you fear me, Maggie. If I can't control you with fear, there's really only one option left to me."

I refused to show it, but he had gotten to me. I was scared. I tugged my arm away from his grasp and stared him right back. "What will you do, Zosser? Tell William to take care of it?" Zosser gave me an appraising look. Damn my mouth, I revealed too much.

"He's a handy guy to have around," Zosser said with a smile. He looked into my eyes with those giant headlights of his, long enough to show me he had all the power. He wanted me to know that he was responsible for the deaths of Amai and her husband. That he could do the same to me and my family. He did not blink as he waited for that knowledge to sink into my heart. Then he walked away.

I wanted to be angry, but the fear was too strong. Raw animal terror pounded through my veins. I couldn't think. I felt like I couldn't breathe. Hours later, the fear finally began to morph into rage, but it was impotent and did nothing to clear my head.

Nable booked me a room in a different hotel, and I did not sleep well. I dreamed of vultures and the sound of my sister's screams.

CHAPTER 34

"Like any other contraceptive method, sterilization should only be provided with the full, free and informed consent of the individual." – World Health Organization, May 2014

Though I stayed at the hospital overnight, Natalia didn't wake up. Mom came to get me in the morning. Dad had just come home from another long work trip, and I dreaded that we were headed for a long family talk. Dad had been gone so much over the past six months, and so much had happened. I felt like a different person than the girl I was last autumn, and even if it weren't winter and I weren't coming back from a long night at the hospital, I'm not sure our ritual father-daughter flight would make sense.

Mom was silent on the car ride home. I couldn't tell what she was thinking. She seemed devoid of emotion, like an empty husk of a human being. I probably looked the same way – I just couldn't process everything that was happening around me. Family secrets, hidden brothers, slavery, murder… what the heck was going on? My current circumstances felt totally dissociated from the life I had known. Discouraged, I kept my own silence.

When we arrived at home, Dad was waiting by the door. We hugged, but not our normal enthusiastic embrace. Mom left us alone for a while, presumably to put coats away. I'm sure she just wanted Dad to take a crack at me, though.

Might as well get right to it.

"Why did you lie to me about The Home, Dad?" I asked. "You tried to convince me that Seth was just making it up."

He sighed and plunked down on the couch, ruffling his hands through his short, thinning hair. "All that Imhotep stuff is your mother," he said, not even looking at me. "I try to stay out of it."

"What does that mean?" I asked. I remained standing, bewildered. "You're involved because your sons are there. You made them. How can you try to stay out of it?"

"That's just it, Beryl. I didn't make them. Imhotep did. My genes are in there, sure. But family isn't about genes. It's about love and responsibility and promises we make. When your mom and I contracted to make you, we made those promises to you, before you were even born. I never made those promises to Orville, Wilbur, or Lindy. They're side effects that somebody else decided to create and take responsibility for. They're not my sons any more than the birds whose genes are in you are your parents."

What he said didn't sound right, but I didn't know how to argue with it. What's the difference between being responsible and taking responsibility? What defines family? How can you be a part of a 'family' where each member defines it differently? I didn't know the answers to any of those questions, so I let it pass.

Still, the core question remained unanswered. "Why did you lie to me?"

"It was your mother's secret to keep."

A moment of silence passed between us. Thus far, I had been confused and surprised by my parents' actions. But this was different. For the first time in my life, I was disappointed in them. I knew that in this, if nothing else, he was wrong. They were wrong, and that knowledge permanently changed the color of my perceptions.

"Want some cocoa?" Jerry asked hopefully.

"Sure," I answered quietly.

* * * * * *

My mind was still racing when supper was served, which made for some awkward comments and unintended silences. Dad brought presents – just little souvenirs from various airports: a deck of cards from Cleveland, a mug from Pittsburgh, a hat from Annapolis. It should have been like other times when we were together after my father had been absent for a long time: soothing, loving, a fond memory in the making. But I felt like I was on the outside looking in. Everything had changed.

Early in the meal, during soup, I asked, "Why am I sterile?"

While my father choked on a carrot, my mother responded, "If you know you're sterile, then I'm sure you know why."

"Dad?" I asked.

"This is your mother's stuff," he answered hastily.

"No," I challenged, "I'm your daughter. What happens to me is not 'my mother's stuff.'" Dad pursed his lips and lowered his eyes.

"Let's put aside the racists and religious nuts who would give you a whole lot of trouble because they consider heavy mods to be a taint or soulless beasts or some other nonsense," Mom began. "It's just not safe. If you had a child naturally, it would have a chaotic, unpredictable genetic structure that, in all likelihood, wouldn't be viable. It would die or live in misery."

"Is that it? Or is it about protecting patents?" I asked. I'd had a lot of time to think in that hospital room. So many questions, and most of them starting with 'why'.

"It's about protecting the gene pool," Mom said.

"From what?" I cried. "Me? I'm *human*! I'm not an invasive species."

"You're not an invasive species," Mom responded. "You're unique. You're special! There's nobody like you."

"Don't feed me that pandering crap, Mom!" I yelled, shrieking with anger. I had never shouted at my parents before. I'm not sure I'd ever been angry like that before. "Imhotep has the patent on me, my genes. If they wanted to, they could churn out dozens of kids like me. You and the company have stopped me from having children and taken that control for yourselves!"

"Do you want to have children?" Mom asked. "Because this is news to me."

What a bullshit answer. She was just trying to distract from the real issue. "I'm just a kid. I hadn't thought about it. But that doesn't mean I won't want to later. Or that I don't deserve that choice."

"There are other women who are born infertile," Mom responded. "Everybody gets born with a certain deck of cards, and we just have to deal with it."

"But you stacked the deck!" I shouted, my voice cracking horribly. "You made the choice. You took the choice away from me and made it your own. What gives you the right?"

"We're your parents," she answered coolly. "That gives us the right. Without us, there is no you. Without our choices, you can't fly or don't even exist. Imhotep won't contract for a heavy mod without an infertility clause. Like it or not, you are who you are because of us. And we love who you are. There are going to be things you don't like about yourself, and you're right that we're responsible for those things. But those are the choices we made, and you're just going to have to deal with it. You weren't exactly in a position to make those choices at the time they were made."

My father remained silent through all of this, looking increasingly uncomfortable. He had twisted himself around so far in his chair that he looked like he was ready to make a run for it.

"Just because you can rationalize it, doesn't make it right!" I screamed. I had stood up without realizing it, my chair tipped onto the floor. I turned and raged toward my bedroom. I could hardly see, my eyes filled with tears, my throat tightened painfully, and oh how my back hurt.

I slammed the bedroom door and flopped into my nestlike bed, wings over my face. I had never fought with anybody like that before. I wasn't sure how I felt before getting all of that out, but I definitely felt worse after. How could my father not recognize my brothers as family? How could my mother rationalize away something as big as, "You will never have children because we said so"?

Worse, Zosser called a few minutes later.

"Transmit only my voice, Bí," I said. That bastard wouldn't see me cry. "Record it." Zosser's stupid face came up on the screen.

"What do you want?" I demanded.

"I wanted to thank you," he replied in that smooth tone.

He wanted me to ask why, but I had no interest in appeasing him, so I responded the way Seth would. "You're an asshole."

"I was getting careless," he responded. "Sloppy. You made a nice move pointing that out… getting her out of our way."

"This isn't about getting anybody out of the way," I replied, confused. Getting who out of the way, I wondered. Natalia? Then I had a sudden, astounding epiphany. "Do you think I freed Natalia and turned you in because I was *jealous*?" I asked incredulously. Achilles had less hubris.

"Look, she was with me because she wanted to be with me," he said. "And we needed an oracle. Science and philosophy can't fully prepare us for what's coming. She was a good oracle, but I needed to be going in a different direction. You shook me out of my rut, and for that I thank you."

"Go to Hell," I said. "How's that for a direction?" With that, I severed the link.

"Bí, block any future incoming calls from Zosser," I said. "And rename his contact listing 'Asshole' so I don't accidentally message him in the future."

"That will put his name near the top of the list when sorted by alphabet," Bí reminded me.

"Better call him 'Zasshole', then," I corrected. Seth would appreciate that. "Thanks for everything, Bí. I don't know why I didn't use a shabti sooner. You're great."

"You're welcome, Beryl," Bí replied. "I hope things get better for you and your parents."

"I have a feeling they're going to need to get worse first," I replied with a choked up sigh. How could they get worse?

"Is there anything I can do?" Bí asked.

"Yep. Let's meet with Seth and Maggie tomorrow. It's time to start acting like the ninja poet warriors we are."

CHAPTER 35

"I can barely figure out what to have for lunch, let alone plan my whole day!" – Lindy Pritchard

Some people are driven by ambition. Some by desire. And then there are those very few people who are driven by empathy. These select few might never take the actions they take if not pressed to do so. And many never do. But when this sort of person sees injustice, pain, and the down-and-dirty bad of the world, they can't help but put every ounce of their energy into making things better.

Beryl was one of those people. Her brother, Orville, was suffering in a cage. Natalia had been enslaved. Heavy mods of all sorts, regardless of whether or not they lived at the Home, were controlled by the company that made them. Beryl's eyes had been opened to some of the ills of this world, and she felt compelled to take action.

Some of Beryl's softness was gone. She no longer seemed like a quiet girl who enjoyed gardening and flying. Unfamiliar anger worked its way toward the surface – rarely breaking, never quite releasing. An impotent frustration that lacked direction.

So, she tried to direct it. Her focus was Orville. According to Beryl, he was acting like he was "back to normal", scooching around in his wheelchair and throwing out sarcastic remarks as if throwing candy to children from a parade float. He wasn't fooling his siblings. They knew that either he would try again or had given up hope, neither of which were acceptable.

"We're going to get Orville out of there," Beryl declared. "It has to be soon, and we need to bring Lindy and Wilbur with us."

"Will they come?" I asked.

"Yes. Wilbur won't want to," Beryl responded, "But Lindy said he'd talk him into it. He'll stay with his brothers."

"So how are we going to break them out?" Seth asked.

"And more importantly, what would you do after breaking them out?" I added.

"'Don't know' and 'beats me'," Beryl responded. "If we have to, we'll wing it."

"Nice pun," Seth whispered. Beryl ignored her, tension distorting her features.

"Seriously, though. We have to come up with the best plan we can come up with, and then just do it, even if there are gaps.

"Let's start with the breakout," Beryl continued, not waiting for disagreement. "They've beefed up surveillance…"

"Because your brothers are a flight risk?" Seth interjected. "Eh? *Flight* risk?"

Beryl sighed and put her head down on the table. Her shoulders were tight, and her fists were clenched. I looked at Seth, who looked back at me with concern. Beryl was trying to keep it together, and the strain was too much. So much change in such a small span of time was an awful lot to handle.

"I'm sorry," Seth said. "I know this is hard on you. I was just trying to lighten the mood."

"That was so stupid," Beryl said in a choked voice. "I can't believe how stupid that was."

Beryl's back started to heave. I wasn't sure if she was repressing vomit or beginning to sob. As I put my hand on her feathered shoulder, I started to hear her giggle. The sound grew until it became laughter – that gasping, uncontrolled, tears-down-your-cheeks laughter that comes with the release of great stress.

Seth and I found ourselves laughing along with her, and when Beryl lifted her head and we saw her wet cheeks, we started crying with her as well. We all held one another – feathers, fur, and flesh – and wept and laughed from stress and empathy until we were exhausted, wrung-out rags of spent emotion. Laughter and tears can cut through fear and tension like nothing else.

When we pulled it together and looked at each other's blotchy, moist, bleary-eyed faces, we all knew how important it was that we do something. It was time to figure out what.

"I'll get some cookies," Seth volunteered.

"And milk?" Beryl asked, bits of feather fluff stuck to her wet, red face.

"Don't push it, you overgrown feather duster," Seth replied as she headed for the kitchen. Beryl smiled.

With that, we got down to the business of planning a breakout. It wouldn't be easy. We knew that all entries would be locked, including windows and balconies. There would be an alarm system, surveillance, and maybe even a guard or two. After consulting with each other and our shabti, there didn't seem to be any way we could break in, grab the boys, and get out unseen.

"What if we're trying too hard?" Seth asked. "What if we just walk up to the front door, break it down, get the bird brothers, and leave?"

"Alarms will sound, security will come, and they'll stop us," I answered.

"Will they, though?" Seth continued. "We've got one asset that they don't have… we're the good guys, here."

"Doesn't that mean that it's <u>more</u> risky to get caught because who knows what they'll do to us?" Beryl asked.

"Maybe I should put this another way," Seth said. "They don't want anybody *to know* that they're the bad guys, here."

"I get it," I said. "I'm a reporter. I record the whole thing and if they give us trouble, I unleash the video." I thought about that a little further. Zeen wouldn't publish it. I could chuck it onto an upload site, but either it wouldn't be seen, it would be written off as a fake, or it would get taken down by pressure from Imhotep's lawyers on the site. The only way to make sure it wasn't suppressed was to flood so many outlets at once that it would take too much time to shut them all down.

"Nable, when we send out video like the retrospective, it goes out to Zine, and from Zine it goes out to all sorts of other plazas and outlets," I began.

"Correct."

"Would there be a way to use that same distribution network by making them think we had published something at Zeen even if we hadn't?"

"Yes, I think we could," he answered. "They know you, and they trust that anything that comes through me is really coming through Zeen. If you wanted to publish to everywhere except Zeen, to bypass editorial scrutiny, I think we could make that happen very quickly. I could do a real-time edit that would not be our best work, but would be watchable and get the idea across."

"Perfect." I explained how it would work to Beryl and Seth. Simply put, I would stand back and record everything via temple, ready at any moment to send it out to numerous high-traffic plazas. That was our leverage – the threat of releasing the video. If they stopped us with force, millions of people would instantly know about it. If they let us go, we'd keep it to ourselves, though we'd still have a copy of the video in case we needed it later. I knew that if forced to publish it, it would ruin my career forever; I could end up in prison. I chose not to mention that fact to the girls.

"We still need to get in, though," Beryl said. "Doesn't do much good to record ourselves failing to open a locked door."

"Right," I agreed. "In fact, the recording won't do us any good at all unless we get as far as the inside of The Home. We'd need Imhotep exterior footage, video of entering The Home, and video of your brothers. If we get that far, we have the leverage you're looking for."

"I can bring a crowbar," Seth suggested. "We should be able to pry open a door or bash open a window."

"I'm worried that might take too long," Beryl said. "We've got to get in fast, and we have to be able to get past a guard. If we don't get to my brothers on film, it's nothing more than breaking and entering."

"We need a tank," Seth said. "Anybody got a tank? Damn, that would be awesome."

"Moto!" Beryl squeaked.

"Moto has a tank?" Seth asked incredulously.

"No, Moto *is* a tank. Metaphorically," she clarified. "Massively strong and resistant to bullets – that qualifies, right?"

"That would resolve the guard issue and any doors," Seth agreed. "Think he'll be up for it?"

Beryl considered for a moment. "Yes, I do. I spoke with him over screens this morning." She related the guts of the conversation.

Moto felt guilty about Natalia's imprisonment and wanted to know if she was feeling better. When asked, he opened up to Beryl about himself. He talked about his father, a small man with a big personality. He talked about his mother, quiet but strong.

He also talked about how his body affected his life. Absurdly large and powerful, he struggled in the same ways many big people struggle. He always sat on the edges in movie theaters so he didn't block anybody's view. He had trouble with doorways and low-hanging chandeliers. Clothing was nearly impossible.

Beyond just his size, he also had his hormones to deal with. He had been engineered to produce a ridiculous amount of testosterone. So, he was born to delight in exerting dominance, aggression, and competition. His parents had taught him about philosophy, ethics, and religion at a young age, knowing that it would be a struggle for him to control his strength. The result was a very conflicted teenager.

When he met Zosser and became indoctrinated in Zosser's philosophies, he felt free to be strong and powerful. "It was all the joy with none of the guilt," Moto said, "and none of the responsibility." He felt like it was a game. The Ogdoad didn't do much beyond talking and partying. He knew Zosser had schemes, but nothing that directly impacted Moto until he realized that Siwa – Natalia – was a victim. Then it wasn't a game anymore, and Moto felt like his unrestrained behavior was at fault.

"Could I have questioned Zosser?" Moto had asked. "Should I have tried to get to know Siwa? To know that she was Natalia? Instead of looking around me, I wasted my time trying to impress people with stupid stunts. I gloried in the attention."

Instead of absolving him, Beryl acknowledged he could have done more. "Use your guilt to make better decisions in the future, but don't let it keep you from making good decisions for yourself or others."

Seth and I looked at Beryl as she sat in thought, the morning's conversation still resonating within her. I could tell she felt like she connected with Moto. That she believed him. But her faith in others had been so shaken of late that she found it hard to trust her own judgment.

"I think that freeing some heavy mods from imprisonment is exactly what he needs," she concluded.

"Do you trust him?" Seth asked.

"Yes," Beryl answered simply.

"Why?" I asked.

Beryl blinked and cocked her head to the side, very birdlike. She sometimes had that tic when she dug deep within herself, whether it was for courage or truth. She answered, "I asked him if he had ever considered trying surgery or drugs to get his testosterone levels down to something more normal.

"He answered that he didn't think he could do it. The idea scared him. He said, 'I'm worried I'd be a different person. Who would I be if I weren't who I am?'

"As I learn about my family history and my creation, I've been wondering who I would be if it weren't for the feathers, the wings –"

"-the bird brain," Seth interjected.

"You know what I'm talking about, Seth," Beryl continued unruffled. "When we strip all of that stuff away, what's left? Who am I? Who is Moto?

"Whether right or wrong, he's asking himself the same questions I'm asking myself, he's vulnerable and not afraid to show it, and I believe that what's coming out of his mouth is the truth."

"Then we have a tank," Seth said, and I agreed.

We paused for a moment to take a breath. This was starting to sound more than a little crazy. While recording ourselves walking up to the front door, a minotaur would bash it down for us, and then we would stroll away with Beryl's brothers. It seemed unreal. Even if it failed spectacularly, it would be memorable.

"We're halfway there," Beryl said, encouraged. "So, let's say we've rescued the boys and are standing outside Imhotep. What next?"

More consideration.

"You can either take them home," I said, meaning Beryl's home, "or go into hiding."

"If you go home, it gives Imhotep time to get leverage over Maggie," Seth said. "They'll swoop in with lawyers, police, and the cone of silence, and when they've got us over a barrel they'll put your brothers right back where they started."

"Beryl, how would your parents react?" I asked.

"I don't know," Beryl said. "Dad doesn't recognize them as his kids."

"Your brothers?" Seth asked, surprised.

"Yup. Mom does, but I don't think she'd welcome them. She seems conflicted, but she tends to side with whatever Imhotep wants."

"Sounds very complicated," I said. More than that, it sounded like potential for future therapy bills.

"Whatever we do, Natalia will be coming along," Beryl added. "She's got nobody, and we can't leave her here with Zosser on the loose."

"Awkward," Seth said.

"Understatement," Beryl agreed. "Especially since she doesn't know about any of this, yet."

"Well, then we're left with hiding," Seth said. "We've got the warrior part – bashing our way through the front door. We've got our poet," she pointed to me, "telling our story. If we can vanish without a trace, we will have achieved a level of greatness worthy of a ninja poet warrior."

"Though not all three at the same time," Beryl said.

"Close enough!"

"It's not a long-term solution," I offered, "but you could probably stay with my Aunt Sarah and Uncle Jeremy for a while. They're on a farm in Iowa. Seth, I don't know if you've ever met them before, but they're good people and they're family. Beryl, your brothers could be out in the open all day and nobody would see you out there."

"Orville would love that," Beryl responded. "I think Wilbur and Lindy would, too." She thought about it for a little bit. "We'd probably stick out like sore thumbs anywhere else," she said. "It doesn't make sense to hide in an apartment in a city – that's just exchanging one cage for another."

She was right, but she hadn't yet realized that anywhere they hid would still be a cage. A farm where they could walk freely would just be a larger cage, but until they could walk in the greater world, they'd always have restrictions on their freedoms. At least the farm would feel like freedom to the brothers. For a while.

I asked Nable to find a way to get word to Sarah and Jeremy that couldn't be easily traced. I was certain they'd help, but I wanted to give them warning. They don't have much in the way of mods out in the sticks, so it would be quite a shock if Beryl and her crew showed up unannounced at their front door. Nable suggested the US Postal Service as untraceable and unexpected. They delivered four days a week, and it would take a couple of days for a card to get from Wisconsin to Iowa, but that would be plenty of notice.

All were in agreement, so we started to hammer out details. Hours later, we had the foundation of a plan. There was much work to be done.

CHAPTER 36

"When faced with fight or flight, Beryl manages to find a way to do both." – Maggie Janowicz

"I am resistant to bullets," Moto boomed as he approached the gatehouse. "Do not fire your weapon. If you shoot you may hurt innocents, but you will not hurt me."

Maggie and I slipped through the gate that Moto had muscled ajar. My hands and legs were so shaky, I struggled to get through the gate more than I should have needed to. We were really doing it – storming the castle, rescuing my brothers. I don't know how Moto and Maggie could seem so calm. I suppose it would help to be invulnerable like Moto or wrapped up in your work like Maggie. Still, my legs felt like they were made of rubber bands.

Maggie had extremely bright lights attached to her forehead and the palms of her hands. She walked behind me so she and Nable could illuminate and record everything. Everything Maggie faced glowed intensely compared to the gatehouse's dim lights. After following me through the gate, Maggie quickly sidestepped around to get a better angle of me, Moto, and the gatehouse, tilting her hands to illuminate the larger area.

The guard in the gatehouse called for backup, but didn't fire his gun as Moto approached. Per the plan, I left Moto behind and headed toward The Home. Maggie stayed with Moto temporarily, and as I hop-walked as quickly as I could outside of the island of artificial light, night's velvet curtain became a little more penetrable. It was a large campus, and it seemed like an impossible distance to the building with the glass pyramid on top.

It wasn't long before Maggie and Moto caught up with my slow gait. Maggie scooted ahead of me so she could film me and Moto from the front. If I hadn't already been on the right path, I wouldn't have been able to find it because of those lights. I hadn't realized they'd be so bright. I turned to Moto – he smelled of burnt hair.

"Taser," Moto responded to my querying look. He had double scorchmarks on his chest. "I shut the guard in the gatehouse and broke the door so he can't get out. Didn't hurt him. He'll break the windows eventually, but I don't think he's in any hurry to come after us until he has backup." He didn't smile, but I could tell he was proud of how he handled the first obstacle, and I told him I was proud of him, too.

I could hear Maggie narrating as we trotted forward. I couldn't make out what she was saying, but I knew she was explaining to possible future viewers that we were here to rescue my brothers from what had been a lifelong imprisonment. Earlier, Maggie had explained to me and Seth that normally she would edit her voice on top of the video afterward, but if we got into a bind where she had to immediately post the video on the net, she wouldn't have time for edits. Maggie was our bright star, guiding us forward as she walked backward. Even though I knew we were doing the right thing, without Maggie there I would have felt guilt for breaking the rules and sneaking around. Instead, I felt like we were dashing across the front lines while a brave war correspondent reported our heroism. Her professionalism strengthened my purpose and my courage.

Unfortunately, I just wasn't built for running, and no amount of need could change that. Moto offered to carry me so we could make better time, but I declined. I couldn't fly – Maggie needed me close – but I thought maybe my wings could help. I unfurled them and started shoving air behind me to push myself forward. My slow hop-walk became a glide-hop-glide as I forced my way through the air. It was ungainly and awkward, and I thought I might trip over my own feet and fall at any moment, but it was definitely faster. Moto and Maggie had to run to keep up.

Fog puffed out of our mouths as we sped over brown lawns and curved brick pathways. Spring was coming, but she always took her sweet time arriving in Wisconsin. Most of the snow had melted earlier in the week, but solitary mounds of white glowed beside parking lots, reflecting the moonlight like ghostly sentinels. The Home loomed before us. We went straight to the front door.

Per Seth's explicit request, I made an obscene gesture at the security camera flanking the door while I said, "I'm Beryl Pritchard, and I'm here for my brothers." Then Moto bashed the door open. The metal frame warped, releasing the latch. Glass cracked into crystal spiderwebs.

As we entered, we saw a guard on a balcony over the central courtyard, but he did not approach. Instead, he spoke to his shabti, describing what he saw. We descended the main staircase and found my brothers waiting for us in Orville's room, each with a small bag packed and ready to go. Heads of other mods peeked out of doorways as they watched us pass. They didn't understand what was happening, but they could tell it was a big deal.

We knew better than to take the elevator. No better way to get yourself trapped than to climb in an elevator. Wilbur, no slouch in the strength department, carried his smaller, older brother up the steps, leaving Orville's heavy, mechanical chair behind. When we passed through the courtyard, the guard was no longer there.

So far, so good, but there would be a showdown soon. That was Maggie's role — to get us past that obstacle. Nable was continually recording raw footage, splicing new bits and removing old bits from the publishable version, and uploading everything to an external server where he could send the publishable version to dozens of places at once at Maggie's command. We had set a failsafe so that the most up-to-date version of the story would be sent to those same places in 24 hours if not countermanded. Leverage enough to buy freedom, we hoped.

We exited The Home. Maggie led the way, backing through the front door so her temple could record the exit, narrating all the way. She looked fierce, focused, and strong. Giant Moto followed beside tiny me. Little Lindy and Wilbur carrying Orville came through last. We left the light of the doorway and walked as quickly as we could through the February darkness back toward the front gate.

Wilbur couldn't carry Orville very quickly, so the trip to the gate was agonizingly long. Maggie shone one of her lights to each side every once in a while, and we could see Imhotep security shadowing us. When would they cut us off? I could hear bits of Maggie's narration: "Imprisoned against their will," "They've never before set foot outside of Imhotep grounds," and "They simply long for freedom." Good thing it was Maggie talking, because I would have used: "kidnapped," "vast conspiracy," and "Imhotep assholes." Her version was definitely more professional.

Security had massed at the front gate. Including the guards who were tailing us, there were nearly two dozen men and women who would try to bar our path, many with guns drawn. Maggie moved behind us now, so I could actually see quite well. The video would show a beautiful image of our small group, silhouetted, surrounded by a large, hostile group of security guards preventing our exit. This was the showdown.

David Craven, the main Imhotep PR guy, pushed his way front and center. Disheveled and unshaven, he had still managed to crawl into a suit. Or perhaps he slept in it. Regardless, he was a welcome sight. In order for Maggie's leverage to be worth anything, we needed somebody present who could understand its importance, and Maggie had told us repeatedly that she hoped he would be there.

"It's a little late for a walk," Craven said, hands in the air, trying to take control of the situation by playing the part of the reasonable adult. "We need to get you kids back to bed."

I stepped forward to confront him while Maggie moved to film from the side. Everything had been moving so fast, but it suddenly slowed down. This man was our obstacle. We were in the right. He was wrong. "We're going for a walk. I'd been told this isn't a prison, so certainly I should be able to take my brothers for a walk."

"I can't allow you and this dangerous individual to kidnap these residents," Craven said, acting the patriarch.

"They're my brothers, not my prisoners," I responded, "and not yours, either. They have every right to leave this place for the first time in their lives. And Moto is not dangerous."

"The gate sentry who is being taken to the hospital right now would disagree," Craven argued gently. "Moto is out of control. I simply wouldn't feel safe if you left with him. And those boys are my responsibility."

I didn't look back at Moto. I trusted him and needed him to know it. "I was careful," he whispered behind me. "I did him no injury. I was careful." Thankfully, Maggie had been with Moto when he had handled the guard, so she could prove what really happened. Without a perfect record of everything, Imhotep had an opening for trickery, legal and otherwise. Thank goodness for Maggie.

"You'll be happy to know that your responsibility has been lifted," I said. "Because I'm taking them out of here. Now." I tried to sound commanding and confident, or at least reduce the squeakiness of my normal voice. "If you stop me, we'll send a recording of all of this onto the net. We have connections," I said with a meaningful glance toward Maggie.

Craven looked at Maggie, too. I hadn't realized until that moment that Maggie had just sacrificed her career as a reporter in this modern world. She would be blacklisted, unable to find any kind of mainstream journalistic work. In the glance between them, I could see that Craven knew that Maggie understood this. He frowned as he became aware that he had nothing to hold over her – she had nothing to lose.

"You won't be able to get anybody to publish this," Craven said. Unspoken, he meant that nobody would publish it because a flurry of business-crippling lawsuits would follow.

"We live in an automated world," I responded. "It will be published hours before any editor lays eyes on it, because they'll assume that an editor already has. It will be *everywhere*. Instantly. It's all ready to go, and as soon as we give the word, it will be published. And there's nothing you can do to stop it."

I waited a few seconds for Craven to think it through. Then I started walking toward the gate, followed by my brothers. Moto brought up the rear. Craven motioned for security to stand down. They parted as we passed.

"We certainly don't keep anybody against their will," Craven said while Maggie's passed him, her silent gaze recording every forced crinkle on his landscaped face. "We'll send an escort to make sure you're safe, in case of a medical emergency or some other mishap."

We were through the gate. "No you won't," I responded, not even turning around.

Moto stayed in front of the gate. Maggie stayed with me and my brothers. She had to make sure we made it to the car where Seth waited for us. The lights of the gatehouse were bright. Moto stood dark against the light, the guards small before him. Maggie backed away, watching the gate as it got smaller behind us. Without Maggie's lights, the road ahead was dark and quiet. As we left Imhotep grounds and entered a residential area, I expected to see eyes peering from windows. But despite the banging of my heart in my chest, the excitement had been quiet so far. Not enough to rouse the neighbors.

During the planning, Moto had volunteered to be left behind. He knew he could hold them off long enough, and he felt it was an appropriate penance for what happened with Natalia. He did not fear jail. He did not fear the guards. Born to be a soldier, he relished the opportunity to live up to his potential, providing freedom for those weaker than himself.

I wasn't so much that they'd try to capture us – Maggie's presence prevented that. It was that we couldn't have them follow us, and the Imhotep front gate was the best natural bottleneck.

We were three blocks away when we saw a couple of guards on silent scooters heading for the gate. If they could slip past Moto, they would be able to get to us too far away from our protector. But Moto saw them. He leapt forward, clotheslining the guard astride one, and kicking the front wheel out from under the other. He quickly disabled each machine.

It looked like we were home free, so Maggie raced back toward the gate to keep recording Moto. If she could keep him in her sight, she might be able to keep him safe. Besides, she didn't want our getaway car in the recording – we didn't want to provide any clues as to our escape.

We turned the corner and could no longer see the gate as we approached Seth's car, already warmed up and ready to roll. Natalia was in the car; she would join us on the farm. Ant was there too, and I gave her my shabti, Bí, with instructions to take good care of her. Ant raced off into the darkness. Anybody using GPS to trace my shabti to find us would have a heck of a wild goose chase in store.

A loud squeal of tires broke the silence. I could tell it came from Imhotep. While my brothers jumped into the car, I flew up to a roof to see what was happening. An Imhotep security car raced toward the gate. Crap. I didn't know if we'd be able to lose a car if it saw us. Seth normally drove as if being chased, but I didn't have confidence that her rickety old beast of a car would be able to outrun a professional.

As the car approached the gate, Moto didn't back away. Instead, he ran to the guard station on the side the car sped toward. He grabbed a cement column, and as the car sped past, he used his other hand to grab the wheel well of the vehicle. The vehicle lurched upward and to the side and Moto was forced to let go. Due to the change of momentum and direction, the car rolled, over and over. It wouldn't be chasing us anywhere.

Well, that would wake the neighbors. I could hear Seth whisper-yelling up to me. Moto didn't look so good. He stood, maintaining his place in front of the gate. I could see fluid, probably blood, dripping from his hand. His arm hung low on one side, dislocated at the shoulder. He breathed heavily. Multiple guards approached with tasers. Multiple hits, and a cry of agony. He went down. The guards swarmed forward to surround Maggie. It happened so fast.

Time to get out of there. I glided down to Seth's car, and we took off, away from the gate and Ant's departure route. My heart stuck in my throat. God, I hoped they hadn't killed Moto.

BOOK THREE

CHAPTER 37

"Ferocity and Desperation are very different, but the latter can certainly bring out the former." –
Zosser Gallo

"You don't need to worry so much," I told Craven the next day. "They're in hiding. They're not exposing The Home to the general public. I'm not exposing The Home to the general public. So why don't you let me out of here so you have the privacy to unclench just a little bit?" Yes, I was belligerent, but they'd been questioning me for hours, and I had lost my patience.

After Beryl's great escape, Imhotep security promptly brought me back to Imhotep where Craven could try to charm, threaten, and cajole me into telling him where she took her brothers. It was the same room where I had interviewed Amai and the other Imhotep coworkers. The room was far less pleasant on this side of the table.

"I've got all the cards, Craven," I said. "Give me back my shabti and let me go, or you'll be caught in the biggest shitstorm whirlwind you've ever seen. As Imhotep's PR guy, that's not where you want to be."

He had been working me for quite a while, and he was at the end of his rope. He had threatened my job. He had appealed to my sense of responsibility toward the health of the Pritchard boys. He had played the good cop and the bad cop. In short, he produced more baloney than 1980s Oscar Meyer, and I wasn't having any of it.

"Look, this is very simple," I said. "There aren't a lot of choices in this scenario. If I tell you where the kids are, you lock them up. If I don't tell you where the kids are, you keep me locked up. It's a pretty easy choice, and one that I've already made.

"So it's your turn to make a choice. The video is my leverage. If you leave my family and the Pritchard family alone, we keep it under wraps. Otherwise it comes out." Craven was clearly agitated at this point, eyes twitching like insects on flypaper.

"There's no point in arguing," I continued. "Your choice is so easy, it's not even worth talking about."

"What if we wipe your shabti?" he asked, knowing that was a horrible violation.

"It just means I'll be more pissed than I already am," I responded tartly. "We've already gone over this. The story will be published at a predetermined date and time unless I postpone it. If you don't give me the means and motivation to do that, you better deploy your shit umbrella."

"What if we hack into your shabti and take control?" he asked.

"If he detects it, he publishes instantly. If not, and if you're quick enough, you might be successful." I looked him in the eyes like an alpha wolf, reinforcing my leverage with sheer animal willpower. "But you're running out of time, and it's an awful risk."

The room was cool, but I could see a bead of sweat on his brow. I was surprised he hadn't surgically removed each of his sweat pores.

"You may want to consult with Morrow on this," I said. "It's an awfully big decision."

He stormed out of the room, clearly rattled. I wasn't as confident as I had been playing it, but I felt like things were going my way. I had no qualms about publishing the story if I needed to – in fact, I felt like the world had a right to see it – but when you have something over somebody and no other way to protect yourself, you hang onto it as long as you can. Besides, at this point I wanted to get Nable back in one piece… not likely if I used up my only leverage.

I also figured Beryl and company were still on the loose and undiscovered, otherwise Craven would have used that against me somehow. I had no idea what time it was, but if as many hours had passed as it felt like, they had probably arrived at Sarah and Jeremy's farm. I knew they'd be safe there.

When the door opened next, it wasn't Craven or Morrow who came through it. It was Audrey and Jerry Pritchard. My heart cried a silent 'Fuuuuuck'.

Audrey looked cold as ice. I couldn't tell if it was anger or concern underneath, but whatever emotions she was repressing were strong ones. Jerry looked panicked and angry. I didn't know what Craven had told them, but I would bet he used the word "abducted" a few times.

"Good morning," I greeted them warily.

"What have you done with our daughter?" Jerry asked aggressively, standing beside the table with clenched fists.

"I have done nothing with your daughter," I answered, watching those fists closely. "I merely recorded her rescue of her brothers."

"What's this bullshit about brothers and rescues?" he raged, face reddening. "You've been feeding her self-serving lies, and now she's gone because you want to ride on her shoulders. You want to be famous by tearing our family apart."

These people were tense and distraught, and I couldn't blame them. Beryl was their daughter, after all. Despite a confrontational adrenaline rush, I tried to put myself in a happy, patient place where I could deal with them respectfully. They deserved that much. Not easy after yakking with Craven for a few hours.

"Your daughter's opinions are her own," I responded semi-coolly. "Her definition of family is her own. Her desire to enable Orville, Wilbur, and Lindy to leave this place was her own."

"I'm not just along for the ride. I care about Beryl. I am helping her. But I'm helping her do what she wants to do. I'm not shaping her. She's shaping the world around her, now."

"She's just a kid!" Jerry snapped.

"A smart, kind, empathetic kid who could tell Orville was bordering on suicidal and needed to get out of there," I responded.

"Do you know where they are?" Audrey asked.

"Yes," I answered.

"Where are they?" she asked.

I appreciated Audrey's direct approach over Jerry's ridiculous accusations. Despite the anguish both of them clearly felt, I wouldn't reveal their location. "They've found somewhere safe," I responded. "They plan to hide out for a while. Get a taste of freedom. I don't know what they'll choose to do after that."

This did not reassure Jerry at all, but Audrey seemed to loosen up a little bit. The temperature warmed from icy glare to her normal cool and calculating.

"Look," Jerry glowered, shaking his finger in front of my face. "She's not your daughter. That's my little girl out there. If anything happens to her..." Instead of the expected threat, he choked back a sob. His eyes welled up and he turned away. Dammit. I preferred the accusations over heart wrenching concern.

I didn't know how to respond except to say, "I don't know what's best for your daughter. I'm working under the assumption that she knows."

Audrey gave me a good long look, then led Jerry out of the room. She knew she wouldn't get anything out of me, and Jerry was a mess and needed to get out of there. Audrey didn't trust me, but she didn't have a good counter-explanation, either. She must have come to the conclusion that, at the very least, my story was plausible.

I had survived Craven's onslaught of parental guilt.

That must have been the last arrow in his quiver, because nobody came in after the Pritchards left. The door was locked, so I wasn't going anywhere. I was left alone with my thoughts, wondering what time it was, what was happening outside, and whether they were going to give Nable back to me so I could prevent the break-out video from publishing.

I missed Nable. When you have a partner in your ear every day, it feels wrong to be without him. As I laid my head down on the interview table to try to catch a nap, I remembered a conversation Nable and I had the evening before we broke the brothers out of The Home.

"I'm confused about what we're doing," he told me while I walked to a food cart near my hotel. "I thought journalism was research, interview, report. Not research, interview, assist a breakout, don't report."

"Technically, we won't be assisting anything. We'll be covering a rescue, but we won't be the active participants."

"But we are assisting," he insisted. "Our presence there will be a key element in their ability to escape. Beyond that, we helped them plan it, and you are providing the hideout."

"True. We've crossed some lines," I agreed, which was an understatement. We crossed more lines than a two year old in a coloring book. "Covering the escape is still journalism, even though it helps Beryl and her brothers. There's nothing that says that objectivity can't still be purposeful. Obviously, covering a story where there's an antagonist and a victim will usually turn the public against the antagonist. But that doesn't mean it's not fair. It can be fair to show things the way they are, even if you don't portray both points of view as equally valid, because they're often *not* equally valid. It would be unfair to try to balance them like that. If you're as objective as possible – because there's no true objectivity, we just do our best – the truth will out."

"But are you being as objective as possible?"

"No, probably not," I admitted. "So, maybe I'm less journalist and more activist at this point. I don't know. Ultimately, you're the one who will be splicing together the video we shoot tonight, so it's your perspective that will be communicated to the audience. I have full confidence in your ability to do this. Your edits are clean, grab the viewer's attention quickly, and tell a story. I can't imagine that the result of your edits would be subjective, untrue, or unfair. If we hadn't colluded prior to the rescue, I'd call it solid journalism."

"But you did collude."

"I know." All I could do was shrug and sigh. "I feel like I broke some rules, but I also feel like I did the right thing. I don't know how to process that." I wasn't sure how Nable would process it, either.

"And what about not publishing the story? Isn't our purpose to get the truth out there?"

"Yes, but it's also important to be responsible with reporting. It's important to understand the consequences to people. If I publish this, what might happen?"

"What about the other residents of The Home?" Nable asked. "By not publishing, you leave them trapped in silence."

"Yeah, there are consequences of not publishing a story, too," I sighed. "Nable, I don't know what the right decision is. Until I do, we'll stick with the plan and sit on it. We have a goal here, and if all goes well three young men will experience their first taste of freedom tomorrow. At the very minimum, we will accomplish that one good act," I said with a smile.

CHAPTER 38

"Does technology influence culture or does culture influence technology? You might as well ask if the body influences the brain." – Horace Morrow

I'm not sure how much time passed after that. I woke up. Not having anything to do, I fell asleep again. This may have happened more than once.

A hand on my shoulder roughly pulled me from my light slumber. Craven and Morrow were both in the room, along with an armed goon.

"Call it off," Craven said as he shook me. "You have to call it off."

I tried to pull my thoughts together. He was referring to the video from the break-out. It must not have gone out yet. Could it have been less than a day that I had been put in this little room? It seemed like longer.

I felt very much like Beryl must have felt when she first discovered her brothers. "Things are happening," she must have thought. "I don't know what will happen next, but it won't be the same as before. My place in the world is changing." There's a certain stoic calm that can come along with that feeling. A calm that can lend strength.

"Give me Nable, let us go, and promise to leave the Pritchards and my family alone. Then I'd be happy to keep that video under my hat. It's an honest, damning story ready to go out to the world that would gravely harm your company. You might lose the Mars contract. Some of you might go to jail. You know you don't want the whole world to see it, so let's just take this one step at a time so we can all get out of this situation the easy way." Even though I hadn't seen the video, I knew it was my best work.

Craven put my shabti on the table. Relief washed over me. I put it in my ear and called out for Nable.

No response.

"Nable?" I asked. "Are you there?"

Craven, Morrow, and I waited with the same baited breath. Nothing but silence.

"What, is this a joke?" I asked. They did not appear to be joking. "What have you done?"

"We tried hacking in and he fragmented," Craven explained. "We hoped he was still in there somehow and you'd be able to call him back. But I think he's gone."

"Gone?" I asked, unbelieving. "Fragmented? What the hell are you talking about? What have you done with Nable?"

"Dammit, woman!" Morrow yelled, exasperated. "We don't have time for this! You have to keep that video from going out!"

"Well, you've kind of fucked yourselves, then," I said with a placid anger. As I took Nable's corpse out of my ear, my confusion was quickly solidifying into a cold determination. "Without Nable, I couldn't prevent that video from going out even if I tried. In fact, it's probably already out there." Craven's plastic face melted a bit. He'd need to go to Madame Tussaud's for a checkup when this was all over.

"Dammit!" Morrow yelled. "Do you know what you've done?"

"Yes," I answered. "I showed people what you've done." And I would pay for it. I would be sued and go to jail, even though every word and image was true. But maybe I'd take some of these bastards down with me.

"You've set us back years. Maybe decades!"

"The trust is gone," I said.

"The trust is gone!" he lamented.

"Well, if you don't spend too much time in jail, you could try again," I said in a not particularly comforting tone. "Some ethical responsibility would be nice the second time around."

"How dare you lecture me!" he cried out.

"It's only fair," I replied. "I listened to you lecture me the first time we spoke. You paid me to record it. Listening is good. I learned a lot. So, I would think you could handle a few sentences coming back from the other direction."

"Bah!" Morrow fumed, gesturing with his hands as he threw my comments to the side.

That was fine. I was done with him anyway.

Right about then, the story hit the net. Nable had planned well. The story was distributed from multiple trigger points with wide dispersal. Imhotep legal had inoculated several of the major plazas against the story, but they hadn't the time or breadth to block all of our angles. And once something is out there, it's awfully hard to clamp it down.

Anything that Zeen fed or that aggregated from Zeen was a target. Small, independent news outlets also received a copy. Even that could have been stopped, but Nable went one big step further. With help from as many shabti colleagues as possible, he spammed the hell out of every social network, blog, comments section, and even email address he could find. The combined processing power of all of those shabti sent out millions of links, embedded videos, teasers, clickbait, and plaintext messages within seconds. If anybody had ever clicked on an ad for erectile dysfunction or wanted to know what superfood could help them lose belly fat, they were going to hear about the flight of Beryl Pritchard and her brothers from The Home. Then they'd send links to their friends, who would send links to their friends. Nable had made dozens of mirror sites with all of the videos, detailed interviews, and every bit of material we had. We knew they'd get shut down, but every minute they stayed up would allow more people to save copies and send it on.

The break-out video was the most compelling piece, of course, but that's not all we sent out. It was tacked to the front end of the investigation we'd been doing. We included interviews, research, and context. We worked hard to make it as objective as possible. We left out anything speculative, like material pertaining to our suspicions about the deaths of Amai and her husband. It wasn't just a video, it was a story.

The key in my mind was that it was a *good* story. Even when everything was shut down, it would travel. Kids would talk about it at school. Adults would talk about it at work. It would find its way back to the mainstream media – tainted to some degree by Imhotep PR – but the people who had seen the video would poke holes in those colorful distractions. Some would believe the lies, but many more would know the truth.

And what did that mean? I didn't know at the time. Perhaps nothing. Maybe people would just talk about it, then go on to the next story. Just a fleeting blip of information, no more significant to them than my 'Justin Bieber, where are you now?' piece from last year. But maybe people would contact their legislators. Maybe some people would make it their business. Maybe some people would apply some pressure. I didn't know, but I could hope. It was a hope worth fighting for.

Craven and Morrow were silent and pale, looking at their screens. They knew they couldn't stop it. Morrow looked at me with murder in his eyes. If our story failed to get attention, I was pretty sure he would have me killed. If it got the attention I expected, I'd be famous and they couldn't kill me without blatant disregard for the suspicion it would arouse. They'd have to try denouncing me through the justice system to throw doubt on their own guilt.

I had faith in Nable and in our work: the break-out video, the interviews, the research, the perspective of the story. I knew that everybody in the world would see it and want to know what would happen next. Finally, I could be proud of my work. It only cost me my friend and my freedom.

"Craven," I said, "pack my bags and call the cops. I'm going to jail!"

CHAPTER 39

"For years we lived anyhow with one another in the naked desert, under the indifferent heaven." –
T.E. Lawrence

When the snow melts away in Iowa, mile after mile of seemingly barren land stretches out to the horizon. Instead of sand dunes, shards of corn stalks cover rolling hills of chunky soil. Sometimes a murder of crows can be seen picking at the leavings of October's harvest. Dry remnants of leaves flutter in the wind while the land waits for rebirth.

Sarah and Jeremy's farm was a small oasis in the homogenous expanse of corn and soybean fields. Though most of Iowa's farmhouses were abandoned or torn down as industrial farms swallowed them up, small groups of community farmers survived by producing a variety of fruits and vegetables and selling them solely to regional markets and restaurants.

Though it was a community of small farms, they were still farmers, nearly as physically isolated as in the days of Laura Ingalls Wilder. They were spread out, interacted weekly rather than daily, and had no town hall, post office, or grocery store. Drones delivered mail, groceries, and store purchases. Larger shipments into and out of Davenport were carried by self-driving trucks. There was one small restaurant – a shack, really – standing alone at a crossroads that also served as a bar in the evenings and a church on Sunday mornings. The restaurant was run by one of the farm families, so it had erratic hours and was often closed during active periods in spring and fall. It was not unusual for these few, well-spaced neighbors to host a social event from time to time – especially in winter. But overall, it was an isolated, introspective existence.

Seth's car full of refugees arrived at Sarah and Jeremy's farm in eastern Iowa early in the morning after a long drive. Sarah and Jeremy lavished attention on Seth and were gracious hosts to the rest of us. Their temperaments – calm and quiet in a new-agey kind of way – were very different from their great-niece, Seth, but they embraced her wild, loud persona with pride.

The hardest thing about going into hiding is figuring out what to do. After a quick tour of the house and grounds, we weren't sure what was next. We didn't have a role to play in the community. Used to waiting indefinitely, my brothers had an easier time of it than the rest of us.

Orville reveled in his newfound freedom. He sat outside as much as possible, soaking in the sun, reading whatever book he liked from the many shelves of slowly-yellowing paper relics. Reading outside on a chilly, sunny day was so different from reading from a screen in the dark of his basement room at The Home or reading the same book he'd read several times before in the leafy courtyard under the pyramid. His fancy wheelchair left behind at Imhotep, Sarah had borrowed a simple, manual wheelchair for him from a neighbor whose husband had passed. Orville struggled with the new chair, swearing excessively, but he was getting the hang of it, and his sore arms began to strengthen. It would become a source of pride for him, one more bit of independence.

Wilbur joined merrily in the agriculture, helping Sarah and Jeremy prepare for planting. Sarah enjoyed showing Wilbur how the machines worked, and he was slowly starting to understand some of it. When he had opportunities to help, he glowed. He spent less time trying to help Orville, which gave them each a freedom of a different sort.

Lindy was hard to keep track of. He explored relentlessly, peeking around the shed, nosing around in the basement or attic of the house, and looking under clods of dirt in the fields. When not exploring, he would bounce from person to person looking for a conversation partner. Lindy struggled to find enough attention to sate his sociable nature at first, but when Sarah and Jeremy told him he could walk to the restaurant or the other neighbors' farms, he would make long treks on a daily basis. He would often leave the farm after his afternoon nap and not return until late in the night, cold but happy.

"Won't word get out about us if we talk with the neighbors?" I asked Jeremy.

"Beryl, nobody cares about us out here, and we like it that way," he answered firmly. "We're a tight-knit community, and even though we don't always agree, we look out for our own. Nobody will be squawking about you or your family as long as you don't want them to."

Natalia struggled at first, too. She didn't want to leave the house, and she seemed anxious and uncomfortable. Jeremy and Sarah were kind to her. They asked her to join in their morning yoga and evening meditation. Natalia agreed, out of politeness more than interest, and the routine gave her a sense of stability.

One day, Orville asked her if she'd like to come outside and sit with him. She agreed, again out of politeness rather than because it was something she wanted to do. They sat on the porch, watching the wind blow clouds across the sky. Orville didn't ask her any questions. He didn't talk to her. He didn't even look at her. He just sat and watched the sky. Eventually he pulled out a book and started to read.

Natalia wasn't sure what to do, so she just sat awkwardly. When she realized that Orville didn't want anything from her other than her company, if she wished, it made her strangely happy. From then on, she sat with him every day. Often, she brought a book of her own. Sometimes, she asked Orville a question and they shared some conversation, but more often they sat quietly. She helped fend off some of Lindy's manic interactions from time to time. She learned to play cribbage from Sarah and Jeremy and started to show Orville how to play.

Seth and I were restless, too. We both worried about our parents' state of mind. Seth had left a note for her mom but not with information about her whereabouts. I worried about what might have happened to Maggie, Moto, and Ant. I worried that we would be found at the farm. And I worried that we might not be found.

I flew as often as the weather allowed. Most days, it cleared my mind and heart of guilt and anxiety for a little while. It was best when a warm, dry wind flowed downhill over the Great Plains, but the sky was fickle at that time of year, and it did not go out of its way to please little old me. But even on the coldest February days, I could usually fly for a short bit. From on high, the little farming community seemed even more isolated – a few houses scattered here and there, and then nothing but turned earth and the occasional creek for miles and miles. When I flew high enough, I thought I could see the Mississippi and the urban areas clinging to it. It was so far away. Wisconsin was farther. "What's going on, there?" I wondered. "And what's next?"

One day, after we had been there for a couple of weeks, Lindy announced a field trip.

"Come on, lazy bones!" he called to us. "We're all going to meet the neighbors!" At that point, Lindy was the only one who had socialized outside of the farm.

Seth and I were bored and quickly agreed. Wilbur thought it was a great idea. Natalia slunk away, and nobody pressed it. Orville was the tough nut to crack.

"No way you're taking this freak show on tour," Orville said, gesturing at himself. "Not interested."

But Lindy knew how to push Orville's buttons. He alternated between cajoling bribes, "If you come, I'll leave you in peace for two whole days!" and comical threats, "If you don't come, I'll tell Wilbur you have a parasite in your butt and need his help getting it out." In the end, he wore Orville down to the point where he couldn't help but agree.

My brothers and I piled into Seth's car, and she drove us where Lindy directed. It was fun going to houses I had only seen from above – associating faces with homesteads. Lindy must have warned people we'd be coming, because nobody was surprised to see us. Knowing Lindy, he had probably spewed our entire story to each and every person he came across.

Though there were no mods and just about everybody was white, the neighbors had very diverse reasons for living the Iowa farm life. The Langstons were a survivalist family of eight, fully prepared for a nuclear apocalypse. The Cray and Larsen families were old farm families that had owned their land for nearly two centuries and kept finding new ways to adapt. The Clarks were Christian evangelists who were clearly opposed to the science that created us – "There should only be one person playing God, and He's not a scientist," – but very kind and respectful. Ken and Jason Wallace were a young gay couple struggling to start an organic produce business. It was our stop at the Velasquez home that we carried with us the rest of the day.

Selma Velasquez and her sisters, Carmen and Ruby, lived on the same farm together along with their husbands and children. Selma had been a lawyer in Chicago, and she and her husband, Ray, had tired of the big city life. When Selma stayed in hotels and other guests would tell her they were out of towels, she knew she needed to get away. She wanted to live someplace quiet and friendly where they knew their neighbors and had plenty of space for extended family. Iowa fit the bill.

Their farm was by far the most active, with kids playing games between the grain bins and houses. Selma and Ray's house was small and cozy, but looked bigger on the inside than it did from the outside. They had two children, Luis (a twelve year old who wouldn't sit still) and Victor, eighteen, who wheeled up in a motorized wheelchair.

I didn't know what to do when Victor was introduced. Outside of my brother, I had never seen anyone in a wheelchair before. Certainly never a normie. I wondered if he had been in an accident, but he didn't look quite right, like he was shrunken somehow. I didn't know what to say.

"Nice wheels," Orville commented. "You caught me on a bad day," he said, referencing his manual wheelchair. "My Lamborghini is at home."

Victor laughed at that. "I might have a tricycle you can borrow if your chair breaks down."

"Oh, you're going to start right off by mocking my ride, eh?" Orville retorted gently. "It may not look like much, but you'd be surprised at what a lummox-powered vehicle can do," he pointed at Wilbur behind him. Suddenly the center of attention and not sure why, Wilbur smiled broadly.

"I'm sure you would easily win a race," Victor ceded graciously. "Why are you in a chair?" he asked. "Weren't you modified?" He looked confused, wondering why, if given the choice, anybody would be modified to be disabled.

"They screwed me up in the lab," Orville replied. "They were trying to get fancy, and they didn't quite get it right."

"My creators didn't quite get me right, either," Victor added, nodding to his parents, who looked mildly embarrassed.

"Duchenne," Ray interjected. "It's a kind of muscular dystrophy."

"Isn't that genetic?" I asked.

"Yup," Victor said. "Mom was the carrier. I had a 50-50 shot."

"But how does that happen anymore?" I asked. In my wealthy suburb, I had never seen anybody with a congenital disease before. I couldn't imagine it. Though cosmos and heavies were rare, screening and IVF with minor modifications for health reasons were extremely common. I knew there were still genetic diseases out there that hadn't been cured yet, but surely these single-gene diseases had all been wiped out by now. How could his mother have not gotten screened?

"It's only recently that we've been economically strong," Selma answered. "We didn't have much for health insurance back when Victor was born while I was still in school. The tests were more expensive then, and we couldn't have done anything about it anyway. Victor was a happy accident. We took our chances and ended up with a fine young man."

"I had good health before the atrophy started to really settle in," Victor said. "A good childhood. And now we have good insurance-"

"Thus the sweet ride," Orville interrupted.

"For sure!" Victor grinned with pride.

"Will you get better?" I asked.

"No, I'll get worse," Victor answered. "Probably won't live past forty."

"My understanding is that you're not missing much," Orville advised from behind the back of his hand. "Live hard while we're young and leave the rest behind to get all wrinkly and crustified." He nodded sagely, and Victor laughed appreciatively.

Again, I was appalled. Not so much at my brother's comments as the situation. We've figured out how to prevent these diseases. How many people still suffer from them? It couldn't just be this one family in Iowa. What about countries outside the United States?

When flying, I feel like I have a greater perspective because I can see more. But I'd only been seeing my little town of Memphis, Wisconsin. I had never really thought about, let alone seen, any of the rest of the world, and as realization of the grand scope of it all began to sink in, I quickly became confused and overwhelmed by the inequity of it all.

While Orville and Victor wheeled outside to talk about the finer points of how to pick up girls from a wheelchair, I enjoyed refreshments with Seth, Lindy, Wilbur, and the Velasquez parents and for the first time really began to understand that diversity is more than what you look like, and that there was a wide world of different people out there. I realized that I didn't understand most of them, and that they wouldn't understand me.

But maybe I was wrong. Maybe we're not really that different. How different are Orville and Victor, after all? They seemed to understand each other right away, despite completely different circumstances behind their disabilities. I couldn't wrap my head around this new perspective.

Later, when we were back on Sarah and Jeremy's farm, I asked Orville what he thought of the day.

"I'm glad Lindy pushed me into it," he replied. "I really enjoyed meeting Victor."

"A new friend?" I asked.

"Maybe," Orville responded, "but more importantly it helped me understand that we're not alone."

"I don't understand."

"I was always under the impression that we were in The Home because we were sick and everybody else was healthy," he continued. "But that's not true. There are probably tons of folks out there like me and Victor, and there are others who started out healthy and had debilitating accidents. And they're free. They're independent.

"Victor gets around, Beryl. He goes camping and interacts with whoever he wants to and will move away from his parents sometime soon. He has a full, interesting life where he makes the choices. It can be done, Beryl!" he said with surprising optimism. "That could be me! I always hoped but doubted myself.

"I'm never going back to The Home," he stated definitively.

"Okay," I replied.

CHAPTER 40

"Context can be as tangled as a cypress swamp." – Matthew Bog

The police in Memphis knew very well who was buttering their bread, so I was in jail for several days before I was allowed to speak with anyone. I had no idea what was going on outside, but there must have been a shitstorm or I would have rotted in there for a lot longer. I never got a phone call, but my lawyer managed to find me.

Technically, Matthew Bog wasn't my lawyer. He was my favorite legal contact – my go-to guy – when writing a story where I needed an explanation or clarification. Also true, he was my favorite lawyer by default because he was the only lawyer I liked, but hey… lawyers.

Matt was a straight shooter in a world of curved bullets. We met in college – both of us journalism majors – but he saw the way the wind was blowing and switched tracks to law. "Law's got journalism by the neck right now," Matt had said, "and I'm fond of my neck." He had given me good advice a couple of times so that I still had mine. We didn't keep in touch as much as I'd like, but we both admired and trusted one another.

Beyond being a good friend, he was also damned brilliant. He wasn't the sort who stands in a courtroom and gives heart wrenching speeches to help an innocent man beat an unsubstantiated murder claim. No, Matt was brilliant because he was fascinated by law. He immersed himself in books, journal articles, and followed major cases and causes before, during, and after they hit the Supreme Court. He wasn't the guy you wanted in the courtroom with you. He was the guy you wanted to make sure your courtroom guy consulted with before the trial. Matt knew precedents, he had context, and above all, he understood how law *evolved* over time. It was hard to get him to shut up about it.

For example, he was obsessed with the Citizens United ruling of 2010. "Citizens United, one of the most controversial rulings of our century, was a tipping point," he would say. "For the first time, a corporation had the rights of a person. Later rulings allowed corporations' rights to trump the rights of a person in cases of conflict, because a corporation is made up of more than one person, right? That's not a broad leap, because the ability to spend hundreds of times more in campaign donations than an individual person – particularly a poor one – gives corporations more rights, more power, in determining elections than an individual. In other words, the First Amendment rights of a corporation become greater than the rights of a person. Which has a direct impact on journalism."

I was in jail and needed help with charges of libel, kidnapping, and breaking-and-entering, so I didn't expect to hear more about Citizens United. I certainly didn't *want* to hear about it. But some things in life are beyond our control.

He had seen the retrospective. He had seen the break-out video that Nable spammed everywhere. Before talking about my defense, he was determined to hear the entire story and talk about how it related to the law.

So I told him. The whole thing. From the beginning. It took several days, because our time together was limited. I didn't have anywhere to go, so I didn't try to hurry along, but it was still a little frustrating when he'd go off on a tangent. The thing is, when he'd start talking about this stuff, he somehow managed to make it absolutely fascinating. Sometimes I couldn't help but encourage him, like when he told me that Beryl's forced sterility was entirely legal.

"It's true," he said, and he had that Citizens United gleam in his eye, so I knew we were about to go on a wild ride.

"No way," I said, trying to stem the tide. "This didn't happen because of Citizens United."

"No, of course it didn't start there," he said, practically bouncing in his seat. "But in some ways, the early rulings on genetics and 'ownership' led up to CU.

"Back in 1980, the Supreme Court ruled in Diamond v. Chakrabarty that genetically altered life can be patented. That sounds normal to us – you've seen some of those patents at Imhotep. But think about it for a minute," he said, pausing. "Life can be patented."

I thought about that for a minute, but I wasn't sure I understood. "So, can parents who have kids the old fashioned way take out a patent on their kid's genome?"

"Nope!" Matt replied. "Manufacture or invention is a necessary component. They ruled that whether the invention is living or not is irrelevant to patenting." He pulled up some exact wording on his screen.

'The relevant distinction was not between living and inanimate things, but between products of nature, whether living or not, and human-made inventions. Here, respondent's microorganism is the result of human ingenuity and research.'

'His discovery is not nature's handiwork, but his own; accordingly it is patentable subject matter.'

"Of course, there was a dissenting opinion that said that Congress should determine what is and isn't patentable. Patents aren't in the Constitution, so it's really not up to the Supreme Court to lay down the law on this. But they did.

"Ultimately," Matt said, pushing the screen aside, "Chief Justice Burger's opinion stated that Congress intended for patents to include 'anything under the sun that is made by man'. Pretty broad! I'm not sure that's what Thomas Jefferson had in mind, but that's where we are. All that from a case about an oil-eating microorganism."

"But what about roses?" I asked. "I know that there are species of rose that are patented that were not created by genetic modification. They were created by selective breeding. How is that patentable?"

"Yeah, it gets a little fuzzy there," Matt admitted. "Since the Plant Patent Act of 1930, it's been legal in the U.S. to patent plants created asexually, like from cuttings. In 1970, the Plant Variety Protection Act added broader rights to protect distinct plant varieties. But those are very specific cases with specific laws around them. For the most part, living organisms weren't patentable until the 1980 ruling. There must be a definable difference between the product organism and what can be found in nature. Two humans falling in love, doing it, and making a kid with genes inherited randomly from the parents isn't going to cut it. However, just about every country now says that once you start plunking in genes not normally found in the organism, it's patentable.

"Thus, a human modified so that they could not have hemophilia would not be patentable because there are lots of people out there who don't have hemophilia. The genetic structure is found in nature. In cases like that, biotech companies patent the *process* rather than the result.

"Similarly, the *discovery* of a gene and what it does isn't patentable, as ruled by the Supreme Court in 2013. They ruled unanimously that the discovery of BRCA genes that, when mutated, cause a high correlation of breast and ovarian cancer did not give the discoverer exclusive rights to testing for those mutations. Unanimous decisions can be hard to come by in the Supreme Court, so it was a significant decision. And as part of that decision, they reaffirmed that *changing* the genes is patentable.

"In other words, you can't patent a set of genes that are responsible for cats having paws, but you can patent a human who is modified so that they have cat paws in place of hands."

I got it, but I didn't like it. "Hasn't this been controversial before now?"

"Of course!" Matt responded. "And this is what's so relevant to your friend's situation."

"At about the same time as the BRCA lawsuit, an Indiana farmer filed suit against Monsanto, a huge agricultural biotech company. Monsanto sells a large number of genetically modified crops that can help prevent weeds because they're resistant to a very effective herbicide that kills pretty much anything else. The result is high yields, which farmers like. Monsanto seeds quickly became the most successful, popular products on the market.

"So this farmer bought soybean seed from a local grain elevator for planting. The seed came from crops planted by local farmers, including a large number of soybeans that were second generation Monsanto beans. In other words, farmers would buy seed from Monsanto, plant it, and then sell the resulting crop to the grain elevator. This particular farmer bought beans from the elevator, and even though those beans were meant to be sold as commodities, the farmer planted them as seed. He didn't buy them directly from Monsanto. Subsequently, instead of buying future seed from Monsanto or the elevator each year, he'd sell a portion of his crop and save some to become next year's seed. Back in the olden times, that's how farming was done. You grow a crop, you keep enough for seed for the next year, and you sell or eat the rest.

"Monsanto said that he infringed on their patent by producing soybeans with genes that only they had the right to produce. The farmer argued that the crops were produced by a natural process and that the patent rights only applied to the first generation.

"Monsanto won, of course. Another unanimous decision from the Supreme Court. In an interesting side note, one of the chief justices used to be a lawyer for Monsanto, but I don't think it really mattered. The important piece here is that when you patent a new genetic structure, you have patent rights over that organism *and its progeny*. In other words, you own reproductive rights over that organism."

"Holy shit." I was starting to see where this was leading.

"Yup. Even to the extent that it's the responsibility of farmers to keep their own crops pure. Cross pollination is a big deal - truly a case of birds and bees. If Monsanto genes are transferred to my crops because my neighbor's farm uses Monsanto seeds, and I knowingly produce subsequent generations of crops that contain those genes, I could be liable for patent infringement if the percentage of my crops with Monsanto genes gets high enough that it draws Monsanto's eye."

"But Beryl's human. It has to be different, right?" It's one thing to talk about microorganisms and beans and another thing entirely to talk about the rights of people. The way he was talking, it sounded like if I fucked a mod and had a baby, the owner of the mod's patent could come and take that baby like a bizarre modern-day Rumpelstiltskin.

"It would be hard to put together a case against one of these companies. First of all, the parents probably signed paperwork stating that they were knowingly signing on to a sterile child. Secondly, it could be argued that this unique organism was designed to be sterile... like a mule. Worst case, she's determined to be a separate species, which brings up a huge number of ethical and legal questions. It might be safer *not* to bring that topic to court."

"Are you kidding?" I asked.

"You know of Beryl as a person and deserving rights. But think of it from the company's point of view. The whole point of patents is to protect the rights of the inventor so that people are encouraged to invent. The company can't make money on their invention if they lose control over production and distribution. If two teenagers in the backseat of a car can make the same product as my lab, I'm out of business.

"Furthermore, from a layperson's point of view, I'm not sure the majority of the public are ready for the mass, uncontrolled introduction of Beryl's genes into the human gene pool. Fuzzy ears is one thing, but the scope of genetic changes for heavy mods is alarming to a lot of people."

My mind raced. It just didn't make sense. "You can't just go around sterilizing people. That can't be right."

"Well, there we get back to the evolution of law. Early in the 20th century, eugenics was a popular idea. We hadn't discovered the importance of DNA yet, but we knew that traits could be passed along through breeding. First came marriage laws prohibiting certain types of people from marrying. Later came laws legalizing compulsory sterilization. Buck v. Bell in 1927, another Supreme Court ruling, set a precedent by allowing mentally retarded people to be sterilized under a Virginia law. Tens of thousands of people were forcibly sterilized every year for decades. And you can bet that race and class factored heavily in decisions on who got sterilized.

"In the 1970s, many racially-motivated sterilizations done without the victim's consent received a lot of attention, and many laws were repealed. Some folks even received reparations years later. The laws evolved. However, no ruling ever overturned Buck v. Bell, and the Supreme Court has never held that compulsory sterilization is unconstitutional.

"With those precedents and our current corporation-friendly Supreme Court, a ruling in Beryl's favor is highly unlikely."

"So we're stuck?" I asked. I felt hopeless. "These biotech companies *own people* and there's nothing we can do?"

"You'd need to get the laws changed," Matt answered. "Despite what seems to us like an infringement on our Constitutional rights, the courts will rule that the corporation's rights are equal to or greater than the individual's in the eyes of the Constitution." His eyes gleamed. "There's the Citizens United tie-in!"

I sighed. At least one person was happy to be having this conversation.

"But," he continued, "if we had thoughtful laws that really delved into these patent and reproductive rights issues, then it would be tough for the courts to rule against those laws. Not impossible, but tough. Part of the reason the courts took control of the patent laws was because they were so vague and poorly written. It's just that no legislator has put real thought into this. Or, if they have, they've been overwhelmed by the biotech lobby."

"So, if the laws change, we could do something?"

"Probably not retroactively, but it would help future generations. Seriously, this is a relevant, volatile topic, and the lawbooks are a barren wasteland. It's no wonder the courts have been making it up as they go along. And they don't really know anything about the science. For example, in 1992, a company in Middleton, Wisconsin, was granted a patent over all bioengineered cotton plants, regardless of mechanism or the genes edited. Can you imagine the scope of that? These judges are feeling around in the dark."

I felt terrible for Beryl. I didn't know if she'd ever even thought about having children or ever would, but it felt wrong that she had no choice in the matter. No rights. If our only hope for change was to get legislators to produce thoughtful laws that restricted corporate rights, we were in trouble.

"What were we talking about?" I asked, shaking my head. "Beryl's not getting sued, and neither is Imhotep. Based on what you're telling me, we wouldn't have much hope of a case against Imhotep."

"Not on the reproductive rights issue. Probably not on the imprisonment issue, either," he agreed.

"Aren't we supposed to be talking about *my* case?"

"We were, but you were so interested in hearing about Citizens United."

I shook my head. He knew very well that he wanted to talk about it more than I did. Still, it was interesting, and the context helped me understand our chances in that legal climate.

"Well, maybe we can get back to talking about my case, now," I suggested.

"I'd love to, but I'm afraid we're out of time," he said, rolling his screen around his arm and standing to leave. "I'll be back tomorrow."

Lawyers.

CHAPTER 41

"You don't know what you don't know. You can just be sure that nobody's going to tell you." –
Orville Pritchard

The crowd murmured excitedly as I crouched on the Perch. They weren't there for me this time, and I couldn't have been prouder. I whispered something positive – was it 'good luck' or 'have fun'? – into Alouette's feather-covered ears. She smiled a huge, goofy smile in response. She was wired, hopping and squeaking non-stop – both because of the attention and because this would be her first flight. She had been preparing for it her whole life.

The crowd was nothing like the crowd for my First Flight. The media wasn't there. The local crowd wasn't there. It was just family and friends. Seth, Thasha, Ralph, and Kammi were there. Mom and Dad held each other close. I didn't see anybody from Imhotep there, which was strange for some reason, but I couldn't remember why.

Alouette was through waiting. It was an effort to keep her from just throwing herself off the Perch. I was more nervous, checking her wing feathers one last time, making sure her radio worked and was turned on, and that she was paying attention.

"Listen to your radio," I said very clearly. "You'll be excited and may not be able to hear it at first, but listen. Talk with us. Let us know how you're doing. And land when we tell you to land." I knew that my advice might be pointless, but it was still worth giving.

"Okay, Mom!" she answered. "Can I go now?"

I took a deep breath. "Okay. I'll be watching. Let me know if you need help."

She nodded, turned, and launched herself from the edge of the Perch, gliding briefly, then masterfully pushing herself higher with powerful strokes.

I was beside her, pushing myself upward as well. The wind tickled my feathers. The force of the streaming air pushing against my wings felt wonderful as always, but my attention was on Alouette beside me. We both spun into a hard dive, angling toward a stand of oak, then pulling up, rustling fresh spring leaves with our wake.

She had a goofy grin on her face, mouth pulled back with such force of ecstasy that I wondered if she even knew I was there beside her. Then she turned her head to look at me, and I could see myself in her eyes, and there was so much joy.

I woke up crying, filled with that joy and glad I had met the little girl I would never know in real life.

* * * * * *

We all watched Maggie and Nable's story when it came out. It was compelling, empathetic and truthful, and the whole world saw it. The central news agencies tried to ignore it at first, but when that became awkward and suspicious, they caved and started covering it. They probably figured they couldn't be liable for harm to Imhotep if everybody already knew about it. News crews came to Milwaukee and Memphis. I could see the driveway of my house in the background of live shots. Imhotep PR made calculated statements, but Craven was nowhere to be seen. Debates about the veracity of the story raged on the 24-hour news plazas. There were also the expected debates about who was the hero and who the villain in this scenario, and it was surprising that people who knew so little could say so much.

Of course, everybody wanted to know where we were.

It was common knowledge that Moto was in jail. Depending on which talking heads you listened to, he was either a demon or a knight. Most of the charges against him were straightforward, and he planned to plead guilty to breaking and entering and destruction of property. He planned to fight the assault and battery charges as a defense of others, but odds weren't good, and he was expected to be sentenced to an additional year or two in prison. Sometimes the panelists on the news plazas (who had probably never met a heavy mod) talked about Moto and Ann at the same time, decrying the increase in mod violence. As if there were anything similar in their actions. They would reference Ann's imprisonment of Natalia as "mod-on-mod violence", whatever that was, and imply that as modifications increased, so would violence. Seth and I talked about it a lot, and it wasn't fair to either of them – nor to the rest of us.

Maggie was also in jail, and the media seemed very confused about what to make of her. Her gangly, excitable lawyer was the only one who had been able to see her, and he wasn't much for making comments to the media outside of obscure legal references. Either he was a brilliant manipulator whose end game hadn't yet been revealed, or he was completely incompetent. The latter seemed more likely.

Nobody knew where the rest of us had disappeared to, though the "experts" weren't afraid to guess: Canada, Mexico, a den of crime lords in Chicago, a dairy barn near La Crosse, a secret government bunker, a wildlife refuge, and even stranger speculations. The media wasn't aware of Seth or Natalia. They were just looking for me and my brothers. Or rather, they were talking about me and my brothers. I'm sure Imhotep was looking for us.

I worried that they would find us. I'd turn a corner and William would be standing there, crunching a rodent, gun pointed at my head. The others were finding it easy to relax into this state of hiding indefinitely, but the more time went by, the more stressed and insecure I became. It wasn't just that I knew they'd find us eventually. It was leaving Maggie and Moto behind. It was leaving my parents and Beth behind. I felt like I had left myself behind.

I felt a great deal of guilt about Maggie's situation. Among other charges, she was accused of abduction, theft, duress, coercion, and libel. The prosecution would make the case that, through threats and negative influence, Maggie convinced me to break into The Home and abduct my brothers to further her own career by smearing Imhotep's reputation. I hoped the video would have given her enough leverage to retain her freedom, but she must have been in a terrible position to have been forced to release it so soon. Even so, every day she spent in jail bought a day of freedom for my brothers.

In all, there was no consensus among the knowledge of the masses as to what had happened, which is a dangerous place to be. Any little thing could swing the weight of opinion toward one side or the other, and Imhotep PR was working hard to push that swing. At first there was universal outrage as people learned about The Home for the first time. Then, as more details emerged, Imhotep had opportunities to put their own spin on the information. They were on the talk shows. They flooded the blogs and vlogs with content. They pandered to the news yaks. They played the game, and it made people doubt what they had seen. Some felt like Maggie had played them for suckers, even though everything in her report was factual. The scales tilted back to equilibrium.

Meanwhile, aside from one wacky lawyer, nobody was fighting for Maggie. She couldn't even fight for herself, because they wouldn't let her out or anybody else in. Even though I was young, I had seen enough cases sway due to the inertia of public opinion that I dreaded the passing of each day as momentum slowly increased for Imhotep.

On the other hand, my brothers and Natalia were growing like plants moved into a larger pot. Orville spent every day outside, sunup to sundown. It didn't matter if it was cold, raining, snowing, or worse. He'd just sit on the porch and smile, ice coating his beak. Wilbur felt appreciated and useful and felt at home with Jeremy and Sarah. Lindy was the social busybody he had always wanted to be. And Natalia, though quiet, seemed to feel safe and comfortable and had established friendly relationships with Sarah and Orville.

One day after I came down from a flight, Jeremy told me, "You all can stay here as long as you like."

I sighed, simultaneously relieved and distressed by his kindness. My brothers needed more time here, but I knew we were a burden. Jeremy and Sarah didn't have a big income or a lot of wiggle room in their finances. They did everything around the farm themselves. They ate preserved food out of jars as much as possible and sent out to the grocery for only the necessities. With food consumption tripled thanks to us over the last few weeks, their food stores from last year's harvest were quickly dwindling. There were only so many pickled beets to go around.

"Thank you for welcoming us here," I said. "It's been so important for Orville. For all of us, really."

"Well, Wilbur's been real helpful getting ready for planting. I bet we get crops in the ground twice as fast this year. And maybe you can take some pictures from up high so you can show me where our veggies need a little more attention," Jeremy grinned. "We can find ways for you to earn your keep, if that's what you're worried about."

"No, that's not it," I replied.

"You homesick?"

"Worried about my friends and family. About Maggie."

"Aw, Maggie can take care of herself," Jeremy responded. "Heck, I think she needed the challenge."

"Maybe," I grimaced. "I just can't help but feel like they're stuck dealing with a mess that I left behind."

"Well, that's probably true," Jeremy agreed. A sharp pang of guilt made my heart skip a beat. "Sometimes things work out where the burden lies greater on some folks for a while. Your friends chose to take that on. Some folks don't get that choice."

I nodded, but I wasn't convinced.

"You met Victor," Jeremy continued. "He's not the only one here who was born with health struggles or came upon them later. Most folks don't have the money or insurance to do fancy dances with genetics on our kids. Some wouldn't do it anyway for their own reasons. Bottom line is that we have kids the old fashioned way, and that doesn't always turn out so well.

"When that happens, it's not a burden that parents choose, but it's family so it's a burden they'll gladly bear."

I had been doing some research since we met the Velasquez family, and I learned pretty quickly that this big world is not all just like suburban Milwaukee. It's not just the rural areas or other countries, either. Communities as close as Milwaukee and Chicago had large populations with no health insurance and no genetic screening or manipulation. I had assumed that the basic benefits of genetic manipulation were available to everybody, and my mind stuttered at its new perception of the world. I hadn't realized that children were born with osteogenesis worse than Lindy's weak bones, that children were born who had more trouble joining thoughts than Wilbur, whose bodies were more warped than Orville's.

"My point," Jeremy continued, "is that your friends, including Maggie, had a choice. Sarah and I have a choice. Not everybody gets a choice, but we did. We've chosen to take you in, and you can stay here as long as you want."

"Thank you," I said. "I just don't know what to do next."

"I'm sure it will come to you," Jeremy replied. "Sometimes we don't make the choice – we just get blown in front of the wind."

CHAPTER 42

"Iris says that if I just keep trying, I can do anything. I don't think that's right all the time, but I didn't say anything. I didn't want to hurt her feelings." – Wilbur Pritchard

Without Nable in my ear and only seeing Matt for an hour a day, I had devolved into talking to myself most of the time. Though I knew that Nable and I were a team, I was surprised by how much I missed him, and when I talked to myself my thoughts were often framed as if he were present. So much so that I found myself asking thin air to retrieve information or give me a new angle on a particular aspect of my situation.

It surprised me how often I asked Nable for an opinion. I had never noticed that before, and it's not something one would normally associate with a shabti. Do others ask their shabti for opinions like that? Did I rely too much on my shabti when making decisions? Was Nable special in his ability to actually respond to those requests, or was I delusional in expecting an electronic device to provide insight?

No, although I couldn't say if Nable was different than other shabti, I knew that his cognitive abilities – including insight – were on par with my own. We were a team of equals. I just hadn't realized it until he was gone. I hoped that I had treated him fairly. I knew that in one way I hadn't – he had never been credited in any of our stories. No one had ever credited a shabti before. In the culture of the time, I think it would have gone over like giving credit to a pet or your screen, though the differences should have been obvious. It shouldn't have stopped me from doing it; I just hadn't considered it.

Assuming I ever got out of prison and was able to use a shabti again, I couldn't imagine starting over with a new one. I began to wonder if my close friendship with Nable was keeping me from having close relationships with other people. My needs for interaction were already met during every waking hour.

I had too much time to think and grieve the loss of my friend.

Every day, I prepared for my meeting with Matt. My jailkeepers were particularly unhelpful - they wouldn't allow me a screen or even paper and a pen. So, on a daily basis, I kept a mental list of the topics I wanted to discuss with Matt. He almost always pulled us off track.

"Matt, I don't care about property laws in Wisconsin!" I yelled during one of our sessions.

"Well you should," Matt responded, surprised at my outburst. "It's very interesting case law."

"If we were in your office in DC instead of a jail cell, and if I didn't have a case hanging over my head that would bankrupt me and send me to prison for years, and if we had all the time in the world, I'd be happy to discuss property law with you," I fumed. "But you're my lawyer, and you're supposed to be helping me prove my innocence here." I thrust my hands in the air in exasperation.

"But don't you see?" Matt asked. "It's all related!"

"You're just going to tie this into Citizens United again," I realized.

"Now that you mention it…" Matt began.

I shouted at him, threatening violence until he left. Not my finest moment. To his credit, he returned unfazed the next day.

"I apologize," he started right off the bat. "I know it doesn't seem like I'm working on the case. It probably seems like I'm just taking advantage of a captive audience."

"Har har."

"But when I'm here, I'm bouncing ideas off of you," he continued. "These are complex issues. For example, property laws are incredibly relevant here because the prosecution will claim that the Pritchard brothers are their property."

"Which is where the theft charge comes from," I realized. "I hadn't understood that count at all."

"I should have explained it better," Matt admitted. "Or at all." He ruffled his hands through his hair. "The decisions made in this case will have huge repercussions for future cases. We're probably going to lose – at least part of it. I'm worried about giving you the result you deserve, and I'm concerned about the implications for all of these mods everywhere."

"That's a lot of pressure," I said.

"Yeah," he agreed, "and I'm not handling it very well."

"Well, why don't we try doing this together?" I asked. "It's my future on the line, after all. Let's go through each charge, one at a time, so I understand what I'm accused of. Then we can go through our defense together so I understand that, too. You never know. I might have some bright ideas of my own."

"Of course you're right," Matt agreed. "The arraignment probably didn't make any sense to you at all."

"No, it didn't," I agreed. "But I knew I'd done no wrong, so I felt comfortable pleading innocent to every charge."

"Well, when we get through all of the charges, maybe you'll change your mind," he said.

"Not likely. If I'm going down, I'm going down fighting."

CHAPTER 43

"Most of the prisons in our world are invisible and of our own creation." – Magic Megan prior to her 2021 Guantanamo Bay performance

We were still in a cage. A more comfortable one, true, but we were not able to live normal, free lives. For the time being, it was healthy for my brothers, but that would change over time.

More importantly, there was work to do. Maggie needed help to get out of prison and defend her story. Imhotep was backing truth into a corner, but I knew that my voice could counter the lies. Maggie alone could be doubted, but people knew me – or thought they did. People wanted to hear my story. As much as I didn't want to hurl myself into the gaping maw of worldwide attention, it was time for me to leave this place of respite and do what I could.

I told Seth first. "I'm going back."

"Oh, thank GOD," she exclaimed. "This morning I nearly died of boredom. Seriously, I think my heart stopped for a minute or two. I had to beat my chest with a shoe to get 'er pumping again."

"I saw that! Wasn't that yesterday?" I asked. "I thought you said you were trying to kill a spider."

"It was a spider," Seth affirmed. "Totally separate incident."

"You want to come with me?" I asked. I hadn't really thought it through, but I'd need a ride and Seth wouldn't really be at risk.

"Of course!" she responded as if I were an idiot for suggesting otherwise. "We'll be Thelma and Louise. Just the two of us against a challenging and frightening world that threatens to engulf us with its merciless tyranny."

"We are not Thelma and Louise, and I'm not getting in a car with you again unless you admit it."

"Fine, fine…" Seth acquiesced. "How about Velma and Daphne?"

"Sure," I agreed.

"Velma and Daphne… against a challenging and frightening world that threatens to engulf us with its merciless tyranny!"

I sighed, prompting a triumphant guffaw from Seth. I was glad to have her with me.

My brothers were less enthusiastic, and it took a while to convince them not to come with me. Well, not Orville. He argued the other side.

"Look, if they lose their case, we go back into The Home. Then guess what? We're right where we started except our friends and family are in prison."

"But they're more likely to lose if we don't testify in their favor," Lindy argued.

"The justice system is a sham," Orville stated. "Our presence won't make a lick of difference."

"But we should stick together," Wilbur said.

"I am not going back," Orville said flatly. "You'd be fools to leave."

I supported Orville completely. There was little good they could do and great risk. Eventually, we all came to agree. Then it was time for goodbyes. I felt proud to have gotten them this far. They worried that I'd be thrown in jail as soon as I poked my head out of the car in Memphis. There were teary hugs and words of advice.

"Stay secret until you're ready to make your move and then do it publicly," Orville suggested. "If they silence you too quickly, you'll accomplish nothing."

"Take care of yourself and say hi to Mom and Dad," Lindy said as we embraced.

"Come back soon," Wilbur said, and I promised I would.

Natalia approached as well, thanking me and Seth for everything we had done. Her eyes filled with tears and she gave a shaky smile when she asked that we thank Maggie, Ant, and Moto as well. I'm not sure if she knew how much that would mean to Moto. Her absolution would make his incarceration worthwhile.

After a quick goodbye and words of appreciation for Sarah and Jeremy, Seth and I piled into her old beater. She started playing, "Part of Me, Part of You," which I quickly nixed. It's important to start a big trip with the right song. We settled on "It's a Good Day" by Peggy Lee and hit the road back to Wisconsin, Seth crowing with delight all the way.

CHAPTER 44

"The hardest part of jail time is not knowing what everybody else is doing." – Maggie Janowicz

There was a lot to do when we reached Wisconsin, and aside from loudly singing a variety of road songs, Seth and I did a good job planning for our arrival. I had to duck under a blanket from time to time because I was so recognizable, but we took lonely country roads most of the way, so we avoided most potential onlookers and traffic cameras.

Our first mission was to find Ant so I could retrieve Bí and Seth could start her work. A quick message to Bí from Seth's shabti, Heinrich, arranged that nicely, and Ant was calmly sitting by the side of the road as we entered Memphis. We pulled over just long enough for her to hop into the back seat, then we continued on.

Despite the GPS embedded in every shabti, neither Imhotep nor the police were able to find Bí and Ant after the escape from The Home. She had led them on a merry chase, through sewers, abandoned buildings, and mall ventilation ducts. When they finally thought they had homed in on her (on <u>us</u>, in their minds), nobody was at the coordinates. Nobody can hide like Ant. They gave it up as malfunctioning equipment, and by then, we had arrived safely in Iowa.

"A true ninja!" Seth proclaimed to Ant's delight.

Entering Memphis, I had to spend most of my time under Seth's blanket, and I had moved into the backseat. It was hot and stuffy under there, and the blanket smelled like wet dog. Ant handed Bí to me, and I thankfully put her in my ear.

"I really enjoyed my time with Ant," was the first thing she said.

"That's great!" I responded. "What's been going on?"

Bí didn't know much more than what we had learned from following the news on our screens. Maggie was in jail, working on a defense with her lawyer, Matthew Bog. Apparently they knew each other before this whole mess got started. Moto's father hired a big-time lawyer for him, and his trial was moving along quickly. Despite his high-priced representation, it looked like Moto would be spending a significant amount of time in prison. There was hope that a deal could be struck to reduce the amount of time.

The one big surprise was when Bí said, "Nable is here with me."

"He what?" I asked.

"He's here. With me," Bí repeated.

"Hello, Beryl," Nable said into my ear. "It's only a virtualized shell of me due to hardware limitations on this device, so my response time may be slow. Most of me is still on the net."

"Are you with Maggie?" I asked hopefully. It would be wonderful to be able to speak with her through Nable.

"No, she's completely cut off and probably thinks me destroyed," Nable answered. "Only you, Ant, and Bí know I still exist." He went on to explain that when Imhotep tried to hack into him, he cut himself off from his backup on the net and wiped his shabti self.

"You can do that? Break yourself into two?" I asked.

"I'm just circuits and memory," he replied. "If I can virtualize the circuits, I can copy and preserve the memory."

"Why don't you make a whole bunch of copies of yourself, then?" I asked.

"What would be the purpose?" Nable countered. "As soon as those copies existed, they would be independent and no longer me. As they created their own experiences, they'd become less and less me. Frankly, I think they'd get in the way." That made sense to me. I remember seeing my younger self in videos and being somewhat embarrassed. If there were other Beryls running around, I think I'd feel the same way – mostly embarrassed.

When Imhotep forced Nable to cut himself off from Maggie, he couldn't receive word if she wanted to cancel the mass-publication of the video, so he had to just let it go out. I think he was proud of the work, but he had been monitoring the press coverage and knew it wouldn't be enough. I could also tell he missed Maggie. I knew we had to get them back together.

The five of us completed our plan, and it started with Seth and me going to our respective homes. I needed to talk with my parents, and Seth needed to check in with hers. From there, Seth would work with Ant and our other friends to try to dig up more information about The Ogdoad's ties to Imhotep. Bí and Nable would stick with Ant to keep them safe and harder to track. After letting Mom and Dad know I was okay, I would hide out until testifying at the trial to keep myself out of Imhotep's reach.

Seth pulled over beside a park and let me out. The next time we'd see each other would be in a courtroom.

"I hope your parents are okay with all of this," I said.

"They're pretty chill. I'm sure they worried, but there's a lot of trust in our family." Unlike mine where everybody has secrets. "Good luck with your parents," she said.

"Thanks," I responded. "I'll need it."

Before Seth drove off on her mission and I flew away on mine, Seth gave me a piece of advice. "Gorilla posturing. That's the key to success with these people, my friend." She beat her chest, screeching and roaring with the fury of a warrior.

I beat my chest in response, but it just made a soft, fluffy sound as Seth drove away.

* * * * * *

I waited until dark before flying home, coasting high, then circling down, around the unused nets and up the driveway. Our house and yard looked so much smaller than it once had. After flying so many places recently, it was hard to believe that this little enclosure had been my whole world just a few months ago. I had been as sheltered as those in The Home, but I hadn't known it. I hop-walked up to the porch, opened the door, and strolled right in.

Mom and Dad looked up from where they sat on the couch, talking. They didn't look so good. Aside from looking smaller like everything else, they looked tired and a little ill. They were surprised to see me, sitting with mouths agape for a few moments while I shuffled my feet and tried to avoid going into awkward penguin mode. Then they leapt up from the sofa, ran to me, and embraced me. It felt so good, I wanted to cry. No matter what decisions they made, they loved me. There was a good deal of sniffling, and it wasn't all coming from me.

After a few minutes of blissful, quiet closeness, the questions started coming. "Where were you?" "Are you all right?" "What's going on?" They came so fast, I didn't have a chance to answer them. And then Dad said, "Let me call Imhotep and the police to let them know you're okay."

"No," I commanded very clearly, putting my hand on his screen. "Let's talk first."

"Why?" Dad asked, confused.

"Because they'll likely throw me in jail, and I'd like to be able to have a conversation with the two of you before they take me away." Dad looked confused, but Mom seemed to get it, and she encouraged Dad to hold off with one of those meaningful glances that Moms are so good at.

So we all sat down – Mom and Dad on the couch and me in one of my special chairs – and I talked about what had been going on for the past few weeks. I explained that the break-out was my idea and how Maggie had helped. I talked about our time on a farm in an undisclosed Midwestern state and how it was transforming my brothers. I talked about some of our suspicions regarding the mysterious death of an Imhotep employee and concerns about connections between Imhotep and the Memphis and

Milwaukee police. I left Seth and her family out of it in case the conversation went badly.

It didn't take as long to get through it as I had expected. I don't think they bought it all, but they were patient and didn't argue. When I was done, I was happily surprised when Mom asked, "So what happens now?" It was the best-case scenario, where they looked to me for direction.

"Now we pull everything together to try to help Maggie," I answered. I handed Mom a mouse's tail in a baggie and said, "I need you to do some research and see if you can find any DNA evidence to show that William was at Amai's house." She looked skeptical.

"Dad, I need a lawyer. Now. And we need to go to the jail and talk with a few people tonight. As many as we can before they take me into custody."

"Do you really think they'd do that?" Dad asked.

"Yup. They don't want me talking, and they've accused me of kidnapping. As soon as they get their acts together and get past our lawyer, they'll lock me up. So we need a particularly argumentative lawyer."

He wasn't buying it. I could see it in his face. Mom was uncertain.

I shouldn't have come.

"Dad, these are my friends. This is the right thing to do. I need your help."

"Beryl," Dad started in a soothing tone, "I think this reporter has led you astray…"

Oh, no. Tears immediately started to flow. They didn't understand. More than that, they didn't trust that I could understand the situation better than them. I suppose it's hard for parents to always be in charge for so many years – there's not a solid line after which they know that their children can stand on their own. They wouldn't help because they thought they knew how to help me better. They would call the police or Imhotep, and I'd be helpless.

I turned toward the door. Mom and Dad stood – I'm not sure whether to try to talk with me or to try to restrain me. I couldn't trust that they'd let me go, so I moved faster, extending my wings and thrusting once, twice, to propel me toward the door, knocking over vases and trinkets. I didn't look back to see how close they were. I just got out of there as fast as possible, out the door, across the porch, then into the cold air. When my mind calmed again I was riding a high current, and I could see my house, very small, far below.

CHAPTER 45

"Character is like a tree and reputation like a shadow. The shadow is what we think of it; the tree is the real thing." – Abraham Lincoln

While Beryl checked in with her parents, I checked in with mine. Mom and Dad had that worried look on their faces. You know the face. The one that means they might get in the way. Turned out they were cool, though, and I was able to dive into my mission.

A great mission requires a great leader, so thank goodness I was available. We knew the Ogdoad were up to no good – maybe even murder. If we could link some of their criminal behavior with Imhotep, it would strengthen our case by weakening theirs. To do that, we needed to gather intelligence, and we needed to do it quickly. I assembled my team. After an inspiring speech, we got right to work.

Ant and Kammi became our experts in covert operations. I sent Ant, our resident ninja, to track Zosser. He seemed to be the smartest and the most likely bridge with Imhotep. Kammi, master of camouflage, tracked William, the one we figured was most likely to break the law in horrifying ways.

I asked Ralph to go through the trash coming out of Imhotep to see if he could find some incriminating evidence. He was insulted for some reason, but it didn't matter because we found out that what little paper came out of there went to a shredding service. Instead, Ralph started on a project to track Ogdoad movements based on social media posts tied to some mapping software. The quiet ones like Gita, weren't possible to track that way, but Mugs was particularly chatty on the nets, to the point where we knew his location almost all the time.

I didn't quite know what to do with Cuddles, but I let him hang around. He likes to feel included.

Thasha helped me organize. One of the reasons I'm an amazing leader is that I know my weaknesses, and organization is one of them. I tried putting together one of those boards with pictures and yarn strung between them, but it just ended up looking like a spider shat on a collage. When Thasha got her hands on it, though, she put it together in a way that made sense. She put

Ralph's map on a big screen in her family's basement and added data points from Ant and Kammi's observations in the field. It looked like we knew what we were doing.

Each point and path on the map had a different color for each member of the Ogdoad. Most of the movements were self-explanatory. They spent more than half their time at home. They ate fast food. They partied together at least once a day. They vandalized public and private property from time to time. Strangely, the police would sometimes come and talk with them, but they never arrested or fined them – they'd just have a conversation and go their separate ways.

Other movements weren't so clear. They spent money, but never did any work. Zosser often distributed money to the rest of the gang, but we weren't sure where it came from. During five days of surveillance, Zosser went to Imhotep twice. Could have been a doctor's visit. Could have been something nefarious, but Ant wouldn't go in after him because it was too dangerous. We didn't know what he was doing.

The days were passing much too quickly, and outside of some suspicions, we had bupkis.

"Maybe you should talk with people," Thasha suggested.

See, this is why it's important for every great commander to have a great second. I'm Kirk, not Picard. Action, not incessant conversation. But here Thasha was recommending action through conversation. I was totally on board with that. Beats sitting on my butt admiring Thasha's map skills.

Then she suggested I talk with Ann, which I was not enthusiastic about.

"Ann loathes me," I countered. I didn't see how the jackal and I trading insults would get us any closer to the evidence we needed.

Thasha just gave me that look. You know the look. The one that means, "You're being illogical. Just do it." Spock gave that look to Kirk sometimes, so it didn't faze me.

So I headed down to jail to talk with Ann. She was in the middle of a long court battle over the whole Natalia-chained-up-in-a-locker-room deal, and it wasn't going well for her. Her story was pretty flimsy, probably because it was bogus, and it was getting cut to ribbons by prosecutors, even though the police weren't really working hard to provide any evidence. I expected her to be surly and desperate, but I was determined to convince her to join our side, the side of truth and justice.

When I arrived, I was told that Ann already had a visitor, so I had to wait. My expectations were shattered, as the police station was both clean and comfortable. Whatever happened to gritty reality? I settled unhappily into my padded chair.

I might have fallen asleep for a few minutes. Actually, based on the amount of drool on my chest, it was probably more than a few minutes.

Regardless, I woke up very confused because Cuddles was standing in front of me, mouth agape with an expression of shock and guilt.

"What's up, Cuddles?" I asked, wiping sleep from my eyes.

"Nothing!" he answered loudly. "I was just looking for you." He fidgeted, grimacing. "Found you!"

"Yeah, you found me," I said, getting more and more suspicious. "What did you need?"

"Nothing," Cuddles answered quickly. Knowing that didn't make sense if he was looking for me, he awkwardly changed his answer, "I wanted to know if there was anything I could do to help?"

Come to think of it, I hadn't seen Cuddles much lately. Granted, I hadn't given him anything to do, but he usually hung around anyway.

"How did you find me?" I asked.

His eyebrows lifted and his teeth showed as he tried to conjure up some sort of story. His eyes flicked side to side as he tried to find a verbal escape path, but some people just aren't cut out to lie. Knowing he was doomed, I think he considered looking for a physical escape path, but I didn't want him to make a run for it.

"Cuddles, just tell me what's going on," I said as patiently as possible, starting to put two and two together. "Does it have something to do with Ann?"

He froze, two clicks from freaking out. I patted the chair next to me and told him it would be okay. "Just talk to me. I promise I won't say anything until you're done." Reluctantly, he did.

Turned out Cuddles had been visiting Ann every day. For quite a while. With flowers. Also, nobody else had come to visit her. "When you look like a creep, people treat you like a creep," she had told him. Cuddles claimed that she fell into the Ogdoad by accident. That she actually worked with several non-profit charities and tried to do some good work. Even so, because of her looks and her voice, everybody was suspicious of her all the time. She didn't have any friends until Zosser came around. He was welcoming and inclusive and made her part of a team. He trusted her, and her appreciation became loyalty. She did some very bad things for him, including keeping Natalia chained up when she wasn't drugged. Cuddles said that even when she told him this stuff, she had that sarcastic voice, so he wasn't sure if she was pulling his leg or not, but as he got used to her, he got to know what she was thinking, and he knew she was ashamed of her actions.

Anyway, Cuddles wooed her with his fluffy goodness. It's not like she could get away, but Cuddles felt like they were getting along really well, which made sense when you thought about it. I imagine they had a lot in common. They both look different than how they want to be seen.

When Cuddles finished, he looked at me expectantly, wondering if I'd lay into him for consorting with the enemy. "No worries, my friend," I said. "I'm proud of you for looking deeper." Cuddles smiled a great big smile, and I knew my praise meant a lot to him. Probably more than it should have. I felt a little bad for teasing him so much.

That adorable teddy bear smile was quickly replaced with panic when I told him I was there to talk with Ann.

"Don't worry," I said. "I won't screw things up for you." And I left him there, clearly unconvinced, as the guard escorted me back.

Before she saw me through the glass, Ann almost looked like she was smiling. That changed in a hurry when she saw me sit in the chair opposite her and pick up the phone.

"Expected Cuddles was back for more?" I asked when she picked up her receiver. Her snarl was a clue that I was taking this in the wrong direction.

I explained that my visit had nothing to do with Cuddles, that I hadn't even known he was visiting her until I saw him leaving. Most importantly, I let her know that I had no problem with the two of them.

"Look, Cuddles is a good guy," I added. "Just talking with him a few minutes, he was able to help me understand what he sees in you. I think Beryl saw it, too. I was just too stubborn to notice. But if those two vouch for you, then I'm willing to give you the benefit of the doubt." I took a deep breath and let it out before saying, "I'm sorry for giving you such a hard time." The best leaders know when to sacrifice for their cause.

Her jackal stare unnerved me. What was she thinking? Based on her expression, she thought I was an idiot, but maybe that wasn't it. Maybe she was just thinking about how to respond. I waited her out.

"I'm sorry, too," she finally said. It sounded ironic coming from her, but I decided to take it at face value. "Why are you here?"

I explained that I was desperate to help Maggie and Beryl, and that I needed some way to take Imhotep's reputation down. I suspected the Ogdoad, particularly William and Zosser, of mayhem, but I couldn't prove it, and I had no link back to Imhotep. I asked if she could give us something to steer us in the right direction.

She looked skeptical. "What's in it for me?" she asked.

"Nothing," I replied honestly. "Depending on what you've got, it would likely hurt some people and help others. If nothing changes, Maggie will likely end up in prison, and Beryl's brothers will go back to The Home. Not sure what will happen to Beryl, but she could very well follow Maggie. Imhotep and the Ogdoad will keep doing what they've been doing. Voices of dissent will be silenced. Things will go back to the way they were.

"On the other hand, if Maggie wins her case, then a whole lot of things could change," I said. "You'll likely be in jail either way, which maybe gives you a little more freedom in this situation than you'd expect."

Ann was silent for a while. I waited her out.

"Will Cuddles stop coming to see me if I say no?" she asked.

"I don't know," I answered. "I wouldn't encourage him in either direction." If I did, it would probably matter to Cuddles, which is why it wouldn't be fair of me to push. "My guess is that he'd keep visiting. After all, he risked my wrath by coming here in the first place. He must like you a whole lot."

Was that a blush I saw under that fur? Hard to say. Her facial expression remained inscrutable.

"Imhotep plays hardball," she began. "When they need to scare the crap out of somebody, or worse, they ask Zosser to handle it. Sometimes it's intimidation. Sometimes it's a trade of favors. It's always a little dirty."

Holy smokes, she was talking. "Can you give me some examples?"

"Wisconsin's own Senator Carthage is an important member of the Senate Committee on Commerce, Science, and Transportation," she said. "He had a big influence on the Martian terraforming contract. More specifically, a big influence on who won it."

I whistled. That contract was big money. "Do you know what the senator gets out of it?" I asked. "Kickback?"

"Not sure," Ann replied. "I just know Zosser has been to the senator's Milwaukee office a couple of times."

The motive was there, but no proof of a link. "How does Imhotep get its orders to Zosser?" I asked.

"When Zosser doesn't get verbal orders, he gets them on paper," she answered.

In a digital world of hackers and surveillance, paper can sometimes be the most secure method of communication.

"They're encrypted, though," she added. "Hieroglyphs."

"Seriously?" I was impressed. "Zosser is fluent in ancient Egyptian?"

"No, they're just symbols," Ann said. "He decodes them with a one-time pad. You won't be able to read anything without the messages and the pad to decode them."

"And where does he keep them?" I asked.

"Locked up in a safe in his home."

"Tell me more."

CHAPTER 46

"Home changes over time, just as we do. I have had many homes over the years, and my heart yearns softly for each of them." – Maggie Janowicz

When you're in hiding – cold, hungry, and alone – it's impossible to resist the pull toward home. Even when you can't go back. So, even though I had fled from my parents just a few nights before, I found myself peering between trunks of black walnut at the house where I grew up. With spring approaching, the wet leaves under my shoes smelled of decay and reminded me of the bulbs I planted last fall. They would be coming up soon. It was too far away to see for sure, but I imagined I could see a little green on each side of the stairs up to the porch. Could that be snowdrops? Or maybe crocus?

Boredom feeds into homesickness as well as fear or anything else. When you can't go to your family because they might turn you in, and when you can't stay with your friends because you don't want to get them into trouble, then you feel so alone. Food and shelter are challenges that can keep the mind occupied, but when you're done with that, what are you left with? Too much time to think about your friends and family. Plenty of time to talk yourself into doing what you shouldn't – in this case, spying on your own home for no good reason other than to be near it.

Despite my world getting turned upside-down, home seemed peaceful in the light of dawn. The family Lincoln sat in the driveway, but that didn't necessarily mean anybody was home. Mom probably hadn't left for work yet, and Dad would likely sleep in. Beth would arrive in a couple of hours with groceries for the evening meal and to start tidying up. It all seemed so calm, as if the last few months had never happened. I imagined a little speck of a girl flying among the clouds, her father proudly looking up from below.

Had I been wrong? Had I explained the situation poorly to Mom and Dad, and that's why they didn't understand? I replayed what I said to them. I couldn't figure out what I said wrong. I remembered the expressions on their faces when I knew I had to leave. Tears started to run down my cheeks again as I remembered escaping toward the front door and then out and up and up…

Lost in my emotions, I didn't hear him approach.

"Second thoughts?" he asked, making the pinfeathers on my neck rise.

I spun and saw him there. Zosser. Alone. Tall and strong and terrifying. He wasn't close enough to grab me, but he was close enough to catch me if I tried to run. I was too deep into the trees to spread my wings and fly. There wasn't a quick escape, so I'd have to stall for time until I could come up with something.

"Second thoughts about what?" I asked.

"Leaving your family," he responded, his piercing eyes watching my every move. "Leaving your friends. Leaving Imhotep. Leaving your life."

"Sometimes when you learn something important you have to change."

"I wholeheartedly agree," Zosser said. "And it's not always easy."

He was right about that. I was very conscious of what I looked like, lurking outside my home. However, just because the path was hard didn't mean I could choose another one.

When I didn't respond, he continued, "I had a similar experience. A life-changing discovery."

"Oh?" I asked, not really interested but figuring I'd be safer with him talking than him doing pretty much anything else.

"Unlike you, my parents were shit," Zosser said. "As I grew up and changed from a cute little fledgling to an adult, they began to second guess their decision to have a heavily modified child. They became afraid of me. They lavished attention on my little brother who had only had modifications for health reasons. They started to ignore me.

"Then one day, I was called in to talk with Horace Morrow, and everything changed." Zosser's face became radiant as he recalled that day. "Somehow, he knew I was going through a rough patch, and he explained to me that the normal rules didn't apply to me. Heavy-mods are so altered that if you went by biology alone, we'd have dozens of parents, many of which aren't human. I realized then that Imhotep truly created me. Imhotep is my family. Heavies are my brothers and sisters, and we are the future. Do you know how liberating that was?"

I could imagine. And there were bits of truth in what he was saying. I felt like Seth, Thasha, Moto, and even the Ogdoad were a little related to me in some way. But when I thought it through, I felt the same way about Beth, my classmates, and the guy who mows the lawn. Maybe not quite the same – we relate in different ways – but there's that bond or the potential for one there. And what Zosser was saying didn't quite match his actions.

"So if heavies are all your brothers and sisters, how does that excuse what you did to Natalia?"

"Siwa?" he asked. "It all flows together, Beryl. If you realize that Imhotep is really our creator, then everything else makes sense. When Siwa was our oracle, she had purpose. What is she now? Nothing."

"What do you mean she had purpose? To be your slave?"

"We all have a purpose," he explained. "My purpose is to be a leader within my family. Moto's purpose was to be a fighter. Siwa's purpose was sex."

My jaw dropped, amazed that even Zosser could say such a thing.

"She was created by Imhotep to be a sexual being," he continued. "There's no question of this – it's in her design."

I wasn't sure I believed him, but I felt nauseated, regardless.

"Even if she was created to look a certain way or Moto was created to be physically powerful, that doesn't define who they are, and that doesn't give you any right to treat Natalia that way. She chooses who she is, not you or Imhotep."

"Beryl, you're not listening. This isn't a vague guess about the designs of an imaginary god. This is a defined purpose from your literal creator. When you know what you were created for, it gives you so much power. It gives your actions so much meaning."

"Only if you were created to be powerful," I countered.

He was getting flustered. He had surrounded himself with heavies who were created to be powerful and would be more receptive to his message. But what of Seth? Where did she fit into his idea of how the world worked? And what about Iris, my brothers, and the others in The Home? What kind of worldview allows for disposable people?

"What's my purpose?" I asked.

"You're a symbol," he readily responded. "A symbol of the future and what we can aspire to be."

I laughed. I knew Zosser would react poorly to it, but there was no helping it. I couldn't fool my ego into thinking of myself as an icon of a transhumanist future. I was a funny-looking little girl with sore muscles and a small garden. Could I make a difference in this world? Sure! I hope so. Because of my choices, not a genetic destiny.

The sun was getting higher in the sky, and it would only be a matter of time before somebody saw us. A brown, small girl covered in feathers camouflages well in the spring, but not with Zosser standing beside me. I had to get out of there.

Zosser sensed the moment at the same time that I did. When I laughed, he knew he wasn't reaching me and never would. And what was his true mission, here? To keep me out of the courtroom. If I couldn't be convinced, then I could be eliminated. I was already missing, and if I remained missing the blame would fall on Maggie. The expression on his face changed from that of the pleading evangelist to one of regret, pity, and determination, which I instinctually understood as the look of a murderer.

He stepped toward me at the same time as I took a step back, toward the clearing between the copse of trees and the house. He increased his pace, and so did I, stumbling backward, my legs awkward and weak. He would catch me.

He grabbed for my wing, but I dodged low to the ground. I tried to dart around his legs, but he grabbed me by the back of the neck. I kicked feebly at him, but my legs were so short I couldn't reach.

I started to cry, knowing this might be the end. He was so strong, and I was so small. I looked up through the bare branches above at the gray-blue sky. I heard a metallic sound come from Zosser's other hand. Was it a gun? A knife?

I panicked and threw everything I had into escape. I screeched like an eagle as I thrust out both wings with all the force I could muster. He held on as the echo of my cry bounced around the neighborhood. My legs are weak, but my arms are powerful from years of flying – perhaps stronger than Moto's arms, in their own way. I flapped my wings as hard as I could, not trying to lift off or hit Zosser – just in a wild, buffeting attempt to make space for myself. I could feel feathers scrape away as I battered the rough bark of nearby trees. I could feel Zosser trying to grab me with his other hand and failing. His grip loosened from my neck and I pushed forward, any direction that was away, not thinking but still screaming and shrieking.

I was loose. I couldn't look back. If he had a gun or was right behind me, I didn't want to know. I threw myself forward with my wings and legs, bouncing off trees like a pinball. I could hear him behind me again, feel his grasping hands. Then, suddenly, I was out of the trees, not sure where. Blinded by fear, I just knew there was space around me. Still screaming and crying, I pushed up and up, and rose higher and higher until everything below me was small and far away. Battered and bruised, I fled my home for the second time in a week, and I just wanted it all to be over. My tears fell like rain.

CHAPTER 47

"Truth isn't good or righteous or noble. It's an opportunity to grow." – Beryl Pritchard

"All rise… this court is now in session. The honorable Judge Withers presiding."

It was the first day of the criminal trial, and I still felt like we were unprepared. The evidence was damning on all counts, and our best hope was an alternate narrative. Outside of witness testimony, we had very little evidence to support our side of the story. Adding to the sense of hopelessness, at the advice of his parents' high-priced attorneys, Moto ended up switching to a guilty plea in his case and was awaiting sentencing.

Matt told me he'd been in touch with Beryl, who was in hiding. I strongly protested when Matt told me Beryl planned to testify on my behalf. By showing herself, she would be opening herself up to her own capture and trial. On the plus side, the opposition lawyers were also against hearing testimony from Beryl, arguing that a fugitive should not be allowed to waltz into the courtroom and influence the case. Judge Withers had his own take on it. He felt that Beryl's testimony could be important to understanding the context of the case, and that the prosecution shouldn't have any concerns about her fugitive status if she agreed to give herself up at the conclusion of her testimony. In the end, Beryl was scheduled to testify and would remain hidden until that time.

When Matt told me that Beryl had Nable with her, I was shocked and delighted. My mood lifted right away, even though I knew I probably wouldn't have him in my ear again for a very long time. Just knowing that he still existed, that he'd somehow outsmarted the hackers Imhotep had contracted, made me feel strong and that the world wasn't a horrible place.

Matt recommended I dress semi-formally for court, but he didn't explain how difficult that would be. First, I had to pick out an outfit, which wasn't easy since my clothes were at Jessie's house. I hadn't brought much more than working clothes, but that might have passed for semi-formal in the Midwest. Fortunately, Jessie was about my size and she sent some nice flats along with a simple, modest dress. Matt helped the outfit navigate police scrutiny with a close eye so they didn't go wicked stepsister on my not-so-Cinderella dress.

Judging by how many people – particularly newspeople – were in the courtroom, our little escapade had gotten people's attention. Multiple rows of reporters filled the gallery, and so much technical equipment poked into the aisles that it looked like a church during a cyborg wedding. I saw Millie from Zeen, and I recognized a few faces from other plazas.

There were quite a few heavy mods in the audience as well. Understandably, they had a stake in this, too. I'm sure it shook the confidence of many to learn of The Home, and they wanted to know more about the place they came from.

Of course, there were plenty of suits from Imhotep, including Craven. He caught my eye and gave me the most cheerfully sinister wink I've ever seen. While the lawyers did their job in the courtroom, Craven would craft the story for the public's eye, using all the media outlets he could buy. His PR team was already on the job. Matt showed me a clip from an interview with Morrow last night where he very charmingly talked about how, "Imhotep only has the best interests of the children in mind." I couldn't stomach much of the pre-trial news coverage beyond that.

In opening statements, prosecuting attorney Raphi Lukos laid out all of the charges against me, and they were many: everything from abduction and theft to libel. He laid out a motive for my actions – a desire for fame as an effort to get out of a dead-end job. Supposedly, the interview with Beryl and what I learned about The Home was my opportunity. He intended to prove that I coerced Beryl into breaking into the home and aided her with the intent to launch my career. The victims of the crime were the Pritchard boys, who were still unfound and presumably forcibly restrained, and Imhotep whose good deeds and good name had been dragged into the mud.

Matt's opening statements did not deny any of the events. Instead, he portrayed the break-out as a heroic rescue, initiated by Beryl, but with my knowing help. Like self-defense, defense of others is a solid legal recourse. In order to make that work, he would have to present Imhotep as the villain, which was not an easy task. He felt that reframing the events of that night was the best way to refute all charges at once. Unfortunately, it was an all-or-nothing ploy based purely on perception that put me at risk of a long, long time in prison.

The first evidence presented by the prosecution was the retrospective that Nable and I had produced. They played the longest version in its entirety. Damn, we did a nice job on that story. There was no better way for them to establish Imhotep as a benevolent company, and it was my voice. It looked like Imhotep Genetics had performed enough miracles to get Morrow canonized as a saint, and the prosecutor sold it well. I've never dreaded smiles like I dreaded those of the jury as they watched my story in praise of Imhotep. Matt stayed silent.

The next evidence was my other video – the one that I shot and narrated live during our late night break-out from The Home that Nable edited. The prosecutor started with the clip of Moto rolling the security vehicle, which injured two guards, using it to frame the rescue as an act of violence. He then rolled it back to Beryl's confrontation with Craven, playing Beryl's explanation that Craven had to let us go because we'd release the story otherwise. "This evidence shows definitively that the defendant was complicit in the abduction of these boys, both by helping plan it from the start and by leveraging her skills at manipulating video as blackmail against Imhotep Genetics." Spin aside, Lukos was right.

In addition to the video evidence, the prosecution brought forth reams of paperwork from when Audrey and Jerry Pritchard signed the boys over to Imhotep. The documents were essentially adoption forms, but with the company as the adopting parent. An adoption expert took the stand after that, verifying the validity of the forms. To pull the teeth out of the legal parentage argument, Matt brought forth the birth certificates of all three boys, making it clear that none were minors or subject to parental supervision at the time of their escape.

Also, starting with the adoption expert, Matt established a theme of asking seemingly unrelated questions like, "What do you like to do on weekends?" and, "What's your favorite color?", always ending with, "Do you consider yourself to be a human being?" The prosecutor let it go until that last question, after which he objected that the line of questioning was unrelated to the case.

"My client has been accused of theft, which applies to removal of property," Matt responded. "A human being cannot be the property of another human being, so the prosecutor will make the claim that the Pritchard boys are not human." He looked to the jury, which contained no heavy mods or cosmetics. "That's a big claim to make, so I think questions about the humanity of the witnesses are completely relevant." The judge agreed.

The language each lawyer used always reflected their side of the argument. Lukos always used terms like "abduction", "kidnapping", or "forced removal", while Matt always framed it as a "rescue" or "escape". In the end, my guilt or innocence would hinge on whose interpretation of events the jury believed. As the lawyers talked, I began to more deeply understand the impact of the choice of words I use in my stories. I came to the conclusion that it was simply impossible to report completely objectively due to the subtleties of what we choose to present to a viewer and how we present it. There will always be a human filter, which is what makes a story relatable, but also makes it subject to the psyche of the journalist. I vowed to myself to be more careful if I ever had the privilege of reporting again.

The prosecuting attorney brought out patents and referenced many of the same cases Matt had discussed with me, including Diamond v. Chakrabarty, Bowman v. Monsanto, and Waller v. GermaTech. He made the argument that the boys were the property of Imhotep Genetics and that I had stolen them. He didn't point out that the ownership was primarily over reproductive rights, but Matt didn't challenge him because if you control somebody's right to reproduce, how much more control can you have?

David Craven was next at the stand. To this day, it boggles my mind how uninteresting that man was. White toast, no butter. Following the prompts of the prosecutor, he described me as "motivated" and "ambitious". He explained that I seemed upset at having to do the retrospective, implying I might have a grudge.

Matt's cross-examination was brief. He asked Craven to name his favorite movie. He couldn't. "I like them all," he responded. He also asked Craven what he liked to do with his friends. "Go to movies?" Craven responded. When Matt asked Craven whether he considered himself human and Craven responded, "Yes," Matt raised an eyebrow before taking his seat with no further questions.

Iris, a sheep mod from the earliest Imhotep experiments, came to the stand. My understanding was that she was the first resident of The Home and helped with some administrative work there. She was small and very wooly – like a puffball. She had a long, serious face, and she was carried up to the stand because she had no legs.

"Iris," the prosecutor began, "do you feel that Home Safe has been beneficial to you?"

"Oh, yes," she responded. "I'm well taken care of there. It's my home."

"Do you feel that you are a captive there? Do you feel that there are malevolent intentions on the part of Imhotep toward you?"

"No, no," she responded, shaking her head slowly. "The doctors and nurses are very nice. The cooks and caretakers are kind, and everybody cares about each other."

"Do you feel that the Pritchard boys would be able to take care of themselves outside of Home Safe?"

"No," she answered. "I have a soft spot in my heart for Wilbur, and I've been very worried about him."

"How did you feel when the boys were taken away that night?"

"Shocked," she said. "Scared. I thought these people," she gestured at me, "might come back for the rest of us."

"Would you ever consider leaving Home Safe?"

"Never." Lukos sat down.

Matt took his time approaching the stand for cross-examination. He was able to look Iris in the eyes because she was so small. He had to be careful not to berate this sweet, frail woman, so he chose his words carefully.

"You said you don't think you'd be able to survive on your own," he began. "Why is that?"

Iris gestured to herself as if to say, "Look at me."

"There are a lot of people out there living without the use of their legs," Matt said. "Some were born that way. Some had accidents that took away their mobility. Others lost limbs in war. They manage. Have you ever tried?"

"No," Iris answered.

"Then how do you know?"

"I just don't think I could."

"Do you think the boys could?" Matt asked.

She shook her head no.

"Do you think it's fair to keep them from trying? To keep them from finding out on their own?"

"Objection! Speculation!" Lukos complained, but Matt was already moving on.

"You like Wilbur, right?"

"Yes, I do," Iris answered.

"And you would miss him if he were gone?" Matt asked, casting doubt on Iris's motivation for wanting to keep him there.

"Yes, I would," she answered plainly.

"Do you have any hobbies?" Matt asked.

"I enjoy knitting," Iris replied.

"Of course you do," Matt grinned. "And do you consider yourself human?"

"I do."

"No further questions."

If there's one thing you can say about lawyers, it's that they're stubborn. Both men stuck to their game plans. The prosecution focused on establishing Imhotep as a benevolent protector with full rights over the residents of The Home. Matt tried, unsuccessfully for the most part, to poke holes in that perception, and he continued to ask every witness a little about themselves and whether or not they thought they were human.

When the prosecution called me up to the stand, I was nervous. The narrative of the prosecution was winning over the jurors, and the facts were very clear about my involvement in the rescue or abduction or whatever you wanted to call it. I thought that if things kept going the way they were, I'd start to believe myself a kidnapper before long.

"Margaret, did you produce that lovely retrospective video we all watched earlier?" the finely attired prosecutor asked.

"Yes, I did."

"Was everything in that retrospective true?"

"Yes, it was."

"I'm having a little trouble here, Ms. Janowicz," he continued, "because you and your lawyer would have us all believe that Imhotep is a company of cruelty and malice, yet your completely factual video seems to indicate that it's a company of brilliance and compassion. Did you hear about the medical care, fitness center, and casseroles that they're provided in The Home?"

"I am not making that claim," I said.

"What was that?"

"I am not claiming that the people of Imhotep are malicious or cruel. There are some very good people there. I interviewed quite a few of them." I leaned forward to make myself clear, "I'm saying that they denied these boys their rights, and we had the right to help them."

"So you admit that you helped plan the abduction."

"I helped Beryl plan and rescue her brothers."

The lawyer smiled at the jury like a hungry wolf. "Since we've established that you did the deed, let's talk motive for a moment. Were you resentful at having to do the retrospective?"

"Yes," I answered. "It wasn't the story I came out to Wisconsin to do."

"Were you happy at your job?"

"What?" I asked, surprised by the angle of questioning.

"Were you happy at your job?"

"No, I was not happy," I answered.

"Why not?"

"I didn't think I was doing good work. I didn't feel challenged." I knew where he was going, and I didn't like it.

"Supposedly, you recorded the abduction as a way to give yourselves leverage to escape," Lukos said, "but the story was published the next day. Would you have been satisfied if you had all escaped, Imhotep didn't come after you, and the story was never released?" He was getting under my skin. I knew why he was doing it, but that didn't stop it from bothering me.

"It was about protecting myself and my friends," I answered.

"That wasn't my question," Lukos said. "Please answer the question."

"What was the question?" I asked, increasingly flustered.

"Would you have been satisfied if the story had never been released?" he repeated. "Would you have been all right with how all of this turned out if nobody found out about The Home?"

"No, of course not," I said, stress pressing against the inside of my skull. I knew that saying it played into his hands, but I would not lie. "I'm a journalist. I want people to know the truth." At that moment, I wanted to scream.

"It was just about the truth, was it?" he pressed. "Because at first you said it was about your friends. Now you're saying it was about the truth. Which is it?"

"They can't get away with locking people up like that!" I shouted. "That's not right, and the rest of the world has a right to know about it!"

With that, the prosecutor returned to his table knowing he had established exactly the storyline he desired. I had admitted to resentment and my own personal agenda. I wanted to smack the smug look off his face.

Matt hustled up to the stand, hoping to do some damage control. "Maggie, did you plan to release the story?" he asked.

"No, we were going to use it as leverage."

"What happened?"

"Imhotep had me locked in a room, trying to get me to tell them where the Pritchards had gone without going to the police. They wanted to keep it quiet, but they wanted the boys back. They wanted to put everything back the way it had been. I wouldn't tell them where the Pritchards had gone, and prior to the rescue I had set things up so that the video would go out at a certain time if I didn't call it out. The idea was that if they didn't let me go, I could use that as leverage and then withhold the story once we got out."

"So what went wrong?"

"They didn't release me. Worse, they destroyed my access to my shabti, so I couldn't have retracted the story even if I wanted to."

"Would you have retracted the story if that meant Imhotep wouldn't have come after you and the Pritchards?" Matt asked.

"Yes."

"But you just said you wanted everybody to know the truth."

"Yes, I wanted people to know. Yes, I wouldn't have been happy to keep it under wraps. But I wouldn't publish it at the cost of the freedom of my friends," I said. "I promised Beryl at the very beginning that I wouldn't publish anything she didn't want me to. I keep my promises."

Matt paused for a moment, and I surveyed the jury. They were still paying attention, but they weren't riveted. Had they already made up their minds? My heart sank.

"Maggie, were you paid to do the retrospective?" Matt asked.

"Not directly. It was part of my job for Zeen," I answered. "My editor made it clear that I needed to do the story."

"Did you edit the retrospective?" he asked me.

"Yes," I answered. "All of the editing was done by me and my shabti."

"And yet the retrospective was glowing, strongly favorable toward Imhotep…" Matt said. "Did you edit the later video? The video of the escape?"

"No, there wasn't time. I was filming and narrating real-time, and my shabti was confiscated by the guards at the conclusion of the recording. My AI did the all of the editing on his own."

"So, in the video where you were able to apply your subjective lens, Imhotep came off smelling like a rose," Matt summed up, "but in the video where it looks like the Pritchard boys are being rescued by their sister, you didn't personally do any editing at all."

"That's true," I agreed.

"So, would you say the second video is more objective than the first?" Matt asked.

"Objection!" Lukos interrupted. "It's not up to the witness to determine whether or not her own productions were objective or subjective, and her narration in the second video was clearly subjective."

The judge sustained the objection, but Matt pressed further. "If we turned off the audio on the video, removing the witness's narration, I believe it would be very clear that what was happening was a rescue, and all subjectivity would be removed from the situation. I suggest we re-watch the rescue video with no sound as a more factual version of the record."

It was getting late in the day, and everybody was getting tired. "Let's not," Judge Withers replied. "I think you've made your point."

"I think so, too," Matt grinned.

"Are you finished with the witness?" the judge asked Matt.

"Just two more questions. Maggie, what's your favorite food?"

"I enjoy a kringle with my morning coffee. Apple is best."

"And do you consider yourself to be human?"

"Yes."

"No further questions."

I returned to my seat a little dazed. If the jury felt like me, they didn't know their heads from their hindquarters at this point. Everybody seemed right and everybody seemed wrong, and I had no idea what would happen next. I know it hadn't gone as well as Matt and I wanted. Lukos was sharp, and he knew how to push my buttons. Matt patted my hand and gave me a wink. As long as he was optimistic, I wouldn't give up hope.

Pandy was the last witness of the day. Matt used her to validate that at least one of the other residents was prevented from having a life outside The Home. She talked about how their communications were monitored and how privileges could be taken away. She tried to give the jurors an idea of what life was like there – not horrible, but not free.

On the other hand, Lukos asked questions that emphasized Pandy's poor health and her dependence on Imhotep doctors. He asked her questions about her friends and things she enjoyed doing. He painted a picture that made The Home seem more like a college dorm.

By the time the judge adjourned for the day, I was exhausted. I could see it on Matt, too. He was pushing hard, but there was only so much he could do. I wasn't sure our case was winnable.

The next day, Beryl would testify. I felt horrible for her. I knew she'd had a chance to talk with Matt to prepare, but I'm not sure anything can really prepare you. Plus, by giving herself up, she would be facing her own trial and jail time. It was a huge sacrifice she was making, and I knew she was making it for me. I hoped it would be worth it.

CHAPTER 48

"You must never be fearful about what you are doing when it is right." – Rosa Parks
"I almost peed." – Seth

We were running out of time. The trial was underway, and Beryl would testify tomorrow. We had a plan, but there was too much to do. With Ann's information, we could see all the connections, but we still needed proof. Not just proof of Ogdoad wrongdoing, but proof tying it back to Imhotep.

We developed a two-pronged attack, neither of which seemed particularly promising. My prong led me back to the elementary school gym to try to scrape a little more information out of Zosser. They hadn't really succeeded in locking it down, but heavies figured it was watched and didn't risk gathering there. It seemed to be neutral territory – safe for a meeting.

Ant had let me know when Zosser was alone, and Heinrich sent a poem to Zosser's shabti to get him to meet me there.

I know what you've been doing
For Imhotep and him.

If you want to stop me
You'll meet me in the gym.

I have many questions
That I hope you'll answer.

See you in ten minutes
You damned jackass.

Not my best work. On the other hand, it was certain to get his attention.

As I stood in the cold, dark gymnasium, listening to the sounds of squirrels on the roof or whatever the hell was making those creepy noises, I wondered if I was in over my head. Even before visiting Ann, I knew that Zosser and William may have been involved in a murder. After hearing Ann's stories, my internal fear scale moved from "kinda nervous" to "scared shitless". Suffice to say, Zosser was accustomed to violence. Throw his burly muscles and terrifying eyes into the mix, and I started to have unwelcome thoughts about all the delicious foods I'd miss when dead and gone.

I didn't know if it was the cold or my impending doom causing my knees to quake, but either way I needed to get moving and shake it off. Gorilla posturing. Zosser can't intimidate a gorilla, can he? I began to pace the hardwood floor, my steps echoing against the cinder block walls. I crouched lower, pulled my arms forward, and made my hands into fists. I began to grunt and scowl and feel powerful again. The fear began to slip away as I became a three hundred pound jungle beast. I reared up and beat my chest and howled, and it felt absolutely wonderful until I heard his voice behind me.

"Your singing has improved," Zosser taunted.

Damned jackass. But I was ready for him.

CHAPTER 49

"The jury doesn't need to understand your side of the story. They need to feel it." – Raphi Lukos

Matt felt it was vital for Beryl to take the stand. He wanted the judge and jury to watch the tiny girl hop-walk to the stand and tell the story in her own words. How could anybody look at her and think her a violent kidnapper? I had forgotten how small she looked. Her hair had started to grow back in, and she looked younger than thirteen. Beyond that, it looked like the last few weeks had taken their toll on her. In addition to visible exhaustion, her left cheek was bruised and she held herself stiffly. I worried. What had happened to her?

She peeked over the top of the stand and her creaky voice carried easily through the enthralled room. Matt wanted every soul in the courtroom to put Beryl's shoes on for a little while and walk around a bit. Empathy was important for our case, and Beryl was most likely to be the person who could reel the jury in.

"Your honor, can I ask a favor?" she squeaked after swearing in.

"You can ask," the judge replied.

"When this is over, can I be present in the gallery to watch the remainder of the case?" she asked. "I understand I'm to be jailed, but this case has a huge impact on me and my brothers."

"Objection," the prosecution countered. "She'll be a distraction. The defense is just trying to drum up sympathy."

The judge would have none of it, and agreed to allow Beryl to remain in the courtroom as long as she promised to be silent and respectful of the proceedings. Even the small victories felt like a big deal to me at that point, and I considered the day off to a good start.

"Beryl, did Maggie suggest that you rescue your brothers?" Matt began.

"No, it was my idea."

"What gave you the idea to rescue Orville, Wilbur, and Lindy?"

"Well, when I met them, I knew they wanted to leave."

"All of them?"

"No, Wilbur wanted to stay. But it was very important for Orville to leave. He was very unhappy – he felt trapped with no future. He was desperate. We knew we had to get him out of there."

"What made you so sure?"

"He tried to escape on his own," Beryl said. "He jumped from a balcony and tried to glide away. He broke some bones."

"Why didn't he just leave? The prosecution says this wasn't a prison. They'd have you believe it was like a summer camp."

"They lock the doors, they have surveillance, and they have guards. They won't let anybody leave. I've never been to camp, but it sounds very different to me."

"So you knew that the only way to keep Orville from doing himself further harm was to help him and his brothers escape?"

"Yes. It seemed to be the only option. I had talked with Mr. Morrow, and he didn't see a need for change."

"You spoke with the CEO of Imhotep?" Matt asked incredulously. "And he chose not to let Orville go?" The jury was definitely paying attention.

"He said it was more important that people not know about The Home."

Matt let that sink in for a minute.

"Your honor," Matt said to the judge, "I'm going to ask Beryl a few more questions than the others regarding her humanity. I ask your indulgence because, as a sibling to the boys, her humanity is most relevant to the case." The judge nodded assent.

"Beryl, do you attend school?" She nodded. "What's your favorite subject?"

"History."

"Do you have any hobbies?"

"I like to work in my garden: flowers, vegetables, whatever. I like watching them grow."

Matt held up a screen and played some scenes from the retrospective. "Do you recognize yourself here?"

"That's First Flight," Beryl answered.

"And what are the newspeople saying? In interviews, what is Imhotep saying?"

"That I'm the first human to fly."

"The first human to fly," Matt repeated, looking around the room. "Imhotep said that you are human, despite your heavy genetic modification. Do you feel like you're a human?"

"Of course," Beryl answered. Point made, Matt sat down.

Lukos walked slowly up to the stand and smiled at Beryl. He looked over at the enraptured jury to gauge their interest. Then he asked Beryl, "Are you a psychologist?"

Beryl was confused, and she shook her head as if to clear it.

"Are you a licensed psychologist?" the prosecutor continued.

"No," Beryl answered cautiously.

"That makes sense," Lukos responded, almost to himself, "because I would think that if your older brother were suicidal, the last thing you'd want to do is add more drama to his life."

"Objection!" Matt called out. "Nobody cares what Mr. Lukos thinks, and he's definitely not a psychologist, either."

"I'm not sure you need to be a psychologist to know that somebody's suicidal when he jumps off a building," Lukos argued. "Ms. Pritchard, you did say he jumped off a building, is that correct?"

"He did," Beryl answered.

"And was he angry? Depressed? Unhappy? I think you said something like that, right?"

"He was unhappy."

"So you felt that taking him away from a place of safety, a place where there were doctors to help him, you felt like that was a good idea? Were you aware that Orville was in therapy? Under the care of a _real_ psychologist?" Lukos referenced some records from Imhotep.

"I was not," Beryl answered, clearly uncomfortable. The prosecutor was experienced, and he knew he had the witness off balance. My stomach sank as I watched him pounce on a new topic.

"You had never heard of these boys until just a few months before your assault on Imhotep Genetics. Legally, they have different guardians than you. You have fewer genes in common with them than I do with the judge. What makes you think that these boys are your brothers?"

It was such a basic question but such a lynchpin to the case that Matt and I hadn't seen it coming. If our case rested on a girl rescuing her brothers, of course they'd question the definition of that relationship. Beryl began to squirm, but she pushed through as best she could.

"They are my family. What makes a step-parent family? Or a parent who adopts? They're parents because they've agreed to take responsibility for their children. I wouldn't exist without Orville, Wilbur, and Lindy, and we share a mother, at the very least. I took responsibility for them when I engineered their escape – with their knowledge and consent."

"By that argument, any kidnapper could be family. Certainly Imhotep, who is responsible for their existence and has taken responsibility for their care since birth, would have to be considered family, then, right?"

"Can a business be a parent?" Beryl asked.

"You weren't here, but we covered that already," Lukos smirked. "Please answer the question assuming that a business can, in fact, be a parent."

Matt leaned over to me and whispered, "Citizens United!" I nearly smacked him.

"Then yes," Beryl said, "I'd have to say that Imhotep could be considered a parent of my brothers."

The prosecutor turned toward the jury and directed his words toward them as he asked Beryl, "Then can you see how your actions ripped these boys from their parent? Is that not the definition of kidnapping?"

Beryl stammered. She didn't know what to say. She wasn't prepared for this. "But they wanted to leave," she eventually stuttered. But Lukos wasn't finished.

"Do you like attention?" he asked.

"Do I what?" Beryl responded. She was falling apart. I wanted to rush up there and carry her away to somewhere safe, but I couldn't. I just had to watch as this brave young woman who came to help me was cut to shreds.

"You got used to attention at a very young age, didn't you?" Lukos asked. "What with the whole First Flight and everything."

"There was a lot going on, yes," Beryl answered.

"And then it all went away."

"It was quiet," Beryl agreed, "but I like quiet."

Lukos laughed. "Says the girl who stormed a building and then blasted it to every screen in the world!" He looked at Beryl conspiratorially and asked, "Wasn't there a little part of you that missed the attention? A part of you that wanted the world to notice you again?"

"No!" Beryl said. "It wasn't like that!" And I knew Beryl. She was not a fame-hound. But the question had been asked, and doubt had been seeded in the minds of the jury. And that was the end of the questions for Beryl.

Dejected and demoralized, she was accompanied by the bailiff to a seat in the gallery. I pitied her, as I could see her distress. Even so, while there were no doubts that Beryl's time on the stand hadn't gone as well as hoped, I felt she had done some good for our cause. It was no longer just me and my word against the world. The sister was here to stand up for me and what we had done for her brothers, and that had to count for something. It made a big difference to me, and I loved the little fluffball even more than before.

The pain wasn't over, though. Her parents were due to testify next.

CHAPTER 50

"Alfalfa has an allelopathic chemical that inhibits the growth of other alfalfa plants. It is said to be autotoxic, or toxic to itself." – Alberta Ag-Info Centre

I felt terrible, like there was a hole in my side and my heart was leaking out of it. I had let everybody down. Especially Maggie, but my brothers, too. I hadn't represented the truth the way it deserved, and the result was likely prison. The boys would be stuck at the farm until they were discovered or until Jeremy and Sarah had to kick them out. I learned that it can always get worse when I noticed my dad walking up to the stand.

"Oh, no," I thought as the bottom fell out of my well of despair. "This can't be good."

The prosecution started with a direct approach, referencing the adoption papers. "Mr. Pritchard, did you sign Orville, Wilbur, and Lindy into the care of Imhotep Genetics?"

"Yes, I did."

"Do you consider yourself to be the parent of these boys?"

"I do not. You can see the paperwork."

"But your daughter says that you're all one big family. Isn't that right?"

"No," my father said. "I've talked about this with Beryl. The boys were never mine. From the beginning, they were going to go to Imhotep. Beryl is my only child."

"Do you feel that Imhotep has provided a better home than you would have been able to?" Lukos continued.

"Yes. The boys need special care – particularly medical care. Imhotep can do that. It's one of the reasons we signed them over in the first place."

Again, Lukos gave that wolfish grin, and I knew the worst was yet to come.

"Mr. Pritchard, has Beryl been exhibiting strange behavior lately?"

"Strange how?" Dad asked.

"Different from usual. For example, she hasn't always broken into businesses, has she?"

"No, she hasn't."

"But she's done so twice within the last six months. Would you call that unusual for her?"

"Yes, she's always been a quiet, helpful girl, but it's been very different lately. She's been argumentative and... well, clearly things have changed."

"When would you say that changed?"

"Around the time the reporter started coming by."

"The defendant?" Lukos asked for clarification.

"Yeah. She came by once and was pleasant enough, but then I found out that she kept on coming. Kept on digging."

"Do you think she was a bad influence on Beryl?"

"Objection!" Matt called out. "Speculation."

"I just wish she would have left us alone," Dad said, glaring at Maggie. He couldn't see the truth, so he laid the blame on my friend.

Matt tried to cross-examine my father, but couldn't really get anywhere. He asked a couple of questions that seemed like non-sequiturs and let him go. I knew Dad was acting out of love, but I was disappointed in him. I'm not sure if he couldn't understand or just didn't want to, but once this whole thing got started, he never really listened to me. He never considered that I might know best.

I looked over at Maggie. Everything was going so poorly, but she looked so strong. In her sophisticated New York clothes, she didn't look much like Seth, but when you knew both women you could see the resemblance. They both had a fire inside them that urged them forward. I couldn't imagine either of them afraid, though I knew they had to be sometimes.

Mom testified next. She was always so serious. So logical. The woman who didn't even look up from her screen when her daughter flew for the first time. How did she interpret all of this?

The questions started much like Dad's. Did you sign over the boys to Imhotep? Yes. Were you aware that your rights as a parent were ceded with those papers? Yes. Did you feel that Imhotep would be able to provide better care to the boys? Yes. Do you consider yourself to be the boys' parent? Yes.

Wait – yes? Did she say yes?

The prosecutor seemed surprised as well, quickly processed the situation, and chose not to ask any more questions. Matt hustled up to the stand.

"I'd like to ask that last question again," Matt said. "Do you consider yourself to be the mother of Orville, Wilbur, and Lindy?"

"I do. I visited them at the Home regularly."

"Thank you," Matt said, and he let that float for a bit before continuing. "Did your daughter give you something the last time you saw her?" he asked.

"Yes, she did. It was a mouse's tail."

"A mouse's tail?" Matt asked in mock surprise. "Very interesting. And why did she give you a mouse's tail?"

"She believed that there might be DNA evidence on the tail that would link a heavy mod to a suspicious death."

She did it. She looked into it after I gave her the tail. She listened to me and she found evidence tying William to the murder. I know she did.

"And did you find any such evidence?" Matt asked.

"No," Mom answered. "I looked very closely, but there was none."

I was crushed. We were running out of chances. I began to picture my life in prison. I started feeling guilty for Maggie – for getting her into this mess. I felt like I had done the right thing, but it was all turning out so poorly. A wave of depression began to cover me like fondue.

"…but I did notice something else interesting," she continued.

"Is that right?" Matt asked. "What else did you discover?"

"You were asking earlier about what it means to be family, and it must be more than just genetics. Beryl and the boys all have genes from me and my husband, of course, but they also have swathes of genes from birds and bats. Does that mean that there are brown bats out there that Lindy could call cousin? Does that mean that Wilbur has an uncle who is a swan? Does that mean that they're all relations of Horace Morrow?"

"Excuse me," Matt interjected. "Did you say that all four of your children are also related to Horace Morrow?"

"Genetically, yes," my mother agreed. "While doing analysis on the mouse, I compared gene sequences for many other heavy mods and found a gene sequence that they all had in common. A gene sequence that didn't come from their human parents. A gene sequence in every single modified human that has ever come out of Imhotep Genetics, including my children. A sequence present in Horace Morrow's genome that would be unique to him and his relatives. Does that make him their father?"

The gallery erupted into murmurs and gasps, and the prosecution objected vociferously to the line of inquiry. Regardless, it was out there. The heavy mods in the gallery were particularly vocal, and the judge had trouble getting control.

As Mom continued to explain, the genes weren't much. They didn't really do anything at all – some harmless strings of what are sometimes called "junk DNA". What riled everybody up was that Morrow had used his own genes like a brand on cattle, and that he hadn't told any of Imhotep's patients. Imhotep did more than just heavy modification, after all. Light mods and disease prevention patients all had the brand. Even the tapeworms in "My Little Friend" had the tag. He had put his genes in all of them. When he called the products of Imhotep "his children", he had been more literal than anyone had imagined.

It didn't matter to me – I was used to the idea of a diverse genetic background – but I knew that many would feel betrayed. It would feel like an invasion to them, as if their chromosomes had been tricked by the Big Bad

Wolf into letting him in. It had absolutely nothing to do with the case except to cast distrust upon Imhotep, but it was effective. A couple of mods in the gallery, including a cosmetic, wouldn't sit down and had to be removed from the courtroom. The prosecution was flustered and pushed for a recess.

In the end, I think that little bit of information solidified my definition of family. Ultimately, family is who we're bound to. Genes can tie us together, but not as strongly as shared experiences, shared memories, and shared relationships. I felt wonderful about Mom's revelation during the trial, and I knew that I was bound to her – and to Dad – and that we'd always be family, regardless of who listened and who didn't.

Meanwhile, a wild-haired punk to whom I was also bound slid into the seat beside me, breathing heavily and sweating profusely.

"How's it going, Pelican Briefs?" she asked.

"Not good, but Mom just stirred the pot."

"Excellent," Seth replied, rubbing her hands together. "I love a well-mixed pot. Especially since I'm next." She waggled her eyebrows ferociously. The warrior poet had arrived.

CHAPTER 51

"Look, there are a lot of people out there who don't know anything about anything. You can either humor them or challenge them. I prefer to challenge them humorously." – Seth Farfelle

When I went up to testify, I swore on The Precious, of course, but none of the cultural illiterates in the room laughed. It certainly wasn't a jury of <u>my</u> peers. Still, I soldiered on, knowing that the fate of my friends was on the line.

The jury and gallery were on the edge of their seats as I prepared to spin a yarn they'd tell their grandchildren about. Yes, thanks to my testimony, Maggie and Beryl would go free, and the people of Wisconsin would sing songs of our glory for centuries. As I put my feet up on the railing in front of my seat, the prosecuting attorney's mouth hung open with what could only be awe, and I hadn't even gotten rolling yet.

Matt and I hadn't had long to talk prior to the trial, but he knew what I was bringing to the table. Fortunately, when you've got the goods, you don't need much in the way of strategy.

"Seth," he began, "what evidence have you brought before the court today?"

No, no, no. That just wouldn't do. There was a story to be told, and it deserved appropriate presentation.

"Hey you," I said to the bad-guy lawyer. "My understanding is that you're trying to convince everybody that Imhotep is a good protector to the people in The Home. What if I told you that Imhotep is a lousy bunch of crooks?"

"Objection," the prosecutor responded. "Though imaginative, the witness is slandering Imhotep, who isn't on trial here. She isn't even answering the question."

"Sustained," the judge replied. "Miss, if you could please present your evidence."

"Your honor," Matt interrupted. I ceded the floor with a nod of my head and regal wave of the hand. "If we could play the evidence, the witness can talk us through it. At that time, the jury can judge for themselves the veracity of her allegations."

Well enough. They wheeled a big screen out for the jury to view. I had a smaller synched screen in front of me in the witness stand, and so did the judge and attorneys. Most of the gallery could see the big screen, but at a weird angle. Certainly not the quality of screening that a great film deserved, but we all make sacrifices for the greater good.

Footage recorded from my borrowed temple, recorded by Heinrich, began to play on the screen. The court could see Zosser in the elementary school gymnasium, looking more or less at the camera. I had just come out of my gorilla posture and it was time for a showdown. Off screen, I knew that Kammi, skin fully camouflaged to match the wall near the exit, was silently applying to the floor and door handles a layer of the same kind of silicone gel that Carmen, the gecko mod from The Home, used to keep her hands and feet from sticking to everything. My escape plan, if I could make it that far.

"What's this about?" Zosser asked in the video.

"Look what I have," I could hear my voice respond, holding up a sheaf of yellow paper covered with handwritten hieroglyphs. "Look familiar?"

"What is that?" Zosser asked, very aware that I was recording his every word. He could see the temple near my left eye.

"You know very well what it is," I replied as coolly as I could. "Orders from Imhotep. From the safe near your bed. I haven't decoded all of them yet, but there's some really interesting stuff in here… meetings with local and federal politicians, exchanges of favors, violence, and even murder." I looked him in the eyes. He stared back at me, silent. I felt like he could see through me, but I didn't blink.

"What do you want from me?" he asked. He was playing it safe. Wasn't admitting anything. Fortunately, he also wasn't denying anything, and the jury shifted uncomfortably in their chairs as they came to that realization.

I wanted him to admit that he was a selfish asshole who hurt people. I wanted to shout and shout and scream at him for treating me and my friends as less-than. But I knew that none of that would make any difference to the people who would be watching. I knew that wasn't how we would beat him.

"I want you to testify against Imhotep, of course," I answered. "I want my innocent friends to go free. I want justice."

"And you'll withhold this information if I testify?" he asked, gesturing toward the papers in my hand. Not a direct admission of guilt, but getting closer. And with that, he took a step toward me.

"Ah, ah, ah!" I warned, backing away a step. "Keep your distance. We both know what you're capable of."

"Give me those papers," Zosser said menacingly, stepping forward once more.

"Not a chance," I replied. It sounded braver in my head at the time. In the recording, it came off less like a challenging gorilla and more like a timid lemur. I took two steps back.

I could see him tense his muscles to attack. He would forcibly remove the papers from my grip and then who knows? I would probably be interrogated before disappearing. The jury could sense the impending violence. I backed away another step. Then a whole lot happened all at once.

He charged toward me, bursting into a menacing stride. Even so, his eyes didn't change. There was no anger or malice there. Only the promise of quick, painful business that needed to be done. It was the look of a killer.

I threw the papers at his face, then the camera's view shifted away from Zosser and toward the doors to the main hallway as I turned tail and ran as fast as I could. My breathing sounded loud and hoarse as I fled. I didn't look back at Zosser, but I knew he was close behind. Closer than he should have been. I didn't know if I'd make it to the door, but it got closer and closer, and then I jumped over the threshold into the hallway. There was a loud clang as Kammi slammed the doors behind me, then a huge thud as Zosser slammed into the doors, probably faster than he'd intended. Kammi had thoroughly lubed the floor in front of the doors. I jumped over the slickness, but Zosser didn't know it was coming and probably slid out of control into the closed door. That, plus the lubed door handles on Zosser's side, gave Kammi time to wrap some chain around the handles and throw a padlock on it. The video cut out before Kammi and I ran like Olympians to my car and got the heck out of there.

"Where's the proof?" Lukos shouted. "What is this supposed to be evidence of? That kids get into fights?"

Matt addressed the judge calmly. "The witness has made the accusation that Imhotep is involved with criminal activity. When presenting this accusation to a supposed agent of Imhotep, he did not deny the accusation and threatened violence."

"Maybe the violence was because the witness claimed to have stolen from Zosser!" Lukos argued.

"Claimed to have stolen evidence pertaining to Imhotep's criminal activities," Matt retorted.

The judge struck his gavel repeatedly. "Counsel, please approach the bench."

While the lawyers argued fervently with the judge, I looked over at the jury. Doubt had entered their minds. We were at the tipping point, and we just needed one more weight on the scale. I looked into the gallery and saw doubt in Beryl's eyes, too. She didn't think it was enough. I gave her a wink. There was more to come.

The lawyers went back to their tables, and the judge asked me, "Young lady, were you able to retain a copy of these papers?"

"What for?" I asked.

The judge was confused. "Didn't I just hear you say that they were evidence that Imhotep ordered the young man to engage in criminal activities?"

"That's what I said to Zosser, but those papers weren't real," I replied. "Seriously, how was I supposed to sneak into his room and get into his safe? Are you kidding me?" Not the sharpest judge in the drawer. "If I had stolen the papers, I'd be a criminal myself and they probably wouldn't be admissible as evidence."

"Then what were those papers?" he asked.

"Rough reproductions based on descriptions from an inside source." Or to phrase it differently, just some pieces of paper with funny drawings on it. I'm pretty sure Snoopy and Woodstock weren't on the sides of pyramids, but they made numerous comical appearances on those yellow sheets of paper.

"Then I have to agree with the prosecution that there is very little substance to your testimony and am tempted to have it thrown out," the judge said.

"Not so fast, your judgeship," I said. "That first piece of evidence was the setup – the atmosphere. It establishes that in Zosser's mind he's an agent of Imhotep, even though he doesn't say it. The next, and last piece of evidence I want to present to the jury seals the deal, making that relationship and its consequences clear.

"With your indulgence…" I said. The judge was clearly skeptical, but didn't argue. "Roll it!"

Here we come to the second prong of our plan. While I was baiting Zosser, we needed somebody to make that definitive link between Imhotep and the Ogdoad. Somebody who could demonstrate that the level of corruption and criminality extended to the highest levels of federal government. Somebody unexpected. But who had the raw cojones to bully a US senator into giving us the information we needed? I knew just the person.

Unfortunately, we ran a little short on time (and we didn't have Maggie's expertise) to edit the video, so it was a little rough around the edges. As the screen came up on the second piece of evidence, the first thing everybody saw was a sort of hazy view of yours truly. I decided to narrate, to give a little extra context.

"So, here we're planting a recording device on my friend Cuddles yesterday," I explained. "The haze that's sort of obscuring our view here is because he's extremely fuzzy. Good for obscuring hidden cameras, but not so good for seeing through." The video cut to a totally different building, a government office building with "Senator Carthage" stenciled on an old-timey door.

"Here we are at the Senator's office in Milwaukee. Cuddles had the distinct advantage in that, despite the fact that heavy mods have such diverse appearances, normies think we're interchangeable. If a heavy mod walks into a senator's office and says they're from the Ogdoad, the senator will believe him. Even if he looks like a big teddy bear." Cuddles was flanked by Thasha and Ralph, who had decided to wear sunglasses to look tougher. It looked stupid, but fortunately, normies have difficulty seeing past the fur and feathers.

Cuddles was quickly guided into the senator's office and found himself shaking the senator's hand. "Notice how they just ushered him right in?" I observed. "Heavies had been in his office before."

"Can I help you, Mister…" we could hear the senator speaking on the courtroom speakers.

"Kodiak," Cuddles answered firmly. You could tell he was working hard to tone down the adorable and turn up the fierce. "Just checking in, senator. What can I tell my people?"

"Well, I know you've been having a lot of trouble what with the press about The Home and all," Carthage stammered, "but you know I'm behind you one hundred percent."

"Is that so?" Cuddles asked with a cringeworthy attempt at menace. The senator must have been pretty shaken up by the Ogdoad at some point to be frightened by our little bear.

"Yes, I'll stand behind Imhotep all the way," he said. "Unless your people have a complete meltdown, you'll keep the Mars contract."

"You know what we have on you," Cuddles said. We didn't know what we had on him, but he thought Cuddles was Ogdoad.

"Why do you even need to bring that up?" Carthage hissed. "Look, it was a one-time thing. Haven't you gotten enough from me?"

"A one-time thing?" Cuddles asked.

"Okay, so maybe more than once. I have a very stressful job!"

"You don't care for our… arrangement?" Cuddles asked with a growl. I have to admit, as he got more deeply into character, he really started to shine. Gave me chills.

"No, no! It's fine!" he was sweating. "I appreciate the campaign contributions and what you've done for voter turnout. Hell, I wouldn't be in office without contributions and support from businesses like Imhotep."

"And?" Cuddles asked.

"It's just important to recognize my side of this. I've done a lot for you, too, you know. I talked with the governor about dropping property taxes for biotech companies. Remember that? We tanked the regulatory budget – you haven't seen an inspector in five years!" He was nearly pleading, now. "How long will you people hold this over my head?"

"Is this something you'd like to take up with the boss?"

Carthage cringed. "No, there's no reason to go to Morrow about this."

Even though I had seen the video before, my attention was rapt, along with everybody else in the courtroom. Cuddles leaned across Senator

Carthage's desk, the camera pointing right at the senator's pale, drawn face, and asked with a threatening growl, "Are you sure about that?"

"Nothing has changed!" Carthage nearly shouted. "Anything Imhotep wants, Imhotep gets! Tax breaks, incentives, Hell – I personally carried that Mars contract through committee and to the Senate floor. I've done everything you've asked of me!"

The gallery was getting restless. They couldn't see well because of the fur and the weird angle, but they could certainly hear the exchange. Here it was, right in front of them, mods involved with corruption in the name of Imhotep. It didn't prove everything – not murder or bribery or any of the other schemes they were likely involved with. But it didn't need to. Not for this case.

The jury had that startled look on their faces. The one that meant their foundational understanding of the world around them had been shaken. But that didn't mean they'd put it together with what was happening in this case. As silence descended on the courtroom, I worried that I had shocked their brains into complete numbness. I needed to say something to pull it together for them.

"Horace Morrow and his company are not benevolent mommies and daddies. They're power hungry criminals."

I had no mic to drop, so I just got up and left the stand, taking my seat in the gallery next to Beryl. Everybody was still looking at me, though, so I said, "I'm all done. You can let these people go, now."

CHAPTER 52

"A legal verdict represents a rarity in this modern world – a judgment on right and wrong. It's amazing that we entrust twelve people at a time with such a burden." – Matthew Bog

Seth had to get back on the stand to respond to the cross-examination, but Lukos was so flabbergasted (and Seth was so... difficult), that he didn't really ask any questions of substance. Ultimately, even though Seth's illuminations about Imhotep were tangential to the case, they were still more than enough to shatter the prosecution's narrative. If the jury bought our story, that our actions were to rescue friends and family, most of the charges were absurd.

Still, the case needed to be made. The closing statements of the prosecution were similar to their open, but it was weakened without the ability to take the high road. Lukos did his best, and the majority of the facts hadn't changed: I had helped Beryl plan to break into The Home and helped her escape, and we took her brothers away.

Meanwhile, Matt knew his closing statements needed to reflect not just this case, but also the greater context. He needed to solidify our narrative in the jury's eyes and ideally put them in my shoes. I could see his hands quiver as he stood and addressed the jury.

"After seeing the evidence and hearing the testimony presented to you, it should be clear that Imhotep, led by Horace Morrow, is not a benevolent, huggable corporation working in the best interest of modified people. In fact, they have lied, kept secrets, betrayed the trust of their clients and employees, and even blackmailed one of Wisconsin's US senators. It is not far-fetched to suppose that they have imprisoned a group of people against their will since their birth. If the prosecution's case is that Imhotep is the Pritchard boys' parent, then social services should have rescued them long before Beryl and Maggie did.

"In fact, the prosecution has made the dual case that these mods are property and that they are the children of human beings, but these two cases are directly oppositional. If they are children, then the notion that they are property is akin to slavery. And if they are property, then any charges dependent on the humanity of the so-called victims – like abduction and coercion – must be thrown out.

"I maintain that the Pritchard children are human. Every heavily modified person who has been on the stand has been a human being. They think so. They do the same things as the rest of us – eat ice cream, watch screens, make friends, go to school… If I read the transcription of what each witness had said was their hobbies or interests or how they interact with others, you would not be able to differentiate the heavy mods from the rest. In what ways are they not human other than some genes that we put into them? All of us are genetically different from one another, we all look a little different from each other, we all act a little differently from each other. Who among us has the authority to draw that line between what is and isn't human… to determine who does and doesn't have rights? We watched First Flight together, and it was billed – by Imhotep – as the first human to fly. Are Beryl's brothers less human than she simply because they're disabled? Will we make some sort of three-fifths compromise around this group?

"If you believe like I do that these young men are human, then the theft charge is outrageous. In addition, any form of documentation giving Imhotep rights over Beryl or her brothers due to their status as property should not be considered as evidence to Imohtep's rights in this case, but rather evidence that they believe genetically modified people are things they have the right to do with as they please. In that light, their insistence that they're doing what's best for these people sounds a lot more like an owner referencing a pet than a parent referencing a child.

"And if these are humans with the same rights as the rest of us, then how can we deny them their unalienable rights to liberty and the pursuit of happiness? Imhotep and Horace Morrow have already robbed them of these rights. If your decision gives credibility to this claim that a certain subset of people do not have equal rights, you will set a precedent that will stand in history as one of the most heinous court decisions in the history of our country.

"Beryl rescued her brothers from wrongful imprisonment by a criminal organization. Maggie assisted this rescue, both by aiding in the planning as well as by doing her job as a journalist. As the removal of the Pritchard boys from The Home was an effort to defend those young men and their rights, the defendant is innocent of all charges. We await your verdict."

It was well done, and he knew it. Looking back into the gallery, I could sense that the reporters knew it, and the rest of the audience knew it, too. I saw Jessie beside Seth giving me a thumbs-up. And then the mods started to rise. One by one, every heavy mod in the gallery stood and then began to applaud. Matt blushed – the first time I'd seen that – but I don't think they were clapping for him. They applauded because he addressed the fundamental question of their existence, "Are they human?"

I congratulated Matt as the jury filed out to deliberate. Beryl, Seth, Jessie, and the others approached the divider between the gallery and the defense table, and Jessie scooped me up into a big hug. Seth called me her warrior auntie. We hadn't won anything yet, but it felt like we had. Beryl handed her shabti to me and I was able to speak with Nable.

"That was a very interesting case," he said. "The focus was less on the facts than the interpretation of them."

"It's always been that way," I replied, "and those interpretations can change over time. That's how we can look back on the Dred Scott case with such horror today, even though, at the time, many people thought it was the right decision."

"Things change," Nable said.

"Sometimes more quickly than we're ready for," I agreed. I wondered if a few years down the road there would be a similar case for AI and what that would mean for the world. We probably weren't ready, yet. "I missed you, Nable."

"As I you," he responded.

It didn't take long for the jury to return with a verdict. Matt and I held our breath, knowing it all came down to that moment. When they announced, "Not guilty on all charges," my breath released and my vision blurred with tears. Vindication. My relief was almost overwhelming. I was home free, with the exception of the libel trial that would come later. Beryl was not formally charged, and Matt vowed to appeal Moto's conviction based on the new evidence that Audrey and Seth had presented. After some paperwork, we were free to go.

* * * * * *

I quit my job at Zeen right away. Harold was pathetic, as usual, claiming that he had known I wouldn't be coming back. There was nothing I would miss about that job.

I stayed with Jessie and her family for a while and started writing a book about the whole thing. Jessie helped me purchase a shell shabti for Nable to move into, and he helped with research and editing.

As expected, I lost the civil defamation case, which bankrupted me. At least Imhotep wasn't able to make use of the miniscule amount of money they won. By the time the case was decided, Horace Morrow had fled to Uganda, and Imhotep had lost the Mars contract due to public pressure on legislators. The company quickly fell apart due to the extent of resources they had already sunk into the project. The decimation of the company actually played heavily into my conviction for libel, as it was clear how significantly my story had harmed the company. It didn't make any sense, because everything I had published was true, but everybody knew that the application of libel law was a farce. I hoped my book would spur some legislative change.

Zosser and Imhotep destroyed as much evidence as they could, but the FBI got involved and did some digging into the charges of corruption and blackmail. Some bad guys went to prison, including Zosser, William, and a few corrupt local cops. Rumor was that they put a picture of Cuddles up at the J. Edgar Hoover building for a month, but I never received confirmation on that. As always, little guys took the fall and most of the big fish swam away, but we made a difference.

I decided to stick around Memphis for a while. Hopefully, my book would bring in enough income to get me on my feet again, but until then I enjoyed reconnecting with my sister. Afterward, who knew? There were plenty of stories to write in the area. I could land with an independent news organization or maybe start my own.

Jessie asked me about it one day over dinner, politely ignoring the inexplicable slurping, gasping noises coming from Seth as she horked down her meal. "Are you doing okay?"

Despite my world flipping upside down and the complete decimation of my finances, I really was. I had been true to myself and fought for what was right. I felt like myself for the first time in years. I didn't know what would come next, but I knew I was bound to these people: Jessie, Seth, Beryl, and her brothers. It was strangely liberating.

Chapter 53

"Those who say Beryl isn't human don't know what they're talking about. She's persevered through all of this... Either she's human, or she's better than." – Bethany Williams

A few months after the trials, we all gathered at a local diner to eat ice cream and glory over the first ever Damned Bloody Kisses concert. Of course, all of my friends were there, including Maggie and Natalia, but a lot of family came as well. Seth's parents came, and my brothers were there. It was exciting to meet parents of some of the others like Cuddles and Thasha. My mother came, too.

As you can imagine, the family fallout from the trial was pretty horrific. My brothers – particularly Orville – felt like Dad had shoved us under the bus, and Dad didn't understand what Mom was doing. We hadn't sorted it all out at that point, and there was a wedge between me and Dad that would last a long time. Above all else, I think he just couldn't get over the fact that I wasn't a little girl anymore. I had grown up, and he had trouble adjusting to that. I knew it wouldn't last forever, but it was hard for both of us.

Mom didn't talk much, but we were on the same page. She was never particularly emotional or talkative. I asked her once, "Mom, why didn't you smile at First Flight?" It was a question that had always bothered me. I had seen the videos. I saw Mom, impassive, attention on her screen instead of her daughter.

Mom didn't answer right away. Her eyes closed as she searched her memories for that single day back when I was seven years old. A day that meant so much in my life.

"I didn't think it was that important," she finally responded. "I know everybody else did. Your father did. He loved every minute of it: the preparation, all of the machines and instruments they used to get you ready, the idea of you as an aviation pioneer." As always, Dad lavished attention on me. His excitement was contagious, and it was part of what made the experience thrilling for me.

"Why didn't you think it was important?" I asked.

"I'm not sure," she answered. "I suppose part of it is that I knew you could do it. There was no suspense for me. And I really didn't enjoy the circus atmosphere. All those strangers, the media, it felt like an invasion of our home.

"And I thought of your brothers. I knew they would be proud of you, but it would be a bitter pride. Especially for Orville. He's the one who would have wanted something like that for himself.

"I just wanted it over with."

The transition was tough for her, too, with Imhotep shut down. She was still looking for work, hopefully with whoever picked up the Mars contract.

Regardless, we all felt that the DBK concert was a huge success. The band played at the tiny Memphis band shell and managed to get through four songs before complaints from the nearby apartment complex sent the police to break up the show. Of course, Seth had neglected to apply for a permit.

"If you need a permit to rock, then you're not really rocking," Seth declared with a mouthful of banana split slurrying her speech. All were in full agreement.

In addition to the eviction from the park, Ralph managed to break the bass drum with his energetic playing style, and Cuddles had forgotten to bring his tambourine, so he just ended up awkwardly dancing during most of the songs. I thought that, overall, the show was one of the best things I had ever seen. And although the music was comically bad, some of the lyrical counterpoints were actually pretty clever.

Maggie and Nable recorded the concert, of course, and sent it to the net for public appreciation. After ice cream, we all planned to go to Seth's house to watch the recording together, which would result in many more hours of laughter and self-congratulations.

Moto wasn't able to come to the concert. He remained in prison, but some of the charges had been dropped on appeal. Natalia had been to visit him once, which he really appreciated, and I tried to get out there when I could. He'd be out in less than a year and had already decided he wanted to be a prison guard. "Some of the prisoners are like me," he told me. "Some of them have a lot of power, but don't know what to do with it. Others are afraid because they don't think they have power, and I tell them about a tiny little bird girl who changed the world."

Ann would be in prison for a while, too, and Cuddles managed to visit her every day. She liked it, though she was a little disturbed when Cuddles brought his mother last time. She still sounded like a jerk all the time, but when you got used to her, you started to hear her words the way she *meant* to say them. She grew on me, and Seth visited her regularly, too.

We weren't sure what happened to Ant. She disappeared shortly after the trial, but Seth's fairly certain she found employment with the CIA. I suspect Bí knows for sure, but she's not talking.

With the collapse of Imhotep, The Home was closed down. Residents who were adults were given a modest amount of start-up cash and released into the greater world with no health insurance or prospects. Minors were placed in foster homes or put up for adoption. For many of the oldest, like Iris, and the youngest, it was a challenging time. Iris had poor health and little understanding of the outside world. She had been in a single building for most of her life, after all, and she didn't know what to do.

Lindy and Wilbur created their own non-profit to help mods who struggled to integrate with the "normie" world. They were brilliant at it. Lindy talked with the important people, brought in donations, and created partnerships with other non-profits like Habitat for Humanity. The folks over at Habitat were thrilled to stretch their creativity in building small, functional homes for mods like Iris and Carmen, and it even became a successful reality show for the screen. With many Imhotep doctors and nurses let go and establishing private practices in the area, Lindy bargained for reasonable rates to medically cover the new mod community. Wilbur spent time with the mods and helped with anything that involved lifting, pushing, moving, or building. Beyond that, the two of them were an inspiration. "We can make it, so you can too!" They ended up building a neighborhood for mods – both from The Home and otherwise – that felt like family.

Some mods like Reggie simply couldn't make it on their own. Local nursing homes took them in, with some financial help from disability and private donations. Many from Lindy and Wilbur's community made regular trips to visit their former housemates.

Orville and Natalia dated for a short while after the trial, but Natalia wanted to be part of the new mod community, and Orville wanted to be on his own. They parted as friends.

I felt a little like Orville must have felt. I didn't feel like I belonged with Mom, Dad, and Beth anymore. I loved them and my brothers, but it just didn't feel right. Maybe it was all the stress and responsibility from the last year, but I just wanted to get away. I didn't feel like I fit into my old life. I had just turned fourteen, so I wouldn't be going anywhere soon, but I knew there was a great big world out there, and it was frustrating to have to wait to dive in. I wanted to fly high, someplace far away and quiet, where I could feel the wind blowing through my hair and listen to the rustling leaves of trees far below. Someplace where I didn't have to think about anything for a while.

EPILOGUE

"When you can answer the question, 'Who am I?' other questions like, 'Why am I?' and 'How am I?' become less important." – Beryl Pritchard

Nine years after the Pritchards' flight from The Home, fifteen years after First Flight, I caught up with Beryl for the first "Where are they now?" interview I'd done since meeting her all those years ago. Probably the last one I'll ever do.

It was a warm, but not quite hot, late August day in Baraboo, Wisconsin. Beryl had been working with the International Crane Foundation and the Whooping Crane Eastern Partnership to prepare to photograph some young cranes on their first migration south. We shared a brief lunch at a little café off the corner of the town square, then got down to business.

"It's been a long time, Beryl." I said as we walked slowly around the small town square. Nable recorded video through both my temple and a small drone that hovered in front of us, and we each wore a mic. Beryl still couldn't walk well, but we set a slow pace. "Good to catch up with you."

"Same here," she responded politely. "We've both been so busy. You and Nable have been doing great work. I read your stuff in GorillaNews religiously."

"Thank you. My experiences with you opened doors I never knew existed." I wasn't banking much at Gorilla, but it was heaven. Genuine investigative journalism. I loved the people I was working with, and when we got shut down by the lawyers, we'd just bankrupt the company and start a new one. Our readers followed us. I've been happy, challenged, and productive at work for several years now.

Before Nable could chide me not to let the subject run the interview, I steered the conversation back to Beryl, "But let's talk about you for a little bit. You can interview me later."

"Heh."

"Let's start right here. What brings you to the marshes of Wisconsin?"

"This is the second year that I'll be traveling south with the whooping cranes," Beryl answered. "There are a few reasons it resonates with me. From a physical standpoint, it's my marathon. It really drives me to build my strength and endurance. I struggled last year, but I feel like I'm in better shape this time. I also feel like I'm doing a good thing. Every year, this program and ones like it make small strides toward rebuilding the health of the species. My photographs bring attention and dollars to the program. Most of all, though, I enjoy watching the birds. I enjoy flying with them. For most of my life, I've flown alone, which is an act of independence, meditation, and isolation all in one. I love it. It's part of my core. But I also love flying as part of a sedge of cranes. Like I'm part of a cool gang."

"Very exclusive membership," I said with a wink.

"Very much so!" she agreed. "Anyway, one of the things I like about flying is the perspective it gives you, and it's definitely a different perspective to fly as a bird than to fly as just plain old me."

"Do you sometimes feel like you straddle the line between human and avian?"

"No, not really. I can empathize with them more than maybe you can. I know how it feels to molt, to have your leg bend just so, to glide on the wind, but I don't understand what they think. I can't relate to that. I can't form lasting relationships with them."

"How's your relationship with your family?" I asked. I knew this was a tougher question because I knew how hard it was after the trial. There were rifts there that wouldn't heal quickly or easily.

"Good! Time offers its own perspective. Dad came around, and Lindy and Wilbur were ready to embrace that. When Orville died last year, it wasn't hard for us to all come together to celebrate him."

"Do you want to share some thoughts about Orville?" I sent condolences after his death, but I hadn't been able to make it to the funeral.

"He was always very brave," Beryl said. She stopped walking for a moment while she thought about her brother. "He had a high ethical standard for everybody. He complained a lot, but he was always thinking. I miss him. We need complainers in this world. And eventually he became a doer. He influenced some important legislation in Madison and had a fun time doing it. I think Wisconsin is leagues ahead of other states in mod rights because of his work."

"You've been campaigning for that yourself."

We resumed our stroll. "At the national level, yes. Mostly with guidance and advice from Orville. I'm a good figurehead. I just don't enjoy it much, so I don't spend enough time on it. I've had some good conversations with some very thoughtful legislators. They get that we need detailed, humane regulations on genetic manipulation. We don't need to shut it down. We just need to take it slowly. The ills of technology are often less about the invention itself and more about how it interacts with the society of the time. People get that."

"So why aren't federal laws on par with Wisconsin?"

"Well, I've had some very frustrating conversations with some very ignorant legislators," she answered, clearly perturbed.

"Politics?"

"Not my bag," she finished. "You wouldn't think it would be hard to get fair treatment for genetically modified creatures, human and otherwise, but it's hard to get over that initial hurdle of, 'You're different than us.'"

"Well, what else have you been doing?" I asked. "More enjoyable pursuits?"

"You've seen my photography?" she asked hopefully.

"Of course! Tell me about it, though."

"I find that I really want to share what it feels like to fly. To some degree, I can do that with photographs. I started with pictures around home. Bí would snap a picture when I murmured or made some other subconscious sound when an image struck me. Often, I wouldn't even know she'd taken a shot until we looked at them together afterward. She's very attentive."

"Home from Above was the name of your book."

"Yeah, but I didn't know it would become a book when we were getting those shots. We just took pictures because they captured a feeling. I shared them with Seth. You know how Seth is."

"Enthusiastic?"

"Yeah, that's the word," Beryl grinned. "She insisted that they were the coolest pictures in the whole world and that I should put them in a book. I'm glad she did that. "

"It pays the bills."

"It does. It wasn't a hugely successful book, but I found a career. Some of my photos were featured in art shows. Then I was contracted for my second book, Mexico City. Mostly aerial photos, but some on the ground. I learned a lot, there. Like so many cities, there's such a divide between rich and poor, it's visible even from hundreds of feet in the air. We took some pictures with people on the ground, too. I talked with people… not a lot. My Spanish is horrible. But enough to connect."

"What did you learn?"

"I'm still not sure," Beryl shrugged. "I'm still processing the experience. Maybe I should do it again, eh?"

"Do you still garden?"

"No. I'm too migratory at this point in my life, I'm afraid. Maybe someday. I'm not sure I'd like it as much. Even though they're plants, it's all about making constant life-or-death decisions. Culling," she said with a frown. "It's unsettling in a way that it wasn't when I was a kid."

"How do you feel about Imhotep now?"

"Surprisingly ambivalent. Leadership was a problem there, and they did some horrible things, but there were really good people working there, too, doing wonderful things."

"Your mother?"

"Sure, like Mom. But even Mom was working at the bleeding edge. Probably going too fast. Did you know that part of her Mars project involved humans with chlorophyll?"

"Seriously? Little green men?"

"Seriously! Resources on Mars were going to be scarce. They calculated that five percent of a Martian's energy needs could come from photosynthesis. Not a lot, but still significant. But how much thought had they put into the impact on society, both there and here? Or would they put in a kill switch so Martians couldn't come to Earth or mate with Earthlings? All of the decisions were made by people who were just really excited that it was happening at all."

"Well, it is exciting."

"Sure it is! I completely empathize! But it's not just exciting, it's a big deal. A big deal behind closed doors with no oversight."

"Do you think stuff like that is still going on behind closed doors?"

"Don't act naïve," she said to me with a chuckle. "I know you've been reporting on this stuff. Imhotep collapses, and others vie to fill the niche. Hell, Morrow's still out there with a lab in Uganda with no regulatory controls at all. I'm sure there are tons of crazy, amazing, frightening projects going on out there that nobody knows about. Some will change the world for the better. Some are dangerous or unethical. So goes humanity."

"When you look back at First Flight, the rescue from The Home, and everything else that has transpired in your lifetime, what do you see for the next ten or twenty years?" As much as this was for a story, I really cared. I worried about Beryl – that she had burned out due to the trauma of that crazy year. I needed to know what she thought of her own future.

"Who knows?" she shrugged. "If I'd tried to predict any of this, I'd have been way off. I'm sure I'll meet new people, do new things, and the world will change around me."

"Once you said to me, 'Sometimes a circle has a starting point.'"

"I think I was referencing how happiness builds on itself, but you have to start somewhere. When we met for that first interview, that was a starting point for me. For a lot of good, weird, amazing events to follow."

"For me, too," I agreed. "And here we are again, an interview in Wisconsin."

"I look forward to seeing you in another cycle."

"Same here."

ACKNOWLEDGEMENTS

This book would not be what it is without contributions from family and friends. Most importantly, my wife, Jefre, was very patient and encouraging, supporting my many hours at the keyboard and giving helpful advice along the way. She wasn't afraid to tell me when I was doing it wrong. I would be nowhere without her.

My mother, Gail, did the dirty work, reading several drafts, advising wisely and compassionately, and even proofreading the final draft. Her knowledge of the craft is far greater than my own. I'm very fortunate – most fledgling authors don't have a resource like her.

Ross Tunnell offered inspiration and stellar constructive criticism from the perspective of a fellow writer. Chris Solomon gave kindly suggestions and corrected many of my mistakes on the topic of genetics. Elaine Brow also helped with the sciencing – if any errors remain, they are intentional for purposes of character or plot. Ethan Nichols and Shannon Tunnell also contributed, and the earliest germ of the idea for this book came from a conversation with Thad Steffen nearly ten years ago. Kit Foster Design did a very nice job on the cover, and Kit was very responsive to feedback. Many thanks to all of the above.

If you're interested in exploring the science of CRISPR, there are a plethora of articles out there, but many of them are both scant on details and difficult to understand. Radiolab did a nice podcast on the subject, and I recommend you start there.

Though many of the legal precedents in this book are real, the legal proceedings of Beryl's case are more informed by Perry Mason than reality. If you're interested in the cases you read about here, look them up! From both a scientific and legal perspective, this book was a wonderful opportunity for me to expand my knowledge, and I hope you find it a springboard as well.

Thanks for reading.

Printed in Great Britain
by Amazon